President CLAY HUNTINGTON, young charismatic, determined to prove his strength and decisiveness . . .

Premier NIKOLAI ANDREYEV, an aging figure torn between his love of country and love of mankind . . .

WHITNEY STOUGHTON, deputy director of the CIA, his vast power tragically vulnerable to a shameful secret in his past . . .

VIKTOR MALININ, using his position as security chief to Andreyev and as lover to Andreyev's beautiful and tormented daughter, Claudia, to pursue his ruthless climb to power . . .

MATT OLDS, special assistant to the President and the only man who realizes the gruesome plot that is pushing the world over the brink into the abyss of total destruction . . .

You will never forget what happens at

THE SUMMIT

"Very fast and very good!"

— Kirkus Service

Other SIGNET Titles You Will Enjoy

THE
SUMMIT

by STEPHEN MARLOWE

A SIGNET BOOK from
NEW AMERICAN LIBRARY
TIMES MIRROR

All rights reserved under International and Pan American
Conventions. For information address Bernard Geis Associates,
130 East 56th Street, New York, New York 10022.

Library of Congress Catalog Card Number: 75-97592

This is an authorized reprint of a hardcover edition
published by Bernard Geis Associates.

 SIGNET TRADEMARK REG. U.S. PAT. OFF. AND FOREIGN COUNTRIES
REGISTERED TRADEMARK—MARCA REGISTRADA
HECHO EN CHICAGO, U.S.A.

SIGNET, SIGNET CLASSICS, SIGNETTE, MENTOR AND PLUME BOOKS
are published by The New American Library, Inc.,
1301 Avenue of the Americas, New York, New York 10019

FIRST PRINTING, MAY, 1971

PRINTED IN THE UNITED STATES OF AMERICA

To

Marion Claudel

Devotion to pure Utopia, and revolt against a polluted society, are the two poles which provide the tension for all militant creeds. . . . To the psychiatrist, both the craving for Utopia and the rebellion against the status quo are symptoms of social maladjustment. To the social reformer, both are symptoms of a healthy rational attitude. The psychiatrist is apt to forget that smooth adjustment to a deformed society creates deformed individuals. The reformer is equally apt to forget that hatred, even of the objectively hateful, does not produce that charity and justice on which a Utopian society must be based.

—Arthur Koestler
The God That Failed

CHARACTERS

The American Delegation

CLAY HUNTINGTON, President of the United States

BENSON REED, Secretary of State

GEN. PIERRE GUSTAV BEAUREGARD LAFFONT,
  Chairman of the Joint Chiefs of Staff

WHITNEY STOUGHTON, Deputy Director of the CIA

MATTHEW OLDS, the President's Special Assistant for
  National Security Affairs

HARVEY ROSS, Press Secretary

BURT EAST, Chief of White House detachment, Secret
  Service

DR. NANCY PADGETT, the President's physician

MISS PRISCILLA LEE, the President's personal secretary

AL CASH }
CHUCK } CIA agents

The Russian Delegation

NIKOLAI IVANOVICH ANDREYEV,
  Premier of the Soviet Union

CLAUDIA NIKOLAIEVNA ANDREYEVA, his daughter

VASILY KAPITSA, Foreign Minister

COL. VIKTOR MIRONOVICH MALININ,
  Chief of Security, KGB

DMITRI TROFIMOVICH MOSKALENKO, an assassin

LEONID BAYEV }
YEGOROV   }
SOKOLOV   } KGB agents
KOLCHAK   }

SEMYON SEMYONOV, a pastry chef

In Washington

GIGI HUNTINGTON, the First Lady

BERNARD MC MANUS, Director of the CIA

CONGRESSMAN LAKE, Chairman of the House Armed
   Services Committee
DR. HOWARD RUTHERFORD, an obstetrician

In Moscow

IGOR LYSENKO, First Secretary of the Communist Party
The Minister of the Interior
The Minister of Defense
GEN. CHUIKOV, Chief of the KGB

In Switzerland

KERMIT HAUSER, retired American Ambassador to
   Russia
NATASHA HAUSER, his Russian-born wife
The President of Switzerland
WILLY MÜLLENER, Minister of Justice and Police
TRACY OLDS, ex-wife of Matthew Olds
CHRIS OLDS, their son
SHIELDS, a retired American stockbroker
ERNST GROSSMANN, Air Rescue Service pilot
RUEDY STÜCKI, a pilot
GROS-CLAUDE, a Swiss Communist
HENRI, a Swiss security policeman
MR. HESSIAN, a schoolmaster

The Yugoslavs

ANTON ILIĆ, President of Yugoslavia
CVETKOVIC, Defense Minister
COL. SUMOZJA, an Army officer

The Press

JENKINS POTTER, Associated Press
ALPHONSE BOREL, *Tribune de Genève*
YURI KIROV, Tass News Agency
JACQUES DU CHÊNE, *L'Humanité*
HAROLD YATES, Reuters
FIDEL GÓMEZ, *A.B.C.,* Madrid
MINORU ITO, *Yomiuri,* Tokyo

Part One

Chapter
ONE

1   Rain fell on the city, a cold, relentless November rain that, in the Alps fifty miles away, might have been the first snow of the season.

The slick, cobblestoned streets were deserted. Occasionally a forlorn Sunday-night car drifted along the lakefront toward the Mont Blanc bridge, its headlights silhouetting the squat, cutback plane trees along the water's edge. Occasionally a gust of wind swept off the lake, rattling raindrops like hail against the window of the hotel room.

It was an old hotel, somewhat seedy for its location on the quay, the room large, high-ceilinged, and crowded with the kind of overstuffed, overornate Victorian furniture Claudia would have expected in a hotel in Moscow or Leningrad rather than Geneva.

Standing at the window, her back to the room, she wondered if Viktor had chosen this hotel because it would remind her of home. No, she thought, Viktor is not sentimental. Calculating, yes, but he is very definitely not sentimental.

Claudia stared across the black, rain-dappled surface of the lake broken by bands of varicolored light. Her father had told her, before they left Moscow, that Geneva was the only city in the world where even the advertising signs could be beautiful—all of a size, all of a height, reflecting across the waters of the lake.

She had no way of knowing. She knew Moscow, still suffering from the wedding-cake Gothic of its Stalinesque period a generation ago. She knew Leningrad, with its canals and the stately Nevsky Prospekt, more a Western

11

city than a Russian one. She knew Tbilisi, the capital of the Georgian S.S.R., where she had been born, a provincial city in the soft light of the south, with the great range of the Caucasus looming beyond. Suddenly, watching the rain, aware of Viktor behind her in the gloomy hotel room, she was homesick.

Her father was at home in all the capitals of the world. Viktor, with his detached cynicism, was quickly at home anywhere, perhaps because he had no real home. Claudia needed roots. Even Moscow had remained alien to her— the glitter of diplomatic receptions, Viktor's ubiquitous Security Police following wherever she went, the cold, clear northern light so unlike the friendly air of Tbilisi, which was like wine, like a caress.

She saw herself at her father's side, riding in the lush foothills of the Caucasus, their horses lathering, her father pleased that she could sit her saddle so well. She could see the look of quiet pride on his face, and then she was galloping, ahead and alone, her father calling in alarm because the path was treacherous, his voice fading, the stallion between her knees moving powerfully and the quick excitement of the moment so sweet because soon her father would overtake her and his words of concern would be, really, words of love. She needed roots, she needed love, and she was denied both now. Her father was too busy, too important. He carried the history of the next twenty years on his shoulders, of the next fifty, perhaps. Viktor used her.

The tolling of bells from the cathedral on its hill across the lake in the Old Town wrenched her back to Geneva.

"Midnight," Viktor said in his deep voice. "The first time we made love, it was midnight. Remember?"

Claudia no longer remembered. She thought she no longer cared. She hated Viktor now for his false sentimentality, but Viktor would have said, gravely, you could not hate if you had not loved. Well, she was tired of Viktor's sanctimonious aphorisms, too. It was over, what had been between them. In its wake was a residue of pain and embarrassment. What am I doing here? she wondered, and at once knew the simple, almost frightening answer. Viktor had asked her to come, and she had obeyed.

"Close the drapes," he said.

She found herself obeying that, too. The room seemed at once warmer but less protective.

"And now, we will talk."

12

"We have nothing to talk about, Viktor."

Claudia heard a small delicate popping sound and turned to see Viktor with his square strong capable hands holding a champagne bottle.

"The wine will be cold enough, I think."

"I'm tired, Viktor."

"You? Tired?" The white, even teeth showed against the broad, handsome Slavic face. "You have more energy than any woman I ever met."

"I'm tired tonight. Really. The plane trip."

Viktor held up the champagne bottle. "Taittinger," he said. "The finest champagne in the world, produced by the most decadent people in the world. It makes our own Russian wine taste like dishwater." He filled two stem glasses and then replaced the bottle in the silver urn. "Try some."

"I'd rather not."

"I said try some."

He did not come to her. That, she knew, was obscurely important, a touchstone for what would follow. She went to him, slowly, her walk provocative in spite of herself. She had good strong hips and long legs that Viktor had always said were the legs of a young ballerina. He was a squat, powerful man in his early forties. She was as tall as he was. When they went dancing at the Rossiya in Moscow, she'd always worn low heels.

She tasted the wine.

"You see? Delicious."

"One glass. Then I'm going back to Villa Krupskaya."

"Nikolai Ivanovich knows you're here?"

"Who else would I be with, my first night in Geneva?"

"And he approves?"

"I'm twenty-six, Viktor. It doesn't matter whether my father approves or not."

"Or else it does matter, and he is a fool."

She set the champagne glass down, surprised to see that it was empty, not surprised to feel her hand trembling. Viktor could always do that to her, in a hundred ways. Why should it be any different, here, at midnight in Switzerland, in a seedy hotel on the shores of Lake Geneva?

"It's late, Viktor. I never should have come. Let me have my coat."

He ignored her, pouring more champagne.

"My coat, Viktor. Please don't be boorish."

"But I," he said calmly and with a smile, "am the most

13

boorish man in the world. The New Russian, as subtle as a sledgehammer. Drink your champagne, Claudia Nikolaievna. I am trying to seduce you."

Two years ago, Viktor's matter-of-factness would have shocked her, had shocked her, in the beginning, in Moscow. But there had been a fascination in it, too—Viktor, the confident male, so completely, so ruthlessly sure of himself, almost as if he were telling her, if not you then someone else. She had found herself responding to the frankness, to the lack of romance, with an eager excitement. Viktor counted on that and played on it, almost like a scientist performing a carefully controlled experiment. Each time it had left Claudia feeling a little less sure of herself, like the small frantic laboratory animal in the scientist's clever maze, learning the path that would bring a tidbit reward, a few moments of love, Viktor's special kind of love, before the remorse.

She must have asked a question, because Viktor was saying:

"You are very good in bed, that's why."

He removed his jacket, loosened his tie, and sipped champagne. He sat on the edge of the bed and began to unbutton his shirt. He did not touch her yet, did not even try to touch her.

"I will prove something to you," he said. "Your coat is in the closet. The door is there. Why don't you go?"

She balled her hands into fists to stop the trembling.

"Because," said Viktor dryly, "you really don't want to go." His chest was muscular and devoid of hair. "You want exactly what I want. It makes no difference if it is for the rest of our lives or just one more night."

"You really are a fool if you think that."

"We are all fools," Viktor said sententiously, "spending our little time from the swaddling cloth to the shroud, mistaking stupidity for idealism, as your father does, or lust for love, as you do. What did you expect? Candlelight and violins? We enjoy each other. That is enough."

"And you," she asked, her face flushed. "What kind of mistakes do you make?"

"Sometimes," Viktor said slowly, "I miscalculate. I miscalculated with your father. He is not courageous, he is merely stubborn."

"That's enough, Viktor."

"Tell me, had I shown more of the sentiment you think you require, would you have come to bed with me?"

She said nothing.

"Well? Answer me. Yes or no will do."

"I—honestly don't know, Viktor."

"But now it is too late? Now if I insist Nikolai Ivanovich is a less than brilliant man with one task left to perform before he is thrown to the wolves, now if I suggest that some of his less-than-brilliance rubbed off on you—"

He raised a hand and wiped his face. She had flung what was left in her champagne glass at him.

"Good," he said calmly. "You are proving my point. When I was a cadet at KGB school in Moscow, they told us that any woman could be seduced if you knew how to reach her. Once you found the way, it was quite predictable and Pavlovian and even dull, unless she had some talent for it."

He reached for a pack of Kazbeks on the night table and lit one.

"Some women, delicate types, must be cajoled. A certain amount of gentleness, and they will respond passively. Others, strapping farm girls from the steppes, you have to fight with. Literally. The bodily contact excites them, you see, until they finally respond with fierce passion," Viktor said, without any passion at all. "Once you find the key, you can seduce any woman in the world. And what is the key to Claudia Nikolaievna?"

She tried to move. She willed herself to move, to run, to get away before it was too late. But he held her there, cobra-like, with his indifference.

"I will tell you," he said, blowing a plume of smoke past her shoulder. "An indifference on my part, and a growing anger on your part because everything I do in my indifference is an insult to you, and then you realize the indifference is after all pretended, because I find you a very attractive woman—"

"Please stop," Claudia heard herself say in a very small voice. But he knew her. He knew her so well. She was lonely and afraid in a world that was too big, her father's world. She needed the one thing it could not give her—love. And she would accept Viktor's mocking, clinical travesty of it because she could find it nowhere else. He had trained her carefully.

"But you don't want me to stop. Do you?"

By then he was completely undressed, seated on the edge of the bed, calmly, infuriatingly smoking. "Now," he

15

said, "you will look at me and decide whether my indifference is real or not. Look at me. Now."

For ten long seconds she wouldn't let her gaze leave his eyes.

"Claudia," he said with mild reproach. "That is not what I mean. Look at me."

And, finally, with a reluctance that was not really reluctance at all, she let her eyes drop, past the muscular chest, the flat belly, the darkness of hair.

"Tell me, is my indifference real?"

Her answer was a whimper. She undressed in a frenzy and struck the lighted cigarette savagely from his hand. He allowed her to mount him and to take his hot hard manhood within her, and for a little while the rain and the hotel room, so far from home, went away, for a little while she went away, back to Tbilisi on that wild stallion ride with love behind her in her father's concern, and then Viktor laughed and turned her over and there were scalding tears of shame and humiliation on her cheeks, but because Viktor wanted her it was as good as it had always been.

2 It had been, Matthew Olds told himself on the two-hour drive down out of the mountains from Gstaad to Geneva, even worse than he had expected.

At least a glance at Chris seated beside him in the rented Volkswagen was reassuring. Too much emotion had finally done its work: Matthew Olds's twelve-year-old son, the collar of his coat turned up against the thick, too-long blond hair that was like his mother's hair, was sleeping.

Matt hoped Chris would stay asleep until they reached Geneva. He did not know what to say to the boy. He hoped a few words of paternal assurance, uttered glibly as the doors of the Leman International School in Geneva closed behind a sleepy Chris, would suffice until next Thursday. Then they'd have some man-to-man talk over Thanksgiving dinner, if that was what Chris wanted.

They drove out of the hills above Lausanne at midnight. Wet snow had given way to freezing rain, but the surface of the Lausanne-Geneva autoroute ought to be all right. Matt could put himself on automatic pilot and think.

Matthew Olds was a big enough man to make the

interior of the Volkswagen seem very small. He was bareheaded and wore a battered old trenchcoat, probably, he knew, as a revolt against the white silk scarves and homburgs favored by the rest of the White House staff. Except for Matt, the men who surrounded President Huntington seemed all of a type, like stones worn smooth and featureless in a fast mountain stream. It was inevitable that some reporter, sooner or later, as Maddox of the Washington *Star* had finally done, would call trench-coat-wearing Matthew Olds the White House's resident private eye.

In the faint light from the dashboard his face was craggy and not quite gaunt, the eyes deep-set, the grooves pronounced on either side of the firm, straight mouth. It was a face that worried men, if they had reason to worry; a face that disturbed women, if they had reason to be disturbed.

The headmaster at the school in Gstaad had had reason to worry. He was a small, fussy Englishman in his forties, a few years older than Matt, a man who had surrendered to dandruff, five-o'clock shadow, and an only mildly offensive B.O.

"Sorry it had to be Sunday afternoon," Matt had said. "I've been damn busy, and I appreciate your seeing me now."

They shook hands. The headmaster's hand was limp and moist. "Ordinarily we don't take many day students," he said, shaking his head and producing a small snowstorm of dandruff flakes. "This *is* a boarding school, after all. Perhaps that is Chris's problem." He sniffed, and the watery eyes behind the thick glasses blinked nervously. "Or shall I be quite candid?"

"That's why I'm here," Matt said.

"Despite the jet set," the headmaster said, "or perhaps because of it, Gstaad for all its glitter is just a village." He smiled faintly, pleased with his turn of phrase. "In a village, there are few secrets. You do understand?"

Matthew Olds, patiently, said that he understood.

And, staring out the window at the mountains etched sharply against the snow-threatening sky at the far end of the valley, the headmaster said: "Chris's mother is leading a wild life. She drinks too much. Every merchant in the village knows it. The international set is aware of it. Worse, she makes herself—may I be blunt, Mr. Olds? You may find this painful."

17

Matt said that he would appreciate bluntness.

The headmaster licked his lips, ran a hand raspingly over the five-o'clock shadow. "I am new at the school, Mr. Olds. I arrived this autumn. I am not married. People talk—the other young bachelors in town, don't you know? I heard it three times the first week I was here." His voice changed; he had a gift for mimicry. He was now a young, footloose American. "There's this blonde. Stacked." He paused. "If you will forgive me, they always used the word stacked." The American voice resumed: "Plays tennis like a man, skis like Kiki Cutter's older sister and is drinking herself one hell of a corrugated liver. In the bed department, no strenuous campaign necessary. She'll do the asking. Kind of athletic and, if you're a gentleman about it, grateful. Got a kid, but he's not in the house much. Comes complete with her own chalet with a view that'd knock your eyes out, not that you're going to have time for the view."

The nervous eyes darted from the view framed in the window to Matt's face. "Dear me, I hope I haven't—"

"No. That's all right."

Chris, the headmaster said sadly, was a bright twelve-year-old. The fact that he was already a freshman in high school indicated that. So did the tests he had taken before entering the Gstaad American School in September. But in two short months he had become a disruptive influence in the school. He did not do his work. He was disobedient, insolent.

Words tumbled quickly from the weak, pursed lips, the sadness tempered by spite, as the headmaster gave concrete examples of Chris's disobedience and insolence. "Such a promising child," he sighed. "But I fear this is not the place for him."

"So you indicated on the phone," Matt said a little stiffly. "Have you told his mother?"

"I preferred telling you, Mr. Olds. Reluctantly, believe me. May I suggest that Mrs. Olds is not a fit guardian for a sensitive boy? Were he living with a parent from whom—"

"I've made arrangements to board Chris at the Leman International School in Geneva," Matt said.

"The International School, I see," sniffed the headmaster. "I had hoped the boy might . . . but a man as involved in the problems of the world as you are . . . The Interna-

18

tional School does take problem children, of course. May I, uh, then assume that Chris will not be with us tomorrow?"

Matt said, dryly, that that was a safe assumption. "Where's Chris now?"

"We try to keep them occupied on weekends. Busy hands, don't you know?" the headmaster said effusively, glad to be talking about something else. "Hiking. It's beautiful country. They should be returning shortly." The headmaster rose, wafting the faint effluvium of his B.O. in Matt's direction. "We'll send Chris's records to Geneva in the morning, Mr. Olds. I do hope he'll fare better there, and I'd like to thank you for your cooperation. Some parents can be rather stiff-backed." The headmaster dwelled for a while with bitterness on the nature of stiff-backed parents. "But of course a man accustomed to dealing with Big Problems—" he capitalized the words— "ought to be able to take a situation like this in his stride."

The limp handshake again, and: "May I ask a rather impertinent question? We cannot help wondering, here in our little Shangri-La, if it was wise for your President to agree to a Summit Conference at this time."

With a straight face Matt said, "I make it a habit never to discuss Summit Conferences on Sunday."

The nervous eyes blinked, a reluctant smile touched the spiteful mouth, there was a third and final handshake at the door, and Matt went to find Tracy's chalet.

Now, driving through the middle-of-the-night emptiness of the four-lane autoroute in the rain, Chris still asleep at his side, Matt wondered if one reason the meeting with Tracy had been so bad was that he had felt guilty about taking time off from his duties. The President and his staff would reach Geneva tomorrow morning; the Russians had arrived today and were already settled into Villa Krupskaya on the lake. The Russians had touched down at Cointrin Airport in their new Tupelov supersonic jet, but our own SST had, over the past few years, encountered snag after snag, and thus far only a prototype had flown, so it would be subsonic Air Force One in the morning.

Matt had reached Geneva four days early, as President Huntington's Special Assistant for National Security Affairs, to set up a preliminary agenda with his Soviet opposite number. He had expected someone from the

Foreign Ministry, but he got a Colonel Viktor Malinin instead. Malinin hadn't been bad to work with. His command of English was excellent and he didn't mind using the language they had in common. Nor had he minded working behind closed doors, being willing to let the propaganda pronouncements await the arrival of President Huntington and Soviet Premier Nikolai Ivanovich Andreyev.

The only disquieting note had been Colonel Malinin's identity. The name and the man were unknown to Matt. He had put a check on him through the Embassy in Bern, drawing a blank. A call to CIA in Virginia was more successful: Colonel Viktor Malinin, they told him, was the new chief of Main Department Seven of the KGB.

Russia's KGB, the Committee for State Security, was a superagency that would make even minds accustomed to the bureaucracy on the Potomac boggle. It was CIA, FBI, and the Secret Service rolled into one. Main Department Seven of the KGB corresponded to our own Secret Service, and why the chief bodyguard of the Council of Ministers should be Premier Andreyev's front man Matt had no idea. It could have meant Andreyev feared for his own safety. But Geneva took Summit Conferences in stride, and even a meeting between God and the devil in the Palace of Nations wouldn't have surprised its unflappable citizens. It could have meant Colonel Malinin was being groomed for bigger things, except that Malinin had just been appointed head of Main Department Seven. It could have meant the Council of Ministers didn't trust their own Chairman, but then why send him to the Summit at all?

Well, Matt thought, we all have our problems, and Secretary of State Benson Reed was less than delighted that Matthew Olds, caretaker of the so-called Little State Department in the White House basement, instead of one of his own deputies, had been first on the firing line for our side.

He had reached Chalet Bambi late that afternoon, after the interview with Chris's headmaster. The first snowflakes had begun to fall. The chalet, with its pitched roof, overhanging eaves, and gingerbread balcony, was perched above a rushing mountain stream. It had a fine view across the valley to the high mountains, and with lights blazing from all the windows against the gathering

20

darkness it managed to look snug and secure. Trust Tracy to run up the biggest electric bill in the Bernese Oberland; she had always been prodigal. But then, Matt was well aware, she had never had to worry about money.

A vintage Mercedes 300SL was parked in the turn-around. The divorce had been almost three years ago; the car was after Matt's time. He parked the up-staged Volkswagen next to it, took a deep breath, lit a cigarette, told himself this needn't be unpleasant if he remembered to act urbane—urbanity being the social grace he had always lacked, according to Tracy—and went up the front stairs.

He pulled the chain, and a corny cowbell clanked over his head. He waited: no answer. He pulled the chain again, got the same no answer, and tried the door. Tracy was a heavy sleeper and always loved her afternoon nap.

The door opened inward, revealing a short hallway, the kitchen off to the left and straight ahead the living room with a high, beamed ceiling, a wall of glass with that view across the valley, and a fireplace with two big pine logs that glowed dully red.

"Hello?" Matt called uncertainly.

He was then on the threshold of the living room. It was a cluttered mess: cigarette butts overflowing a couple of big ashtrays on the cocktail table near the fireplace, two not-quite-empty glasses, an empty bottle of Johnny Walker Black on the hearthrug, a cashmere sweater that he recognized tossed across the back of the sofa, a pair of soft velvet après-ski boots near the bar.

He debated leaving the chalet, driving into town, and phoning, because the trail of clothing—a frilly blouse, one wool sock—went up a flight of stairs to what would be the bedroom level. But he wanted to talk to Tracy before their son came home. Maybe Tracy was up there alone; you could undress that way in an alcoholic fog, he supposed. Who knew what Tracy was like now? No man's clothing was in evidence, anyway. Maybe her companion of the late afternoon, if any, had left.

He climbed the stairs noisily, called hello again, and got no answer again. A hallway at the top, brightly lit like the rest of the chalet (*Humor me*, Tracy had said more than once, *isn't it silly, but I'm scared of the dark*) and three doors, two of them shut and one a few inches ajar, with no light behind it.

Suddenly he froze there, on the landing, wishing he had

waited downstairs, wishing he had left the chalet, wishing he had driven back into town to phone. What he heard, standing there, not moving, was a rhythmic sound, a squeak followed by a thump, the cadence at first slow, and then faster for a while, and then slow, and then faster again, and faster still, and then a man's voice cried out, a long drawn-out shuddering "aahhhh," and a woman's voice, Tracy's voice, thickened, spent, said a name over and over again, "Ruedy, Ruedy, Ruedy," and he heard their hard, irregular breathing and after a while with a lewd chuckle Tracy said, "Why, what a perfectly lovely way to spend a Sunday afternoon."

He must have moved. He wasn't aware of it. A floorboard creaked.

"Chris? That you, Chris?" Tracy called out shrilly. "Go on downstairs, Chris. Have some cocoa, you must be cold. I'll be down in a minute."

He stood there for another moment, feeling ridiculous, and the words just came out: "I don't want any cocoa."

"Who is it?" Tracy cried. "Good Lord, *Matt?* Is that you, Matt?"

There's this blonde, he thought. *Stacked. In the bed department no strenuous campaign necessary. She'll do the asking. Kind of athletic and if you're a gentleman about it, grateful.*

He felt nothing, except that he had walked up there, not quietly, and they hadn't heard, and he had called out, and they hadn't heard—and it might have been not him but Chris.

"Matt? Give me a few minutes to—"

"Tell him to get dressed and get the hell out of there. Is there a back way? Tell him to use it. The boy'll be home any minute now."

Then he went downstairs to wait.

3 What Tracy Olds called Matt's lack of urbanity was regarded, by President Clay Huntington, as an asset rather than a defect. Matt, the President often said, had rough edges. To someone who didn't know him or, like his ex-wife, knew him but didn't understand him, his frankness was alarming and his penchant for taking direct action could be frightening. Had he carried a State Department portfolio, his sometimes unthinking, sometimes ruthless honesty would have been embarrassing.

Matt was no diplomat. The Benson Reeds of the world would never understand him. The Viktor Malinins would think they understood him and would enjoy the prospect of horse-trading with a man so unsophisticated. But Secretary of State Reed had learned, by the third year of President Huntington's term, that Matt was probably closer to the President than any man in the Administration, and Viktor Malinin had discovered, in three days of conferences, that Matt's apparent directness had an odd shifting, elastic quality. Anyone who regarded Matt's directness as simplicity or his candor as ingenuousness was in for a surprise.

Less than a year after Matt had become the President's Special Assistant for National Security Affairs, the papers were already saying that Kennedy had his Sorensen, Johnson his Moyers, Nixon his Kissinger, and Huntington his Matthew Olds. But they waited, the papers did, with a certain restrained glee, for the inevitable disillusionment and fall from power. Sherman Adams had stumbled on his own impeccable morality; Jack Valenti had been laughed out of the West Wing of the White House, the victim of his too maudlin adulation of Lyndon Johnson.

And Matthew Olds?

"If you want to keep this job, and you can be damn sure I want you to," the President had once told Matt, "keep a couple of things in mind. First, stay out of the limelight. No TV appearances, no lectures, nothing in print, and when you leak something to the press, it's not from you, it's from a source close to the President. Your public life begins and ends about six inches from this desk, even if you wind up on a fact-finding mission to Ulan-Bator.

"Second, your private life. You don't have any."

"Well, in a way I don't," Matt had said. "Tracy's getting a divorce."

"Good Christ," the President said. "Will it be messy?"

"The only messy thing that ever happened to Tracy, she says, was me. No worry there, Mr. President. A real surgical divorce."

"Presidents," the President said with a wry grin, "are encouraged to have private lives. Presidential assistants are faceless. Get into policy difficulties and I'll stick my neck out for you. It's going to happen sooner or later with Secretary Reed, or maybe with the CIA, and I don't want you to lose any sleep over it. But after hours keep your nose clean. If you don't, watch how the papers jump on you." The President wasn't grinning then. "And watch how I pretend we never met."

Until now, Matt had managed to remain faceless and reasonably clean of nose. The President made that easy. There is not much time left for kicking up your heels after a sixteen-hour workday.

"My, how you've changed," Tracy said from the stairs. "I never knew house-cleaning was one of your virtues."

She was wearing a knee-length, pale-blue quilted house-coat, and her blonde hair, brushed and gleaming, hung down her back. She was tall, with the full-blown figure of Sophia Loren. She had put on considerable weight, and Matt had to admit it was becoming. Seeing her for the first time, he'd be inclined to think, here is one sexy broad.

"Or were you trying to remove the evidence of the orgy before Chris came home? He's late, by the way. I'm a little worried."

"I came straight from the school. They've—"

"Where, no doubt," Tracy interrupted, her blue eyes narrowing, a weary, superior smile touching the full lips, "that nasty little Mr. Hessian has been telling tales."

"They've expelled Chris," Matt said

The blue eyes widened. "Expelled him? I knew he was having some difficulty adjusting, but—give me a minute, will you?"

Her way of taking a minute was to go to the bar, find a fresh bottle, thumbnail the seal, and pour herself a stiff straight slug. "Want one? Maybe we're both going to need it."

"No thanks."

Tracy tossed back half of the four ounces she had poured for herself and said, "You'll be able to talk them out of it. You've very good at talking people out of things."

"I'm not going to try," Matt said.

Tracy gave him a blank look. "But there isn't any other school in Gstaad that—"

"That's right."

She looked at him, the blue eyes very narrow now. "What are you trying to tell me?" she asked, hovering over him.

24

"Not trying to tell you anything, least of all how to run your life. Sit down, Tracy."

Obediently, looking subdued, she sat in an overstuffed chair facing the fireplace. The hem of the quilted blue housecoat rode up several inches. She had very good legs, and when she saw Matt glance at them she chuckled, not quite the way she had chuckled upstairs, and said, "We had a lot of good times together, didn't we, Matt?" and he knew it would be very unpleasant.

"How much do you drink these days?" he asked.

"Drink? I don't understand what you're driving at."

"On the average day. Half a bottle? A whole bottle?"

She pulled the quilted housecoat down, the hem reaching her knees again. "I don't see where that's any business of—"

"Before I drove up," Matt cut her off, "I registered Chris at the Leman International School in Geneva. It's a good school, one of the best. I'm taking him back there with me tonight."

She finished her drink in a quick, nervous gulp, looked at the bottle, and at Matt, and didn't get up to pour another. "You—you can't ride roughshod over people like that," she said.

Jerking a thumb in the direction of the staircase, Matt asked, "How often does that sort of thing go on?"

Color flooded Tracy's face. "Don't I have a right to my own private life?"

"The door was open. Anybody could have walked in on you. It could have been Chris."

"We're not married any longer. What I do doesn't reflect on you, or your precious position. You have no right to intimidate me like this."

"I said Chris could have walked in on you."

"Don't shout at me." Tracy's lips were beginning to tremble. "I'm discreet. I usually ... Maybe I was a little careless this afternoon. We had a little too much to drink. ..."

A little careless, a little too much to drink, and a village that wanted to know everything and was small enough and ingrown enough to have its wish, and maybe after enough of it some of Chris's classmates would greet him with knowing leers, maybe they already had, maybe he already knew— Don't let yourself feel sorry for her, Matt thought. Pity is a luxury you can't afford.

25

"Look at me, Matt. I'm only thirty-five. I mean you can't expect me to go through life without . . ."

Her voice broke, and then she was crying, great wrenching sobs torn from the remembered body, and Matt crossed to the window and stared out at the darkness and the snow falling, and he said:

"Chris's coming with me tonight. No arguments, Tracy. I'm sorry. That's the way it has to be. You kick up a fuss and I'll get a lawyer up here from Geneva who'll do some digging, and if you don't think they'll give me custody, which by the way I'm not asking for now, you're nuts."

She sat there, trying to compose herself, and he could see her reflection against the blackness of the window, and after a while she got up and did pour herself another Scotch, drinking most of it before she managed a small hollow laugh and said, "Well, the newspapers always did say you were a ruthless son-of-a-bitch. Are you going to tell Chris, or shall I?"

"Tell me what?"

There was Chris, in the hall, wearing a toggle-coat, his cheeks rosy from the cold, his too-long blond hair covered with snow.

"Daddy? Daddy, you're here, you're here!"

And Matt was holding the boy in his arms, and they were pounding each other's backs when Tracy said, maliciously:

"We have a surprise for you, Chris. Daddy's going to take you home with him."

"You mean to live with him? In Washington? Oh, boy!"

Which lie took some undoing. He went upstairs with Chris, and they talked. He bounced all over the world for President Huntington. Why, last year he had logged almost seventy thousand miles. They'd have no home life. Chris would hardly see him at all. Washington was a lousy place for a kid to grow up alone. But Chris liked Switzerland, didn't he? Chris allowed, the glow of delight fading from the blue eyes that were so like Tracy's eyes, that he really dug the Swiss scene. There was this school in Geneva, Matt said. Chris said in a flat voice that he'd heard of the International School. Kids from broken homes, he said, with unexpected twelve-year-old wisdom. Kids nobody wants, castoffs. Why can't I go with you? Chris did not ask, Why can't I stay here? Their agreement

26

on that, an agreement that would remain unspoken, Matt decided, was a place to start.

You're exaggerating, Chris, he said. Castoffs, Chris said again in the same flat voice. Not just castoffs, Matt said. A lot of kids from diplomatic families, from twenty different countries, the UN and its agencies, not to mention the American corporate families. It's a damn good school. Get out of there with decent grades and you can just about name the college you want. Oh, am I going to college? I want to be an actor. Do they have acting schools in college?

For a while it was all right. They talked about acting as a career and Chris dropped, with twelve-year-old awe, the names of some movie families who owned chalets in Gstaad.

When am I going?

Tonight, as soon as you pack.

Nobody wants me.

He wished, afterward, that Chris had cried. But Chris's eyes remained dry, his voice remained flat, and he got a bored, terribly blasé look on his face and he said, Tonight's as good as any night, I guess. You got snow tires on the car? It's snowing up a storm. Matt thought he had snow tires on the car. Is it okay if I say good-bye to some of the guys at school? I've got some stuff over there anyway. My locker. Sure, I'll drive you. No thanks, I'll walk.

After Tracy gave him his dinner, Chris put on the toggle-coat and walked, Matt having decided that the headmaster could put up with his disruptive influence a little while longer. The little while turned out to be three hours, and for the first hour Matt and Tracy sat in the big living room of the chalet like strangers in a waiting room. Matt was grateful for that. Tracy still remembered, at least, that it was no good arguing with him once he had made up his mind. That was Tracy's own very genuine urbanity—she hated scenes.

She got up, after the waiting-room hour, and said, "I'll pack his things." She packed them and remained upstairs until Chris returned. Her good-byes were said up there. Chris came downstairs lugging two huge suitcases, and Matt ran to help him with them.

"There's a trunk, too," Chris said in that flat voice. "Mom's shipping it by train."

27

"When I was your age—" Matt began with a hopeful smile.

"You're not my age now. I'm my age. Let's blow this joint."

They loaded the car in silence in the softly falling snow. Chris got in and slumped down and immediately pretended to be asleep, and then after a while he really was asleep.

Chapter
TWO

1   Monday dawned bright, crisp, and cold. The tarmac of Cointrin Airport was clear, but snow lay on the ridges of the Jura Mountains to the north.

Blue and white and shining, Air Force One taxied across the runway, following a jeep with the words SUIVEZ-MOI in large letters on its back. The jeep and the four-engined jet came to a stop, the nose of the big Boeing expertly placed over the arrowhead painted on the asphalt.

A red carpet had been unrolled; the self-propelled flight stairs reached the hatch of the Boeing just as an Air Force sergeant in dress blue opened it from inside and stuck his head out into the clear Swiss air; and then, swiftly, the Presidential party was descending.

The Ambassador had come down from Bern, functionaries of both Swiss Federal Government and the Canton of Geneva lined either side of the carpet along with a contingent of UN people, and the Geneva police in their white pith helmets stood on the observation deck and the runway, looking for trouble that did not materialize. There was polite Swiss applause from the observation deck as President Huntington came jauntily down the flight of stairs, but nothing that indicated he would be the Saviour any more than Russian Premier Andreyev, who had arrived the day before. The Swiss, Matt knew, had played host to Summitry before, and they could be forgiven a certain jadedness.

28

In deference to the Ambassador and the State Department he represented, Matt remained in the background. The top Federal official from Bern made a small speech of welcome in German and his cantonal colleague did the same in French. Then President Huntington moved along the receiving line, smiling into faces and flashbulbs, shaking hands. He wore no coat, despite the chill. His thatch of unruly hair, blowing in the wind that swept across the tarmac, almost matched the color of his tan whipcord suit. He had the gift of making a fixed, public smile seem warm and sincere. Some people said it was because he was crazy enough to like being President. He was forty-six years old, having entered office three years ago at the same age Jack Kennedy had. The same people who liked the public smile saw a resemblance between Kennedy and Huntington, too: both young, both with the same jaunty, optimistic appearance and outlook on life. And while Kennedy had often worn a brace for his back, President Huntington walked rapidly and easily but with a noticeable limp. He had almost lost the leg in Korea.

Comparison of the two Presidents could, and did, go further. Both came from backgrounds where money had never been a problem. Kennedy had spoken with an educated Boston accent; Huntington spoke that rarest of native American speech, educated New York. He had been born and bred in Manhattan, and had entered politics there. Unlike John Lindsay, though, he had been wise enough not to let his career founder in the political quicksand of New York's City Hall. Kennedy's glamorous wife had been educated abroad; so had Huntington's. Kennedy had followed an immensely popular Republican President into the White House. Huntington had followed an immensely unpopular Republican President into the White House. Kennedy had spoken always of vigor, pronounced "vigah." Huntington spoke always of courage, pronounced "courage." Both had, effortlessly—which, Matt knew, was the only way you could ever have it— tremendous charisma.

President Huntington strode to the battery of microphones at the end of the red carpet, thanked the dignitaries, and turned to the crowd.

"It is only fitting that representatives of the United States and the Union of Soviet Socialist Republics ... beset by mutual difficulties ... and hoping to resolve those difficulties ... have journeyed to this most international of cities ... in this most neutral of countries.

"If we have the courage ... to live in peace ... as the Swiss have wisely lived in peace since long before there was a United States or a Union of Soviet Socialist Republics ... then a bright new era may yet dawn for mankind.

"This is the opportunity presented to Premier Andreyev ... and to me ... in your city and your nation."

A raised hand then, to still the applause, and a sudden radiant smile. "May I end this on a personal note? I bring greetings to the people of Switzerland ... from my wife ... who as you know spent her childhood in your mountains. She would love to be here at my side but ... as you also know .. certain conditions make that impossible."

The condition, as the Swiss and everyone in the world did indeed know, was the imminent arrival of a Huntington heir, and the personal note, as Matt knew it would, got warmer applause then the brief political statement.

Then President Huntington was striding quickly, despite the limp, toward the first of a line of limousines waiting on the tarmac. His eyes roved the crowd; he saw Matt and winked. The wink was eloquent, for it seemed to say: Okay, we gave them their official reception. Now, friend, you and I get to work.

Soon the waiting limousines would be moving. Soon others would take their place, to await the arrival of the Boeing airbus carrying the lower-echelon Presidential staff. Before the morning ended, much of official Washington would have been moved to Geneva—the Secretary of State, the Chairman of the Joint Chiefs of Staff and his aides, the CIA people, and the Secret Service at the Hotel Beau Rivage with the President, the overflow—second-level experts on Russia, on the Balkans, on our own defense capabilities—at the big Intercontinental Hotel. The transplanted White House, Matt thought wryly, and the transplanted Executive Office Building, ready with position papers, with task forces to tackle any problem, with a communications center to contact any part of the world. But, as it did in Washington, with only slight deference to the grinding gears of bureaucratic machinery, decision would rest with the Chief Executive and a very few close advisers. That was President Huntington's way.

Matt got into the third car and settled back. Soon they were rolling, flanked by motorcycle outriders, through the airport gates.

2   Several hours later, sleeves rolled up, a fresh pack of cigarettes and a large bottle of beer at hand, Matthew Olds sat in his room at the Hotel Beau Rivage in Geneva, just down the hall from the Presidential Suite. In front of him on the table were a portable typewriter, the same battered Hermes he had used as a young foreign correspondent years ago, and a stack of yellow paper.

The President wanted a report. Ordinarily it would have been easy. Ordinarily, at high-level meetings like the one that had ended half an hour ago in the Presidential Suite, there was reasonable agreement. But this time the discussion had become heated and Matt found himself at loggerheads with the Secretary of State and the Deputy Director of the CIA.

He stared at the empty paper.

How to report on that fairly?

Maybe, Matt thought, I should have kept my big mouth shut. But you don't keep your mouth shut—big or otherwise—when you hear two of the most influential men in the Administration advocating a policy that could force a nuclear confrontation with Russia.

Well, one of the most influential men, anyway. Secretary of State Benson Reed's power lay in the office, not the man. But Whitney Stoughton had the President's ear, all right, and he sure had bent it today. The press usually said that, next to Matthew Olds, CIA Deputy Director and Plans Division Chief Whitney Stoughton had more influence on President Huntington in matters of foreign policy than anyone else in the Administration.

All right, Matt thought. Next to Matthew Olds.

He glared at the battered Hermes and the still-virgin sheet of paper, took a swallow of beer, and told himself that no one was paying him to straddle fences. His thoughts drifted back to the morning.

The rasp of an electric razor had come from the open bathroom door. "Coffee here yet?" President Huntington's voice called. "What time is it, anyway? There's nothing like a trans-Atlantic flight to foul up the internal clock."

31

"Ten-thirty, Mr. President," Matt said. "Here comes the coffee now."

Burt East, chief of the Secret Service contingent that had come to Geneva, opened the door to admit a waiter wheeling a service cart. The President sat down, put his long legs up, inserted a cigarette in a stubby black holder, lit it, and poured coffee. Burt East followed the waiter outside.

"Put your feet up and relax, Matt," the President suggested, buttering a croissant. "We've got a few minutes before the ExCom tells us how to run the world."

The ExCom was, officially, part of the National Security Council. Like Kennedy and Johnson, but unlike Eisenhower and Nixon, President Huntington rarely convened the entire Council. It was, he often said in private, too unwieldy. Instead, he got together a few people whose ideas he respected and, as he put it, let them toss the thing around. This was the Executive Committee. Its members varied from situation to situation, and even then it left the President less than delighted. "I want advice, not a debate," he had once told Matt.

Now he asked, "Anything on for today?"

"Just a reception at Villa Krupskaya tonight, Mr. President. Tomorrow morning Secretary Reed and Foreign Minister Kapitsa meet to approve the agenda Colonel Malinin and I dreamed up."

"Fine," the President said, stubbing out his cigarette. "And do me a favor, Matt. Cut out that Mr. President stuff until the ExCom gets here."

"How's Gigi?" Matt asked.

"The general shape and dimensions of a tent in a stiff wind. She sends love." President Huntington buttered another piece of croissant and bit into the flaky pastry. "What about this Colonel Malinin?"

"Smart. Speaks in pithy little phrases, like he wants to sell them to the *Reader's Digest*. Or like he doesn't want you to know what he's really thinking. And, he's way up there."

"Meaning what?"

"Meaning he's more than Main Department Seven of the KGB. How much more, I don't know. Just a feeling I got, doing business with him."

"It wouldn't surprise Whitney Stoughton," the President said. "The way CIA sees it, Chairman Andreyev's in trouble at home. Either this is his last chance to get his point across, or else he's lost and he's simply here as Lysenko's mouthpiece."

"Does Whit think Lysenko's taken over in the Kremlin?"

"On the verge of it. Would that make Malinin Lysenko's boy?"

"Either way, it figures," Matt said. "If they're still fighting, Malinin's here to defend Lysenko's interests. If Lysenko's running the show himself, Malinin's here to keep an eye on Chairman Andreyev."

The President nodded. "That's about what Whit said. If he's right, we're in trouble. They've got their hawks and doves, same as us. And Lysenko is all Hawk. With him running things, nobody's going to have time to build any fallout shelters."

Matt said nothing. The understatement, the euphemism were part of President Huntington's famous unflappable cool. But whatever words he used, the threat to the world was the same. Nikolai Ivanovich Andreyev, Chairman of the Council of Ministers, Premier of Russia, was the Kremlin dove. Igor Lysenko, First Secretary of the Central Committee of the Communist Party, was the Kremlin hawk. Give all power to Lysenko and what you'd have was no time to build any fallout shelters. What you'd get were acts of provocation, a new Berlin, another Vietnam, and, eventually, a drift toward all-out war.

There was a knock at the door, and Burt East's bland, freckled face appeared. "They're right on time, Mr. President," he said. "It's a quarter to."

"You check them for concealed weapons, Burt?"

East looked startled, then smiled. "You mean, trust nobody, Mr. President?"

"Something like that," President Huntington said, glancing at Matt before the door opened wide to admit the members of the ExCom. Matt knew that the joke, if it was a joke, had been lost on Burt East. Given the climate of opinion in the States these days, the members of the ExCom had a certain inclination toward hawkishness themselves.

Matt studied them, all men he had worked with except one, while chairs were drawn up, cigarettes lit, pads and pencils readied, and the usual small talk made.

Secretary of State Benson Reed was a small, spare Vermonter in his early sixties. He had been Governor and had served a term in the Senate before campaigning unsuccessfully for the Presidential nomination that went to Huntington.

Benson Reed, Matt knew, resented him. Reed was more than twenty years Matt's senior and should have had a clear field as the Administration's foreign-policy spokesman. But for the second time in recent years there was a so-called Little State Department in the White House basement, and Matt ran it. Reed, in his three years as Secretary of State, had been something of a disappointment to the President. He had a gift for acerbic understatement that endeared him to the press, but he leaned too heavily on the slow-churning wheels of his department's bureaucracy.

Whitney Stoughton, the second man to enter the sitting room of the Presidential Suite, was something else again. He was Boston and Newport, Groton and Harvard. A bachelor who had once been a suitor of Matt's ex-wife, his name was linked frequently in the society columns with some of the most glamorous and some of the wealthiest women in the country. He had served in Moscow with the State Department before making the switch to CIA. As Deputy Director and Chief of its Plans Division he currently held down the toughest and most controversial desk in Central Intelligence. He was urbane and clever and ambitious and, at forty, still had his youthful blond good looks.

General Pierre Gustav Beauregard Laffont, Chairman of the Joint Chiefs of Staff, was a Louisiana Creole from an old military family. Tall, swarthy, and poker-faced, he wore a gray worsted suit and a trim little military mustache. He seemed ill at ease without his uniform. The neutral Swiss, Matt thought with a smile, would let you hold Summit Conferences until all the brown-and-white cows came down from all the high pastures, but they wouldn't allow foreign uniforms on the streets of Geneva.

The fourth man to enter the room had not flown over with the Presidential party. He was even taller than General Laffont, and lean and straight despite his almost eighty years. He was, Matt observed, the only one who hadn't chucked his outer garment in the anteroom. He was wearing a toggle-coat like the one Chris had worn last night. He took it off, tossed it negligently on a chair. The ruddy face split in a wide grin under the thick mane of white hair as he crossed the room to shake hands with the

34

President. He wore, under the coat, a pair of baggy corduroy trousers and a heavy turtleneck sweater.

"Mr. President," he said. "Good trip?"

The President got up. "Always a pleasure to see you, sir."

He meant it. He had often told Matt he wished Kermit Hauser had been twenty years younger. Hauser was, according to the President, the best Secretary of State the United States never had. He had spent forty years in the department as a career officer, including two stints as Ambassador to Moscow and a few years' leave at the Institute for Advanced Study at Princeton. He had always been a maverick. Retiring after his second tour of duty in Moscow, he had married his fourth wife, a Russian woman half his age. Like many superannuated ex-diplomats, he had put himself out to pasture in Gstaad. He had driven down to Geneva at the President's request to sit on the ExCom.

A fresh pot of coffee arrived, the small talk dwindled, and President Huntington said, "Gentlemen, we have some problems to discuss."

Which had been, Matt realized, sitting over the battered Hermes in his room, as low-key an introduction to the fact that we might be going to war with Russia tomorrow, or next week, or next month, as you could get.

He looked at his watch. Still a couple of hours to do the report before he had to dress for the party at Villa Krupskaya. He leaned over the machine and, using two fingers on each hand, began to type.

3

To: THE PRESIDENT
From: MATTHEW OLDS
Subject: NSC EXCOM MEETING, MONDAY, 24 NOVEMBER

Only conference we'll have before the Summit gets underway, so of course everyone had to get his oar in—yours truly included.

CAST: The President, the Secretary of State, Ambassador Hauser, General Laffont, Whitney Stoughton, Matthew Olds.

Secretary Reed in good form. Sounded knowledgeable. Probably is, up to a point.

Gave us background on Russo-Yugoslav conflict.
Russia had ideological red face—pun Reed's—
due to Yugoslav experimentation with so-called
market socialism. Market socialism step
toward capitalism, worked well for Yugoslavs.
Post-Tito flirtation with outright capitalism
and increasing ties with West followed. Iron
Curtain neighbors, recognizing a good thing,
move in direction of market socialism—eventually outright capitalism?—themselves.
Russia, threatened with economic revolt in
satellite countries, fears political revolt
would follow.

Second point equally important for Kremlin,
according to Reed. Russia's growing Mediterranean fleet relies on Egyptian and Algerian
bases. But who ever heard of stable government in Egypt or Algeria? Invasion and conquest of Yugoslavia, on any pretext, would give
Russia what she has coveted since Czarist
days—her own deep-water Mediterranean port at
Rieka.

Reed eloquent in outlining reasons why Russian takeover of Yugoslavia must be prevented.
If not, Greece and Turkey—Eastern arms of
NATO—all but isolated; Italy's Adriatic Coast,
west of Yugoslavia, vulnerable to attack;
neutral Austria virtually surrounded by Communist Bloc troops. More: all of Western
Europe so demoralized that Austria and Finland
could be next targets—eventually Berlin—
until bit by bit Russia gained control of
continent. And, if Russia allowed to control
vast industrial output of Western Europe,
Kremlin could set timetable for a Third World
War—and win.

The President: Nobody will win a Third
World War.

A small silence, with everybody considering
the possibility of atomic Armageddon.

The President: The Russians know that as
well as we do. That's why Chairman Andreyev is
here in Geneva.

Whitney Stoughton: Chairman Andreyev can't

blow his nose unless Lysenko sends him a box of Kleenex from the Kremlin.

The President: Hold that for later, Whit.

President asks General Laffont for up-to-date evaluation of the tactical situation.

General Laffont less convincing in civilian clothes. Looks smaller, less sure of himself, but his remarks not debatable. Russia's powerful fleet, led by three _Moskva_-class carriers, already steaming from Alexandria and Mers-el-Kebir for the Adriatic. Aboard the _Moskva_ carriers are VTOL jets, MiG-27's, carrying atomic weapons. At same time, US Sixth Fleet building steam in Naples. We must show flag too. Naval confrontation seems inevitable.

Soviet Bloc troops observed by Orion reconnaissance satellites on maneuvers in Rumania. Four mechanized infantry divisions and elements of two more identified. This, General Laffont insists, is diversionary deployment. Russian invasion of Yugoslavia, when it comes, will be across flat Hungarian plain in direction Subotica-Belgrade.

Pentagon's best guess: Russia will attack Yugoslavia before end of November, giving Red Army three weeks to move in and mop up before snow blankets northern part of country.

Whitney Stoughton, poised and very sure of himself, next. CIA Plans Division had been active behind the scenes. Contact already made with Yugoslavs. Sixth Fleet could expect big welcome in Rieka. More: Belgrade airport and big expansion of airport at Cilipi, south of Dubrovnik, means American airborne forces can land. Would also be welcome. Stoughton's activities coordinated with General Laffont. Five American airborne divisions, in Reforger-like setup, could be in Yugoslavia inside twenty-four hours. Stoughton, Laffont, and Yugoslavs awaiting go-ahead.

General Laffont: Policy-making is not my concern, but give us the green light, Mr. President, and we can have Yugoslavia garrisoned before Russia has a chance to move.

The President: No, that's right. Policy-making is not your concern, General.

A pink face for General Laffont.

Secretary of State Reed: Well, it is my concern. The 1972 mutual defense treaty with Yugoslavia clearly states that in the event of attack . . .

The President: I know what the treaty says. Nobody's been attacked yet. We're here to prevent that.

Some discussion, not heated, of what happens if Russia does attack. Agreed that we must go to Yugoslavia's defense, with even White House resident-dove Matthew Olds concurring reluctantly. The point being that stopping a limited aggression now could prevent a far bigger war later. Reed makes the old Hitler comparison, which is valid. First the Rhineland, then Austria, Czecho, finally Poland. Early on, Adolf could have been stopped. By the time Poland's turn came, too late to stop him short of World War. Same could be true of Red Army now. If Russia moves, a limited response might prevent all-out hostilities.

Back to problem: What can be done to prevent attack?

Kermit Hauser, dignified, calm, commanding enormous respect, gives a history lesson.

World faced with period of dangerous upheaval because cast of characters on the stage of history has changed so rapidly.

In France, Pompidou and the last vestiges of Gaullism are gone.

In Spain, Franco is gone.

Yugoslavia makes her way, too satisfactorily to suit Kremlin, without Tito.

Kosygin gone in Russia, and later Brezhnev.

Hauser's question a good one: What have the new Russian leaders inherited?

Back in fifties, Khrushchev said: We will bury you. In late sixties Brezhnev, responding more subtly to Czech revolt, promulgated Brezhnev Doctrine. Moscow claimed right to intervene in any socialist country departing from practice of Soviet-style Communism.

Attempted to barter a free hand for Kremlin in East, according to Hauser, in return for giving us a free hand in the West.

But new Russian leaders have no intention of giving us free hand in the West, while their own free hand in the East is really something. And they seem determined to bury us on middle ground that is neither East nor West.

Yugoslavia one example, outside Soviet camp since 1948. Middle East another example. Because lines not clearly formed there, danger of nuclear confrontation exists.

Hauser brings up 1972 Big Four Conference, following Ten Day War between Arab States and Israel. Even with Russian support, Arabs fail to make Israel surrender gains that protect her borders. Brezhnev does some saber-rattling, is left looking worse than silly. Four months later—exit Brezhnev. Nikolai Ivanovich Andreyev becomes Chairman of Council of Ministers, or Premier, and Igor Lysenko becomes Communist Party Boss. Andreyev regarded in West as dove, Lysenko as hawk.

Crucial question for ExCom: Which one wields the real power in Russia?

Secretary Reed: Show me a time in the past when the Premier was more powerful than the Party Secretary.

Hauser: I can't, Mr. Secretary. But that doesn't mean it isn't happening now.

Reed: Lysenko controls the Party machinery. That's where the power is.

Hauser: And Nikolai Ivanovich is Chairman of the Council of Ministers. That's where the decisions are made. And he is an honorable man. (Note: Honorable, in this context, would sound strange from anyone but Hauser.) If he is here to talk, he'll talk. He says what he thinks, and I've known him to act on impulse. Remember his flight to London?

Everybody remembered Andreyev's flight to London. State Department wags still talk of it as the Big One-and-a-Half Conference. Two Russian cosmonauts, returning from moon, make

39

emergency landing in Devon, with British help. Six hours later, Andreyev is at Number Ten Downing Street. Sincere thanks, and three days of conference with Prime Minister Dawson.

Whitney Stoughton: So he acts on impulse. What does that prove?

Hauser: As a result of that visit, Andreyev agreed that Russia wouldn't meddle in the Gibraltar dispute—and made it stick in the Kremlin. Don't underestimate him. If he wants to talk, there's a chance for peace.

Stoughton: Or maybe he wants to talk so they can attack Yugoslavia while we're at the conference table.

The President: We're here to talk with the Russians. We're going to talk. Right now there are three points to consider. One, is Russia ready to move on Yugoslavia? State thinks so, and the Chairman JCS agrees. Two, if Russia moves, do we stand a better chance of averting total war by going into Yugoslavia ourselves or letting Russia get away with it? We seem to agree on that one: If we let Russia get away with it, the risk of general war increases. Three, can we hope to prevent the invasion, here, at the conference table with Andreyev? The answer, gentlemen, is that you can be damn sure we will try. Nobody wants war, not even a limited war.

The President, Matt remembered, leaning back from the typewriter, had let the one word, war, hang in the smoke-filled air of the room.

That one word meant everything to civilization in the last quarter of the twentieth century, for if the word became fact there would be no civilization. It was a word that defied imagination. You could, if you had to, picture a Pearl Harbor, where a fleet had been destroyed, or a Dresden, where a city was turned to rubble in a single night, or the dehumanizing brutality of a brush-fire war like Vietnam. But you could not conceive of President Huntington or Chairman Andreyev using their nuclear go-codes to summon the end of the world—a thousand missiles with nuclear warheads streaking for Russia, a thousand streaking for the States, and in the morning

President and Chairman possibly safe in their deep shelters but the great cities vaporized and two hundred million people dead.

Matt lit a cigarette and began typing again.

Toward end of meeting, Stoughton and Secretary Reed advocating same policy, but for different reasons. Reed insists on honoring treaty with Yugoslavia. Stoughton urges striking first, before the Russians do.

Both push for direct military aid to Yugoslavia, now. General Laffont keeps nodding agreement but is subdued after Presidential rebuke and says nothing. Kermit Hauser, smoking pipe, also says nothing. Matthew Olds sticks his two cents in.

Olds: I keep remembering the Cuban missile crisis in '62. Remember how the Kennedy brothers handled it?

Reed: Exactly what do you have in mind?

Olds: Khrushchev. We had to let him retreat without losing face.

Stoughton: We used a naval blockade.

Olds: Sure we did. But the ship we boarded—and we boarded just one—flew the Panamanian flag. We didn't touch the Russian Merchant Marine. There was also plenty of talk about invading Cuba, but we didn't. We gave Khrushchev the chance to pull out on his own hook, and he did.

Reed: This is a totally different set of circumstances.

Stoughton: We didn't go into Rumania. Or Hungary and Czechoslovakia before that. I don't have to remind you what happened.

Olds: Go into Yugoslavia now and we could have nuclear war on our hands.

Reed: That is an unwarranted assumption.

The President: Mr. Hauser?

Kermit Hauser: I would say that Mr. Olds is right. The focus of contention has shifted, in the past decade, from southeast Asia to southwest Asia and the Balkans. The Kremlin can't afford to let us steal a march on them there.

41

Stoughton: Then this Summit is a waste of time.

Hauser: I was never aware that an attempt to prevent nuclear holocaust was a waste of time.

Stoughton: Am I supposed to tell the Yugoslavs we don't move in? They'll love that.

Reed: And am I to inform Ambassador Djeba that the United States is not prepared to honor the treaty?

The President: Keep your shirt on, both of you. If you mean, am I turning this over to the Pentagon before the Russians attack, the answer is no.

Stoughton (very dramatic, getting up and scooping up his papers): Then we're wasting our time here. I guess I should have realized a former foreign correspondent knows more than the Secretary of State.

The President (loud): Sit down, for Christ's sake. This is no popularity contest.

Stoughton: It's not even a discussion.

The President: I said sit down.

Stoughton (sitting): I'm sorry, Mr. President.

Stoughton glares at Matthew Olds. The President does not quite grin. (Note: This is nothing new. The President almost seems to encourage Stoughton-Olds arguments. To draw them both out more?)

The President: Now, Whit, I want you to keep your lines open to Yugoslavia. You can tell them we won't tolerate a Russian takeover.

Stoughton (somewhat mollified): Is that the official word?

The President: That is the official word. And Benson, you can tell Ambassador Djeba we'll honor our commitments—when and if it's necessary.

Secretary Reed backtracks, suggesting we might bring a couple of bargain points to the conference table. One: if Russia removes the pressure on Yugoslavia, we curtail our efforts to establish a stable, dead-center government in France. The Sedoux party could be left to stew in its own juice. Two: Israel. We could agree to a Russian demand for a pullback to the pre-1972 borders.

Olds: That would be a bad mistake. We're here to prevent an open act of aggression, not to horse-trade.

Secretary Reed grumbles but says nothing. He considers himself a horse-trader from way back.

The President gets a faraway look in his eye. That's the only way I can describe it. We've all seen it before.

The President: You're right, Matt. No horse-trading for now. But if Andreyev agrees to leave Yugoslavia in peace, there's nothing I'd rather do than sit down and talk with him. I mean a real Summit. All the problems that make this the most interesting and most terrifying century in history. The population problem. A billion people living at starvation level. International health. The way we pollute the air we breathe and the water we drink. Disarmament. A means of controlling our military-industrial complex at home and their steel-eaters in Russia. We can do it. Sooner or later we've got to.

That's the Huntington dream. Can it happen in our lifetimes?

Stoughton (bringing the ExCom down to earth with a jolt): Then how about a position of strength? Rattle a few sabers. Put the Pentagon on Prime Alert—

The President: The Pentagon is on Prime Alert. Right, General?

General Laffont: Right, Mr. President.

Stoughton: I mean, let the Russians know we've put the Pentagon on Prime Alert.

Olds: No. It ought to be kept under wraps.

Stoughton: It can't be kept under wraps.

Olds: Well, not for publication, then. The Russians have their own reconnaissance satellites. They'll know. But we don't have to broadcast it.

Stoughton: Why the hell not?

43

Olds: There's no point telling the world we're as cynical as the Russians, that's why not.

Reed: I'll have to go along with Whitney.

Stoughton: Why not put it to a vote?

The President (smiling): A vote? That would make my job easy, wouldn't it?

Stoughton: What's the use? The two of you had it all figured out before the rest of us walked in here.

The President (ignoring that): The important thing is, we're ready. The Sixth Fleet will be leaving Naples this afternoon. The Reforger apparatus is on standby. Five airmobile divisions, fully equipped, can be—

Stoughton: Are sitting in their bases in the States because an ex-foreign correspondent is afraid we'll get a bad press if we use them now.

Olds (hot under the collar): That's the second time you've said that.

Stoughton: I'm sorry if I hurt your delicate sensitivities.

Olds: Well damn it, Whit, we're trying to give the President some useful options.

Stoughton: Options? The President? Not from where I sit. From where I sit, you've been—

Olds: We've tried to take all the options into—

Stoughton: Is that the imperial we or the editorial we?

The President: SHUT UP, BOTH OF YOU!

Both shut up, very chagrined.

The President: The Sixth Fleet is sailing, the Reforger apparatus is on standby. We're ready to move if we have to, but we're going to talk first.

Kermit Hauser: I can guarantee that Premier Andreyev will not sit down with us in treachery.

Stoughton (sarcastic): I'm glad someone can guarantee it.

Hauser (to the President): Did you know Andreyev is a sick man?

Stoughton: I had a report or two to that effect.

Secretary Reed allows himself a thin smile.

Hauser: Forgive me, but I have been rather out of touch.

The President: Gentlemen, let's put the lid on now. If I don't call Gigi soon—you know pregnant women. I'd like to thank you all. It's been a fruitful discussion. (Goes to the white telephone with the eight-button console that has just been installed.) The way I see it, everything depends on what Chairman Andreyev has up his sleeve, and the only one who can tell us that is Andreyev himself.

Which is how we leave it—hope or despair, peace or war, in the hands of a sick man at Villa Krupskaya, who may or may not be the real boss of Russia. But at least, for the moment, we've clipped the wings of our own hawks.

Matt pulled the last sheet out of the typewriter, read what he had written, shrugged and took the papers down the hall to the Presidential Suite.

He wondered if he had been accurate or merely hopeful. Had the wings of our hawks really been clipped? The first meeting of the ExCom, really, had ended on a wait-and-see attitude. And the memo he had just completed would not be the only report on the meeting.

Whitney Stoughton, now, was probably on the phone with CIA Director McManus in Virginia, or sending a cipher through the secret machinery of the Plans Division to his contacts in Belgrade. Secretary Reed would give his assurances to the Yugoslav Ambassador. General Laffont would certainly be in touch with the Pentagon, giving the Sixth Fleet its sailing orders, making sure the Reforger apparatus was ready to move five divisions a third of the way around the world in a matter of hours. Before the day ended, the military might of the United States would be poised like a sprinter in the starting blocks.

And Russia? Was Chairman Andreyev preparing for war, too?

On the way into the Presidential Suite, Matt passed a small man seated in the foyer with a large attaché case on his lap. It contained, Matt knew, the go-codes that the President had to activate to fire our nuclear missiles. The operation, from the time the attaché case snapped open anywhere in the world, took less than three minutes.

Chapter
THREE

1 Nikolai Ivanovich Andreyev, Chairman of the Council of Ministers of the Union of Soviet Socialist Republics, Premier of Russia, was attempting a neat, precise bow with his black tie.

"Foolishness," he mumbled, getting it wrong and pulling the end free again. "What happened to the clip-on?"

"You told me not to bring it, Father," Claudia said.

"I did? I must have been mad." The bow came out wrong again, and Andreyev untied it.

Claudia managed not to smile. "Here, let me."

She stood in front of him and deftly tied a perfect bow. She studied the dear, loved face six inches from her own without seeming to study it. Her father was looking well. His cheeks had color and the dark, near-sighted eyes behind the pince-nez lenses were sparkling. The spade-shaped beard, still a glossy Georgian black despite Nikolai Ivanovich's fifty-four years, had been trimmed before the flight from Moscow. He was breathing normally. He was broad-shouldered and no taller than Viktor, no taller than Claudia herself. Despite his complaint about the bow tie, he was a fastidious dresser. The black dinner jacket and studded formal shirt suited him. For a man who had had the second of two severe heart attacks less than a year ago, he was looking very well indeed.

She stepped back. "There. You will be the handsomest man at the party."

Nikolai Ivanovich picked up a pair of military hair-brushes and began to brush his hair back. He was very vain about what hair he had left, two wings of it, as glossily black as the beard, on either side of the high bald dome.

Claudia sighed elaborately. "When I marry," she said, "I will be quite accustomed to waiting for my husband."

She was already dressed in a brocaded green satin floor-length sheath. She wore a single strand of pearls.

46

Green satin ballroom slippers peeked out under the hem of her dress. Her black hair, so dark it had blue highlights, was piled on her head, accentuating the fine cheekbones and the large dark eyes.

"And do you have a candidate in mind?" Nikolai Ivanovich asked, not quite teasing.

"Where can I find someone as good as my father?"

"You saw Viktor last night?"

The glow left her eyes. "He showed me something of Geneva."

"In the rain?"

"It's a beautiful city, even in the rain," Claudia said, as last night came hurtling back. Viktor's hold on her, she told herself, was purely physical. He could, even when she was furious with him, bend her to his will. A look, a touch of his hand, or worst of all the infuriating game he played with her, and her own will melted. Away from him she could say: Viktor Malinin, Colonel, KGB, is an opportunist. It is not me he wants. He wants what I can give him, a place close to the seat of power.

Or does he? Politics yesterday afternoon, and lust last night in the rain. The political argument had frightened her. Viktor had belittled her father. Nikolai Ivanovich, Viktor had all but said, was an anachronism. There was a time for détente with the West, but that time had passed. Nikolai Ivanovich was still living in an era of post-Vietnam goodwill. Events had passed him by.

Viktor's words had been sarcastic and taunting. It was almost as if he had dared her to denounce him, but that didn't make sense—unless, of course, Claudia thought with sudden alarm, Viktor wanted to go on record as being critical of her father prior to Nikolai Ivanovich's fall from power.

"Nervous?" Nikolai Ivanovich asked.

"What? I'm sorry, I was—daydreaming."

"Your first party outside Russia."

"My first anything outside Russia," Claudia laughed. "Maybe I am a little nervous."

"Don't be." Nikolai Ivanovich stepped back. "You look wonderful."

"But my English—"

"Your English is fine," Nikolai Ivanovich assured her. Languages were a hobby with him. He spoke English, French, and German fluently. "And believe me it is an

47

accomplishment to speak the second most difficult language in the world as fluently as you do."

"The second?" Claudia asked cautiously in English. "What is the first?"

"Russian," her father said in mock despair. "Just as we Russians are the most difficult people in the world."

They laughed together, and there was a moment of closeness, and then Claudia said, "Father, Viktor said some things yesterday." She was suddenly glad to be speaking English; the words she had to say seemed, in a foreign tongue, somehow less ominous. "Are you—in trouble at home?"

She watched him closely. The dark eyes, so like her own, seemed to go opaque. Her father could become infuriatingly self-contained. He waved a hand vaguely, shrugged, waved the hand again. "I told you, we are the most difficult people in the world. One way or another I am always in trouble. Two hundred and fifty million individualists in a socialist society, how can it be otherwise?"

"I mean," Claudia persisted, "trouble with Secretary Lysenko?"

"Claudia, Claudia," her father chided her gently, vaguely, unsatisfyingly. "I am probably the stubbornest man in Russia. Comrade Lysenko is probably the second most stubborn. Between us we try to govern. Don't worry your pretty head about it. This evening you will sparkle. When there is trouble, really bad trouble, I will tell you."

"Promise?" Claudia asked, feeling very young.

"Of course I promise. Look at you, so solemn. Now smile. What time is it?"

"Seven-thirty."

"Time you went down to greet our guests."

"Aren't you coming?" Claudia asked in alarm.

"So you can waltz down that ridiculous staircase on my arm?" Nikolai Ivanovich shook his head. "To teach a child to swim—you drop him in the water. This party is for the small fish, anyway. President Huntington is aware of that. He will try to be the last guest to arrive, and he won't stay long. I will time my arrival with his. It is a game, diplomatic protocol. Besides, it is better for our football players. Let them worry about us one at a time."

The football players Nikolai Ivanovich referred to with his mild scorn were their personal bodyguards. Former footballers for the Dynamo Sports Club, the athletic club that was the pride of the KGB, they now served in Main

Department Seven under Viktor Malinin. Nikolai Ivanovich, a man who liked to plunge into a crowd with a big fatherly smile on his face, did not like bodyguards.

"Now go," he said. He went to the door with her, kissed her on the forehead, then changed his mind, kissing her on both cheeks and hugging her. "You smell delicious. Enjoy yourself at the party."

When he opened the door the two hulking footballers waiting in the hall came to attention.

"Comrade Yegorov," Nikolai Ivanovich said, "you will find Colonel Malinin downstairs and ask him to escort Claudia Nikolaievna. Comrade Bayev, you will wait outside in the car park."

"In the car park, Comrade Chairman?" repeated the hulking Bayev, surprised.

"In the car park. When the American President arrives, you will let me know."

A moment later Claudia was standing, uncertain and alone, at the top of the broad, curving staircase waiting for Viktor. She wished she had a cigarette, decided it would be unseemly, then remembered that her cigarettes and her makeup were in the small beaded evening purse she had left in the apartment. There was still no sign of Viktor. She went back and entered without knocking, going to her father's bedroom where she thought she had left the purse.

Nikolai Ivanovich had removed bow tie, dinner jacket, and stiff white shirt. He looked at her, startled. A plain dark suit was folded neatly across the foot of the bed.

"My purse," she said. "I forgot my purse." She saw it on the dresser, got it.

Their eyes met.

"I thought I would take a nap," Nikolai Ivanovich said. Then his eyes followed her gaze to the dark suit folded on the foot of the bed. All he said was: "Go now. Viktor will be waiting."

Viktor was waiting. "You are looking lovely, Claudia Nikolaievna," he said formally, as if last night had never happened.

She took his arm. They went downstairs toward the sounds of the party.

2   She found Viktor's attentiveness infuriating.

He lit her cigarettes for her, kept her champagne glass

filled, introduced her to second-string American diplomats with their blandly confident faces, made small talk at her side as if he were a social aide. His coolness made her want to scream.

She made the necessary small talk. It was her first diplomatic reception outside the Soviet Union, though she had served as her father's hostess for several years at home. She was complimented on her beauty. The Americans were more gallant than the Russians.

Soviet women, she said. Yes, a woman's role in the Soviet Union is whatever she wishes to make it. But how can I generalize? We are a vast country. The distance from Leningrad to Vladivostok is greater than from Leningrad to New York. Do you mean Georgian women, or the women of the Uzbeks? We Georgians have always made much of our women. Our old kings we remember, but it is a woman, Queen Tamara, whom we adulate. Among the Uzbeks, on the other hand . . .

Thank you, she said. I learned it in school and from my father. He is the fluent one in your language, not I.

The American women present—there were not many of them—awed her. They seemed so natural, so confident. They wore very little makeup. No lipstick. She was glad she had worn no lipstick herself. They talked calmly, capably, on a hundred subjects. They were easy and comfortable among men. She envied them. What would she be, she thought, if she were not Nikolai Ivanovich's daughter? True, she had risen through the ranks to become, at a very young age, Second Secretary of the Communist Youth League—but would that have happened if she had been plain Claudia Andreyeva from Tbilisi in the Georgian S.S.R. instead of the daughter of the Comrade Chairman?

Would even Viktor have wanted her, have loved her for two years, except for her father? Viktor, who now wanted to cast her off. Viktor, who had all but said that her father's days as Chairman were numbered?

Among physicians, she said, seventy-five percent are women.

Cocktail-party smiles and another glass of champagne.

No, she said, I'm afraid my father doesn't discuss those things with me.

Ah'm from Georgia, ma'am. An odd, drawling accent. Are you from Georgia?

The babble of conversation increased, the men's voices

louder, the women's more brittle. Third-drink level, an American voice informed her, it's standard at all cocktail parties. The balding American went away with a Russian girl with not-quite-green hair. This year, in Russia, dyed hair was almost universal.

Foreign Minister Kapitsa smiled at her, had a duty sip of champagne, and waddled off toward the hors d'oeuvre table, a plump penguin of a man in search of food.

Viktor was no longer at her side.

She suddenly felt overwhelmed. It wasn't the noise and the strange faces and the necessity of cocktail-party talk. It was much more and much less. It was Viktor, and the way he had used her and no longer wanted to use her. It was her father, and his bad heart, and the trouble with Comrade Lysenko, if there was trouble with Comrade Lysenko. It was a plain dark suit on the foot of her father's bed, and no answers to the questions she hadn't asked. It was not knowing who she was, or if she was anyone except the daughter of Nikolai Ivanovich.

I want to be me, she thought. I want to be me.

"Well, who else are you?" an American voice said.

"What? I beg your pardon?"

"You said, 'I want to be me.' "

She felt her face coloring.

"Don't worry. You didn't exactly scream it. More like a mumble, actually. You're not alone. Ten minutes at a cocktail party and I want to start climbing walls, too. It's one of the dangers of being a diplomat."

"You're a diplomat?"

"Well, not exactly. I work for the President. I'm Matthew Olds."

"The Special Assistant for National Security Affairs," she said promptly. "I'm impressed."

"I'm impressed you knew."

"Pravda says you exert a very strong influence on your President."

"Then *Pravda*'s kinder to me than the New York *Times*. Need a refill? Or some food? That's quite a spread there. The Chairman's really outdone himself. At the Russian Embassy in Washington, it's usually Ritz crackers and slices of Kraft American cheese."

"Chairman Andreyev is a Georgian," Claudia said. "We Georgians are famous for our hospitality."

"You're Georgian, too?"

"Yes."

"What do you do here, anyway?"

Claudia waited three seconds and then said, "I suppose you would call me a social aide."

"In Geneva with the UN or what?"

"No, I came from Moscow with the Chairman's party."

There was another three seconds of silence, this time a comfortable silence. He was tall and looked dashing—dashing was the only English word she could think of—in his dinner jacket. His dark hair was shaggy around the ears and collar, as if he had his hair cut, with reluctance, only when someone led him to the barber's chair. Thirty-five, she thought, or perhaps forty. The eyes were dark. The craggy face, with its deep brackets around the mouth, seemed too solemn, until he smiled. He was beginning to smile now. The smile started in his eyes and changed his whole face.

"Something is funny?" she asked.

"Man over there. American. He just now said he misses the good old times of Khrushchev. Khrushchev, he said, was predictable. Do you miss the good old times of Khrushchev?"

"I was just a little girl then."

"What's your name?"

"Tamara," she said quickly. She had been waiting for him to ask, the name ready on her lips. She wondered how long she would be allowed to be Tamara.

"Matt," he said.

"What?"

"Oh. I see the problem. A name and a word. It's what friends call me."

"Matt. Of course. Short for Matthew. But short," she said, "is one thing you are not."

He smiled again. "Anyone who can make a play on words in a foreign language has a pretty good command of it."

Her standard response, that her father's English was ever so much better, remained unsaid. She felt light-headed and reckless. She wanted to go on being Tamara, just plain Tamara from the Georgian S.S.R., as long as she could.

"It is," she said, "one reason why I am a social aide."

"I'm definitely in need of some social aid," he said.

"Really?" She spoke the one word coolly, with a raised eyebrow, almost, she thought, as one of the confident American girls would have said it.

52

"Uh-huh." He drew a finger across his throat. "I've had it up to here with cocktail parties, or with this particular cocktail party. I'd like to go somewhere quiet and talk. Can you?"

"Can *you?*" she asked.

"I probably ought to stick around. Maybe that's why I want to take off."

"I really ought to 'stick around' myself."

Then she saw Viktor and the footballer Yegorov, across the big crowded room, looking in her direction. Viktor was talking animatedly, Yegorov nodding. She didn't want to stop being Tamara, not yet.

"But you talked me into it," she heard herself saying. "Just let me get my coat."

"Great. Meet you at the front door?"

"No," she said quickly, "better not. I really am supposed to stay. Not that they'll miss me once I'm gone," she lied. "There's a driveway that goes from the kitchen door to the highway. Can you meet me at the top?"

"I'll find it," Matthew Olds said, and he watched her make her way through the crowd and up the big, curving staircase.

The apartment was empty.

Nikolai Ivanovich's dinner jacket hung neatly in the wardrobe. The plain dark suit was gone. His coat was gone.

For a moment Claudia stood there. She placed a cigarette between her lips and then removed it, unlighted. She went to the window and looked out—a star-filled night, and the surface of the lake black and calm. Distantly across it she could see the winking lights of France. Here, a few kilometers east of Geneva, beyond the Palace of Nations where her father would confer with the Americans, the lake was wide, the view magnificent.

Where was Nikolai Ivanovich?

She bit her lip. She almost decided not to meet the American.

Her father had taken the trouble of dressing in his dinner jacket for her benefit. Probably, she guessed, he would soon appear downstairs, pince-nez low on his nose, bow tie askew, as if he hadn't gone out at all. But where had he gone, and why? Viktor's taunting words came back to her. She ought to go downstairs and wait.

But she couldn't. Viktor might talk to her, or one of the

53

footballers. Nikolai Ivanovich, he is resting? Like most women she knew she could tell a small lie convincingly. But a big one?

She decided to wait fifteen minutes. Perhaps in fifteen minutes he would return. She smoked the cigarette, and another one. He did not return.

She got her suede coat, opened the door, and peeked out. The long hallway was deserted. I could wait here, she thought. But she knew her father. If Nikolai Ivanovich wasn't ready to talk, her urging would only embarrass them both. Putting out the second cigarette, she wondered how much she was rationalizing. She knew she wanted to see the American.

Swiftly, she shut the door behind her and went down the length of the long hall, past the top of the curving staircase, to the kitchen stairs. She descended the two flights quickly and entered the smells and bustle of the kitchen. A waitress was heading with a heavy tray of hors d'oeuvres for the swinging doors. Two chefs were making more of the delicate little open-faced sandwiches. The old Ukrainian pastry chef, the one with the enormous white moustaches, was sitting at a table with his head on his hand, gazing mournfully at what was either a glass of water or a glass of vodka. He looked up.

"Good evening, Claudia Nikolaievna," he said.

"Good evening, Semyon."

The waitress with the heavy tray swung around and stared at Claudia before going through the swinging doors.

What the kitchen staff knew, Claudia was sure, all of Villa Krupskaya would know tomorrow. She shrugged. She was twenty-six, she had gone out to meet a man.

She wondered how Nikolai Ivanovich had accomplished it. This was the only way out, except for the front door. Perhaps old Semyon, whom he trusted, had somehow managed to clear the kitchen for her father's departure.

Time enough later, or tomorrow, Claudia told herself, to trade confidences with him. Right now she was Tamara, and a feeling of unfamiliar recklessness propelled her out the kitchen door into the cold, clear night.

3   Matthew Olds was waiting, in the Volkswagen, at the head of the driveway. Cars sped past on the Geneva-Lausanne highway. He looked at his watch. She's not coming, he thought. Well, give her five minutes.

It was, he thought, what the French call a gratuitous act, doing something for the hell of it. He ought to have stuck the party out. You never knew what tidbits of information could be picked up over a glass of champagne in a crowded room where, sooner or later, someone talked too much. But he had ducked out of such parties before, in Washington and elsewhere, and he supposed the President had got the message.

Matthew Olds did not like cocktail parties.

Matthew Olds did like the girl Tamara.

It was a quick judgment and after ten minutes alone with her, driving along the lake into Geneva, he might regret his decision, might learn she had a mind as subtle as—what was that old Garbo role?—Ninotchka. You capitalist lackey nogoodnik, me dedicated lady socialist. Well, he could always turn the car around and return to Villa Krupskaya. Probably still make it in time to greet the President, too.

Come to think of it, she did look like Garbo. Tall, and those fine high cheekbones and the big dark eyes just a blink away from laughter, and the lithe, controlled way she walked. Whatever else she turned out to be, she was one attractive woman.

Maybe, Matt thought with faint self-mockery, what I need is an antidote to that interesting meeting with Tracy last night.

He had almost missed the rendezvous himself. He'd pulled the VW out of its slot in the parking lot and driven to where he was now waiting. A large bulky figure had loomed out of the darkness.

"May I see your papers?" he was asked in a Russian accent.

Matt had showed his diplomatic passport.

"For fresh air, Mr. Olds?" The passport was not returned.

Matt smiled. "I'm waiting for a lady," he said.

A silence, and then frank, appreciative laughter, and the slap of the passport against his palm. "The same the world over, eh? Good luck to you, comrade."

The bulky figure had drifted away into the darkness.

Fifteen minutes later, Matt thought: Well, five more minutes, but this is absolutely it.

Footsteps crunched on the crushed stone of the driveway.

"High heels and gravel, what a combination," her voice

said, and then he was out of the car, around to her side, and opening the door for her. She wore a dark suede coat with a flaring skirt and fur collar. "Where shall we go?"

"Drive," he said. "Into town. Geneva's special at night. The lights on the lake."

"I know. My father—always told me."

"Your father's here?"

"A cook. He is the pastry chef. Had you stayed longer you would have sampled some of his pirogi," Tamara said quickly.

Matt sensed that she was lying. Well, okay, her old man has some kind of security job. So what?

He started the car. A figure loomed out of the darkness again—probably the same man who had asked for his passport. Matt kept driving.

When the American President arrived at eight-forty, Viktor Malinin realized Nikolai Ivanovich had not yet made his appearance. He looked around the ballroom of Villa Krupskaya, not anxious as yet, but curious.

He did not see Claudia anywhere.

"... said you were a pleasure to work with, Colonel," the American CIA man Whitney Stoughton was saying.

"He did? That was very kind of him."

Some more small talk, and then Malinin excused himself and went upstairs.

Yegorov the footballer was waiting outside the Chairman's apartment.

"They in there?"

"The Comrade Chairman is."

"How long have you been here?"

"I was downstairs most of the time, Comrade Colonel."

"Where's the daughter?"

Yegorov gulped. He was beginning to sweat. "Out," he said.

"Out? What do you mean, out?"

"Bayev saw them. She entered a car, a Volkswagen, with Mr. Olds, the Special Assistant for—"

"I know who Olds is," Malinin cut him off. "Where did they go?"

"Bayev followed them into Geneva."

Yegorov blinked sweat out of his eyes and looked at his watch, which wasn't a watch at all. It made a faint rasping sound, and a voice, Bayev's, could be heard.

"They are walking in the Old Town, Comrade Colonel," Yegorov said.

"I can understand Russian, comrade. Tell that imbecile Bayev to find out what they're up to." Malinin shook his head. "Here, let me."

He lifted Yegorov's arm as if it were a mechanical gadget and told that imbecile Bayev to find out what they were up to.

Then Yegorov waited outside the Chairman's apartment and Malinin ducked into his own room. A few minutes later he heard footsteps—Nikolai Ivanovich and Yegorov on their way downstairs. He waited, then slipped out into the hall, unlocked the door of the Chairman's apartment, and went inside.

Malinin went to the wardrobe first, running a hand quickly over the garments hanging there.

Nikolai Ivanovich's overcoat felt slightly cooler than the rest.

He had gone out, and he had returned, and now Claudia was in Geneva with Matthew Olds.

Viktor Malinin spent ten more expert minutes in the apartment, learning nothing else.

He went down the kitchen stairs thoughtfully.

4   They drove into town and crossed Mont Blanc bridge and parked in the Place du Molard on the Left Bank.

Matt had been mostly silent on the short drive. It was enough to watch the girl Tamara out of the corner of his eye, to observe her wide-eyed scrutiny of the dark lake, the sailboats drawn up on shore and covered with canvas for the coming winter, the imposing stone façades along the quay, and, across the water where the lake narrowed and became the Rhone River, medieval buildings huddled together on their hill and crowned by the floodlit towers of St. Pierre.

"It is the Rhone, isn't it?" she asked, as they followed a rattling tram across the wide, low bridge.

"That's right."

"Someday," Tamara said in a little-girl voice, "I would like to follow that river—down through Provence, and the old Roman ruins. Is it true all the trees lean in one direction, bent by the mistral? And earth the color of terra-cotta, and olive trees and cypresses? How beautiful it must be!"

Matt remembered a holiday in Provence with Tracy, shortly after they were married, while he had still worked as a newspaperman. The gnarled trees had indeed all leaned to the south, like an army of bent old men marching before the wind. In Les Baux, high on its windswept plateau, the once great city crumbling to ruins and now five hundred years from anywhere, they had met an old classmate of Tracy's, Gabrielle Germaine duPont, called Gigi, and recently Gigi Huntington, bride of the freshman Congressman from New York. The four of them spent a few days prowling the ruins, spending too much money dining at the Beaumanière, then driving down to Cannes in Clay Huntington's Jag.

Once, a little drunk on champagne at the casino in Cannes, Gigi had said: "You see that man over there?" That man over there, cautiously playing red and *impair* at the roulette table, was her husband. "Someday he's going to be President."

"That's interesting," Tracy said. "What makes you think so?"

"Because he wants to be."

Two days later, on the beach, Clay Huntington told Matt: "If you ever get tired of filing cables from Oran or Oslo, I can use you. I mean it, that's an offer. Just say when."

Six months later Tracy had talked Matt into saying when.

Now in the Place du Molard in Geneva, Matt said, "Are high heels and cobblestones as bad as high heels and gravel?"

"Tbilisi is a city of cobblestones. Why?"

"There's a restaurant I know up in the Old Town, and it's more fun walking there."

"What a lovely idea," Tamara said. "I'm starving." She studied him. "Candlelight and violins?"

"As a matter of fact, yes. Is that okay?"

"Okay," Tamara said. "I love that word. But it's better than okay. It's perfect."

They got a small table in a corner of the upstairs room of the Chandelier. The maître d' looked at them and seated them side by side without asking. The violinist, who had been leaning over the service bar sipping a glass of wine and looking bored, came right over as if he had been waiting for them.

58

"Ask him, can he play gypsy music?" Tamara said.

The violinist, a small, narrow-shouldered man with an enormous nose, beamed at them and played gypsy music.

Matt found himself watching Tamara and enjoying the gay-sad gypsy violin through her enjoyment of it, as he had seen Geneva through her eyes, walking up the steep cobbled hill to the old Roman Bourg-de-Four, window-shopping at the antique stores along the Grand-Rue on the way to the restaurant. Whatever else she was, she was no Ninotchka.

"Now something Russian," Matt said, and the violinist glanced at him, smiled at Tamara, and played *Dark Eyes*.

They ate smoked salmon and filet Stroganoff and drank dry white Dézalay and rich red Vosne Romanée, very old and lovingly decanted by the sommelier, who smiled at them, appreciating them as the violinist had.

"In Russian restaurants," Tamara said, looking around the small room with its dark-paneled walls and candlelit intimacy, "the tables are lined up like soldiers on parade and if you're lucky the waiter comes in half an hour."

"In American restaurants," Matt said, "anywhere but New York and San Francisco, the crucial question is: How do you like your Idahos, with butter or sour cream?"

"What is an Idahos?"

Matt told her.

"In Russia," said Tamara, "we call *soupe du jour* thumbsoup, due to the clumsiness of our waiters. We also—" She frowned. "That isn't fair of me. Restaurants. Who cares about restaurants? Shall I also say a poet sometimes cannot write what he wants to write, or that we pollute the waters of Lake Baikal, once the purest waters on earth? I'm giving you the impression I don't like my country. I love it. I love Mother Russia," she said, only slightly defensively.

"We are the New World, not you," she went on, didactic now, surprising him with her vehemence, as if she wanted to convince herself. "In the socialist society, envy, greed, poverty, even hatred—all are purged. Money is of no importance. Every man, every woman, contributes what he can of his labor, his ability, his talent. Every man, every woman, is rewarded only according to his needs. Why, in a short time there will be no crime in my country. The state, even the state will wither and die. And as for war—"

It was a set piece, and she delivered it well but, delivering it, mouthing the propaganda of *Pravda* and a hundred little newspapers from Byelorussia to Vladivostok, she was not the Tamara whom Matt had found so attractive.

He took a chance and said, "Look, that's the dream all right. Marx and Engels had it, and maybe Lenin started with it, and before that it was the dream of the French Revolution too, in a way, and maybe all the revolutions that swept Europe in 1848. But it's not the country you live in. Your state isn't withering away; it pervades every segment of life in your country. The abolition of private property hasn't ended man's inhumanity to man. The state can be a master more brutal than any—"

"That's enough," Tamara said. She was pale.

The long-nosed violinist, standing a little way off, unable to hear their words but with their strained faces in plain view, shook his head sadly, returned to the service bar and nursed his wine.

"Hey, take it easy," Matt said. "Nobody with half a brain can be patriotic unless he's willing to criticize, too. Any moron can mouth platitudes. Stuff me full of Idahos from Maine to Forida, or give me built-in obsolescence in the car I drive or the refrigerator my wife uses—"

"Are you married?"

"I was. Anyway, they can ruin the landscape with neon-blight and plant suburban subdevelopments like toadstools all over the place. And whatever you do, don't think of the common good, that's being corny. And let us not forget television. But you know what? It still works. Two hundred and thirty million people and, more or less, one law for all of them, and most of them happy, if people are ever happy, and a Constitution and a Bill of Rights to protect them, sometimes against themselves— No, I'm a patriot, Tamara, same as you," he said, wondering if he were being defensive, too. "But some healthy self-criticism never hurt anybody."

There was a silence.

"End of speech," he said, a little lamely.

With no expression on her face Tamara said, "If you think your suburban—what did you call them, subdevelopments?—are ugly, you should see the blocks of new apartments outside Moscow or Leningrad."

Then Tamara smiled, and his hand found and held hers on the red-checkered tablecloth. The violinist sighed and smiled too and played for them softly in the background.

"Why are you no longer married?"

Matt shrugged. "The usual reason. Got together far too young and kind of became two different people and drifted apart."

"You are too dedicated?"

"Or she's too frivolous, or a bit of each."

"You have children?"

"A boy. He's in school here in Geneva."

"He likes it?"

"He doesn't go around saying what he likes. He's a funny kid. All up-tight."

"Maybe he would rather live with you."

"No homelife if he did. I'm on the move too much."

"Too dedicated?" Tamara asked again, and added with a half smile: "But, as someone once said, some healthy self-criticism never hurt anybody. Maybe being too 'dedicated' is an excuse. Maybe you really value your freedom too much."

"I never thought of it that way," Matt admitted.

"Your President, is he very dedicated, too?"

"He's a strange one," Matt said. "He's dedicated all right, but he likes the good life, too. He's courageous, but he understands what it is to be less than brave. He wants peace, but it has to be a peace we can live with."

"Does he think there will be war?"

"Not if he can help it, there won't."

"That's not what I asked you."

"He's a fighter," Matt said. "He'll fight for peace."

"I would like him, I think," Tamara said. "From what you say, he reminds me of my father."

Her hand moved nervously; she spilled the last of her wine.

"The pastry chef?" Matt said.

He smiled; Tamara did not smile.

"I lied to you," she said after a while.

"Is your father in politics? Or a security job? What difference does it make?"

"My name is not Tamara."

"Okay," Matt said, waiting.

She withdrew her hand and looked away from him and spoke very softly, "I am Claudia Andreyeva."

The violinist finished playing with a flourish. He executed a small smiling bow and Matt stuffed some franc notes in his hand. The violinist returned them. "No, it was a pleasure playing for you," he said.

"You're not Swiss," Matt said.

"White Russian," said the violinist. He went away. By then they were the only diners left in the upstairs room of the restaurant. It was very quiet.

Matt began to laugh.

"You're not angry with me?"

"Angry? Hell no. I was just thinking, trying to have an ideological argument, about Russia, with you. That's too much."

"Because you thought the daughter of Nikolai Andreyev would be too—doctrinaire?"

"Something like that," Matt said, and then it was Claudia's turn to laugh.

"What's so funny?"

"My father. He is the least doctrinaire man I ever met. He always tells me the Young Communist League has turned me into a—a spouter of ideology. Am I a spouter of ideology?"

"Only when you've had too much Vosne Romanée to drink."

Claudia stared at the empty bottle in exaggerated sadness. "And now, it is finished."

"And now I'd better be getting you back. You weren't supposed to leave, were you?"

"Not," said Claudia, "on your life."

"Then what do we do? Take you to the front door and ring the bell and say, 'Here's your daughter, Premier Andreyev'? That wouldn't go over very big."

"Leave me outside the villa." Claudia squeezed his hand. "Are you sorry we came?"

"Claudia, look," Matt began, fumbling for words. "This would have been easy to say if you were Tamara the baker's daughter. But now whatever I say would be the wrong thing."

Her big dark eyes were glowing. "Then why don't you pretend I'm Tamara from Tbilisi?"

"Okay," Matt said, feeling strangely shy. "Tamara, I'm glad we met and glad you don't like cocktail parties any better than I do. I'd like to see you again."

"But," she said, teasing, "a man of your dedication? Could you fit me into your schedule?"

"I'll try. Tamara was always my favorite Russian name."

"Georgian name. I am Georgian, not Russian."

"Correction noted."

"We Georgians are very impulsive, the Latins of the U.S.S.R., you might say," Claudia said. "I like you, Matt Olds, and I want to see you again."

Matt grinned at her. "Always quit while you're ahead," he said, and called for the check.

Five minutes later they were outside on the Grand-Rue. At first they walked arm in arm, but then, where the narrow street began to descend to the lake, a gusty wind sprang up, propelling Claudia faster and faster along the uneven cobblestones until she looked over her shoulder at Matt, grinned, and was running. He jogged after her, two and then three paces behind.

At the bottom of the steep hill he overtook her, catching her arm and turning her. Her face was radiant, her long dark hair flying, and it seemed the most normal thing in the world for him to draw her toward him and kiss her.

She pulled away, stiffly, the joy gone from her eyes. "No, Matt, please."

Matt heard the pounding of footsteps and turned to see a man rushing at him.

The footballer Leonid Bayev was sitting over a carafe of red wine in the ground-floor room of the Chandelier. Bayev had a headache. He liked red wine, but red wine always did that to him. He was also worried. When Colonel Malinin was angry, you knew it. Malinin's voice had really barked at him over the wristwatch radio.

Bayev was a big man, built, people said, like a water-storage tank, with no definition between shoulders, waist, and flanks. He hadn't gone to flab yet, though, a risk that ex-athletes faced. He was solid and powerful, and took pride in his strength.

He was also frustrated. Could he help it if Premier Andreyev had instructed him to remain in the parking lot until the American President's car arrived? Could he help it if the American Matthew Olds had lied to him, claiming he was waiting for a lady?

But no, Bayev thought, that had been no lie. The American had cleverly failed to specify which lady he had in mind. Bayev had tried to stop them, but they had driven right by.

The drive into Geneva, the walk up the hill, and now two hours here, and the red wine, and the headache that felt like a band of steel closing on his forehead.

And what sort of provocation upstairs?

Bayev wished he were still wearing the blue and white jersey of Dynamo Moscow, guarding the goal against the red and white of Spartak, the Red Army team. Life had been good then, a hundred thousand fans in Central Lenin Stadium, all cheering themselves hoarse for Leonid Bayev.

And now?

Now, he had his strength and an astonishing swiftness of reflex, the pay was good, at home he lived inside the Kremlin walls, he really shouldn't complain as long as they told him what to do—except for Claudia Nikolaievna. His feelings about Claudia Nikolaievna gave him no peace. She was the most beautiful woman he had ever seen. He dreamed about her at night, often—incredible, impossible dreams from which he awoke breathless and spent—but in her presence he was awkward, oafish, unable to do anything but lick his dry lips or sometimes, when she said a kind word, feel all warm and melting inside. He would die for her, with a smile on his face, because he could not live with her.

They were coming downstairs.

Bayev turned away. They passed close to his table. Claudia Nikolaievna did not see him. They got their coats. Bayev paid quickly for his wine, got his own coat, and went outside. Follow them on foot back to their car, he thought, drive his own car after them to Villa Krupskaya, and that would be that.

He looked down the street, his head throbbing fiercely.

Claudia Nikolaievna was running, the American chasing after her swiftly.

Bayev loped after them, not seeming to move very fast, but his huge easy strides soon closed the gap.

In time to see Claudia Nikolaievna struggling to get away from the American.

Claudia turned, breathless, with the pressure of Matt's hand on her arm. His face swam toward her, and at first the thought of a kiss, a single kiss, in the darkness, after they had run down the hill like a pair of children, pleased her. She liked this big, gentle American, who could criticize his country but love it too, who seemed to understand her ambivalence about her own country, who made her feel relaxed and confident in her womanhood in a way that Viktor had never made her feel. But Viktor, she thought. Last night the meeting with Viktor, the way

Viktor could bend her to his will, and the loveless coupling that Viktor had made her initiate, sitting there, nude, arrogant, sure of himself, sure that she would ...

She stiffened, turned her lips away, pulled back from him, her eyes stinging. "No, Matt, please," she said.

Then something hurtled past her and struck him. Matt lurched three steps back and sat down heavily on the cobblestones, and the something that had struck him was a man, was Comrade Bayev, who worked for Viktor, and who now leaned down over Matt, dragged him to his feet and shook him, shouting into his face in labored English: "You—you—how do you dare?"

Claudia cried, "Comrade Bayev, stop!" and at the same moment Matt brought up both hands, hard, chopping Bayev's hands away from the collar of his trenchcoat.

They stood there, panting, the squat, wide Russian and the tall American, ready to fight. Bayev will kill him, Claudia thought.

She got between them, facing Matt. "I'm sorry. It's my fault. He's my bodyguard."

Then she turned to Bayev. "It's all right. We had dinner. There's nothing here for you."

"It is late," Bayev said. "This is a strange city. I will drive you back to Villa Krupskaya."

Claudia told Matt, "He wants to take me back. Did he hurt you?"

Matt shrugged, and then she could see the tension leaving him. "Your boy throws a pretty mean downfield block, but I guess I'll live."

She had no idea what a downfield block was. "You're all right?"

"Remind me," Matt said, "to clear it with Main Department Seven before we see each other again."

"You're angry with me."

"I don't like being manhandled," Matt said, but then he managed a smile. "Don't mind me. It wasn't your fault."

Bayev said, "Claudia Nikolaievna is going with me. You wait here. Five minutes here. You understand?"

Claudia wanted to say something, anything, that could take them back to the mood they had shared in the restaurant. She could think of nothing.

Their eyes met. At least if I had let him kiss me, she thought, and then she fell into step with Bayev. She looked back over her shoulder once, and saw Matt watching them.

Chapter
FOUR

1 Including the new wing that had been completed early in the decade, the Palace of Nations, roughly shaped like the letter S, had a continuous façade almost half a mile long. Built on a hill overlooking the lake, it had tall cathedral-like windows and a look of permanence that belied the failure of the old League of Nations and the sometimes-failure of the UN.

It had seen halfhearted sanctions against Mussolini fail in the 1930's and Nazi Germany's cynical withdrawal from the league. It had died during the Second World War along with the great hope of the League. It had been resurrected after the war as European headquarters of the UN, but New York was where the action was, and it had not really come alive again until the early seventies when the General Assembly began to meet alternate years in Geneva. Once again it could dream the good dream, the words of Robert Cecil written in huge letters in the lobby under the bas-relief that reminded Matthew Olds of Michelangelo's *Creation:* THE NATIONS MUST DISARM OR PERISH.

Matt walked quickly across the polished marble floor, heading for the stairs that would take him to the third floor and Salle IX, the small conference room where he would sit down with Secretary of State Reed, Russian Foreign Minister Kapitsa, and Viktor Malinin to iron out the agenda for the Summit. His ribs still hurt from the encounter with one of Malinin's goons last night. He debated registering a complaint with Malinin, then decided against it. The KGB man's mistake was a natural one —perhaps he had seemed to be chasing Claudia. Put bland-faced Burt East in the same situation, Matt had to admit, and he might have reacted even less gently.

Three American reporters were waiting at the foot of the stairs.

"What's on the agenda, Mr. Olds?"

Matt gave them an intentionally weary smile. "That's what I'm going upstairs to find out."

"Give us a break, Matt."

"Just Yugoslavia, or the whole works?"

"Will Kapitsa want to drag in the Middle East?"

"Kapitsa," Matt said, "always wants to drag in the Middle East—but that's off the record."

"What about Soviet Bloc troops massing in Rumania?"

"Ask Comrade Kapitsa."

"Ah, come on, Matt."

"Look," Matt said, making his way through them to the stairs, "I'm a working stiff, same as you. Secretary Reed and Foreign Minister Kapitsa will issue a statement after the meeting. Anything I say now would be premature. I don't envision any problems, so it ought to be a short session. Why don't you have a cup of coffee and wait for the word from Secretary Reed?"

But, Matt thought bleakly three hours later in Salle IX, his assessment had been wrong. The agenda meeting, which should have taken half an hour because he and Malinin had seen eye to eye last week, was getting nowhere fast.

Vasily Kapitsa, the pudgy Soviet Foreign Minister, had stubbornly brought up every problem in the East-West book.

Israeli aggression, he said.

Sédoux and the right-wing extremists in France, he said.

Spain's geographic and moral right to the Rock of Gibraltar, he said.

Russia and Yugoslavia, he said, constituted a small problem, strictly between the two nations involved, that should be no concern of the United States—unless, of course, Secretary Reed and the President were willing to consider the other, graver problems, in which case Yugoslavia could find a place in the agenda.

Kapitsa spoke Russian in a chirping, birdlike voice. The UN interpreter, seated at the conference table rather than in the glass-enclosed booth, translated a full octave lower but managed to catch the Foreign Minister's chiding tone. Kapitsa's assistants from the Ministry sat on either side of him, looking bored. The State Department's Balkan specialists, flanking Secretary Reed, cast puzzled glances in

Matt's direction. This was not what he had led them to expect at all.

Reed himself came as a pleasant surprise though. Yesterday in the Presidential Suite he had brought up the advisability of horse-trading with the Russians on the very points Kapitsa was mentioning, but now he put on his best pinched dour New England look, shook his head, and said a firm no to every extraneous item dragged in by the Russian.

Once he cupped a hand over his mouth, leaned across to Matt, and said, "Just what the devil is going on here, Olds? We didn't come three thousand miles to hear this tired old refrain. I thought you said—"

"I know what I said. I don't get it either."

Viktor Malinin's strong, wide-cheekboned face remained impassive. Kapitsa's raking up of old coals did not surprise him. If anything, Malinin's cold dark eyes seemed to regard Kapitsa with approval, like those of a teacher watching a clever pupil who has learned his lessons well.

If what the Russians had in mind was to delay the Summit, Matt thought, they couldn't have found a better way to do it. Matt had been firm on that point with Malinin all last week. "We don't want the usual Summit propaganda circus," he had said.

"I agree completely," Malinin had said.

"We keep it simple. One subject."

"Absolutely," Malinin had said. "Only Yugoslavia. Nothing else."

And now?

Now Matt said, "I'd like to ask Colonel Malinin a question." His voice was so scornful that Secretary Reed gave him a sharp warning look.

"Can you tell me, Colonel," Matt asked slowly, "what happened between last Friday and today to make you do such an about-face?"

"What happened? Nothing happened," Malinin said mildly in his deep voice. "The final decisions of my country for an agenda are the responsibility of the Foreign Minister. I thought you understood that. If my own ideas differed somewhat from those of Minister Kapitsa, I apologize."

"Differed somewhat?" Matt repeated. "You're trying to shove a whole new agenda down our throats."

"You can always turn it down."

68

Secretary Reed chuckled. "I thought it pretty clear that I *was* turning it down."

Malinin looked at Minister Kapitsa.

"In that case," Kapitsa said, "perhaps it would be best if we adjourn until later this after—" He paused. Did Malinin shake his head? "Perhaps it would be best if we adjourn until tomorrow."

"The first plenary meeting was scheduled for tomorrow," Matt reminded him.

"Without an agenda, there can be no plenary meeting," Malinin said.

"Did you ever intend for there to be one, Colonel?" Matt snapped.

A few seconds of strained silence, and then Secretary Reed and Foreign Minister Kapitsa made conciliatory noises, and it was agreed they would meet again on Wednesday morning. It was also agreed to issue a joint statement saying that the first meeting had been fruitful. Fruitful, in diplomatic parlance, meant difficult but not hopeless.

Outside, Secretary Reed asked Matt, "A little rough on them, weren't you?"

"They're stalling. They know we can't accept their blanket agenda."

"Yes, that's true. It's a common enough Russian tactic when they're waiting for instructions from the Kremlin."

"But why? What's changed things?"

"Olds," Secretary Reed said with a faint smile, "I'd love to have you in the Department for a few weeks. If I taught you nothing else, I'd try to teach you patience."

Matt let that go. The Secretary of State's disapproval of his brusqueness was something he had come to expect. "Did you get the impression Colonel Malinin was running the show?"

"Perhaps more than he ought to have. Still, don't let Kapitsa's appearance fool you. It would be a mistake to underestimate him. Besides," Reed added dryly, "you may have given them the same impression Malinin gave us."

2   It looked like an ordinary telephone.

When it rang, in answer to the call he had put through twenty minutes before, Viktor Malinin gritted his teeth and picked up the receiver.

"I have the First Secretary on the line now," said the Villa Krupskaya operator.

Malinin looked at his watch. Fifteen hundred miles to the east, the gilt hands of the huge clock at the west entrance of the Kremlin would be pointing to four-thirty. Inside the walls, past the gold-domed cathedrals, the ornate palaces, the Ivan the Great bell tower, Igor Lysenko, First Secretary of the Central Committee of the Communist Party, would be sitting alone in his office on the second floor of the sand-colored building that stood in the center of the vast fortress compound. He would have finished his tea by now, Malinin knew. Every day Secretary Lysenko took an hour in the afternoon to sort out his thoughts. This retreat was sacrosanct. Were the Kremlin going up in flames around him, Igor Lysenko, his detractors claimed, would sit there at the big desk, gazing moodily out of the window at the courtyard and the row of ancient bronze cannon, pondering. He had much to ponder today, and Viktor Malinin did not like it.

This was Malinin's second call of the day to the Kremlin. He waited, listening to the whispers of distance in the receiver. The telephone was a scrambler, and in the unlikely event that an electronic spy succeeded in plugging into the circuit here in Switzerland, he would hear meaningless sounds that only became words at the receiver in Malinin's hand and at First Secretary Lysenko's desk.

"Malinin," the voice said, startlingly clear.

It was a harsh, rasping voice, a voice made for the casual utterance of four-letter words, unmistakably Lysenko's. Malinin's face felt flushed. He was a man of tremendous self-confidence—until he heard that voice.

"Yes, Comrade Lysenko."

Lysenko insisted on that form of address, suggesting with the low-key salutation an equality that could not be.

"The meeting?"

Malinin licked dry lips. "A complete success. We have delayed twenty-four hours."

"Comrade Kapitsa was unhappy with the delay?"

"He accepted it."

"Review, please," rasped Lysenko's voice, and Malinin quickly sketched the meeting in Salle IX of the Palace of Nations.

"Olds will be the difficult one," Lysenko said. "The Embassy in Washington predicted that. Have you rapport with him?"

"Until today."

"What happened today?"

"Olds accused me of deceitfulness."

"Re-establish rapport," Lysenko said, as if two words of peremptory command could solve the problems of delicate diplomatic relationships.

"I will try, Comrade Lysenko."

"By all means 'try,' " said Lysenko, putting an emphasis on the word that made it sound like an admission of failure on Malinin's part. "Have you 'tried' to discover where the Premier went last night?"

"These things take time," Malinin said vaguely. He doubted that he would ever find out. Andreyev had left before the party, had been gone about an hour, had returned. He had ducked out of Villa Krupskaya through the kitchen, returning the same way. A maid had admitted that. The old pastry chef, who was loyal to Andreyev, had admitted nothing so far.

"And the daughter's escapade? You've learned more?"

"No," Malinin said. "Dinner in Geneva with Matthew Olds."

" 'With Matthew Olds.' I see."

"Bayev was there."

"Within earshot?"

"No," Malinin admitted. "A man, a woman, and a bottle of wine. That's all."

"You know that for a fact?"

"It can be surmised. They never met before."

"Let me do the surmising," Lysenko rasped. "What else?"

"Nothing. Well, Bayev thought they might have been struggling."

There was a sound across fifteen hundred miles of scrambler, and though he had heard it before it took awhile for Malinin to realize the First Secretary was laughing.

"Is Bayev reliable?"

"He's very loyal."

"And perhaps stupid?"

"Comrade Yegorov is the bright one."

"And where was Yegorov last night?"

"Here," said Malinin lamely.

"Listen, Malinin," Lysenko said. "You have a simple job. To watch the Premier, to keep him in line. But what do you do? You let him disappear last night, and you

71

allow the daughter to walk off with Matthew Olds. Are you that inept?"

"No, comrade. I hope not, comrade."

"Aren't you getting it any more?"

"Getting what, comrade?"

"The daughter. Surely you can keep her in line. You've been fucking her for two years."

Well, thought Malinin, unsurprised, if Lysenko knows, he knows. But Malinin could feel the sweat starting in his armpits.

"This is not the time to break off that relationship."

"Yes, comrade. I mean, no, comrade."

"Which do you mean?"

"This is not the time to break off with her."

"Listen to me, Malinin. Comrade Andreyev has one final task to perform for Party and country. You must see that he performs it adequately. He is no fool. It won't be easy for you. It is particularly difficult now because Nikolai Ivanovich has departed from the script. You must delay the Summit until you learn why, and I must delay Operation Minaret as long as the Summit is delayed. Only Andreyev can convince the Americans not to go to war over Operation Minaret. You must see that he does."

"He opposes it."

"He has made that quite clear. And do you also oppose it?"

The unexpected question made Malinin all but shout his answer. "Of course not!"

"The point is, Malinin, his ideological opposition is irrelevant, as yours would be. We need him—for now. We need his popularity in the West. Thirty years," said Lysenko suddenly.

"Comrade?"

"He has worked thirty years for the Party, for history. It is his life. It is a Pavlovian response by now. Find out what he has been up to, Malinin. And then see to it that he salivates."

The rasping voice became a shade warmer. "How old are you, Viktor?" Not Malinin, not even Viktor Mironovich. Just Viktor. Fatherly, almost.

"Forty-one, comrade."

"General Chuikov is an old man, ready to retire. You would be the youngest chief of the KGB since Shelepin. Even I, myself, was in my late forties when I took

72

command of the KGB. It was the single most important step in my career. You understand, Viktor?"

Malinin said that he understood.

"For a deserving man, an ambitious man, it can lead anywhere. Are you ambitious, Viktor?"

"I try to do my work, comrade."

"Your work, shit. You're ambitious. We all are. Only Nikolai Ivanovich is no longer ambitious. Do your work. Do history's work. An ambitious man who has to live with his own failure is a very sorry specimen."

Viktor Malinin felt cold sweat trickling down his sides. The veiled menace, the not-quite-stated promise, a deft administration of the carrot and the stick—and Malinin had no idea where he stood.

"I understand, comrade," he said, and realized he was talking to an empty line.

3 Claudia felt sorry for the footballer Bayev even before she lost him in the crowded aisles of the Grand Passage department store.

It was after lunch. She had asked Bayev to drive her to the Grand Passage, as her father had instructed, and Bayev had called for a car and driven expertly through the heavy traffic along the quay and across the Mont Blanc bridge. He found a parking space on the Place du Molard, where the American Matthew Olds had parked the night before.

She walked past the clock tower and along the side of the open-air flower market, with Bayev following dutifully six paces behind like an Oriental wife. She noticed a taxi rank near the arcade at the side entrance of the department store, and knew that her father had taken even that into consideration. "Go in the front entrance," he had instructed her. "Set a slow pace. Bayev will be entranced by the merchandise, too. The lifts are beyond the leather-goods display. When you see one that is almost full, move quickly. If Bayev is left behind, get off on any floor, take the stairs down. Otherwise, try again. You will find taxis at the side entrance. You understand, my dear?"

"Yes, Father," she had said, understanding only the mechanics of it.

"Then repeat it to me, please. Also the errands, and where we are to meet afterward."

She had repeated it all, lighting a cigarette nervously.

73

"Good. That is exactly right. Don't smoke," Nikolai Ivanovich said. "You look nervous when you smoke."

"I am nervous. I don't understand why—"

"Later," Nikolai Ivanovich promised. "You would be more nervous if I told you now." He looked at her worried expression, shook his head, and said, "I shouldn't have said that."

"No." She managed a smile. She put the cigarette out and sent for Bayev.

Now, in the Grand Passage, she knew that Bayev would have hell to pay later. In his own way, Viktor was as contemptuous of failure as First Secretary Lysenko was.

The display of perfume and toiletries, of frilly blouses and lingerie, of good Swiss chocolate, of gourmet foods you wouldn't dream of finding even in the new *culinarias* springing up in the Moscow suburbs almost made Claudia forget why she had come here. But then she saw the briefcases and the wallets and the luggage, and beyond them the bank of lifts, and her father's careful instructions, put to the test, worked like magic. She waited, examining handbags, and saw a lift filling rapidly with shoppers. She waited a few seconds longer, until the starter began to move in front of the door, and then she walked past him quickly and inside the crowded lift, turning in time to see two arms barring Bayev's way and the doors sliding shut. Bayev had not even been alarmed. She knew where the car was parked, didn't she?

She got off on the second floor, found the stairs, went down two flights, saw Bayev nowhere, walked to the side entrance and outside. Four taxis were waiting in a row. She got into the first one.

"Place du Cirque," she said.

It was that simple. But she knew Viktor would find out. Poor Bayev.

There were two other customers in the shop near the Place du Cirque. One was paying for a pair of tinted glasses. The other followed a man in a white smock through a curtain in the rear of the shop. For an eye test, Claudia thought.

"Mademoiselle?"

"These should be ready this afternoon," Claudia said, producing a note her father had given her.

The shopgirl looked at it. "For a Mr. Hauser, of course. A rush order."

The girl opened a drawer behind the counter and took out a pair of eyeglasses, the rims heavy and black, the bows heavier still.

"Leather case? Or plastic?"

"I beg your pardon?" Claudia said.

"The leather cases are fifteen francs, the plastic ten."

"I—the leather, please."

The name Hauser had startled her. It could have been coincidence, but she knew a man named Hauser, or rather her father knew him and she had met him once or twice, years ago, when he was the American Ambassador to Moscow.

"That will be seventy-five francs."

She paid with a hundred-franc note, got her change, and left.

Was it the same Hauser, or had her father simply used the name?

A pair of hair clippers were next, bought in a hardware shop on the Rue du Stand that specialized in knives and surgical instruments. Claudia's final purchase was a quilted black anorak. She held the lightweight parka out at arm's length, deciding that a Swiss forty-two would be just about right for her father.

On the street again, she looked at her watch. Twenty after three. Her father had said three-thirty at the Metropole. "Ask for Mr.—no, here," he had said, scribbling something, folding the sheet of paper, and handing it to her. "Look at it just before you reach the hotel. That will be better."

She looked at it now.

Mr. Hauser, her father had written.

Again that name. But why? Because you couldn't register in a hotel without a passport? Then had Mr. Hauser, Mr. Kermit Hauser, formerly the American Ambassador to Moscow, registered for her father last night, when Nikolai Ivanovich had left Villa Krupskaya? Had Mr. Hauser ordered the eyeglasses this morning? So that her father's name would be connected with nothing?

And the purchases. In the West, what did her father look like? Or even at home, in the caricatures in *Krokodil*?

A pair of pince-nez.

The dark, carefully groomed, spade-shaped beard.

A fastidiousness in the way he dressed. Nikolai Ivanovich would never be seen, in a city, without jacket and tie. *Krokodil* called it his bourgeois cosmopolitanism when *Krokodil* dared a dig at Nikolai Ivanovich.

The heavy, dark-rimmed glasses for the pince-nez.

The hair clippers to remove the beard.

The sporty anorak—the late November afternoon was sunny but cool, there were other anoraks on the street—in place of the jacket and tie.

Nikolai Ivanovich Andreyev, Chairman of the Council of Ministers of the Soviet Union, Premier of Russia, was going to disappear.

That alone made sense.

4 The knowledge pursued her to the dingy exterior of the Metropole Hotel on Quai General Guisan. She cast a fugitive's glance over her shoulder before going inside, almost dropping the package that contained the anorak. She went up the stairs to the concierge's desk.

"Mr. Hauser's room, please." She was relieved to hear that her voice sounded calm.

The concierge ducked his long nose toward the registration cards in a folder on the desk. "Room 308."

"Is he in?"

The long nose lifted; the key rack was consulted. "Yes, mademoiselle. Are you expected?"

A man came up the stairs, studied Claudia, and walked across the green and white marble floor to the checkroom. He removed his coat, adjusted his jacket, and headed for a sign that said BAR. Men stare, Claudia told herself, especially Frenchmen, and the Genevois are more French than the Parisians, or so Nikolai Ivanovich always said. Relax. It's going to be all right.

"Are you expected?" the concierge asked again, taking in Claudia's uncertainty with a small, knowing smirk.

Claudia said she was expected. She crossed the marble lobby to the lifts, pressed the button, and waited. She wanted to hide. She could feel the concierge's eyes on her back.

The doors slid open. She was inside a self-service car. She pressed three, and as the doors shut she caught a glimpse of the top of the concierge's head. He wasn't even looking at her.

Third floor, and a carpeted hallway. Inside, the Metropole was surprisingly luxurious after the gloomy stone exterior. She stood before the door of 308, knocked. She heard footsteps at once. Would it be her father? Or Mr. Hauser?

It was Nikolai Ivanovich. He looked at her face, shut the door behind her, and then took her into his arms.

She could hear the soft, snipping sound of the hair clippers. Five minutes of that, and then water running in the bathroom sink. Her father began to whistle a theme from Shostakovich's Third. Once he made up his mind about something, Claudia knew, he tended to be euphoric. Nikolai Ivanovich was an optimist.

Claudia got up and went to the window. Across the Rue du Rhône she could see the display windows of the Boutique Danoise. It was almost four o'clock. Late-afternoon traffic surged heavily along the street. A two-car tram rattled past, advertising Du-Bon-Dubonnet on its display card.

Her father's voice called: "Claudia."

She turned away from the window. She gasped.

It wasn't her father.

It was a stocky middle-aged man who looked unexpectedly American.

The bushy wings of dark hair had been combed across the bald dome that Nikolai Ivanovich always referred to as his high forehead, his intellectual's forehead. The black-rimmed glasses made the face seem narrower, drawing attention away from the wide cheekbones. He exuded a faint scent of after-shave lotion. The jaw, its skin pinkish and soft as a baby's, looked naked. He wore the black anorak casually, unzipped, a white shirt open at the collar under it.

"Well?" With his optimist's smile, hardly recognizable without the beard.

"I'd never recognize you in a million years."

"Yes, it is rather odd, looking in the mirror and seeing a stranger. I almost expected to see a Chinese."

"A Chinese?"

"When Chinese officials come to Geneva, they stay here at the Metropole. Cheaper than the other good hotels. Every nationality has its preference. The Latin Americans—"

"Father," said Claudia.

"I am talking too much? I always talk too much when—"

77

"Father," said Claudia, but she looked at his face, his new face, and she began to smile.

"Yes. Well," he said. He cleared his throat.

"Tell me," Claudia said.

"Perhaps it would be better," Nikolai Ivanovich said, "if you told me."

Their eyes met. Claudia looked away. Despite the evidence before her, until the words were spoken she couldn't be sure. It was like a dream, a bad dream, only there would be no waking from it to a familiar bedroom and in the kitchen the breakfast samovar bubbling.

"You are—going away," she said in a very small voice.

"We are going away."

She swallowed hard. Her father, her country, love for him, love for Mother Russia, the second wrench in her life. The first had come when she was very young, when her parents divorced. Her mother had died two years afterward, in an automobile accident. She had gone to live with her father. He had taught her love of country. And now this? How could it be?

"I am Russian," Claudia said, the words sounding foolish to her own ears. "I am not going."

Her father's new, unfamiliar face took on a pained look. "Trust me. I am asking you to trust me."

"I will never defect." The word, the monstrous word, was out.

"That is an unfortunate choice of words, my dear," Nikolai Ivanovich said slowly. She had hurt him. "There is a greater morality than love of country."

He sounded sententious then, like Viktor mouthing one of his aphorisms.

"You sound like Viktor," she said, wanting to hurt him again.

"Last night you were worried. The way Viktor was acting, the things he said. Viktor was right. My time is running out."

"You rule Russia," she said flatly, knowing that wasn't quite true. As Chairman of the Council of Ministers, Nikolai Ivanovich headed the government. First Secretary Lysenko ran the Party. Between them, they governed Russia. And, in dialectic terms, much of the history of Communist Russia stemmed from the conflict between government and Party.

"The Presidium of the Central Committee of the CPSU," Nikolai Ivanovich said dryly, "rules Russia. Ten

78

men, ten equals, with two rather more equal than the rest. The Premier. The Party Secretary."

"Comrade Lysenko? Then do what must be done here and go home and fight him."

Nikolai Ivanovich sighed. "I have tried to do too much. I had grand schemes. To run the Party through the state apparatus, rather than have the Party run the state through its bureaucracy. To fight the steel-eaters for more consumer goods. To live in mutual trust with the West. When I was young," Nikolai Ivanovich said sadly, "I believed imperialism an abomination. I still do—no matter whose imperialism it is."

"Go home and fight. You can do it."

"Claudia, I have lost. Comrade Lysenko's steel-eaters, his imperialists, are a majority in the Presidium and the Council of Ministers. It is too late to fight. Whatever I do, I will be deposed. I knew that when we came here. And yet I thought . . ."

"What did you think?"

"Honor. That I would go back and face them. But I can't."

"You can't defect."

He shook his head slowly, pain in the dark eyes behind the unfamiliar glasses. "There is a greater morality than mere love of—"

"Those are words, just words," Claudia cried. "You can't decide for me. I'm a grown woman."

"I have to decide for you. Please don't make it any more difficult than it already is."

"I'm not going. You're afraid," she said spitefully, on the brink of tears, loving him but still wanting to hurt him. "You're afraid to go back."

"I'm afraid that if I go back—"

"You see, you admit it!"

"there will be war, all-out war, and what will going back prove then? No, there are things I must do. For Russia."

"You don't even sound like my father now. It's crazy, what you want to do. I'm not going."

"I can't leave you behind. You would be a hostage."

"You can't make me go."

He stood there, looking at her, his shoulders slumped, a tired, aging man with defeat in his voice. "No, I can't do that. I tried to make it easy for you to accept. The glasses, the clippers. Surely you must have known, when you came here—"

"I knew. I didn't want to believe it, but I knew."

"If I leave you behind, I would be powerless to act."

"If I go with you, I would—hate you for the rest of your life."

"So," he said, his face expressionless. "So, I see."

He reached out a hand to touch her, and she drew back. The reaching hand retreated, clutched at his chest. He doubled over and sat down. He was gasping. His face looked chalky and by the time she realized what was happening it was covered with sweat. His lips worked, but there were no words. He made a faint sound in his throat. He managed to lift one arm and point. The arm fell.

The bathroom. She ran there. Nothing on the shelf above the sink. On the floor, an attaché case. She opened it, in a frenzy. Toilet articles, a large envelope, the hair clippers, the pince-nez, a fresh shirt, his dark jacket neatly folded. She tore the jacket out, fumbling in the pockets. Keys. A comb. A pack of cigarettes. He wasn't supposed to smoke. A small bottle, plastic-stoppered. The pills.

She rushed back into the bedroom. He hadn't moved. His face had gone gray, his mouth was open. The angina.

She put a single small white tablet in his mouth, worked it under his tongue. The big blood vessels were there, the doctor had said, and almost instant absorption of the medicine. She sat beside him, cradling his head on her lap. The frantic breathing slowed to normal. She stroked his forehead, his temples. After a short while he sat up, the color returning to his face. The medicine worked like that, swiftly, a miracle. It always did. Fifteen minutes, the doctor had said, and you would never know he'd had an attack. It is dangerous only if the medicine is not available at once. Otherwise, an inconvenience, just a small inconvenience. She wished she had the doctor there, now, to see his small inconvenience.

"Well, that was rather dramatic, wasn't it?" Nikolai Ivanovich said in a weak voice. "Help me get up."

"You're not strong enough. You have to rest."

"Help me up. . . . I am expecting . . ."

She helped him to his feet and he stood swaying and then took a slow, careful turn around the room. "So," he said, "as good as new."

He walked like an old man. She had seen that happen before. A good night's sleep, or even a decent nap, and he would be back to normal. One more time, she thought. He had survived the doctor's small inconvenience one more time.

The telephone rang. Nikolai Ivanovich picked up the receiver, listened, said yes three times, and hung up.

He looked at her. "Downstairs," he said. "In ten minutes."

This was not the time to argue. This was the time to help. But she could see them, in a year, or two years, in a safe house of the American CIA, living anonymously, unable to go out without protection, father and daughter like partners in a dead marriage without even sex as a palliative, totally wed, despising each other.

They waited five minutes. She brought him a glass of water. She repacked the attaché case and helped him to the lift.

"Back entrance," he said, and they went outside together, arm in arm, to the Rue du Rhône. They walked two blocks. A car was waiting at the curb, its engine idling. A tall old man sat behind the wheel.

Chapter
FIVE

1 All afternoon Matthew Olds had been badgered by the press. The American TV, wire service, and newspaper contigent alone numbered two hundred, but if anything the foreigners were worse. They asked the same questions Matt had been asked dozens of times in Washington, questions about the nature of his job as President Huntington's Special Assistant for National Security Affairs, questions for which he had no real answers.

Ordinarily, in Washington, he had his staff to fall back on. Some of them, less familiar than Matt with the cynical world of journalism, were eager to talk. They said, "Mr. Olds? Well, he has no ax of his own to grind. It's a question of letting the President know what the options are. He draws on the operational agencies—like State,

Defense, CIA—to come up with the Big Picture. That's Mr. Olds's job."

Or maybe, Matt thought wryly, Clay Huntington wanted him around because old friends make the best sounding boards.

Here, in Geneva, he did not have his staff to fall back on. "Secretary Reed," the President had said before Matt left Washington, "won't operate at top efficiency if he thinks you're upstaging him at the Summit. But I'm going to want you there, and I hope you won't mind going alone."

Matt had not minded going alone until the reporters jumped on him. They had waited in the corridors of the Palace of Nations, they had ambushed him in the lobby of the Beau Rivage, they had been camping outside the door of his room down the hall from the President's.

What could he tell them? The meeting in Salle IX had gone well enough, he said; the participants had agreed to meet tomorrow. Weren't the heads of state to have met tomorrow? These things are flexible. Had they agreed on an agenda? They were working on it. Give us a break, Matt—what's the line on this Colonel Malinin? Colonel Malinin, Matt said, was free to answer any questions about himself. Will the agenda be the stumbling block? It was basically, Matt evaded, Secretary Reed's show. I just keep the President posted. Keep him posted, hell. Keep *us* posted, Matt, give us a break, huh?

They had not given Matt a break. They had even waited outside Whitney Stoughton's room, where Matt had dined alone with the CIA Deputy Director and Plans Division Chief in an attempt to bury the hatchet. The attempt had seemed successful, with a lot of don't-mind-me's and we're-all-working-under-pressure's.

What's CIA got up its sleeve, Mr. Olds? They in contact with Belgrade yet? You'll have to ask Mr. Stoughton. Mr. Stoughton had wisely locked his door and turned in early.

But Matt felt restless and edgy. It was not yet ten o'clock. A fast two sets of tennis or a swim would have let off some steam. A walk, really striding out along the lake in the cold, clear air, might help.

Matt went downstairs and outside, crossed the quay, turned left on the lakefront promenade, and began to stride. A few reporters tagged along. Hey, who do you think you are? Harry Truman? Tall and rangy, Matt covered a lot of ground. The reporters, scurrying after him, almost running, had to take two steps to his one. He walked faster, enjoying himself, beginning to take a perverse satisfaction in the chase. The sound of panting beside him, and then dropping behind, and one final question in a ragged voice swallowed by the wind: Mr. Olds, if you had to name one Russian you could get along with, who would it be?

He did not answer the pointless question, wondering what inept feature writer had dreamed that one up. Then the reporters had dropped well behind, and he turned to see them drifting back toward the lights of the big hotels. He was finally alone, the first time in the long frustrating day, and he kept walking.

One Russian? All right fellows, I'll give you one Russian. She called herself Tamara, after the Queen of the Georgians, but her name is Claudia and her old man runs the show for the U.S.S.R. and—this is not for publication—I can't get her out of my mind.

Matt kept walking, beyond the new high-rise apartments between the Palace of Nations and the lake. The wind changed direction, buffeting him from behind. He turned and saw the lights of the city along the water and across it. This far from town, traffic had thinned out. He had come a good three miles.

He cupped his hands over a match to light a cigarette. A car pulled to the curb and a man got out quickly and approached him.

2 The footballer Bayev did not like to admit he was afraid of Comrade Moskalenko.

Moskalenko, he supposed, held higher rank than he did in the KGB. But he had never seen Moskalenko in uniform. Moskalenko always wore an ill-fitting dark suit with wide lapels and baggy trousers, and everyone called him comrade, only that. He was a small, sallow-faced man with pipestem wrists and tiny hands. Bayev could easily flex him over a knee and break him in half, but the knowledge of that did not diminish his fear of Moskalenko. Comrade Moskalenko had the coldest, deadest eyes he had ever seen, and everyone said Moskalenko did his work very well.

Moskalenko worked for that unnumbered subdepartment of KGB called Mokryye Dela, the Department of Wet Affairs, which under Shelepin years ago (when Bayev was still a happy footballer) had replaced the old terrorist organization SMERSH. Chauffeur was Moskalenko's cover job. Moskalenko killed people. Or, if he didn't kill them, he destroyed them in the process of obtaining information. The wet of Mokryye Dela, the Department of Wet Affairs, people said, had a color. It was red—for blood.

Bayev's colleague Yegorov took a rather sanguine approach to Comrade Moskalenko. "He doesn't drink, he hates women, he minds his own business," Yegorov would say. "You mind your own business and he's just a skinny little man with bad breath."

It had been Bayev's decision, a decision he now regretted, because it meant working with Moskalenko, to pick up the American Matthew Olds. Yegorov, almost to Bayev's surprise, went along with the decision, probably because Yegorov was as frightened of Colonel Malinin as Bayev was of Moskalenko.

Claudia Nikolaievna had vanished in the department store.

The Premier, taking his afternoon constitutional, carrying his attaché case as habitually as some men carried walking sticks, had asked Yegorov to buy him a package of cigarettes in a crowded *tabac.* You did not argue with the Premier, especially when he hated the whole idea of bodyguards. Besides, when Yegorov entered the *tabac,* three Main Department Seven security men were waiting on the sidewalk with Nikolai Ivanovich.

When Yegorov returned with the package of cigarettes, one of the agents came running out of an adjacent bookshop. Yegorov did not see the Premier anywhere. The man said, "He went out the back way. A taxi."

Yegorov gave the agent a blank look. "He's gone?"

He was gone.

"Did you get the license number?"

"A crowd recognized him. They were all over the place. I couldn't."

Yegorov considered for a moment. He looked at the traffic racing by. No amount of frantic searching would find the Premier now.

"All right," he said. "Get back to the villa."

Alone, he ascertained that there was no other taxi driver who could identify the Premier's cab for him.

"Beautiful," Colonel Malinin had said an hour later,

while Yegorov fidgeted and Bayev held his head in his hands. "Can't you idiots do anything right?" he shouted.

He could not, he said, call in the entire security staff. Maybe there was some very simple reason why the Premier and his daughter had vanished, separately, at approximately the same time. Maybe they would return, to give Bayev and Yegorov the chance to lose them a third time.

Maybe Colonel Malinin was whistling in the dark, but neither Bayev nor Yegorov suggested that.

"I'll give you pair of shit-heels until morning. Bring me some answers that make sense or you'll be freezing your atrophied balls off guarding the border with Outer Mongolia."

They were dismissed. Bayev did not know what the word atrophied meant, but he got the message. The Colonel, probably, had been on the phone with the First Secretary. That always made him furious.

"The American Matthew Olds," Bayev told his colleague a few minutes later. He reminded Yegorov that Claudia Nikolaievna had been with the American last night. "We pick up Olds and question him."

Yegorov frowned. "I don't know. Olds is an important man."

"The Premier is missing," Bayev said. "Claudia Nikolaievna—" his throat constricted, and it was hard for him to finish— "is missing."

Yegorov said after a while, "We'll get Moskalenko."

"Moskalenko?"

"What do you know about interrogation? What do I know? Comrade Moskalenko can milk a man dry in a couple of hours."

And Bayev, knowing Yegorov was right, almost wished he were freezing his atrophied balls off—whatever atrophied meant—in Outer Mongolia.

They were lucky. They drew a car from the Villa Krupskaya motor pool, a Citroën DS, and drove to the Beau Rivage. They waited, Bayev smoking a cigarette, Yegorov sucking on a mint.

"And now?" Yegorov asked mockingly.

"I can phone," Bayev suggested, "with a message from Claudia Nikolaievna. To meet her somewhere."

"Good, I like that," Yegorov said, and Bayev opened the door of the Citroën and started to slip out from behind the wheel. With one foot on the pavement, he froze.

"That's him now."

"Where?"

"Coming out."

"With an army," Yegorov groaned.

Matthew Olds left the brightly lighted hotel entrance and crossed the quay, the small army of reporters following him. They set out along the lakefront, walking fast.

Yegorov got out of the car. "I'll go on foot," he said. "Drive ahead of them. Stop when you have to. Keep them in sight."

Yegorov began to walk, on the shoreward side of the quay.

Forty-five minutes later, beyond the city limits of Geneva, Bayev U-turned the big Citroën and came up behind Matthew Olds. As he turned, the headlights caught the solitary figure of Yegorov crossing the quay two hundred meters beyond the American. The American was cupping his hands over a match.

Bayev got out of the car. He left the engine running.

He came laterally at Matthew Olds and Yegorov came up from behind. Both had guns in their hands.

"What the hell is this?" the American said, seeing only Bayev.

"In the car," Bayev said in his guttural English and the American moved very fast, shooting the lit cigarette with thumb and middle finger at Bayev's face. The cigarette struck Bayev's cheek, sparks flew, and Bayev shouted. The American turned and ran—straight at Yegorov.

And Yegorov swung the automatic in a short arc that ended against the side of Matthew Olds's head.

3   Before World War Two a Hungarian Communist named Alexander Rado (code names Dora and Albert) was sent to Switzerland as the Soviet Union's chief resident spy.

Rado, under the unassailable cover of an anti-Nazi German expatriate, was able to send Moscow, among other things, the date of the Nazi attack on Russia, information which Stalin disregarded. Badgered by Swiss intelligence and the Gestapo, Rado's network was finally destroyed.

86

But a Swiss listening post remained of vital importance to the KGB. Rado's successors went underground—no difficult feat in Geneva where, by the early seventies, there was a sizable Communist party.

The KGB network had a *yavka*, a safe house, in the village of Coppet, a few miles east along the lake. An old yellow stone château, it stood isolated high on a terraced hillside. The vineyards actually produced a creditable white wine sold in three cantons. The *patron* of the château, a Swiss Communist named Gros-Claude, took his orders from Moscow, relayed via Bern by the Second Secretary of the Soviet Embassy.

It was here at the château in Coppet that Moskalenko was waiting. He had spent the day, Bayev knew as he drove between the stone gateposts, interrogating the pastry chef Semyon Semyonov.

The entire left side of Matthew Olds's head ached.

Not much of an ache until he moved. When he moved, the pain shot from his left temple down to his jaw. Experimentally, he opened his mouth and shut it. He ran two fingers gingerly along his cheek. Nothing broken, he decided, almost with surprise.

He lay there, in a small room, on a bare mattress. Bronze bedstead and a single window on the night. It was cold. He was cold. A shaded lamp on a night table shed dim light. He looked at his watch. After one in the morning. He'd been unconscious how long—an hour and a half, two hours?

Despite the shooting pain in his head, he swung his legs to the floor and lurched to the window. He looked out. It was a long way down, too long. The door—locked from the outside. A sink in one corner of the room, with a slow, insistent drip. He was thirsty. He drank icy water from the tap. He fought a queasiness and went back to the bed and sat on its edge and tried to think, his head down between his knees.

The lakefront, the car, a man with a gun, his attempt to get away. He had seen the man before.

Then he knew. The barrel-like build, the hang-dog face. The same man who had accosted him after the dinner with Claudia.

Her bodyguard. What was his name, Bayev?

Suddenly the queasiness overcame him. He made it to

the sink and threw up chokingly and waited a while and drank some more water.

Bayev came for him at precisely two o'clock.

There were three of them in the room. Bayev had mournful eyes to go with the hang-dog face. He sat in a corner of the large room, on an overstuffed chair, an automatic held loosely in his hand, resting on his knee. He fidgeted, recrossing his legs, resting the automatic on the other knee. The second man was huge, wider even than Bayev, and taller. He stood at the mantel of a cold fireplace, one elbow leaning comfortably on the marble slab like a man posing for a picture. He was holding an automatic too, casually, but it was there.

The third man was thin, sallow of face, and wearing an ill-fitting, old-fashioned suit with wide lapels and baggy pants that crumpled at his shoetops. He looked sleepy. He yawned. He said, in good English, "Shut the door," and Bayev leaped up and pulled the intricately paneled double doors shut and sat down and crossed his legs again. The huge man at the fireplace thumbed a peppermint from a foil-covered roll and popped it into his mouth.

An ornate chandelier with candle-shaped bulbs lit the large room brightly.

"You will now tell us about last night," the sallow-faced man said.

Bayev blinked his mournful eyes. The huge man sucked his peppermint.

Last night, Matt thought. Dinner with Claudia, that had to be it. Two hours of her time unaccounted for—the paranoid worries of the Secret Police.

"Last night," the sallow-faced man went on, "you took Claudia Nikolaievna to the restaurant Au Chandelier on Grand-Rue. You remained there almost two hours. Why?"

"I hate cocktail parties," Matt said lightly, a sense of relief sweeping over him like a wave. "I talked her into having dinner with me." Tell them the innocent truth, he decided, and in a few minutes they'd be bowing and scraping in apology. Their mistake might even be a lever he could use against Malinin later.

Sallow Face smiled with his mouth. He had bad teeth. The pale eyes remained expressionless. He took three steps and stood in front of Matt. "What kind of fool do you take me for?" he said. He looked up at Matt and slapped his face hard, forehand to the right side, backhand to the left. The shooting pain jumped in Matt's head. He grabbed the frail wrist and turned it, and Sallow Face squawked and banged off the wall and sat down.

Peppermint left the fireplace on the run.

"No," Sallow Face said. He got to his feet. "Not yet."

"I don't know what kind of a stupid game you think you're playing," Matt said slowly, "but this is where it ends."

Sallow Face thought that was very funny. He giggled.

Matt tried again. "Do you know who I am?"

"We know who you are, Mr. Olds. We even know what you are thinking—that we are acting like lunatics. That when we are finished, our behavior will have destroyed any hopes for the Summit. But you are wrong. Assume we release you. How would you prove you were here? And just where are we, anyway? In Geneva? Five miles from Geneva? Fifty? Across the border in France? Would your President call off the Summit over an allegation you could never prove? Only a fool would do that.

"And if we don't release you?" Sallow Face went on in his dry, thin voice. "People disappear, Mr. Olds. Even in Geneva, even high officials of the American government. Who would connect your disappearance with us? In fact, we would probably be wiser to make you disappear than to release you."

Matt said nothing. The queasiness had returned, and with it a sinking feeling in the pit of his stomach. Sallow Face had a point, a perfectly valid point that could mean Matthew Olds, Special Assistant to the President for National Security Affairs, was going to die.

"Whether you are released or eliminated depends on your cooperation and on my gratitude," Sallow Face said patiently. "Shall we try once more? Last night—"

Matt shook his head. "Get Malinin."

Sallow Face ignored that. "There are many ways of making a man talk," he told Bayev professorially. My own preference is to test his tolerance of pain." He addressed Matt again: "Every man has his limits, Mr. Olds. Do you know yours? Or will you give me the considerable pleasure of helping you learn them?"

Bayev licked his dry lips. Peppermint stared off into space.

"I generally use this," Sallow Face said. He held a pair of bright-red plastic sticks, each in the shape of a policeman's billy but smaller, attached at one end by three nylon cords.

His hand moved more swiftly than Matt would have thought possible, and the blunt ends of the two toy clubs caught him at the belt line. He suddenly and shockingly couldn't breathe. There was no pain; pain he would have understood. He doubled over slowly, trying frantically to breathe. His knees thumped on the floor.

"Where is Claudia Nikolaievna, Mr. Olds?"

The hand that held the toy moved again. The nylon cords, perhaps three inches in length, were draped over Matt's arm. Sallow Face squeezed the ends of the sticks. It was like a vise closing.

"Where is she, Mr. Olds?"

The sticks were raised. Matt came quickly and obediently to his feet, to ease the pain.

"Where *is* she?" He repeated the words blankly. He was startled, and he hoped it showed on his face. The blind terror that had come with the inability to breathe became a reasoning fear that, in its own way, was even worse. Because to test his tolerance of pain with a question he could not answer was one way of killing him.

A brightness flickered in the eyes in the sallow face and then seemed to go out, like a candle guttering. The shock, Matt thought. He can see it on my face. I can't answer his question. He knows that now.

"Last night," Sallow Face said, "you made certain arrangements with Claudia Nikolaievna."

The red plastic sticks closed on Matt's arm.

"I said I'd like to see her again. That's all."

"And you saw her again today?"

"No."

"In the Grand Passage?"

Matt watched the face. The eyes narrowed before pressure was applied to the sticks. "No."

"Why did you wish to see her again?"

"I just wanted to see her."

The eyes narrowed. Matt's face was bathed in sweat.

"Come now, Mr. Olds. Boy meets girl? You can do better than that."

Matt looked at the eyes.

"Is there a CIA safe house in Geneva?"

"I don't know."

"Where is it?"

"I don't know."

"You took her there?"

"No."

"You arranged for her to go there?"

"No."

"Where is it?"

The eyes narrowed.

"I said I don't know."

"She mentioned her father?"

"Her father?" Matt repeated.

"Last night, you talked of her father?"

Interrogation, Whitney Stoughton had once told Matt, was a two-way street. Sometimes the interrogator revealed more than he learned. Sometimes that could not be helped.

"No, we—wait a minute, yes," Matt said carefully, thinking of Whitney Stoughton's two-way street, the sadism of Sallow Face meaning nothing now, the interrogation that could flow both ways all that mattered. "Her patriotism," he said. "It was something about her patriotism."

"Her father didn't approve of it?"

"She didn't say that."

"But it was implied?"

"Maybe," Matt said.

"This afternoon?"

"I told you. Last night."

"But she had more to say about it today?"

"I didn't see her today."

"Not at the Grand Passage?"

"No."

"Not even when you saw her father?"

"I didn't see her father."

"Begin again with last night," Sallow Face said.

"We had dinner," Matt said wearily, and Sallow Face shot more questions at him, and new combinations of the same questions, and occasionally the eyes narrowed and the sticks closed, but Matt, now that he was learning something, was learning more than they were learning, could find a place away from the pain where he could think.

They were running scared. They had to be running scared if they had brought him here. But why?

The first Summit meeting had been put off a day. Because Claudia had vanished? Would that have been enough to postpone the Summit? Matt didn't think so. Unless—

". . . her father?" Sallow Face was saying.

Andreyev? Had Premier Andreyev disappeared, too?

Sallow Face sighed. He released one of the sticks and jerked the device off Matt's arm. The arm hung numbly, heavily at his side.

Sallow Face threw his hands out wide, palms up in a gesture of frustration, the red plastic sticks dangling.

"Shall we show him Semyon?" he said to no one in particular.

4 A flight of stairs going down, and at the bottom a vaulted stone ceiling, great oak casks lining the walls, the sour smell of new wine. Sallow Face led the way, followed by Matt and Peppermint in lockstep with Bayev behind them.

Another flight of stairs, going up. Sallow Face groped for a light switch at the top.

Matt smelled gasoline and wine, saw three nondescript trucks, not small, and a Citroën DS sedan. Beyond the car was a pair of galvanized-iron doors, padlocked. The stone floor was slick with grease. An assortment of automotive tools hung on one wall of the garage.

Peppermint led the way toward a frosted-glass door on the opposite wall.

"This one," said Sallow Face in his lecturer's voice, "was as stubborn as you. But I had five hours with him today. I would like you to see the results."

The results, Matt suspected as they neared the door, would not be pretty. But he had to admire the technique. Show him one victim of Sallow Face's handiwork and he would be disinclined to become another.

A shove from Bayev, and Matt stood to one side of the frosted-glass door. Sallow Face unlocked it and stepped back. Peppermint pulled it open just as a silhouette loomed beyond the frosted glass.

Bayev shouted a warning.

The silhouette became a man. In the instant before he moved, Matt saw that he was a fat man, and not young. He was naked to the waist and shivering. Raised blue welts covered his chest. He was clutching a length of heavy knotted rope in both hands. His left eye stared wildly. The right eye swollen shut, the size and shape of a big purple plum. A white moustache, large and luxuriant, flowed over the left side of the mouth and across the cheek almost to the ear. On the right side, where the moustache had been, the lip was torn, giving the face a fixed sneer.

The man snarled and sprang up out of his crouch, swinging the length of knotted rope.

Then several things happened at once.

Sallow Face stepped forward and raised the plastic device, holding only one stick, the other swinging free from the nylon cords like a flail. Bayev moved to shut the door. The flailing red stick struck his shoulder. He howled. The automatic sprang from his hand, and it almost seemed that he had thrown it carefully in the injured man's direction. A big hand caught, turned, and cocked it.

Three shots rang out deafeningly.

Peppermint slammed back across the garage, slid down the rear fender of the Citroën, and fell, dropping his gun. The fat man fired again. Nobody else was hit. Sallow Face tried to catch the bare arm in the vise of the red plastic sticks but the fat man, already moving, shook them off and lumbered toward the galvanized-iron doors.

Bayev ran for the Citroën and the second gun.

The fat man, paying no attention to him, calmly stood in front of the galvanized-iron doors, held the automatic close to the padlock, and fired. He tore at the lock with his free hand, but it held fast. He reversed the gun and used the butt against the lock. He looked over his shoulder at Bayev.

Bayev was crouching over the second gun when Matt reached him and kicked the gun across the stone floor.

The fat man yanked the lock out of the hasp, pulled the doors apart, and slipped through.

Running, Matt shouldered past Bayev. He reached the doors. Something brushed his head and clanged against the galvanized iron—the red plastic sticks.

Then Matt was outside in the darkness, jogging around the side of the château and down a sloping dead-straight driveway between rows of trees dimly seen in the starlight. Ahead he saw a gatehouse, and light. He veered to the left, between the trees and over a thin frost that broke crisply underfoot. He heard shouts and saw flashlights bobbing in the darkness.

He reached a high stone wall and stood there panting, the lights coming closer. He backed away from the wall and collided with the trunk of a tree. Then he was on top of the wall, vaguely aware that he had climbed the tree to get there. He hung by his hands and let go.

He ran, and there was the highway and the dark gleam of the lake, and after a while the stone buildings of a town and the only sound his running footsteps on the cobblestones. His throat felt raw and he couldn't catch his breath. He slowed to a walk.

He saw the *gendarmerie* sign under an arcade, brightly lighted in the night. He went in there.

And elderly man in a gray uniform looked at him.

He was going to say something, but once he started he knew he wouldn't stop, and this was not for the Swiss police, not now and maybe not ever; it was for Whitney Stoughton and the CIA.

"Oui, monsieur?" the elderly man in the gray uniform said.

"The hotel Beau Rivage," Matt said.

"In Geneva, monsieur?"

"Call them, please. Room 405," Matt said, quite calmly, in adequate French, and he heard the elderly policeman ask, politely enough, if he was drunk.

He denied being drunk.

The elderly policeman asked to see his papers, and he found and showed his diplomatic passport and heard the sound of the elderly policeman's voice, on the telephone, and sat down on a hard bench and was promptly asleep.

Chapter

SIX

Memoranda

From: CLAY HUNTINGTON
To: NANCY PADGETT, M.D.

Thanks for your quick report on Matt Olds. After the look I had at him, it's good to know he's suffering from nothing worse than a swelling behind the ear and a badly bruised arm-- provided I've interpreted the Doctor Nancy chicken scratches correctly.

It comes as no great shock that Matt wouldn't

take a sedative. He's a stubborn type who never
wants to miss any of the action. Besides, he has
some business with the CIA this morning. When
that's over, see if you can play Lucrezia
Borgia and slip your medicine into his coffee or
something.

Meanwhile, why not get some sleep yourself?
Five-thirty is a hell of a time to start the day.

From: WHITNEY STOUGHTON
To: THE PRESIDENT

Herewith, a preliminary evaluation of the
Matthew Olds debriefing. Olds was interrogated
by the undersigned and agents Charles Colter
and George Norman for an hour and forty-five
minutes beginning at 0600 this morning. A tape
of the interrogation was studied by staff.

1. Subject was picked up by N. S. Yegorov and
Leonid Bayev of the KGB. Both are Main Depart-
ment Seven, under Colonel Malinin. Yegorov
heads the detail responsible for the safety of
Premier Andreyev. Make that ''headed'': Subject
believes Yegorov was shot dead this morning.
Leonid Bayev's special responsibility is the
Premier's daughter.

2. Subject was taken to KGB safe house not
far from village of Coppet. Subject's testimony
locates safe house between 1.2 and 1.5 kilometers east of village and three hundred to
three-fifty yards north on hill. Expect KGB
will do some moving. Our residents will cover.

3. Interrogation of Subject by KGB specialist named Dmitri Trofimovich Moskalenko.
Identification made via Moskalenko's trademark:
A pair of sticks attached by nylon cords.
(Note: It's a variation of an old Okinawan device for flailing grain, and equally effective
for cracking skulls.) Moskalenko high up in
special terrorist section of KGB known as Department of Wet affairs—like our own ten-
slash-two people, the ones we don't admit we
have. Moskalenko reputed to be a killer.

4. Subject convinced, on basis of questions asked, that daughter of Premier Andreyev

has disappeared. Also thinks Andreyev is missing. CIA evaluation confirms daughter's disappearance as definite, Premier's disappearance as probable.

5. Subject encountered Russian prisoner at safe house. Identification made via photograph. He is Semyon Semyonov, pastry chef by trade but chess-playing crony and confidant of Andreyev. Escaped with Subject's help, is now missing. KGB interrogation of Semyonov tends to support Subject's belief that Andreyev has vanished.

6. Kremlin power struggle apparently won by First Secretary Lysenko. Struggle obvious for almost two years--Lysenko fronting for hawks and steel-eaters. Andreyev for doves and consumer-goods people. Andreyev knows too much, is likely running for his life. Question: Any possibility he wants to defect?

7. Defeat of dove faction in Kremlin, leaving Lysenko's policies unopposed, increases danger of war.

8. Suggest advisability of sending Subject back to Washington for his own protection. Sometimes an interrogator reveals more than he learns, which seems to have been the case at KGB safe house last night.

Subject's life could be in danger.

From: CLAY HUNTINGTON
To: SECRETARY OF STATE REED

Delighted you could get appointment with Foreign Minister Kapitsa for early this afternoon.

Two things to remember. First, Olds was picked up by the KGB because he took Andreyev's daughter to dinner. Period. Let's keep them guessing about what we know—or think we know.

Second, push Kapitsa. Tell him I'm mad enough to pull a Khrushchev and walk out on the Summit unless I get an apology from Andreyev— in person—and Andreyev's assurance that the responsible parties will be punished. We can expect Kapitsa to deny the whole thing, but that doesn't matter. The important thing is

your insistence on a behind-the-scenes meeting
between Andreyev and me. Andreyev wants this
Summit as much as I do. If available, he'd
agree to meet. If the answer is no, we can be
pretty damn sure Andreyev is missing. Which is
what we're trying to find out.

Good luck.

From: BURT EAST
To: THE PRESIDENT

I can't go along with CIA. Now that Matt's
reported to them, Stoughton & Co. know as much
as he does. The Russians will realize that.
Chances are Matt is safe here.

From: CLAY HUNTINGTON
To: WHITNEY STOUGHTON

It's possible that Andreyev wants to defect,
but I doubt it. Wouldn't he have found a way
to contact us by now if that was his intention?

We have to assume he has something else up
his sleeve. Get to him before the Russians do
and you'll find out what it is. How's that for
an easy assignment? If it means using your own
ten-slash-two boys, the KGB has it coming.
Just find Andreyev, and nobody will ask how you
managed it.

From: CLAY HUNTINGTON
To: BURT EAST

I'll take your advice on Matt Olds. Probably
selfish, but I want him here. Can you put a
couple of men on him whenever he leaves the
hotel? Better not let him in on it. You know
Matt. He'd spend his waking day trying to lose
them.

From: CLAY HUNTINGTON
To: SECRETARY OF STATE REED

No surprise that Kapitsa seemed genuinely
disturbed, though willing to admit nothing. As
you say, he's a diplomat, not a KGB thug.

No surprise either that he turned down the

meeting with Andreyev. We can now go ahead with
the assumption Andreyev is missing.

From: MATTHEW OLDS
To: THE PRESIDENT
    The only Swiss newspaperman I know who
seems to fit the requirements is Alphonse
Borel, political columnist for the Tribune de
Geneve. We met while I was with the AP bureau
in Moscow and were pretty close for a while.
Borel is very Swiss, neutral but leaning toward
us. He's also convinced Clay Huntington is the
best thing that happened to the United States
since John F. Kennedy.
    Do I see him today, or what?

From: CLAY HUNTINGTON
To: MATTHEW OLDS
    Get in touch with Borel as soon as you
can. Sorry we can't talk this over in person,
but I'm up to my ears with such vital things as
that Thanksgiving dinner in Bern tomorrow.
    Tell Borel you think Andreyev is missing.
Off the record, of course. He doesn't get to
quote you. What he does get is a sensational
rumor, probably correct, which he's free to
print. If he does print it, every paper on the
Continent will pick it up. The Russians aren't
used to living in a goldfish bowl, and I'm hoping it will throw them off balance long enough
to let us find Andreyev before they do.
    On completion of mission, you report to
Doctor Nancy. You take whatever medicine she
prescribes. That's an order.

    "That winds it up for now, Pris," the President told his
private secretary. "Just get me the Ambassador in Bern on
the phone, please."
    "Yes, sir," Miss Priscilla Lee said.
    "And Pris? One more thing. Would you wire Gigi about
five dozen roses for Thanksgiving?"

98

Chapter
SEVEN

1 There were, Viktor Malinin knew, two classic ways to move up in the Soviet power structure.

You could work your way up through Komsomol, the Communist Youth League.

You could climb through the ranks of the KGB, the Committee for State Security.

Nikolai Ivanovich Andreyev, Chairman of the Council of Ministers, Premier of Russia, had taken the Komsomol path.

Igor Lysenko, First Secretary of the Central Committee of the Communist Party, had clawed his way up through the KGB jungle.

Viktor Malinin, like Shelepin before him, had used both routes. He had been a member of Komsomol since his fourteenth birthday. While still in his twenties he had made the good guess of condemning Boris Pasternak in a speech delivered to the Moscow Youth League in the Sports Palace. Pasternak had already rejected his Nobel Prize, awarded after the pirate publication of *Doctor Zhivago* in Italy. That did not stop Malinin. He had stood before fifty thousand screaming, clamoring young Communists and said that to call Pasternak a pig was slandering the pig because Pasternak had dirtied his feeding place, something even a pig wouldn't do. Those older members of Komsomol who had criticized Malinin for wearing two hats promptly changed their tune. *Komsomolskaya Pravda,* the Youth League organ, singled him out for special favorable attention. He was a second secretary before he was thirty.

The second hat Viktor Malinin wore meant hard, grueling work. He had been graduated by the KGB Institute in Moscow, the KGB language school, and the Juridical Institute. He had been assigned to Main Department Five, the watchdog department, and had spent several years in the army, as a KGB spy reporting to Lubianka on the activities of the Military Intelligence Directorate, the rival espionage organization. He came to the attention of Lysenko, then the KGB chief, when he uncovered a Military Intelligence plot to discredit him. He came to the attention of Nikolai Ivanovich later as Claudia's suitor. He made colonel and was given command of Main Department Seven. Nikolai Ivanovich may have regretted it afterward. He had never told Malinin to his face that he was an opportunist, but Malinin could see which way the wind was blowing.

When the lines hardened between the hawks and doves in the Central Committee, Malinin had no trouble picking a winner. Before he left for Geneva, Lysenko had all but promised him candidate membership in the Committee, provided he kept Nikolai Ivanovich in line. On the phone Monday, Lysenko had dangled an even bigger carrot—top spot in the KGB and the general's shoulder boards that went with it.

Not bad, Viktor Malinin thought, for the son of a Tula track-walker. The KGB chief, if he knew how to exploit his position, could be the third most important man in Russia, after the Premier and the First Secretary.

From there it was just a small step to the very top.

It was also, Malinin knew, sitting at the scrambler phone a few minutes after noon on Thursday, a hurtingly long way down—a fall bigger men than Malinin had taken, and for less reason.

One reason for Malinin's imminent fall was spread on the desk before him in his Villa Krupskaya office.

ANDREYEV, OÙ EST-IL?, the blue headline said. Where's Andreyev?

It was a good question. It was a question that in a single minute, in a single decision taken by First Secretary Lysenko, could write an end to Viktor Malinin's once promising career.

A photograph, taken not long after the Premier's heart attack, shared the front page of the *Tribune de Genève* with the accusing headline. Nikolai Ivanovich looked old, tired, worn out. The pince-nez sat slightly askew on the bridge of his nose, and even the beard seemed wilted.

The article managed to say very little in great detail. An expedition, Malinin thought. A clever fishing expedition. It spoke of the power struggle between Premier and First Secretary, and put the power struggle in the historic context of other such struggles. It pointed out that, except for a brief appearance at a Villa Krupskaya party Monday night, Premier Andreyev had not been seen in Geneva. It gave thoughtful consideration to what the writer called an unexpected Russian postponement of the first direct confrontation of the heads of state. Three reasons, the writer said, could account for this postponement. Andreyev, known to be in poor health, might be seriously ill. Andreyev, known to be at odds with First Secretary Lysenko, might have been deposed in absentia. Andreyev, possibly in more serious trouble at home than the Western press was aware, might have fled.

The Russians, the writer concluded, could quell these disturbing rumors only if Andreyev made a public appearance.

Since the early edition of the *Tribune de Genève*, Villa Krupskaya had been in a state of siege. Colonel Viktor Malinin, as chief security officer, was a prime target of the journalistic assault.

He had no comment.

The Premier's health, said the Premier's personal physician, was excellent, all things considered.

Foreign Minister Kapitsa could not be reached for comment.

The Premier's daughter could not be reached for comment.

When the phone on his desk buzzed, Malinin shoved the incriminating newspaper aside. His hand shook.

"Malinin," the voice rasped in his ear.

"Yes, comrade." Comrade. He had got that right.

"The daughter walked out of a department store and disappeared. Correct?"

"Yes, comrade."

"The father walked out of a bookstore and disappeared. Correct?"

"Essentially," said Malinin, gripping the phone harder.

"Essentially? Did I leave any details out? Such as your unredeemable stupidity? Where were you? Where was Yegorov?"

Malinin almost said, buying a package of cigarettes. He did not say it. He said crowds. He said surprise. He said a taxi.

"You are too old," the rasping voice said, "to go back to making pretty speeches to the children in the Moscow

101

Sports Palace. But apparently you are too incompetent for anything else."

"Yes, comrade."

"Don't yes comrade me."

Malinin, otherwise an articulate man, always became tongue-tied in the face of Lysenko's anger. "No, comrade," he said.

"Yes comrade, no comrade, shit. Kapitsa will buy you time. He is very good at it. You will use that time to find Nikolai Ivanovich. Switzerland is a small country."

"He might have crossed the border into France," Malinin suggested. The thought did not make him happy.

"What for? If he is ready to become a capitalist lackey, sooner or later he will go to the Americans. The Americans are in Switzerland. The American President is in Switzerland. Can you imagine our position if Nikolai Ivanovich defected?"

Malinin said that he could imagine it.

"You are a very original thinker," Lysenko said dryly. "Calling in Moskalenko, was that one of your original ideas?"

"I—" Malinin began.

"The Second Secretary at the Embassy in Bern sent a cipher to Lubianka, details supplied by a Swiss national named Gros-Claude. Who shot Yegorov?"

"The chess-master Semyon shot him. Semyon was undergoing interrogation when—"

"And the body?"

"Bayev took care of it. Clothing and identification burned. The face smashed with a jack handle. The body buried. It will never be found." Malinin was eager to discuss these details. He knew they interested Lysenko, a former commander of the KGB.

"Semyon escaped," Lysenko said. "Find him and you may find Nikolai Ivanovich."

The knuckles of Malinin's hand holding the phone were white with strain. Was the Secretary playing with him? This was the second indication he had given that Malinin would not be recalled.

"We'll find him," Malinin said. "He can't get far. He's hurt. Moskalenko—"

"And the American?" the rasping voice cut in. "Just how badly did that sadistic little prick Moskalenko hurt him? And how much did his interrogation reveal?"

102

"I don't know," Malinin admitted uneasily. "Moskalenko doesn't report to me. If he overstepped his—"

"From now on he reports to you."

"Then I'll keep him out of the picture from now on," Malinin said, guessing that was what Lysenko wanted to hear, pleased that Lysenko wanted Moskalenko to defer to him. "He's trouble."

"The shit you will. He's not trouble, he's *in* trouble. So are you. Maybe one of you will redeem himself."

"I appreciate the chance, sir."

"Comrade," said Lysenko in mild reprimand, but his voice softened somewhat. "Listen, Viktor, I still have faith in you. I don't make mistakes about people."

"I'm grateful you feel that way, comrade."

"I don't want gratitude. I want results. Find Nikolai Ivanovich." There was a pause. "And stop him."

"Stop him, comrade?" Malinin asked in amazement.

"Before he can talk to the Americans. Any resources you need are at your disposal, Viktor, anything at all. Nikolai Ivanovich must be silenced. To spirit him home is one way. To kill him is another. He's a sick man. He could die of 'natural causes.' Or perhaps you could put the blame on the Americans. I rely on your judgment."

Malinin could picture Lysenko in his sanctum in the Kremlin, the thick shoulders hunched, the bulbous Leninesque head thrust forward, the small eyes burning with resolution, the fingers of one big peasant hand drumming impatiently on the desk.

"I understand, comrade."

The dangling carrot was jerked away. "I said results, Colonel Malinin. I require results, not comprehension."

"I will try—" Malinin began.

"Try? History is a difficult mistress, Colonel. There are no rewards for trying."

The line went dead. Malinin replaced the receiver slowly and went to the window. It was a cold blustery day. A few hardy November sailors were out, their small craft scudding swiftly before the wind. Across the water, perched on a lushly green hillside, were the villas of the very rich, snug and insulated in a way that Malinin would never be. East of them, the lake widened and the shoreline spread flat to the French border, with the mountains of High Savoy looming beyond. Had Nikolai Ivanovich crossed over? Malinin did not think so. No, the *starik*, the old man, was here in Switzerland. He would defect to the

Americans. Nothing else made any sense. It was why he had fled, with Claudia. To dirty the feeding trough in a way the scribbler Pasternak never would have dreamed possible.

Malinin wondered if his own condemnation of Nikolai Ivanovich, to Claudia, had hastened the defection, made it inevitable. Perhaps it had been a mistake.

He thought of Claudia. His loins tightened. With those long supple legs, and the way she could move, she was magnificent in bed. He had taught her that. He had trained her carefully, as a plaything for himself. Every nuance the way he liked it—the wanton, attacking female, mounting him, then subdued and conquered by him, overturned by his power, until she was begging for more, calling his name finally and crying out that she loved him.

Love? he thought. There was no such thing as love. There was power, the display of it, and the uses of it.

And there was history. If you were lucky enough and ruthless enough, you could even train history, as you could train any other mistress. Yes, Malinin thought, the First Secretary was right. History was a difficult mistress. But a rewarding one.

And, sometimes, a very patient mistress.

Malinin crossed to the far wall of his office, where a single large painting hung. The paint had been applied in gobs—with a trowel, or by hand, or maybe with the idiot artist's bare feet. Nikolai Ivanovich, in his bourgeois cosmopolitanism, had decreed in favor of abstract art. This example of it looked like a wart and a puckered scar on a rhinoceros's hind leg.

Shoving the painting aside, Malinin turned the dial of the wall safe and opened the small round door. He removed a Manila envelope, unfastened the string, and took out the contents.

Nikolai Ivanovich, Lysenko had said, must be silenced.

But if the Americans reached him first? What then?

History was a very patient mistress.

Malinin looked at the negative and the pair of black and white prints. The negative itself was fifteen years old. Malinin congratulated himself. He might have used the photograph before. He had waited, patiently. The man was climbing as he, Malinin, had climbed.

The man could fall, as easily—more easily and more resoundingly—than Malinin.

The Americans took those things rather too seriously,

Malinin thought. A strong Puritanical streak in their national character. Playing right into Malinin's hands.

He chuckled, studying one of the prints taken from the fifteen-year-old negative. The reproduction was excellent, despite the coarse grain of the high-speed film. The picture had been taken with a German Exakta, the 35-mm SLR model favored by the KGB. Every detail was sharp and clear.

There was no mistaking the face. The American had come a long way since that time fifteen years ago, in Moscow.

The photograph showed three men in a hotel room. The lampshade, the ridiculous colored-glass lampshade, could only be Moscow. The room showed signs of a drunken orgy. An empty vodka bottle, resting on its side in a corner. Another, not quite empty, standing on the night table between the beds. A blanket on the floor, and cards and money on that. Clothing here and there—a shirt, a jacket, a pair of shoes, a single shoe.

One of the men, in his underwear, his face turned to the wall, his arms sprawled out, drunkenly asleep on a bed.

A second man, on the second bed, sitting on the edge, his face cut off by the top of the picture. You used their kind when you had to, Malinin thought, but if you permitted them to be identified, their usefulness ended.

The man whose face was cut off by the top of the picture sat on the very edge of the bed, his hands flat on the mattress on either side of his thighs. His pants were down.

A third man, down on his knees, bent over the unidentifiable man's turgid male member. The third man had grasped it with his right hand. A look of mingled pain and pleasure was on his rapt, slack-mouthed face.

Even though the eyes were shut, softly shut with too much vodka, too much desire, there was no mistaking the face.

Perhaps we are ready now, friend, Malinin thought. Find Nikolai Ivanovich. Find him before we do. I'll congratulate you. I'll send you a little gift.

Won't you be grateful? Won't you do my bidding—and history's?

2 Alphonse Borel was a bouncy little man with a shock of bright-red hair who spoke not quite colloquial

American. He had a round face and twinkling eyes, and the jolly manner hid an astute mind. He was fifty, give or take a couple of years. He had been a newspaperman for twenty-five of them.

For their second meeting he met Matt at the café on the Île Rousseau, at the western end of the lake. The café was all but deserted and would soon shut for the winter. An elderly American couple, bundled in coats against the brisk wind, sat at the only other occupied table. The man gestured with his head, and spoke in a stage whisper. Matt couldn't quite hear the words, but from the look of curiosity and then mild awe which followed, he could imagine what had been said in the flat, pleasant accent of the Midwest. See that fellow there? That's Matthew Olds, Special Assistant to the President.

Except for the American couple, and the waiter who took their order, and the swans and ducks in the pens at the edge of the water, Matt and Alphonse Borel had the café to themselves.

"Christ, Matt," Borel said in an aggrieved voice. "You didn't warn me that it would be like this. I had to get out of the office. The office won't be safe for days. I swear, they come out of the woodwork."

"Who?" Matt said.

"The nuts. The well-meaning crackpots who caught a glimpse of Andreyev. They've seen him everywhere. It's the fornicating beard," Borel said with a grin, proud of his use of the word fornicating instead of the four-letter word. "That and any pair of glasses that can pass for pince-nez."

Borel took a hefty gulp of his Campari and soda. "In the first three hours, one hundred and fourteen people called to say they'd seen your boy Andreyev, and of course we'll have to check them all out."

"Anything promising?" Matt asked. That had been their agreement yesterday. Whitney Stoughton couldn't publicly state that Andreyev had vanished, couldn't publicly ask for any leads to his whereabouts. The *Tribune de Genève* could do both.

"I doubt it," Borel said. "You would be amazed how many stocky, middle-aged types wear beards and glasses in Switzerland. Let me see—Andreyev was spotted near Le Salève, of course, fifteen times. That's the French border. He was seen in Schaffhausen twice, in Bern a dozen times, in Zurich five times, in Lausanne, in Montreux, in

106

the Bernese Oberland, and on a pedal-boat in Lake Lugano feeding stale bread to the swans. Not to mention every street corner in Geneva."

"What about the girl?" Matt said. Borel had agreed to make no mention of Claudia in his article.

"Sixteen identifications so far in company with a beautiful girl," Borel said unhappily. "Those are the ones we're checking carefully. We have five in Geneva, two in Montreux, four in the Oberland—"

"Never mind," Matt said. "I get the idea. Have the police been to see you?"

"I've had a couple of calls from the Minister of Justice and Police," Borel said, still more unhappily. "Do you know him?"

"Willy Müllener? He was working with Burt East on security arrangements before the President got here. He seemed a pretty capable guy."

"He is. He didn't just phone. He sent the Security Police around to the office. They wanted me to reveal my sources, of course. I told them I had no sources. Just put two and two together, I said."

"Did they believe that?"

"I doubt it, but don't worry. I came here rather shiftily. I wasn't followed." Borel frowned. "You'd better know what you're talking about, though. I could look pretty silly if Andreyev decided to hold a press conference at Villa Krupskaya."

"He won't. What about the Security Police? They'll be poking around on their own, won't they?"

"In their own quiet, patient, Swiss way. Absolutely."

"They any good?"

"They are superb," said Borel, and when Matt showed him a pair of raised eyebrows, he elaborated: "I mean that. The Security Police of a small, well-run country are bound to be good. No awesome amount of real estate to cover, and an intimate knowledge of every town and village when they need it."

"Sure, but aren't you forgetting the mountains?"

"We Swiss," said Borel, "come as close to taming our mountains as anyone can. But nobody tames the Alps. Why? What do you have in mind?"

"I'm not sure. Figure Andreyev has to get away by himself for a while. A man can lose himself in a big city, say the size of Zurich or bigger. Or he can lose himself in country, real country. Like the Alps." Matt looked at his watch. "It's almost three o'clock. That's got to make forty-eight hours anyway that Andreyev's been gone."

"What makes you so sure of that?" Borel asked.

Matt shook his head. "Sorry. I can't say. Just take my word for it. Forty-eight hours. That's a long time, when you're on the run."

"Assuming he ever intends to stop running," Borel said.

"They just depose them these days," Matt said, thinking of Claudia. "They don't kill them. The last one they killed was Beria. That was a long time ago."

"Ordinarily," Borel persisted, "I'd say you were right. But these are no ordinary circumstances. For one thing, there's the Summit."

"Sure, and Yugoslavia," Matt said uneasily. "I see what you mean. Lysenko will have elaborate plans for the Yugoslav takeover, including a trumped-up excuse for Russian intervention. If Andreyev can quote chapter and verse on it, where does that leave him?"

"It leaves his life in danger. I don't think I'm exaggerating, Matt. There's even some possibility that he's already been eliminated."

"Assassinated? Here in Switzerland?"

"Here in Switzerland," Borel said, "is where he happens to be. I don't consider it at all strange that he hasn't surfaced—if he's still alive. Far from it."

"He wouldn't just run," Matt said. "He'd want a place to hole up. He's a sick man. But even more important, if he's been kicked out of his job, he'd want some life insurance. He could get it by taking someone else into his confidence. That would be his protection. But maybe he wants to do it right, or carefully, or—hell, I don't know. He goes into hiding for a while—"

"To put it all in writing?" Borel suggested.

"Maybe. I like that. Andreyev's a careful man, almost pedantic. To put it all in writing. Why not?"

"And show it to whom?" Borel asked slowly, rocking back on his chair.

"Us," Matt said promptly.

Borel's chair came upright. He leaned across the table. "The Americans? That's not Andreyev. That's not in character."

"Why not?"

"Did you ever read anything he's written? Andreyev has almost a—well, call it a mystical feeling for Mother Russia. What you're suggesting would be betraying his country. He just wouldn't do it."

"I'm not so sure of that," Matt said. "Look. This is where President Huntington draws the line. Lysenko's got all he's going to get. He won't get Yugoslavia without a fight. Not that the President wants one. But if he has to risk limited war now, to prevent total war later, he'll do it. Be very sure of that. Be very sure Andreyev knows it, too. Maybe he figures Lysenko's got to be stopped. A confrontation in Yugoslavia could escalate. Maybe Andreyev figures he's the only one who can prevent it."

"Matt, you're forgetting his mystical feeling for—"

"What happens to Mother Russia in a nuclear war?" Matt asked softly. "Which way does this mystical feeling push him then? A hundred million Russians dead because Andreyev *didn't* stop Lysenko?"

They stared at each other across the small café table. In the pens, an angry swan hissed. A two-car tram rattled noisily across the nearby Mont Blanc bridge.

"*Mon Dieu*," said Borel, forgetting his fine command of colloquial American. "*Mon Dieu*, what a story if you're right. It must be tearing the man apart."

3 The Presidential Thanksgiving message was the brainstorm of Press Secretary Harvey Ross. Presidents, he had pointed out, spent Thanksgiving Day at home in the East Wing of the White House, they did not spend it abroad. It was a time for the family, and maybe a fire on the hearth, and—guess what?—a turkey dinner with all the trimmings.

If the President could not have his Thanksgiving dinner at home in the East Wing of the White House, the least he could do was nibble a traditional turkey leg on American soil. This meant the big black limousines with the Presidential seal on them, the Secret Service, Swiss motorcycle outriders, a dozen cars crammed with reporters, the ululating wail of police sirens to speed the motorcade's way through four cantons. The nearest American soil was the Embassy on Jubiläumsstrasse, a quiet residential street in Bern, and that was where the President went.

Harvey Ross did the thing up brown. A split-screen setup, with Gigi looking serene in a pink brocade maternity dress in the White House family dining room and the

President looking confident and urbane in the dining room of the Ambassador's residence on Jubiläumsstrasse in Bern, was tried, and proved successful.

In an aside to Matt while flashbulbs popped, the President hefted his turkey leg and said, "If you want to know the truth, I hate turkey."

He liked his champagne better. He raised a goblet of Taittinger, and Gigi a goblet of Great Western, the best of both continents, to show, Harvey Ross said, international solidarity. On the TV screen it almost seemed that the President and the First Lady were clinking glasses. The fact that Gabrielle Germaine Huntington was drinking her champagne at one in the afternoon in Washington and Clay Huntington drinking his at seven in Bern didn't seem to bother anyone. The Embassy staff, watching a monitoring screen, applauded enthusiastically. Gigi was surrounded by a few close friends and five dozen long-stemmed yellow roses.

Everything, in fact, in the words of Harvey Ross, was coming up roses.

They had Thanksgiving dinner, and the Constellation satellite beamed the President's message of restrained hope back home. Then, after the President's off-the-cuff remarks to the Embassy staff, telling them what a fine job they were doing, they all went outside to the waiting cars.

And in the crowd across Jubiläumsstrasse, watching them, watching the Marine guards standing at rigid ceremonious attention in the flamboyant dress uniforms that almost made them look like ushers at the Bolshoi or the Theater of Comedy in Moscow, a bald fat man wearing clothes stolen from a farmhouse in Coppet, his right eye swollen shut and painful, debated walking up to them and saying, with the little English he had, "Good afternoon, I want to defect."

He remained where he was. He had stolen a few francs as well as the farmer's clothing, and he would not starve. He had hitchhiked to Bern with the idea of defecting. Geneva would have done as well, but the truck that had finally stopped for him, despite his appearance, was heading in the opposite direction. The driver of the truck had made a grinning reference to his black eye, but the fat man's French was not good enough to follow it. There had been a newspaper in the cab of the truck and on the front page he saw the photograph of Nikolai Ivanovich. He had asked, in his execrable French, and the driver had told him what the newspaper said.

The newspaper said that Nikolai Ivanovich had vanished. If the bald man defected, there would be an American safe house, like the Russian safe house in Coppet, and hours of questioning by the CIA, days of questioning, and meanwhile, what of Nikolai Ivanovich?

No, the bald man decided. Perhaps he will need me.

He watched the Americans enter their sleek black cars, and then he shuffled down the street and around the corner in the direction of the Tierpark.

Chapter
EIGHT

1 An urgent coded message and half a dozen laser-photographs transmitted by the Pentagon reached the Chairman of the Joint Chiefs of Staff shortly before eleven that night.

Fifteen minutes later, General Laffont entered the Presidential Suite, his swarthy face grim. An aide followed him, carrying a viewer for the transparencies.

"Hold it a minute, General—unless the Big Balloon is about to go up," the President said with a faint smile, resurrecting Pentagon jargon more than a decade old. The Big Balloon, then, had meant nuclear war.

"It just could be, Mr. President," General Laffont said in a restrained voice. "You'd better have a look at these right away, sir."

The President sighed. He was wearing a dressing gown Gigi had given him on his last birthday and administering a severe lesson in Red Dog to Matt, Whitney Stoughton, and Burt East. Stoughton and East had been cleaned out, and Matt wasn't doing much better. The President had a big untidy pile of Swiss coins heaped in front of him. He tossed his cards on the table, face up. "You might know," he said. "Two kings, a jack, and a nine. All suits covered. I was going to bet the pot."

He turned to Laffont. "Well, let's have it, General. Was I too optimistic in my speech this afternoon?"

"You'd know better than I would about that, sir," General Laffont said.

Burt East struck his own chest twice with his clenched right fist, burped, and nodded solemnly. "That," he vowed, "is the last time this Carolina boy will ever eat three turkey legs at one sitting."

Silence after that. They had dispensed with the ritual of proving they were just a bunch of guys sitting around a Red Dog table, Matt realized. It was part of the Clay Huntington cool, a way of not taking yourself too seriously until you had to.

General Laffont cleared his throat portentously while cards and coins were swept from the table. His aide placed the battery-operated viewer on a chair and spread a map on the table.

"Northern Yugoslavia," General Laffont said. "The scale is twenty miles to the inch."

He jabbed a finger at the map. "This is Szeged, a Hungarian rail junction across the border, thirty miles northeast of Subotica." He moved the finger. "This is Peć, another railhead, just north of the border town of Miholjac. The distance from Peć to Szeged, not quite a hundred miles. We generally figure a full division for every twenty miles of front, and the Kremlin plays it the same way."

General Laffont had been leaning over the map, his left hand flat on its surface. He straightened and looked directly at the President. "We've had an Orion satellite on a swing that brings it over the area every hour and twenty-five minutes at an altitude of a hundred and seventy-five miles. I'd have liked less, but you know the problem we've been having with the Orions."

Matt knew the problem. Ever since the Huntsville team had developed the Orion, a reconnaissance satellite that could alter its orbit at the flick of a switch and, in a matter of minutes, do a pin-point scouting job anywhere on earth, the Russians had been insisting on territorial air space up to a hundred and fifty miles. We'd lost a couple of earlier Orions as a consequence.

"Not that it matters much," General Laffont said. "The new laser recon cameras, at a hundred and seventy-five miles, transmit at an apparent visual distance of just under

112

a thousand feet. That's close enough, even at night." He nodded to his aide. "All right, Major."

The major touched a button on the viewer, the screen lit up, and the first transparency was inserted. They all gathered around to look. The picture had a gray, ghostlike quality. It was an aerial view of a long freight train in a marshaling yard.

"Could have had it blown up, but there wasn't time," General Laffont said. He gestured to the major, who produced a magnifying glass. It was hardly necessary.

Tanks and half-tracks were being off-loaded from the train.

"That's Szeged," General Laffont said, and at a gesture the major replaced the first transparency with another. "And that's Peć." Although the camera had captured only an instant in time, the evidence of the photographs was unmistakable. A steady stream of military hardware was pouring down the ramps from the big freight cars.

"The rest of them," General Laffont said while the major showed his other pictures, "were taken during the next three swings on the Orion's orbit. They show initial troop and hardware deployment—" he went back to the map— "opposite Novi Knezevac, Subotica, and Sombor. Then," he said, "the Orion stopped transmitting. The Russians shot it down, of course."

Matt knew there was no point in protesting the loss of the expensive piece of equipment to Moscow. Territorial air space was still an uncertain concept at best, and nobody had written any international law to deal with the violent demise of spy satellites.

"Pentagon Intelligence sees elements of five infantry divisions in the hundred miles of front between Szeged in the east and Peć in the west," General Laffont said. "We know that the First and Fourth Ukrainian have been maneuvering in Hungary. We haven't identified the others. A division every twenty miles of front, Mr. President. That's an invasion force."

"Or a defensive alignment," the President suggested thoughtfully.

"Defensive?" Stoughton repeated the word. "Against Yugoslavia?"

"That's what they'd call it, under Lysenko's policy of noncontamination," the President reminded Stoughton. "As an excuse to seal off the Yugoslav border so that Ilić's so-called counter-revolution doesn't contaminate the

Iron Curtain countries." Ilić was the President of Yugoslavia.

"Who said anything about sealing the border?" Matt asked. "It's not the whole border, it's a hundred miles of what looks like invasion front."

"I know, Matt. I'm just saying this doesn't have to be the real thing. Lysenko still has a convenient excuse, and a convenient way out, if he wants to use them."

"It's an invasion front, all right," General Laffont said quietly. "From Szeged in the east and Peć in the west— here, look at the map—the Red Army could send two columns down on Belgrade. It's a textbook situation, without any real terrain to stop them. Besides, in the last four transparencies you saw the initial deployment of five infantry divisions. But that wasn't infantry you saw offloading at the railheads. Those were two tank divisions."

"Any tactical atomic hardware?" the President asked.

"We don't know yet." The Chief of Staff smiled grimly. "I'd say we'll learn that, sir, after the first shot is fired."

The President took a circuit of the room, his limp more pronounced. He looked tired. The necessary ceremonial trivia of his office, like the seventy-mile-an-hour motorcade to Bern and the nibbling at the turkey leg, often had that effect on him. Once President Huntington had confided to Matt that he wished there were two Presidents, like the apocryphal story that every ocean liner had two captains—one to drink cocktails with the passengers and the other to run the ship. President Huntington, unlike some of his predecessors, wanted to run the ship.

He inserted a cigarette in the stubby holder and took a light from the major.

"General," he said, "how soon can you get another Orion up? I want it in low orbit, with two more backstopping it. When the first one stops transmitting, send the second one up. When the second one—"

"They'll shoot them down," General Laffont protested.

"Let them. I want them to know we're on top of this. Whit, have your people get in touch with their Yugoslav contacts. Firm up your plans for an air drop on Belgrade and that airport near Dubrovnik. Supplies—and troops too if necessary. If we give the word, I don't want any delays. Burt, where's Secretary Reed?"

"The Secretary pooped out on us," Burt East drawled. "He's not one of the young folks, he said."

"Wake him up. I want him to assure President Ilić

114

we'll take any measures necessary to guarantee the territorial integrity of his country. Where's Harvey Ross? I want a press conference at nine o'clock."

The President resumed his pacing, the limp less pronounced, the cigarette holder jutting at a rakish angle. His suddenly restored confidence was contagious. An electric current seemed to flow through the room.

"General, how soon can the Sixth Fleet pay a courtesy call in Rieka?"

"Elements of the fleet including the carrier *John F. Kennedy* are steaming west of Trieste right now. By tomorrow morning, if I send the signal right away."

"Send it. Matt, I want you to—"

The telephone buzzed, and on the console the green light was flashing. It stopped them all short. The green light meant the CIA in Langley, Virginia, and CIA Director McManus would authorize its use only in case of emergency.

"Shall I—" Stoughton began, but the President shook his head, went quickly to the phone, and picked up the receiver. It was, Matt knew, one of three scramblers served by the console—the other two being Pentagon and Matt's own Little State Department in the White House basement.

"Clay Huntington," the President said into the phone. "How's it going, Berney? Sleep, hell. We've got a hot one. You probably ... What? I see. Sure, go ahead."

CIA Director Bernard McManus was a courtly Southern gentleman who ordinarily wouldn't dream of interrupting anyone, let alone the President. The news, Matt knew, could only be bad.

"I see," the President said again. "When? How long will that take? Okay. No, no orders, Berney. Just keep on top of it. Right, I will."

The President hung up. He turned slowly away from the phone and stubbed the cigarette out carefully.

"More from the Yugoslav border?" General Laffont asked.

"Not the border. Belgrade." The President shook his head. "It looks like I'm going to start earning that quarter of a million buck salary they pay me," he said. His voice was soft, his eyes hard. "An hour ago," he went on gravely, "President Ilić was shot to death as he was leaving a special session of Parliament. There are riots in the streets. Cvetković, the Defense Minister, says the

115

situation is out of control. Berney tells me the riots are organized and the situation, at this time, is very definitely not out of control. It's the excuse Lysenko needs. Cvetković is his man in Belgrade. Which explains your invasion front, General. The Russians are conveniently ready to move. And it looks like they're going to."

2 When Matt got back to his room, he found three message slips alongside the telephone. All three asked him to call the same Geneva number.

The number meant nothing to him. Who the hell do I know in Geneva? he wondered. His thoughts were elsewhere. After the McManus bombshell, Secretary Reed had joined the President to draft a message to the Yugoslav government on the assassination. "Why don't you take a break and get some sleep, Matt?" the President had suggested. "Doctor Nancy's orders. Starting tomorrow you probably won't have time for any."

Sitting on the edge of the bed and removing his shoes wearily, Matt dialed an outside line and then the number. The President, as usual, was right. Matt's head ached dully and his arm was stiff. He felt light-headed with fatigue.

"*Allô?*" a voice said in French. There was background laughter and the sound of music, an accordian playing *La Vie en Rose*.

"This is Matthew Olds. I have a message to call—"

"Who?"

"Matthew Olds. O-L-D-S."

"Ah, yes, Monsieur Olds." The voice said something else, but the laughter and music drowned the words out.

"What? I can't hear you."

"The child, I said. He is asleep in the back room."

"What child?" Matt said irritably, thinking of the assassination and the Russian troop build-up. "What are you talking about?"

"He says he is your son."

Matt groaned. Chris, he thought, and Thanksgiving dinner and that man-to-man talk his twelve-year-old son might or might not have wanted. He'd forgotten all about it. There was no reason why he couldn't have taken Chris along to Bern. Probably Chris would have gotten a kick out of it. You take him away from Tracy, he thought, because Tracy's not a fit mother, and you toss him bag and baggage into a boarding school and promptly forget about him.

"Okay, sure," Matt said. "I'll be right over. How long's he been there?"

The music swelled, the voice was lost.

"Where is it, anyway?" Matt asked.

"The Café Rendezvous on Rue des Étuves. You know Rue des Étuves, monsieur? It is—"

"I'll find it," Matt said. Maybe she isn't a fit mother, he thought, but who ever said you were a fit father?

Rue des Étuves was a narrow, curving, cobbled sidestreet close to the quay. It was a place of sleazy cafés, their dirty plate-glass windows steamy in the cold night air. The street at this late hour was crowded with drunks and semidrunks wandering from café to café, buying a few hours of oblivion with their beer and cheap brandy.

The Rendezvous was a café like all the others, with an inset doorway and a heavy curtain hanging beyond it to keep out the cold night. Except for the plump, tired-looking barmaid, there wasn't a woman in the place. An accordionist sat on a stool playing *Under Paris Skies*. Faded travel posters decorated the walls, giving a glimpse of worlds the café-sitters would never see. Every seat was occupied. A pinball machine in one corner lit up with the word "tilt," in English, and the player cursed softly.

Matt went to the barmaid. "I'm Matthew Olds. I'm looking for my son," he said slowly in French.

The tired-looking face nodded. "But of course, in back, monsieur." She jerked a thumb toward a dark doorway behind the bar while giving Matt a slow and careful scrutiny, as if wondering what sort of father would meet his son here at this hour. Matt thanked her and started to move past her, but her hand dropped on his shoulder. "Monsieur, probably it is none of my business. The boy, he has been crying."

"All right," Matt said, more brusquely than he had intended, and brushed past her.

In the faint light from the main room, he saw cases of wine and beer stacked along one wall, shelves of glassware, a sink, a two-burner electric stove, a couple of chairs, and a table. Chris was asleep on a daybed, with the long wheat-colored hair like Tracy's down over one eye. Someone had covered him with a checkered throw.

117

He was lying on his side and in the hollow of his body a big black cat lay curled up. It was purring softly. The yellow eyes gleamed at Matt; the cat stretched, arching its back, and moved languidly off the bed, past Matt and out of the room.

Chris stirred, sighed, and turned over on his back, his face looking innocent and untroubled. Matt watched him for a moment longer, then touched him gently.

"Chris."

Chris made a noise and turned back on his side.

"Chris. Come on, boy."

His son's eyes opened suddenly. For the space of a heartbeat there was a look of eager vulnerable relief in them, and then they blinked and hardened defensively. Chris sat up, not saying anything.

"I guess I kind of forgot," Matt said. "I'm sorry, Chris. I'm really sorry."

"Yeah, sure. You must have been busy."

"I was busy," Matt said. "But that's no excuse."

"It's okay," Chris told him. "I don't care."

Silence. Chris reached down to stroke the cat, then realized it wasn't there any more.

"You have something to eat?"

"Sure. They kind of felt—they took a shine to me, I guess. Wine with supper and everything."

"What are you doing here, anyway?"

"It's a holiday," Chris said. "Thanksgiving, you know? All the guys left school. When you didn't show up I just started walking, that's all." The twelve-year-old eyes looked at him steadily. "Did you call or anything?"

"No," Matt said after a while.

"I called your hotel. They said you'd gone to Bern. I know you're busy and all."

"Chris, listen. I should have taken you with me," Matt admitted. "I just clean forgot."

"Well, anyhow, they didn't know what time you'd be back at the hotel. I called from here. This cat started getting friendly. I hung around. I called a couple more times, and they they asked me did I want something to eat. I was pretty hungry, I guess. I conked right out after supper."

"Still sleepy?"

"Not any more."

"What time're you due back at school?"

"Eleven," Chris said.

It was ten after twelve.

"What kind of guy's your headmaster?"

"Mr. Müllener? Oh, he's okay, I guess. Kind of strict, though. His brother's the chief of police or something."

"You mean Willy Müllener, the Minister of Justice? I didn't know they were brothers. Anyway, want to spend the night with me? We could have Thanksgiving-plus-one breakfast. I'll call your headmaster. Think I could square it with him?"

"Yeah, sure, a parent. They always give special consideration to parents," Chris said, without any enthusiasm.

"Then I'll call him."

"Okay," Chris said. "Honest, Dad, you don't have to. I'm not mad or anything."

No, Matt thought, just a little bit hurt, just a little bit in hiding inside yourself. He tousled Chris's hair, and knew at once that it was the wrong gesture, too predictable, too meaningless, the gesture of a father who has no real relationship with his son. He went outside to find the phone.

Finally, Chris was asleep between the crisp sheets of the other bed in Matt's room at the Beau Rivage. It was after one-thirty. They had talked desultorily, about Chris's work at school, about the drive to Bern and the fact that President Huntington hated turkey, about the possibility of Chris flying back to Washington for his Christmas holiday. Chris said he had a friend at school whose parents had a chalet in Klosters, and he had been invited to ski there. Would that be all right? Matt said whatever Chris wanted would be all right.

Now Matt sat at the window in darkness, his chair tilted back, his long legs up on the sill, a tall Scotch and water in his hand, watching the rippling prismatic bands of light on the surface of the lake.

Kids from broken homes, he thought. How do you do it? Just how do you go about making them feel wanted and reasonably secure in a world that might go up in smoke tomorrow? He hardly knew the boy. He saw him once a year, at Christmas, and a weekend here and there when he was in Europe on business for the President. Between planes and when he could spare a few hours of his time. No wonder you don't know each other, he thought. No wonder you're almost strangers.

He finished his drink and stood over Chris for a moment, looking at the stranger who was his son, peacefully sleeping now, the young face untroubled. Then he climbed into bed.

As he drifted off to sleep he thought, unexpectedly, of Claudia. What was it she had said? Why don't you take him home to live with you? Because he had no home, no real home. In Washington he often put in sixteen-hour days in the White House basement. His work. His work was what mattered. A woman could try to understand' that, but never entirely succeed. She had said, "Maybe being too 'dedicated' is an excuse. Maybe you really value your freedom too much."

Chris called out in his sleep.

"Everything okay?" Matt said, sitting up. No answer.

Matt lay back and shut his eyes. He could still see Chris's face, the hair and the eyes that were so like Tracy's, and then the face dissolved, changed, and it was a woman's face he saw as he finally fell asleep, the high cheekbones, the dark eyes—Claudia's face, as he tried to kiss her.

He spoke her name once, softly, in his sleep, but he did not know that.

Chapter
NINE

1 "Get the hell out of my picture!" shouted a TV cameraman.

"Shove your goddamn picture," growled a press photographer.

The picture in dispute was of the interior of the Council Chamber of the Palace of Nations, crammed now, on Friday morning, with more than five hundred reporters, photographers, and TV technicians. They lounged around the walnut delegates' tables and sat on the black leather chairs; they stood in clusters along the mottled marble walls under the high ceiling with its painting of the ramparts of Salamanca; they overflowed to the visitors' gallery above the great hall, looking at the view of the lake through the floor-to-ceiling windows; they glanced every now and then, expectantly, at the huge bronze doors through which the President of the United States would come.

Harvey Ross shook his balding head, took off his shell-rimmed glasses, and polished them. Finally he raised two pudgy arms, leaned forward across the speaker's table, and spoke into the microphone the President would use.

"Clear the floor, find seats somewhere," he said. "Move it, boys, please, just move it."

They moved it, some of them adjusting plastic hang-on-one-ear earphones, listening to Harvey Ross's instructions translated into Russian, French, and Spanish. Uniformed ushers helped them find seats, but for the next five minutes the general movement was considerable, and considerably chaotic.

Matt looked at his watch. "Okay, Harv," he said finally, when the hall was as quiet as it would get until the President arrived, "you might as well give them the general setup."

Harvey Ross mopped his sweating face with a wad of Kleenex. "You call this a press conference?" he said. "It looks more like a nominating convention." He winked at Matt. "Republican convention, that is."

The Press Secretary raised his hands again and leaned toward the mike. "Simple ground rules, boys," he said. "The President will have a statement to read, and then you're free to ask your questions."

"Sure, Harv," someone called, ignoring his microphone, "but will he feel free to answer them?"

There was laughter, somewhat strained, somewhat self-conscious, and Harvey Ross said, "Just identify yourselves and your papers, and ask your questions."

"What about background, Harv? Can't Mr. Olds give us a little background."

Matt shook his head almost imperceptibly, and Harvey Ross said, "The President's opening statement will serve as background."

It still lacked a few minutes of noon, but Matt already felt as if he had put in a full day. He had been up at six-thirty, his right arm stiff but less painful, to take Chris back to the International School. An hour later the President had said: "Get me the Council Chamber of the Palace of Nations." With Harvey Ross in tow, Matt had come banging on the doors of UN headquarters. It took

121

an hour of arguing to convince the Assistant Secretary General to open the Council Chamber for the President's press conference.

Summit Conference of 1955, the Assistant Secretary General said; Berlin Conference of 1958, the Nuclear Disarmament Conferences, the Big Four Mideast Conference of 1972. And now a *press* conference?

A press conference held by a national leader, under sufficiently unusual circumstances, would not demean the famous old hall, Matt said, while Harvey Ross sweated.

The Indian Assistant Secretary General was very much afraid . . .

Well, Matt said easily, we could always call off the press conference, which had already been put back a couple of hours, and tell them you refused, personally, to grant the necessary facilities.

The necessary facilities were granted.

Now the Assistant Secretary General, looking unhappy but resigned, was waiting inside the bronze doors of the Council Chamber. Promptly at noon, they opened to admit the Presidential party. Convoyed by half a dozen Secret Servicemen, flanked by Secretary of State Reed and General Laffont, President Clay Huntington came striding into the hall, his limp hardly noticeable. He was wearing the old whipcord, Matt saw; a shade under-dressed for the occasion, but it was what the President called his good-luck suit. He had been wearing it on election night just over three years ago. Maybe, Matt thought, he'd need the whipcord luck this morning. The press conference was necessary, but opening it to live TV coverage seemed a chancy proposition. The President had insisted on it. "Not a word out of Villa Krupskaya yet about the whereabouts of Andreyev," he had told Matt, "and it looks like they're still waiting for instructions from Moscow on the assassination. Why not get all the mileage we can out of the contrast?"

"Three cheers for the open society," Harvey Ross had said in a subdued voice.

The President had looked at him sharply. "It's my neck that goes on the chopping block, Harv," he said with barely restrained sarcasm. "I'll do the very best I can not to trip over my tongue."

"Ah, don't mind me, Mr. President," Harvey Ross said contritely. "My ulcer's kicking up this morning."

It was, Matt thought now in the Council Chamber, a

day for ulcers all right. As the most charismatic world leader since Jack Kennedy, President Huntington didn't have to worry about his image. But what he said, or didn't say, might push the Russians to the Summit table or cut the legs out from under it. If, Matt thought, there was still any hope for a Summit Conference with Andreyev missing, Yugoslav President Ilić shot dead, and the pro-Russian Yugoslav Defense Minister coming in on cue to ask the Russians to put down what CIA Director McManus called a phony civil war.

Matt stood up as the President approached. More than five hundred newsmen stood up. The TV cameras began to roll. "Ladies and gentlemen," Harvey Ross said, "the President of the United States."

The President, still flanked by Secretary Reed and General Laffont, remained on his feet. "I had hoped," he said slowly, "to enter this historic chamber earlier this week and shake hands with Chairman Andreyev and get down to the very serious business of seeing that no country, or no country's leader, would be careless enough, or reckless enough, to trigger a Third World War. I am still here for that purpose and I still hope that Chairman Andreyev, or anyone else delegated by the Council of Ministers of the Soviet Union, will meet with me here. But the very grave events of last night make my appearance here, alone, essential at this time."

Pouring water from a carafe, the President continued: "I have a short statement to read, and then I'll be pleased to hear—" he did not say, Matt noticed, answer— "your questions. The statement is this: At 0700 Geneva time I instructed the Secretary of State to send the following cable to the Foreign Minister of Yugoslavia—quote: 'The President and the people of the United States grieve with the government and the people of Yugoslavia at the senseless slaying, last night, of President Anton Ilić. We Americans have also suffered the loss of great leaders cut down in their prime. While it does not diminish the loss to say the republic carries on, this is in fact what can, and does, and must happen. The President of the United States, in this tragic time, has asked the State Department to assure the government of Yugoslavia that the United States, under the terms of the Treaty of Belgrade, will take any steps necessary to insure the political independence and territorial integrity of the Federal Socialist Republic of Yugoslavia.'

"That is the text of the telegram sent by the Secretary of State to the Foreign Minister of Yugoslavia. The American government has also informed the Yugoslav government, through the appropriate channels, that Vice-President Ingersol will represent the United States at the funeral of President Ilić.

"And that, ladies and gentlemen," the President said, "is the end of the written statement."

The President drank a glass of water while a hundred hands flew up around the Council Chamber. A score of voices called out. Harvey Ross shook his head ruefully. The President, his head framed by the blue and white UN flag and the American flag, smiled a thin smile.

"One at a time and when you're recognized," Harvey Ross pleaded, and indicated a gray-haired man to the left of the speaker's table.

"Jenkins Potter of the Associated Press, Mr. President. I hope you can clarify the phrase 'any steps necessary to insure the political independence and territorial integrity of Yugoslavia.' "

"At this time I can offer no clarification. The statement speaks for itself. Its political implementation will be determined by internal events in Yugoslavia. Its military implementation, if any, will be determined by events outside that country. The key words remain 'political independence and territorial integrity.' "

"Does 'military implementation' mean what I think it means?" Jenkins Potter asked.

"That depends on what you think it means, Mr. Potter," the President said dryly, and there was laughter.

"Jacques duChêne, *L'Humanité*," a man said. *L'Humanité* was the mouthpiece of the French Communist Party. "Is the President implying that military implementation of the Treaty of Belgrade will depend on the activities of a third power?"

The President flashed a smile. "If the alternative to that question is, Does the United States have any intention of going to war with Yugoslavia, I think Monsieur duChêne can answer the question himself."

"Which third power?" duChêne persisted.

"Whatever third power threatens the territorial integrity of Yugoslavia."

"Would you care to name—"

"I think that's enough of that line of questioning," the President snapped.

"Alphonse Borel, *Tribune de Genève*, Mr. President. In your opening remarks you said 'anyone else delegated by the Council of Ministers of the Soviet Union.' Would you care to amplify that, sir?"

"Well, if Secretary Lysenko cared to take Chairman Andreyev's place here, I'd be pleased to meet with him at the Summit."

"Has the President any indication that Chairman Andreyev will not be able to meet with him?"

"I'm an avid reader of your column, Monsieur Borel," the President said.

More laughter in the Council Chamber. The President wasn't the only avid reader of Alphonse Borel, and although his story had been picked up by the world press, Borel was the only one who'd gone out on a limb with it. His face colored, but he managed a game smile.

"Could the President tell us how long the American delegation is prepared to wait here in Geneva?"

"We're here to do a job," the President said. "We'll stay here until the job is done—or until we learn it can't be done."

"Harold Yates, Reuters, Mr. President. Defense Minister Cvetković of Yugoslavia has declared a state of emergency, and has requested Russian help to prevent the internal situation from deteriorating into—"

"What's the question, Hal?" Harvey Ross asked.

"If the Russians move in, what happens then? There are reports that units of the American Sixth Fleet are nearing Rieka."

"Units of the American Sixth Fleet," the President said, "should be anchoring in Rieka harbor right now, their flags at half-mast in tribute to President Ilić. I hope that the Russians will think twice before heeding what may be a premature call for help. I would also like to point out that while the United States and Yugoslavia have signed a mutual defense treaty, known as the Treaty of Belgrade, I am aware of no such arrangement between the Soviet Union and Yugoslavia."

"My question—" the Reuters man began.

"I think your question, for now, can better be answered by Villa Krupskaya."

"Yuri Kirov, Tass Agency. Is the President accusing the Soviet government of ulterior motives in answering a cry for help from a fellow socialist state?"

"No," the President said.

125

"Does the President suggest that the Soviet government would use the tragic death of President Ilić as an excuse to foist upon the socialist government of Yugoslavia control from outside?"

"No," the President said, "and I hope the Soviet government doesn't plan on doing it."

"Does the President think—"

"When necessary, Mr. Kirov."

"If the President glibly evades questions that are couched in concrete terms," said Kirov hotly, "what precisely is the purpose of this press conference?"

"That sounds like a rhetorical question, Mr. Kirov. It's the third one you've asked. I feel rhetorical questions are best answered by those who ask them," the President said.

Kirov got up. Half a dozen men near him got up. They all stalked out through the exit under the visitor's gallery, the eyes of the TV cameras following them. A babble of conversation accompanied their departure—a departure which, Matt knew, was not entirely unexpected.

"Fidel Gómez, A.B.C., Madrid. Does the President know anything of the whereabouts of Chairman Andreyev?"

"I know that he's not here in this room, and I wish he were."

"Minoru Ito, Yomiuri, Tokyo. Would the President care to say whether 'any steps necessary' includes the possible use of atomic weapons? Would the President condone their use under any circumstances?"

"I would deplore it, Mr. Ito. I think—or hope—that the responsible leaders of any government in the world would also deplore it."

Harvey Ross looked at his watch. The President nodded.

"Just one more question," the Press Secretary said, and half the hands in the Council Chamber were raised. Ross looked at Matt, who said, "Borel," and Ross pointed at the Swiss journalist.

"Alphonse Borel again, Mr. President. If the Tribune's speculations about the disappearance of Chairman Andreyev are correct, would the President care to suggest a motive?"

"That's a tough one, Monsieur Borel. Do you mean hypothetically, and if he were a free agent?"

Borel nodded. "Hypothetically then, and if the Chairman were free to act as he wished."

"I believe Chairman Andreyev," the President said, "to be a man of peace. That is why I agreed to meet with him here in Geneva. I believe that any actions he has taken, or is taking, or will take, are in the interests of peace. Does that answer your question?"

"Yes, sir," Borel said, and his eyes twinkled guilelessly as he asked: "Would you say the same for Secretary Lysenko?"

The President half hid a smile and looked at Harvey Ross, who stood up and said, "I'm sorry, ladies and gentlemen, but that really is it."

The President went to the bronze doors and out.

2 The Associated Press bulletin on the press conference was favorable, a fact which surprised no one. Jenkins Potter had always admired President Huntington.

Radiotélédiffusion Suisse, in its midafternoon broadcast, said the President had, under the circumstances, displayed remarkable honesty.

Corriere della Sera of Milan, the first newspaper out with the story, complimented the President on his adroitness in handling the questions he could not—or would not—answer.

Other afternoon papers on the Continent followed Milan's lead.

"We're in," Harvey Ross told Matt at six o'clock that afternoon. He was grinning like the press agent for a new Broadway hit when the opening night reviews began to come in.

They were drinking coffee in what the balding Press Secretary called his shop, a small room one floor below the Presidential Suite in the Beau Rivage. Two teletype machines, one operating now, the other silent, stood on a table along one wall.

"Here comes Frankfurt," Harvey Ross said, and the yellow paper moved through the roller as the keys tapped out the report from Frankfurt, which said that the charismatic leader of the United States, while answering fewer questions than he had evaded, still managed to convey his dedication to peace in a troubled world.

Alphonse Borel came in, his eyes twinkling, his red hair windblown. He rubbed his hands together. "Cold out there. When the *bise* is blowing like that it could mean snow in the mountains tomorrow. Well, how does it go?"

"Beautiful," Harvey Ross said. "From Sweden clear down to Italy—beautiful."

Borel removed his topcoat and slid into a chair, smiling at Matt.

"What's so funny?" Harvey Ross asked.

"You Americans," Borel told him. "The way so much of life can be reduced to a popularity contest."

Harvey Ross looked hurt. "How's that again?"

"It's the other teletype that matters," Matt explained. The other teletype, its yellow paper still blank, was a direct wire to the press attaché's office in the American Embassy in Moscow. It had been set up at Matt's suggestion and had been sending a twice-daily translation of relevant material to Geneva, excerpts from *Pravda* in the morning and *Izvestia* in the afternoon. Which, Matt knew, explained Borel's presence. The *Tribune de Genève* relied on the wire services for Moscow coverage. Borel, coming to the Beau Rivage, would get half an hour's jump on the news from Moscow.

"The Moscow line?" Harvey Ross said, rubbing his bald head. "Who cares what Moscow thinks? Nobody expects them to like the press conference, for crying out loud."

"It's not what they think about it," Matt said. "It's how they respond. The President made news today, Harv. The Kremlin will want to upstage him."

"To suggest a meeting with Lysenko," Borel said, "was clever. Lysenko won't come, of course, which puts Moscow in the unenviable position of having to call off the Summit unilaterally if Andreyev is—unavailable. Is he unavailable, Mr. Ross?"

"Search me," Harvey Ross said. "I get the notion the pair of you know more than—"

"Let it go, Harv," Matt said. "Alphonse is just fishing." The second teletype had begun to clatter. "Here comes Moscow."

The three men leaned over the machine as the words began to appear.

(IZVESTIA, NOV 28)--AMERICAN PRESIDENT HUN-
TINGTON MET WITH THE PRESS TODAY IN GENEVA IN AN
ATTEMPT TO JUSTIFY HIS GOVERNMENT'S REFUSAL TO
ACCEPT A MEANINGFUL AGENDA FOR THE SUMMIT.
JOURNALISTS FROM MANY COUNTRIES WALKED OUT OF
THE COUNCIL CHAMBER OF THE PALACE OF NATIONS,
WHERE THE MEETING OCCURRED.

"Just Russia, not even her satellites. You call that many?" Harvey Ross asked indignantly. "They're not newspapermen, they're fiction writers."

"Hold it, Harv," Matt said as a line of X's ran across the yellow paper. "Here comes more."

PROFESSOR P. G. MELNIKOV OF THE NEUROPSYCHO-
LOGICAL INSTITUTE OF MOSCOW CENTRAL HOSPITAL
TODAY INDICATED A PRELIMINARY REPORT ON THE
CONDITION OF CHAIRMAN ANDREYEV WOULD BE
FORTHCOMING SHORTLY.

Matt looked at Borel, whose face remained impassive. "It had to come sooner or later," the Swiss newspaperman said: "That's one way of coping with a high-level defector."

MEMBERS OF THE COUNCIL OF MINISTERS HAVE
FEARED FOR WEEKS THAT THE CHAIRMAN RESUMED HIS
WORK ON BEHALF OF THE REVOLUTION TOO SOON AFTER
HIS SEIZURE LAST APRIL. COMRADE ANDREYEV'S
DETERIORATING HEALTH COMES AT A DIFFICULT TIME
IN SOVIET RELATIONS WITH THE IMPERIALIST CLIQUE
OF THE UNITED STATES.

"Eh bien," Borel said. "They're writing off Andreyev. A sick man, and the Neuropsychological Institute means mentally sick. There goes your Summit, my friend."

Matt felt as if he had been kicked in the stomach. The weeks of planning for the Summit, the fencing with Malinin here in Geneva, the hope of averting a confrontation over Yugoslavia—all of it canceled by a few lines on a teletype message from Moscow. There would be no Summit, at least not with Andreyev. When would the ax fall—tomorrow, the next day? A morning bulletin in *Pravda*, an evening story in *Izvestia*, the report of the Neuropsychological Institute, expertly detailing an examination that had never taken place, and the world would be told that Andreyev had suffered a nervous breakdown, or worse. Then Lysenko would be free to act.

The teletype was clattering again.

COMRADE LYSENKO THIS AFTERNOON ASSURED THE
VALIANT REVOLUTIONARY LEADERS OF THE SOCIALIST
REPUBLIC OF YUGOSLAVIA THAT THE RED ARMY WOULD

NOT STAND IDLY BY WHILE COUNTER-REVOLUTION-
ARY BANDITS PUT BELGRADE TO THE TORCH. THE FIRST
SECRETARY OF THE CENTRAL COMMITTEE OF THE CPSU
RESPONDED TO A CALL FOR HELP FROM YUGOSLAV DE-
FENSE MINISTER CVETKOVIC AFTER THE ASSASSINA-
TION OF PRESIDENT ANTON ILIC LAST NIGHT BY
RIGHT-DEVIATIONIST TERRORISTS IN THE YUGOSLAV
CAPITAL. COMRADE LYSENKO ANNOUNCED THAT RED
ARMY TROOPS EVEN NOW ASSEMBLING IN THE PEOPLE'S
REPUBLIC OF HUNGARY WOULD ENTER YUGOSLAVIA IN
BROTHERHOOD AND FRIENDSHIP.

"Matt, I'd like to ask you—" Borel began, grim-faced.

"Not now," Matt said, tearing the yellow paper from
the teletype. "Sorry, Alphonse. The President will want to
see these."

Matt picked up his jacket and headed for the door.

The teletype began to print again. "Matt," Borel said
gently, almost apologetically, and Matt returned to his
side to read the words that could, that probably would,
mean war.

(TASS NEWS AGENCY BULLETIN)--AT NINETEEN
HUNDRED HOURS TODAY MOSCOW TIME RED ARMY
TROOPS CROSSED THE YUGOSLAV FRONTIER AT THE
BORDER TOWN OF SZEGED IN RESPONSE TO YUGOSLAV
DEFENSE MINISTER CVETKOVIC'S URGENT APPEAL FOR
HELP. ALL ALONG THEIR ROUTE THE SOLDIERS OF
THE GLORIOUS RED ARMY WERE GREETED AS LIBERATORS
BY THE PEOPLE OF YUGOSLAVIA.

Matt said nothing. There was nothing to say. He tore
that one from the teletype too, and ran for the door.

Chapter
TEN

1 During his first six months on the Presidential staff,
Matt had drawn his salary as a speech writer. That was

before President Huntington discovered that Benson Reed had limitations as Secretary of State. Writing speeches for the President, unlike writing speeches for the Presidential candidate, was not a full-time job, and Matt had found time to write a history of the war in Vietnam, based in part on his experiences as an AP correspondent there.

The President had read the manuscript and liked it. "Stick around, Matt," he had said. "I like the way you handle contemporary history. Wouldn't surprise me if one of these years you wrote a history of the Huntington Administration."

That was, Matt had thought then, a little too much like the Kennedy-Schlesinger relationship for comfort. Schlesinger had never been in the inner circle of Kennedy advisers, and Matt had begun to taste, and like the taste of, power even as a Presidential speech writer. His special sphere had been foreign affairs, and he quickly learned what others had learned before him: To write speeches for the President was one way, one surprising way, of wielding power. What the President said he would do the President was likely *to* do, and Matt, like speech-writer Sorensen in the Kennedy Administration, soon became part of the Presidential inner circle.

The change was one of degree rather than kind when he took over the Little State Department in the White House basement. One reason the President could give him the more imposing title, and the more obvious power that went with it, was Matt's book on Vietnam. It came out at the right time, when the war had been over long enough for the nation to look back on it with some degree of objectivity. It was well received. Matt celebrated its publication by moving into the office in the White House basement. Shortly after that, the President had brought up the subject of a history of his Administration again.

One of the things that ought to be included, he said, was the very basic difference between a Democratic and a Republican Administration. "Democrats innovate," he told Matt. "Republicans consolidate. I'm more likely to get things done than Nixon, and more likely to trip over my own feet doing it."

The President had smiled. "And another thing. Republicans tend to bring Big Business into government. They run it like a board of directors. Democrats bring the intellectuals to Washington, and they're so busy being imaginative, not to mention opinionated, that they forget all about

131

the mechanics of government. You know what I think? Two Democratic administrations to one Republican administration would be about the right combination, but don't quote me at the precinct level.

"Sometimes, when things get hairy, I'd rather be a Republican. Which is very definitely not for the boys on the precinct level. I'd have a glorified board of directors then, and I'd make a statement of policy, and we'd have some polite talk about how to implement it. I wouldn't have a bunch of intellectuals in a free-for-all, each one of them convinced he can handle the job better than I can. Maybe, in certain ways, some of them can, and without actually saying it they get the idea across. Keeps things kind of interesting, don't you think?"

Interesting, Matt decided at eight-thirty that Friday night in the Presidential Suite in the Beau Rivage, was hardly the word. For an hour and a half he had heard, and had been part of, the kind of talk no outsider would ever associate with the second meeting of the Executive Committee of the National Security Council.

After reading the reports from Moscow, the President said, quietly, "Okay, let's toss it around."

They tossed it around, not quietly.

Secretary Reed wanted to honor the treaty with Yugoslavia at once. He did not say how.

Whitney Stoughton said how. He urged dropping five airborne divisions on Yugoslavia first thing Saturday morning.

General Laffont said that was feasible. General Laffont further said it was the President's duty to return to Washington, tonight, aboard Air Force One, because Washington was where he belonged on the eve of war.

Matt said, wait.

"Good Lord, man," Secretary Reed said. "What do you mean, wait? Yugoslavia has been attacked. Tass blatantly says so, and we've seen an Orion picture verifying it. The President signed a treaty with Ilić in Belgrade, didn't he? We've known all along that a limited war now can prevent all-out war later, haven't we? How can you sit there—how dare you sit there—and say wait?"

"A couple of things puzzle me," Matt said. "Since when do the Russians spell out their moves for us before they make them? I think Lysenko's—call it testing the air. He wants to see how far he can go."

"You're puzzled, all right," Whitney Stoughton said. "You call invading Yugoslavia testing the air?"

"The other thing," Matt said, "is Andreyev. There's hope there—if we can find him."

"They've written Andreyev off," Stoughton said. "In a few days or a week, they'll give us the medical diagnosis. No, Andreyev's out of it."

"He's not out of it yet. He could hurt Lysenko plenty, if he talks. Who do you think shot Ilić?"

"What does that have to do with anything?" Stoughton asked irritably.

"The Russians manufactured an excuse for the invasion by assassinating Ilić. Maybe Andreyev can hang that one around Lysenko's neck."

"Then find him," Stoughton said. "I've tried. Did it occur to you he could be dead? Natural causes, or maybe the Russians killed *him?*"

"We're losing sight of the big issue," General Laffont said, fingering his clipped military moustache. "Do we go into Yugoslavia now or don't we? Go in right away, and we could occupy the south and west of the country in a matter of hours. Wait for the Red Army to move in, in force, and we'd face enormous casualties just trying to get our troops in. If we're going to move at all, we can't afford to wait even five minutes, gentlemen."

"Maybe I'm thinking about another set of casualties," Matt said.

General Laffont looked at him. "Nuclear war?"

"Put American and Russian troops in Yugoslavia, and you tell me it couldn't happen. There's got to be another way."

General Laffont took a deep breath, stood up, looked at the President, and said slowly, "If we fail to act now, tonight, it would be a clear case of dereliction of duty."

The President nodded. "I'd say that's putting it right on the line, General."

"I'm sorry, sir. I never meant you *wouldn't* act."

The President said, "Just what alternatives did you have in mind, Matt?"

Secretary Reed's face darkened angrily. "There are no alternatives. Wait, and you'll be playing right into Lysenko's hands. Where does he go next if we let him take Yugoslavia? Now is the time to stop him. It doesn't have to mean nuclear confrontation. It might even prevent it. We've fought limited wars before."

"Not with Russia, we haven't," Matt said.

"The treaty of Belgrade specifically says—" Reed began.

"We're not talking about a piece of paper," Matt interrupted, his voice sharp. "We're talking about what happens if the Russians miscalculate, or if we do. You're always telling me I don't have enough patience to be a diplomat. I'm saying the time for patience is now. How would you like to be responsible for the death of two hundred million people, Mr. Secretary?"

"The nuclear syndrome," Stoughton said deprecatingly. "We've had a national guilt complex on the subject for thirty years. Don't you think the Russians know that? Don't you think they're banking on it?"

Secretary Reed's face was pinched and bleak. "Patience?" he said. "Good Lord, man, we can't afford patience. The longer we delay sending our troops in, the more it helps Russia."

"Just a minute, Benson," the President said quietly. "Nobody's decided to send American troops anywhere yet."

Reed looked at him. His lips were a thin tight line. "General Laffont called it dereliction of duty," he said in a harsh whisper. "I would go further. I've been in government thirty years. I've held elective office. I know the terrible responsibility." Reed was speaking with an aloof dignity now. "The responsibility is destructive. It can tear your heart out. But a time comes when you must face it. If you fail to face it, Mr. President, that is worse than dereliction of duty. If you refuse to honor the treaty with Yugoslavia, a treaty you signed, a treaty the Senate ratified, I could not be true to myself unless I took it to the Congress." Reed met the President's eyes with his own steady gaze. "It is grounds for impeachment, sir."

2   There was a shocked silence. Benson Reed had collapsed back into his chair and was breathing hard. General Laffont bowed his head, chin on chest, like a man at prayer. Stoughton, shifting his weight from one foot to the other, stared down at the floor. The President stood with his back to the room, gazing out the window. Reed, Matt knew, was a man of tremendous integrity, as hard with himself as he was with others. It must have damn near

134

killed him to say those words. It was no threat. It was a statement of intention.

The President turned to face the room again. With small, precise motions he put a cigarette in the stubby black holder, placed the holder between his lips, lit the cigarette. He said nothing.

"We're all hot under the collar," General Laffont said self-consciously. "That's understandable. I'm sure the Secretary didn't mean that literally."

"No, he meant it," the President said softly, his face expressionless. "Matt, what are those alternatives you had in mind?"

Matt glanced at Secretary Reed, who averted his eyes scornfully, glanced at Stoughton, whose handsome face wore a faint, patronizing smile. Even General Laffont, despite his embarrassment, met Matt's eyes with an angry look before he faced the President and said, "This is the wrong time to search for alternatives. The only alternative was the Summit Conference. We knew that when we came here, Mr. President. It didn't work."

Just where do you begin? Matt wondered. He could sense that they had all but convinced the President, sense that Huntington had turned to him as a last resort before bowing to their will. Maybe, Matt thought, they were right. Maybe a show of force was all Lysenko would understand now. But still—

"You said dereliction of duty, General," he began slowly. "I say it would be the worst kind of dereliction of duty if we sent in American troops prematurely."

"How can you call it premature?" Secretary Reed snapped. "Give the Red Army enough time to consolidate its position and the cost in casualties when we finally moved in would be on your hands."

Matt shook his head. "I keep going back to Andreyev. The days when a major power can walk roughshod over its neighbor without reckoning with world opinion are over. If we can find Andreyev, this whole thing could still blow up in the Kremlin's face."

"How long do we wait?" Stoughton said. "A day? A week? Is that how we stop the invasion, by waiting?"

"Yugoslavia hasn't called on us to honor the treaty yet."

"Do you wait for the drowning man to ask to be rescued?" Reed asked. "Who's going to call on us? President Ilić is dead. Cvetković is a Russian puppet."

"I'm not arguing with any of that, Mr. Secretary. Let me finish. I was going to suggest that in a way the only one who's calling on us to intervene is Russia. Just what do we know about this so-called invasion? We know what Russia wants us to know. Our information comes from a Tass bulletin."

"That's not entirely correct," General Laffont said. "You're forgetting the Orion picture."

"Conveniently forgetting it," Stoughton suggested.

Matt ignored that. An Orion photograph had been radioed from the Pentagon a few minutes after Matt had taken the Tass release to the President. It showed Red Army troops moving south from Szeged in battalion force.

"One picture," Matt said. "A single battalion moving toward the border. And then what happened?"

"They shot the Orion down," General Laffont said. "So we could no longer follow their movements. We expected that."

"Sure, but what was it they didn't want us to see? If they were really moving in in force, Whit's Yugoslav contacts would have sent a Mayday. But there hasn't been a peep out of them."

"They could have been blown," Stoughton said. "Don't tell me their silence makes you optimistic? That doesn't make sense."

"No, not optimistic. Cautious. There are too damn many imponderables. Not hearing from your contacts could mean they're not convinced this is the real invasion. They're afraid to cry wolf. And the way Russia immediately supplies us with a blow-by-blow account of the invasion, that makes me wonder too. All we know for sure is that a single battalion approached, and probably crossed, the border. That's a breach of Yugoslav sovereignty but it's no full-scale invasion. It's almost as if Lysenko is daring us to move in."

"What on earth for?" Reed demanded skeptically.

"Because he's unsure of his ground. If we do move in, Russia and the States fight a war—possibly a limited war—on Yugoslav soil. And once we're committed, who's going to remember that the Red Army moved in first? Lysenko could even claim it was a punitive raid because his troops were attacked at the border. Where does that leave us?"

Matt lit a cigarette. "I'll tell you where it leaves us," he said. "In the position of helping Lysenko fight the war he wants to fight. He chooses the time and the place. We wrestle with supply lines five thousand miles long. That's if we move in. But if we don't? If we find a way to buy some time—an ultimatum, for example?"

"You mean speak loudly and carry a small stick?" Secretary Reed asked contemptuously.

"I mean Andreyev could turn up. It doesn't have to be an ultimatum. We could ask for an emergency session of the Security Council."

"That did a fat lot of good when the Red Army took over Rumania," Stoughton said.

"It's not the same thing. They didn't have Andreyev to worry about then."

"How many times do we have to tell you Andreyev's out of it?" Stoughton said wearily.

"I'm not convinced of that. Andreyev's disappearance could have made Lysenko desperate. If he tricks us into moving now, we could wind up playing right into his hands. It's a war Russia could win, thanks to their short supply lines. And they've got a good enough propaganda machine to make us share the blame for starting it. Whatever Andreyev had to say, then, wouldn't mean a hell of a lot. But if we waited? One battalion, that's all. I tell you, Lysenko's waiting, too. Because if Andreyev shows up in the next day or two and starts talking, Lysenko's had it. He knows that. He's gambling. There won't be any real invasion unless the KGB finds Andreyev and kills him. Or unless we follow Lysenko's script and give him his war. That's why Tass reported the invasion. If he's going to get away with it, Lysenko needs our help. What you're proposing would give it to him."

There was a long silence. Then the President spoke. "You suggested an ultimatum or the Security Council, Matt. Anything else?"

"The hot line. Call Lysenko."

Another silence. Those were the only alternatives Matt had to offer, and if he'd guessed wrong about Lysenko, they were worse than useless. He looked at the doubt on the President's face and felt deflated. An ultimatum or the Security Council bought a day or two of time, but unless Andreyev reappeared like the god from a machine in Greek tragedy, Lysenko would profit from the delay more than we would. The hot line hardly seemed better. Lysenko was not Andreyev. No hot-line conversation with

President Huntington in the middle of the night would make Lysenko back off.

Maybe Reed, Stoughton, and Laffont are hard-headed enough to see that there's only one answer Lysenko will understand, Matt thought. And maybe I'm not.

"I've listened to all of you, gentlemen," the President said, "and everything I heard made sense. We could sit up all night arguing, but that would only harden the lines of disagreement. It's time for me to make a decision. As Benson said, he's free to take his objections to Congress if he doesn't like it. I appreciate his honesty, just as I appreciate Matt's reluctance to go to war and Whit's reluctance not to go to war.

"One question, Whit. Will Cvetković resist an air drop on Belgrade and—what's that other place?"

"Cilipi. Cvetković will try, but from regimental level on down we'll have the Yugoslav Army on our side."

Listening, Matt realized he had lost. In another moment the President would announce his decision, would align himself with the hawks, would meet Lysenko's invasion with what amounted to an invasion of our own. In another moment the cipher clerks in the communications center here in the Beau Rivage would be sending their coded messages to the Pentagon, to the Sixth Fleet, to the Reforger Army units in Kansas and Texas. In another moment the government draftsmen at the Hotel Intercontinental would be drawing the blueprints to weld the machinery of the State Department and the Pentagon into a single political-military entity. In another moment the Press Secretary and his staff would be preparing releases to explain the American position to our allies, to placate the uncommitted nations of the world. In another moment all the vast machinery of government would be grinding, and there would be no turning back.

Despite his own stand, Matt felt almost a sense of relief. They're professionals, he thought. They're specialists. Reed with thirty years of public service, General Laffont with a long Army career behind him, even Stoughton, fed information by the vast, secret, efficient network of the CIA. Who was Matt to stand against them? A reporter turned foreign affairs expert? A sounding board for the President?

Maybe this wasn't the time to hide behind the fear of nuclear Armageddon.

The President turned to face General Laffont. "General," he began, then abruptly pivoted, paced the length of the room, and said hoarsely, "No, damn it, I want another opinion."

He picked up the phone. "Pris, get me Kermit Hauser in Gstaad."

3   Waiting for the call to go through, the President switched the phone to the conference speaker.

But what advice could the former dean of the diplomatic corps give them? It was not Hauser they needed, Matt thought. It was Andreyev. Only Andreyev stood between them and war, and Andreyev had dropped off the face of the earth.

"Clay Huntington, Mr. Ambassador," the President said, and Kermit Hauser's firm voice came over the conference speaker:

"This is one for the books, Mr. President. I was reaching for the phone when it rang. To call you."

The President gave Matt a blank look. "You were?"

And Kermit Hauser said, "I have Chairman Andreyev here with me. Wrestling with his own private angel, you might say. There is a chance, a very good chance, that he is ready to defect."

Part Two

Chapter
ELEVEN

1 The mountains, geologically speaking, were young.

Seventy million years ago—just a tick of the geological clock, Nikolai Ivanovich Andreyev thought—great shifting changes in the crust of the earth had forced these mountains out of silt at the bottom of an ancient sea, squeezed them into stone, and thrust them upward with unimaginable pressures as the sea receded, until they became peaks, ridges, glaciers, lakes, forests, upland meadows called *alps* in the language of the first human inhabitants.

And how long had people lived here? The lake dwellers, who built houses on stilts and fished the cold waters of the mountain lakes—five thousand years? The herdsmen, who followed their cattle into the green upland meadows and thought those meadows the whole world—a thousand years, two thousand? The blink of a geological eye.

And history? History that men wrote and rewrote to suit their petty little fancies? The history of the Communist Party in Russia, a history that enslaved men even as they invented it, because in the final reckoning they held themselves accountable to it?

That history was not yet sixty years old.

What did it matter, Nikolai Ivanovich wondered. What did any of it matter, alongside these mountains, young mountains seventy million years old on a small planet that circled a very ordinary star? And yet we think our little actions, our small hopes, our pygmy conceits are everything, everything.

He was tramping through a woodland of pine and fir and larch on Saturday morning with Kermit Hauser, both their faces red with the cold wind that swept down off the peaks. Sometimes the low cloud cover cleared, and then the high peaks soared into view, seeming to move against the sky. Sometimes the clouds rolled like thick smoke across the slopes. The ground underfoot was soft and springy, like a peat bog, with how many years of pine needles?

Kermit Hauser plunged ahead and reached the shore of a small lake. Dead reeds stood in the shallow water and a rickety wooden dock jutted out over it. Hauser turned and waited at the end of the dock, his mane of white hair blowing in the wind, his blue eyes under the tufted white brows gazing up at a high escarpment, where a mountain stream plunged, branched, and dropped a thousand feet. The falls looked like gossamer, but Nikolai Ivanovich could hear their roaring. Time, distance, perspective, all were confusing in the Alps.

"Feeling all right?" Hauser asked.

The walk had been Nikolai Ivanovich's idea, his small, pointless defiance. They had driven a few miles from Gstaad to a village called Lauenen, where the road ended, and had hiked up a cattle track from there. A car had followed them at a discreet distance. Its occupants, Nikolai Ivanovich supposed, were in the woods somewhere close by. The American CIA, keeping their distance, not intruding, but there. Well, what had he expected?

"Of course I feel all right," he said. His arms and legs tingled. The mountain air exhilarated him. He felt strong and young and capable. And if his heart was beating too hard, almost alarmingly hard, what of it? "I'm no invalid," he said, and smiled. "But you, old man, what about you? You're old enough to be my father."

Kermit Hauser smiled back at him. Tall, white-thatched, red of face, the strong blue eyes twinkling, he looked like an unexpectedly benevolent Old Testament God dressed for winter.

"Perhaps," he said, "I should take it easy." It was said, Nikolai Ivanovich knew, for his benefit rather than Hauser's. Kermit Hauser, despite his almost eighty years, looked as if he could climb an Alp in the morning, eat a hearty lunch, climb down in the afternoon, and then drink you under the table all night.

Hauser pointed beyond the waterfall. "My own special place," he said. "Small children and doddering old men, I suppose, must have them. This far you could take a small car. Up there, the cattle track narrows. A two-hour climb on foot, and you're above timberline, on top of the world. There's a Swiss Alpine Club hut there. Just the hut and the silence. It makes you feel wonderfully small. I get away there to think sometimes. A man could lose himself there for twenty years. It's tempting." Hauser grinned. "My wife talks too much."

Hauser's wife, his fourth wife, was Russian, half his age and currently off on a shopping trip in Paris.

The wind that had been whistling through the tops of the fir trees died down. The last patches of blue sky were gone. Clouds had rolled in to hide the snowcapped peaks.

"Snow coming," Hauser predicted. "You can tell, when you've lived in these mountains long enough."

"How?" Nikolai Ivanovich asked. Everything about these mountains fascinated him. He felt strangely excited and happy, as if he had come home after a life of exile. That was odd, he thought. No two countries could be more different than vast Russia with its distances, and tiny Switzerland with its mountains. No two people could be more different than the Russians with their old, unrelenting, almost Oriental suspicion of foreigners, and the Swiss, who delighted in welcoming the world to their mountains. The tidy cities, the blue lakes, the wild mountains—a man could be happy here.

Then the mood passed. If an exile could be happy anywhere, he thought.

"How can you tell? The way the wind's blowing. We get our weather from the north."

A wind from the north, and a walk in the woods with an old friend, and soon it would be winter, the steppes frozen for two thousand miles east from the Ukraine, the snow falling on St. Basil's, falling on Red Square, falling on the flat northern plain of Yugoslavia— Would the world see another winter?

I hold the seasons in my hand, Nikolai Ivanovich thought. I can give them winter, spring, the rebirth, summer—but at what price to me?

And there was Claudia.

Am I doing the right thing? he thought, in an agony of doubt, and realized he had cried the words aloud.

"I don't know," Hauser said truthfully. "I think you are."

They heard a sound in the woods beyond the clearing—the CIA.

"Have I traded the KGB for that?" Nikolai Ivanovich demanded. "Not our Secret Police, but yours? Is there a difference?"

"There is a difference." Kermit Hauser said gently.

"Will they call me Judas?" Nikolai Ivanovich cried, flinging his arms in a wide, wild gesture. He was breathing hard.

Still gently, Hauser said, "You're not doing it for thirty pieces of silver, Nikolai."

"I'm doing it—yes, I'm doing it for . . ." For what? To give men a breathing spell, so that they could make the same mistakes again, a few years from now, in another place, with even more destructive weapons? So that the dream, the Utopian dream, could go on a little longer, beguiling men with its promise, then betraying them because they betrayed themselves? What was it that polluted such dreams, contaminated them, made a mockery of them—what but human greed?

A Lysenko, gambling with the world, because he insisted on a world in his image.

But if he stopped Lysenko—and he knew that he had to stop him—there would be others. You did not usher in the millennium by bringing down one tyrant.

The Communist creed, when warped, he thought, his mind clear suddenly, the self-torment gone, bears a remarkable resemblance to the Secret Police mentality. That is because, for both, the end justifies the means.

One way to the top, in the Party, was through the Secret Police. It was the way Lysenko had taken. It was the way taken by two out of three rising Party members these days.

A great nation, ruled by the graduates of the KGB.

Not Mother Russia, which he loved. The pollution at the top, only that.

It must be stopped.

And history had put him, had put Nikolai Ivanovich Andreyev, in a terrible position.

He was the only one who could stop it.

"Yes," he said, repeating Kermit Hauser's words, "there is a difference."

They walked off the dock, back among the firs and larches, in the darkness and silence of the woods in the young, seventy-million-year-old mountains.

"I am doing it," Nikolai Ivanovich said, "for Russia."

When they left the cattle track and reached the road where Kermit Hauser's car was parked, it had begun to snow.

2   The closer Natasha Hauser came to Gstaad, the less her middle-of-the-night decision to return home early pleased her. The decision had been reached Friday night in her hotel room in Paris. Perhaps if it had been one of the really fine Parisian hotels, the Ritz or George V, perhaps if she'd had a suite instead of a dreary little room in a small hotel a few blocks from the Opéra, she'd have been able to sleep. But it wasn't and she hadn't, and she'd surprised the concierge at—what was it?—four in the morning, demanding her car and, after some argument, getting it. The servant classes these days just didn't know their place. Marrying Kermit, leaving Russia where, theoretically, there was no such thing as a servant class, she thought she'd put all that behind her. But even the family in-comer (a polite way of saying maid, in Russia) back in Minsk, when she was a little girl, had more manners and knew her place better than the Parisian concierge or, come to think of it, the insolent little shopgirls along the Rue St. Honoré.

Natasha Hauser had planned on two weeks in Paris— shopping, the theater, the three-star restaurants, the excitement of the Champs Elysées in autumn, when most of the guidebook-and-camera-toting tourists had gone, giving the city back to the Parisians. And all of it, she thought now, vaguely disappointing—too small an allowance, given grudgingly by Kermit, to make the shopping trip worthwhile, her knowledge of French rustier than she had thought, so that even some small enjoyment of what had been second-rate theater was all but impossible, the restaurants crowded, the service indifferent, the food disappointing, and the French, returning to their city, scurrying like tourists themselves. Why, they were in such a hurry these days that Paris almost seemed like New York. There had not even been the possibility of a casual flirtation, because no Frenchman was casual these days.

Shortly before five Saturday morning, the padded bench that passed for a rear seat in her Porsche loaded down with the trophies of her holiday, Natasha had driven out of Paris. Speeding through Avallon, Beaune, and Yverdon, she wondered if she could make Gstaad in six hours.

She looked at her watch now: Ten-thirty and she was already heading up into the mountains. Another half-hour ought to do it, she thought, pleased with herself but angry with the weather. It was going to snow. She could tolerate these mountains in fine weather, when you could ride up in a cable-car and see for a hundred miles. But once the winter snows had set in, the Oberland was an abomination. Perhaps as Kermit had suggested five years ago when they had built the chalet in Gstaad, she ought to have taken up skiing.

Kermit was always making suggestions like that. He skied himself, slowly but with grace despite his age; he played tennis and he hiked, putting on his boots and disappearing for two or three days into the mountains. It was unseemly. If a man didn't act his age (my God, she thought, that husband of mine is almost eighty), he became, finally, grotesque. Even his—appetites. Was it seemly for a man Kermit's age to enjoy bed? Kermit did enjoy it, as one way, she supposed, of proving he wasn't a doddering old relic. Lovemaking was a romp for him. In bed he was playful and puppyish. It was unseemly. That word again. It described Kermit so perfectly. Couldn't he realize she was White Russian? There was a depth to the White Russian soul, a grave passion, a solemnity, that cried out for very different treatment in bed.

It had all seemed so different, six years ago in Moscow. Kermit Hauser, the retiring American Ambassador, recently but not too recently a widower, the dean of the diplomatic corps, one of the most respected men in Moscow, had offered her the world. He was then just past seventy; he had looked fifty. She was then in her mid-thirties; she had looked a plump and pretty White Russian twenty-five. He was cosmopolitan, suave. He swept her off her feet. She had gladly left her job as an Intourist guide, gladly exchanged her Russian passport for an American passport.

To vegetate ten months of the year in a picture-postcard village in the Alps?

With a husband who was almost eighty and refused to act it?

There was money, but less money than she had thought. Too much of it had gone into the chalet in Gstaad, too much of it into bad investments; and too much of what remained, she suspected bleakly, though she had never seen Kermit's will, would go to that ridiculous American

146

institution, charity. Scholarships to this college or that, for would-be State Department careerists, he was always saying.

And what would be left for her when he died?

A wave of self-pity engulfed her. She felt trapped. She still had her body, a little plumper now; she still had the looks that had appealed to Kermit in Moscow, if you didn't study the round pretty face too carefully for the telltale signs of aging—the network of wrinkles around the eyes, the looseness of skin under the jaw.

Trapped, she thought, tromping on the accelerator to force the white sports car powerfully forward. Enough money, perhaps, for a shabby existence in a small apartment in Paris or Rome, pinching pennies, making do with last year's fashions, watching the world pass her by, as it was passing her by now.

There had to be a way out. She had to find a way out before it was too late.

3 Claudia, wearing warm furry boots, white stretch pants, and a medallion-stitched lime-colored anorak that the fine old gentleman had insisted on giving her as a gift their very first day in the mountains, had finished the day's shopping. She felt anything but trapped.

She felt delighted with herself. The language of Gstaad was that sing-song variety of German known as Schwyzerdütsch, but most of the friendly shopkeepers could speak French and English as well. Claudia had decided to do her shopping in French today, and she had made herself understood easily.

And the things you could buy! She was carrying two large plastic bags. A can of Danish ham, a duck from the Netherlands, French wine in liter bottles, a small jar of fine caviar for her father, a British soft drink called Bitter Lemon, canned fruit juice from the United States, Swedish smoked salmon, the delicious local bread, pastries, and cheese. She felt like a walking culinary United Nations.

Best of all, loaded down with groceries, the mountain wind blowing in her hair, she could be herself. No one knew her here. There were few pictures of Claudia Nikolaievna Andreyeva in the West, and none of them resembled the tall girl in the lime-green anorak. ("It is a Bogner," Mr. Hauser had said with gentle pleasure, "and you more than do it justice, my dear.")

147

She was just one among many foreigners in the mountain village, and in just a few days she had become friendly with many of the shopkeepers. She had even learned a few phrases of the sing-song German dialect. On Thursday she had window-shopped the *sporthaus* on the single main street of town. Skis and ski clothing decorated the windows for the approaching season. A young man had struck up a casual conversation in French. He worked in the ski shop, he said. His father owned it. During the season he taught skiing. Did she ski? No, Claudia had said, and they talked some more, and before Claudia knew it they were walking together around the corner of the café of the Bernerhof Hotel. More talk, inconsequential laughter, a glass of beer. They parted friends without knowing one another's names. Yesterday morning there had been the young English couple in the low-slung Triumph. They had stopped her on the street to ask directions. She could even tell them where the Bernerhof was. They chatted amiably, inconsequentially for half an hour. Yes, Claudia had said, she was new to these mountains herself. But already she loved them.

At first her father had been doubtful about her going out. She had overheard his conversation with Mr. Hauser.

"What if somebody recognizes her?"

"Relax, Nikolai." She had smiled in the kitchen. Nobody ever called her father Nikolai. It seemed only half a name without the patronymic. "Nobody's going to recognize her. Have you seen the pictures of her in the Swiss papers? They're five years old—a frightened little duckling. She's a beautiful young woman now."

"It is still taking an unnecessary risk," her father had said.

"You're wrong, Nikolai," Mr. Hauser told him. "The risk is negligible, and it's necessary. She'd go stir-crazy just sitting around while a couple of old codgers decide the fate of the world. Let her see these mountains. Let her feel this place. She needs it. You've cut her off—"

"I had no choice."

"—from the world she knows. Let her discover a new one. Believe me, there's no risk."

There hadn't been any risk, and Claudia had reveled in her three days in the village, her three days in the mountains. She could see the mountains from the main street, what Mr. Hauser called the pre-Alps, rising green and wooded against the deep-blue Alpine sky. The wide cuts in the woods were ski runs; she could see the towers and the cables that, a month from now, would take the skiers up. And, at the southern end of the valley, ten miles away, loomed the real mountains, the high Alps, their white fangs biting at the sky.

She had walked in the foothills, through the glades of fir trees, across the incredible deep green of the Alpine meadows. It had been a mild autumn. A few small dairy herds had not yet come down from high pasture for the winter. She would pass the brown and white cows on the upland meadows, their great bells clanking as they browsed, the herdsmen greeting her with a hearty "Grüss Gott." She would pass them on the main street of town, the bells clanking in unison, the black and white dogs barking, the herdsmen in their velvet jackets smoking their curved pipes, breathing the good crisp mountain air and enjoying life.

The heights were dizzying. Once she had climbed very high, to the first station of a cable-car, following the overhead wires, unused now, until she reached a large wooden building. She found herself on top of the world, the emerald-green valley spread below her, the village toylike, the mountains rising beyond, changeless, serene. She had felt, then, an unexpected urge to cry. It overwhelmed her. What's the matter with me? she thought, her eyes stinging. She stood there, buffeted by the wind, the tears streaming down her face.

If she took three steps forward—just three—she would fall a thousand feet.

She took a step, and another, trancelike.

Terror? Remorse at abandoning the only home she had ever known? Pity for her father? Fear of the unknown future?

She heard a distant cowbell. The trance broke. The tears became laughter.

Terror, remorse, pity—not those at all.

Incredibly, it was joy. A sublime, painful burden of joy, like the final triumphal theme of Beethoven's Ninth Symphony, building out of a minor key, a joy that needed human voices to express it—the sky, the changeless mountains, the small changing unknown thing called life, her life, and whatever happened, whatever was going to happen, she loved it.

That had been yesterday afternoon. She brought the intensity of her joy down to Mr. Hauser's chalet. She sang

149

while preparing dinner, a sad, stirring song about the Don Cossacks, but at dinner she drank too much wine and the urge to cry came over her again. Then, later, the American President called.

"I will see him," Nikolai Ivanovich told Mr. Hauser. "Only him, no one else. Make him understand that."

Mr. Hauser made him understand that. "He wants you in Geneva," Mr. Hauser said. "The invasion. He can't leave now."

"No, I will not go to him. He must come to me. He will understand that, I think."

Mr. Hauser spoke on the phone again. The American President understood. He would come when he could. Tomorrow, he hoped. Tomorrow, if there wasn't war. Meanwhile, he would send someone. Not to talk. To watch.

Claudia put her wine glass down. "His assistant, Matthew Olds?"

"The CIA," Mr. Hauser said.

"Naturally," said Nikolai Ivanovich. "The CIA."

Now on Saturday morning, loaded down with her two bags of groceries, Claudia climbed the hill to the Hauser chalet. It was a big two-story house, weathered timber above, white stucco below. It was, according to the wrought-iron lettering on the white wall, called Chalet Elborus—named with a small amusing perversity, here in the Alps, for the highest mountain in Russia.

Claudia trudged past the wall and into the car park at the side of the house. She paused before the door and turned for a final view of the mountains, their peaks now lost in clouds. She thought it might snow soon.

As she turned back to the door, putting down one of the bags and taking out her key, she heard the powerful roar of a sports car and the squeal of protesting tires.

A white Porsche came slewing into the car park. It braked hard, the front end dipping, and a woman got out. She had a round pretty face and was wearing a mink jacket and a ridiculous little hat that managed to look stylish. She glanced at her watch and nodded and said, out loud, "Six hours exactly."

Claudia, with a shopping bag in one hand and the key in the other, looked at her.

"Is it Chalet Elborus you want?" the woman said, in English. "I'm Mrs. Hauser."

Claudia felt her heart racing. She thought Mr. Hauser's wife—Mr. Hauser's Russian wife—was in Paris.

"We're house guests," she said lamely, after a silence.

"Yes?"

"My—uncle and I."

Claudia turned her back and fumbled with the key. She dropped it in her haste and picked it up. She wished her father would return with Mr. Hauser.

"That's a surprise. Kermit told me nothing about any house guests."

"No. It was all very unexpected."

The woman smiled an open, guileless smile. "What's your name, dear?" she asked in Russian.

She could recognize a Russian accent as easily as Claudia could.

"Tamara," Claudia said, and went into the kitchen to unpack the groceries. It was rude, but she didn't want to talk. She didn't know what to say.

4   The chalet just north of Chalet Elborus belonged to a retired American foreign service officer who wouldn't arrive until the season began. Whitney Stoughton had arranged, through the Embassy in Bern, to occupy the place. Arriving at midnight Friday, he had been joined by four CIA agents who came in two cars during the early morning hours. He did not know the men personally but supposed they were competent. They were the entire ten-slash-two contigent in Switzerland and West Germany.

Now, just before noon on Saturday, two of them were still off somewhere in the mountains with Kermit Hauser and Chairman Andreyev. Another had followed the daughter on foot into town. The fourth remained behind in the borrowed chalet.

Seated at a second-floor window, Stoughton slowly lowered his field glasses. The window commanded a view, obstructed partially by a stand of pines, of the side entrance of Chalet Elborus a hundred yards away.

"That was Hauser's wife," Stoughton said.

"Russian, isn't she?" asked the agent named Al Cash, a stoop-shouldered, slow-moving man of about thirty.

"She's Russian all right. And the girl looked frightened."

"Maybe we ought to move in there," Al Cash suggested.

"That would be exceeding our orders," Stoughton said irritably.

Cash looked surprised. Stoughton, as Plans Division Chief, was one of the two Deputy Directors of the CIA and even closer to the President, it was said, than the Old Man McManus. "Since when do you have to take orders from anyone, Mr. Stoughton?" he asked. "I still think we ought to move in there."

"Not yet," Stoughton said thoughtfully.

Hauser's Russian wife and Chairman Andreyev's daughter had entered the chalet. Stoughton tilted his chair back from the window.

Some people, he thought, live in a tree. Like Matt Olds. Matt had stubbornly insisted it was too soon to commit ourselves in Yugoslavia, basing his judgment on the unlikely possibility of Andreyev's turning up—and what happened? A last-ditch call from the President in Geneva to Kermit Hauser here in Gstaad had produced Andreyev and made a hero of Matt.

For a while last night Stoughton had assumed Matt would draw the assignment of keeping an eye on Andreyev. But the President had tapped Stoughton for the job.

"Can you round up some of your ten-slash-two boys?" he had asked.

Stoughton had said that he could.

"Once you're up there, keep out of sight. Just watch the place. No contact unless absolutely necessary."

"How come?"

"It's a question of his dignity. He'll talk to me, no one else. The last thing he'd want is an interrogation by the CIA."

Stoughton nodded doubtfully. "I know, but—"

"No buts. A wrong move by us and he could still change his mind."

Stoughton shot a quick glance in Matt's direction. A sign of smugness, then, would have made him explode. There wasn't any. Matt's face wore a troubled expression.

"Maybe you ought to go right up there," he told the President.

"I wish to hell I could."

"What's stopping you?"

The President smiled. "One disappearance is enough for now, thanks. I'm staying put until we find out what the Red Army's really up to."

Even that, Stoughton thought, was no reprimand of Matt. Far from it. In a way the President was admitting that he was reluctant to leave Secretary Reed and General Laffont alone with an explosive situation while he was off conferring in secret with the Russian Premier.

Sometimes Stoughton was convinced that foreign policy on the very highest level was made by just two people—the President and Matt Olds.

It infuriated him.

Putting the glasses to his eyes again, he could see nothing but the empty road and the car parked beyond it.

Don't make contact unless absolutely necessary, the President had said. Impatiently, Whitney Stoughton wondered how much latitude that gave him.

5   "Call me Natasha, dear."

Standing in the kitchen doorway, smiling, Mrs. Hauser was speaking Russian.

"Do you like to cook? Most modern Russian women, if they are trained for a career, think it is beneath them."

Claudia was poking holes in the fatty duck with a fork. She placed the duck in the oven of the electric stove. "I guess I'm old-fashioned. I like to cook," she said.

"Your uncle is a lucky man."

Claudia grated orange peel for the sauce. The duck sizzled in the oven.

"How long have you been here?"

"A few days."

"Did your uncle come for the Summit?"

"No," Claudia said quickly.

"Perhaps I know him. Tamara is a Georgian name."

"We are Georgian."

"From Tbilisi?"

"Yes."

"Where the Chairman was born."

Claudia rubbed a knuckle raw against the grater.

"Do you know him?"

"No," Claudia said. "We don't move in those circles." Where are they? she wondered. Why don't they come back? Please, why don't they come back?

"What, as the French say, does your uncle do in life?"

"He's an economist," Claudia said, and knew at once that was a mistake. Nikolai Ivanovich, before entering politics, had been an economist.

153

"I see." Natasha had entered the kitchen. Her smile was unctuous. "Can I help?"

"No. Everything's under control. But thank you anyway."

"Have you been reading in the papers about the Chairman?"

Claudia nodded. She began to peel an onion.

"Do you think he's really gone?"

"I don't know," Claudia said.

"I wouldn't blame him. Kermit says he was having trouble at home."

"I don't know about those things," Claudia said.

"Yes, why should you worry your pretty little head about them?"

Claudia diced the onion. Her eyes were tearing.

"Where are they—your uncle and Kermit?"

"Walking in the mountains."

Natasha went to the window. "They'll be back soon. It's beginning to snow. I would like to meet your uncle."

The paring knife slipped. Claudia cut her finger.

"Here, let me help you."

"It's nothing."

But Natasha insisted. She produced Band-Aids and first-aid cream, and busied herself bandaging the little cut.

She could feel the hand of the girl who called herself Tamara trembling.

Twenty minutes later, Natasha was in a hot tub, soaking the fatigue of the long drive from her body.

It was, for a woman almost forty, still a good body. She pampered it with creams and massages at the sauna in Gstaad. The massages were pleasurable, the masseur a simple bovine youth with big capable hands who studiously looked anywhere but at Natasha while kneading her flesh. She could tell that her body excited him. Perhaps there was something there worth looking into. He might be properly, excitingly worshipful.

In the tub she stroked herself with feline contentment. The large breasts were still firm, the slight softness at the waist nothing that a few more deep knee bends each morning wouldn't take care of, the legs long and supple to her touch. The unblemished skin felt silken.

Forty. Almost forty. It would be a terrible birthday. The line, she thought; once you crossed it you were middle-aged. Once you crossed it there was nothing to look forward to but decline—the good muscle tone deserting you, the skin going slack, the breasts sagging, the stares of simple gratifying lust you got on the streets a thing of the past.

Natasha's White Russian mother, who had been born of the minor nobility before the Revolution, had once told her that a woman needed her body before she was forty and money after she was forty. Her mother had had the first, but not the second. It was an uncomplicated philosophy, and Natasha believed in it devoutly.

She ran more hot water into the tub. Her mind wandered.

That girl, how Natasha envied her. She was a natural beauty. And young—how old was she, in her mid-twenties? Her whole life still ahead of her.

Claudia Nikolaievna Andreyeva would be about her age. Natasha had seen the occasional rare picture of her, back in Russia, when the Chairman's daughter was barely twenty. After Svetlana, the Kremlin carefully kept its women under wraps. A tall girl, and coltish, with those enormous melting dark eyes.

The same eyes the girl who called herself Tamara had. That much was certain. As for the rest, six years was a long time.

But if she is the Chairman's daughter, Natasha thought. If she is—

In the kitchen she'd been so frightened she could hardly talk. Her cold hand had trembled under Natasha's touch. From Tbilisi, and her uncle—her father?—an economist.

Of course, the newspapers could have been mistaken. Nobody knew for sure that the Chairman had vanished. It was all speculation, only that.

But if he had?

If First Secretary Lysenko was ready to oust him at home, as the Paris papers had suggested, and if he wanted to defect to the Americans, Kermit would be the perfect contact.

They had been friends for years, Kermit and the Chairman. She had heard it said that Kermit had convinced the Chairman, when Andreyev was still Second Secretary for Relations with Communist Countries, that a certain amount of internal freedom in Czechoslovakia would do more for Russo-Czech relations than outright suppression. And there was Kermit's meeting with Andreyev two years ago in Vienna, after the Rumanian freedom-fighters had been crushed. Kermit had urged the same policy; Andreyev had brought it home to the Kremlin only to lose the point to Lysenko. Or so Kermit said, and whatever other shortcomings he had, her husband was neither liar nor braggart. He exerted a strong moral influence over the Chairman, no doubt about that.

It seemed only natural that Andreyev, at his tether's end, would come to Kermit for advice. Even more so since he was already here in Switzerland.

Natasha raised a leg and soaped it languidly.

The more she thought about it, the more she was convinced.

The girl was Claudia Nikolaievna Andreyeva. Those eyes. She had to be.

A woman needed her body before she was forty and money after she was forty.

They would pay. They would be delighted to pay. Oh God, how they would pay.

Natasha dwelled on that for a while, a soft, pleased smile on her face.

A town house on the Île St. Louis in Paris, she thought, what the French call a *hôtel particulier*. Or an old carriage house in a mews in Belgravia in London. Money for clothes, for jewels, to travel in style instead of on the niggling allowance Kermit gave her. All the wealth she could possibly want, given in gratitude, for one phone call. Kermit would never even have to know.

The fittings at St. Laurent and Givenchy, Cartier's for an occasional bauble, Birger Christensen for a really fine sable, and the whispers that would follow her regal passage down the boulevards of the world's sophisticated cities. Who is that striking woman? Deposed nobility, a contessa, beautiful and mysterious . . .

All of life, all the good years ahead, for one phone call. Wait until Kermit returned with the uncle, to make sure? No, Kermit would see it on her face. If she was going to call, it had to be now.

Putting on her dressing gown she went to the telephone in her bedroom. What was the name of the villa? Yes, of course, named for Lenin's wife. She dialed *Auskunft* and asked, quite calmly, for the number of Villa Krupskaya in Geneva.

156

Chapter
TWELVE

1 By early afternoon it was beginning to snow hard.

The view from the front windows, Whitney Stoughton thought, was like one of those child's toys—a small glass globe full of water, with a toy Alpine town at the bottom, and when you shook the globe, white flakes fell on the tiny chalets and the two church steeples.

The view from the side window that looked out on Chalet Elborus was more disquieting. Through the falling snow, past the already snow-laden branches of the pine trees, Stoughton saw Hauser's car drive up. British make, probably a Rover. Stoughton put the field glasses to his eyes and saw Hauser and Chairman Andreyev get out. They kicked snow off their boots and went into the chalet.

"The Chairman?" Al Cash asked.

Stoughton nodded.

"And Hauser's Russian frau home sooner than expected. I don't like it."

Stoughton wasn't wild about it either.

Would the woman recognize Andreyev?

Despite the lack of beard, despite the heavy-framed glasses, despite the new hair-comb, she probably would. A talk with the daughter first, she'd had plenty of time for that. The daughter would be unsure of her ground. A shy type at best. Those big frightened eyes.

If Natasha Hauser had pumped her and *then* saw the resemblance?

Calm down, Stoughton told himself. She's no Russian now. She's married to an American. Maybe even happily, if anybody is ever married happily. Maybe even a loyal American herself, now.

"This crummy job," Al Cash said. "It can drive you nuts." Cash had flat, cold, emotionless eyes. He was not the first ten-slash-two agent Stoughton had dealt with, and wouldn't be the last. They always made him feel uneasy.

(Small talk: What kind of year did you have? How many people did you kill?)

"Meaning what?" Stoughton asked.

"If you obey orders, maybe you live long enough to get a pension, but sure as hell no medals. If you say screw the orders, you either get a reaming from Langley, Virginia, or you make a good guess and all of a sudden you're a hero. Me, I've got a hunch."

"That we ought to go in there?"

"Yeah," Al Cash said. "The frau bothers me."

"The President expressly forbade—" Stoughton began, realizing he sounded pompous.

"Yeah, well, that's your department, Mr. Stoughton. It was only a hunch."

The two agents who had followed Hauser's car to Lauenen came in, their hair snow-covered.

"Like a witch's tit out there," one of them said.

"For this I had to leave Munich," the other one said.

They poured and drank coffee. Al Cash joined them.

The intentional low-key, low-brow attitude, Stoughton knew, was a pose. These were college-educated men. But they one-syllabled their way through twenty years of tedious, sometimes dangerous, often brutalizing work—if they lasted that long. Maybe the affected attitude made it easier for them to live with themselves. It took a special kind of psychological makeup to earn a ten-slash-two rating. Ten-slash-two people could kill on assignment, not merely in self-defense.

But still, in contrast with Stoughton's, their work was easy. They could have a hunch, and they could say screw the orders, either meaning it or just letting off steam because someone else stood between them and where policy was made.

Stoughton stood in that position. Except that policy was made, most of the time, by Matt Olds.

Who wasn't here. Who was back in Geneva minding the shop with the President.

It wasn't really a question of policy anyway. It was a question of judgment. If the Hauser woman was a real threat, Stoughton knew he ought to go in there.

What, actually, did he have to lose? A little talk with Andreyev, what harm could that do? And if he finally came out and said he was going to defect, if Stoughton's admiration and sympathy got him to say it, with Hauser as a witness?

158

Otherwise the President would come here, and all the credit would go to Matt Olds.

Or worse. Sooner or later, if the President still couldn't leave Geneva, he'd send Matt. And Matt would waltz in, shake the Chairman's hand, and luck into it again.

Stoughton sighed. He drank a cup of strong, tepid coffee.

"Al?" he said. "I'm beginning to think that hunch of yours could be right."

2   The President put the phone down wearily. "That was our old friend Congressman Lake," he told Matt.

Congressman Lake was Chairman of the House Armed Services Committee.

"Hawkish as usual?"

"A screaming eagle," the President nodded unhappily. "What's the good of spending seventy billion a year on defense, he said, if we have no intention of using what it buys? A nation that wants peace prepares for war, he said."

"Why didn't you tell him who said that first?"

"The Romans? He probably never heard of them."

"Or what happened to them," Matt said.

Congressman Lake's call had been one of many. They had started coming in at midnight Friday, a reasonable enough hour from the callers' point of view, considering the time difference between Geneva and the States. They had kept coming straight through the night and Saturday morning. The Secretary of Defense, the Majority and Minority Leaders of the Senate, even, unexpectedly, the United States Attorney General, and a former President.

None of them approached the situation with the same war-fever as Congressman Lake, but all favored some quick, decisive counter-move. They said honor the treaty. They said police action. They said don't let Russia get away with it. The Attorney General had taken a page out of Benson Reed's book. "If anybody brings this to the Congress," he said, "I'd hate to prepare your defense."

Even Jenkins Potter of the AP had come white-faced into the Presidential Suite, after Huntington had agreed to see just one reporter late Saturday morning.

"The story is we're going to let them get away with this," he said.

159

"Where'd you hear that?" President Huntington asked him.

"No orders for the Pentagon at all. That's what our bureau chief says."

"Well, that's right, Mr. Potter. No orders yet."

"I can't believe it. Do you want this Administration to go down in history as the one that finally sold out to Russia? From lack of courage?"

"I don't want history to call it the Administration that took us into war, even limited war, unnecessarily."

"Unnecessarily?" Potter repeated. "Can I quote you?"

The President looked at his watch. "You can say that as of eleven-forty Saturday morning I still wasn't convinced of the necessity of war."

After a while Potter said, "Andreyev?"

"I can't hear you, Mr. Potter."

"It's got to be Andreyev. Nothing else makes any sense."

"As of eleven-forty-and-a-half Saturday morning," the President said with a faint, tired smile, "I have no comment on Andreyev."

"But that could change?"

"I think that could change, Mr. Potter. Off the record."

Jenkins Potter relaxed visibly. "Off the record, of course, have we found him?"

"We know where he is. That is not for publication."

"Is he alive and in good health?"

"And ready to talk. Yes."

Jenkins Potter grinned. As much as anything, it was Potter's widely syndicated column that had made Clay Huntington a Presidential candidate three and a half years ago, Potter's column that had helped Huntington oust the incumbent from the White House in a close election.

"Forgive me, Mr. President," he said. "I should have known better. Accusing you of lack of courage. When do I get to print this?"

"I have to see Andreyev first. I can't yet."

"No. I can see that. Yugoslavia. Plus fielding the complaints from Washington. They've been all over you, haven't they?"

"Let's say that if Mr. Gallup took a poll today, I wouldn't be the most popular man in the United States. In fact, if everything that went on here last night were known, I'd get the poll's second-lowest rating." The wide

160

Huntington smile flashed then. "Matt Olds here would win hands down."

"It was Olds who convinced you to wait?"

"That's right. And if my meeting with Andreyev comes off, you can print it. Quoting the usual anonymous high Administration source."

"When will you see Andreyev?"

"I had hoped today. But I can't be in two places at once."

"Meaning you wouldn't trust Secretary Reed to mind the store?"

"I guess I'm a lousy executive," the President said. "I wouldn't trust anyone to mind the store. That—"

"Is not for publication," Jenkins Potter said ruefully. "But how long can you leave Andreyev waiting?"

"Matt will go up and see him today, if Andreyev is willing."

"Where? You said up. Is he in the mountains?"

"No comment."

That was the first Matt had heard of the President's plans for him. He listened with only half an ear to the rest of the interview. No, the President said, off the record, we couldn't be certain Andreyev wanted to defect. He wanted to talk. That was the important thing. He could lay bare Lysenko's schemes, might even bring about Lysenko's fall from power.

And then what? Jenkins Potter asked.

And then a new collective leadership in the Kremlin, the President mused. Men like Foreign Minister Kapitsa, or the younger technocrats a step away from the top. Men who dream of bringing Russia into the last quarter of the twentieth century with an improved standard of living. They could do it—without Lysenko.

They could even make Russia something she's never been, either under the Czars or the Commissars.

A mature, responsible member of the community of nations.

If we met them halfway.

And if Lysenko didn't lead them to war first.

Jenkins Potter went, after a handshake, with a glow in his eyes.

"What do I tell Andreyev?" Matt asked.

"Find out what he's prepared to do for us, or for Russia, because he'll realize it's the same thing now. And I think you ought to go easy on the idea of defection. He

161

brings it up, or it doesn't get mentioned. What's the daughter like?" the President asked abruptly.

"Claudia? I don't know." Matt felt uncomfortable. "She's warm and imaginative and—well, eager to meet life and—"

The President smiled. "Does she like you, too?"

Matt said nothing. He shrugged.

"It's a place to start. Andreyev won't just open up to you. That's assuming he'll agree to see you at all." The President went to the phone. "While I call and find out, why don't you rustle up Burt East? I want you to take him along. And while you're at it, tell him to pull his boys off you."

"How's that again?"

"Whit wanted to send you home for your own protection. I had Burt put a detail on you instead."

Matt shook his head in mild disbelief. Then he went to find Burt East.

He was back in ten minutes.

"Burt thinks he ought to stick around."

"A more important body to guard?" The President laughed. "I'll talk to him. His boys can take care of me."

"Then Andreyev's answer is yes?" Matt was surprised it had been that easy.

"You made quite an impression on Ambassador Hauser, I gather."

There was a knock at the door. Burt East came in, his freckled face creased in a frown.

"My job is here," he said. "Push me and I could make that stick. I'm not kidding, Mr. President."

"I know you're not, but Matt needs your help. There are five hundred reporters in Geneva, all waiting for the big story of the year to break. Not to mention the Russians. I want you to get Matt up there without being followed. And another thing, Burt. The Russians could find out where Andreyev is. If they do, I want you there."

They evaded the reporters' questions in the lobby and took two taxis and a tram to a café on the Left Bank. Matt waited there while Burt East went around the corner to rent a car. He used traveler's checks made out in the name of the phony passport he was carrying.

In a few minutes he returned to the café, still on foot. "Be awhile," he said. "They're giving us a VW with snow tires on all four wheels. They said it was snowing up a storm in the mountains."

3 A call to the Russian Embassy in Bern produced the necessary information.

Swiss National Highway 20 was the only through road in the valley.

It came in from the northeast, looped to the west where it met National 76 at the town of Saanen, the administrative center for the valley, and then went south through Gstaad and climbed, fifteen miles beyond the village, to a mountain pass. There was a three-man police force in Gstaad, a five-man police force and a small airport in Saanen. In this weather, no planes would be flying.

If you set up checkpoints north and south of Gstaad on National 20, you all but sealed off the village. If you set up a third checkpoint at the little railroad station, that completed the job.

There were other roads in the valley, but they went nowhere. They climbed a few kilometers into the mountains, petered out to cattle tracks and then footpaths and then nothing.

Viktor Malinin and his KGB agents slipped out of Villa Krupskaya in pairs. They rendezvoused in Coppet, where three cars were waiting. They met rain at Châtel-St.-Denis, and the rain turned to a wet snow by the time they reached Bulle. A few miles further, the snow began to stick.

One car pulled off the road after the convoy passed through Saanen. It drove in among the trees of an abandoned camping ground, out of sight of the highway. A second car went ahead, south toward Gstaad.

Malinin and the occupants of the third car waited for ten minutes on the shoulder of the road. A single large trailer-truck passed, then nothing. Malinin looked at his watch, pulled out the stem, and spoke into the watch:

"Verify your positions."

"Two hundred meters off the highway and facing out," came Moskalenko's voice from the car in Saanen.

"A side road, three kilometers south of Gstaad," came another voice. "Near a trout hatchery."

There were three KGB agents in each of the other cars, and four in the command car with Malinin. He did not foresee any trouble, but in the unlikely event of it, those two other cars were his insurance.

"We're going in," he said. "Keep your radios open."

But first he handed something to the footballer Bayev. "Put them on," he said, and Bayev went out into the snow, did something to either side of the hood, and returned inside. They turned right at the big blue and white highway sign that said GSTAAD—3KM. Wind and the car's own speed swirled snow at the windshield and made the little American flags now on both fenders flutter stiffly from their miniature standards.

The highway was still covered in patches, but snow already lay several inches deep in the fields. They entered the village. A few cars were parked on the street. The shop windows were brightly lighted. They looked snug and secure in the gloomy afternoon.

A policeman in a greatcoat trudged by, wheeling his bicycle. Malinin smiled. A country cop on a bike, he thought, that's what we'll have to face if anything goes wrong. Not that anything would.

Two agents were let off at the railroad station, leaving Malinin, Bayev, and a man named Sokolov in the command car.

When they drove under the railroad bridge, a toylike train, all lit up, passed overhead. The little train, the cop with a bicycle, the brightly lighted shops, the cozy chalet architecture everywhere—all had an unreal quality, like something out of a fairy tale. It seemed, Malinin thought, a place where violence could not happen.

Nor would it. If all went well, Chairman Andreyev and his daughter, drugged, would be aboard the Chairman's own TU-144 on the way back to Moscow in a few hours.

Well, perhaps some necessary incidental violence.

On the phone the woman Natasha Hauser had asked for money. A very large sum of money. Malinin had enjoyed himself, bargaining with her like an American shopkeeper. They had agreed on a sum that would be paid over to a numbered account, in dollars, in the Union Bank in Geneva. Despite the bargaining, it was still an enormous sum.

Its size was irrelevant. The woman would never get it. She would get Moskalenko instead.

4 "Bless old Papa Hertz," Burt East said.

It was snowing hard by the time they passed through the small market city of Bulle. There were slushy patches on the road. The Volkswagen, with snow tires on all four wheels, forged reliably ahead.

"How much farther?" Burt East asked.

"An hour in this weather," Matt said. "Maybe a little less."

Burt East shivered. "On the other hand," he said, "to hell with Papa Hertz." The heater in the little car didn't work. "I hope they've got central heating in the Ambassador's chalet."

5 Natasha was upstairs with one of her frequent headaches. Kermit Hauser brought her some hot tea and aspirin.

"How was lunch?" she asked.

"Delicious. The girl's a marvelous cook."

"House guests," Natasha said irritably. She sat up, her plump bare shoulders exposed over the fluffy featherbed, and took the aspirins with a swallow of tea. "All I wanted to do was rest, after Paris. But the girl is nice. A real beauty. What's her uncle like?"

Natasha sounded overwrought. She was often overwrought. Catch her at a calmer moment, Hauser thought. This was not the time to discuss Andreyev. He wished his wife hadn't returned so soon. He wished, wryly, that he'd had better luck—or better sense—marrying. They had little in common. She had seemed brighter in Moscow. Her encouragement of his attentions had been flattering. A foolish old man's final fling, he thought. But the final fling had led to marriage as, probably, Natasha had planned all along. He wondered if she regretted it now. Sometimes they spent as much as fifteen minutes a day talking about something besides the weather or what they were going to eat. Natasha's attitude in bed oddly and frustratingly reversed their ages. She was like a woman who tolerated, with sour amusement, a small child's silly game. Which is my own fault, Hauser decided. The next time around I shall allow myself to become properly flabby and dried out, as befits a man of my age. Sometimes, he was aware, they didn't even like each other. Still, at his age, to divorce would be even more fatuous than to marry.

"What's he like?" he said. "We get along fine. He likes to take long walks in the mountains."

"Not in this weather."

"No, but we got a good one in this morning. Halfway up to my hut."

"You and that hut. The way you talk, you'd think you own it. Sometimes I think you'd rather live there."

"It is a thought," Hauser said dryly.

"Call the maid," Natasha said. "Do you know the number? I'll want her here in the morning."

Hauser hated what he called the clutter of servants around the house. The maid had not been in during Natasha's holiday. "All right," he said, but decided to be senilely forgetful for another day or so.

As he set the tea tray on the night table, the doorbell rang.

"I'll get it," he called downstairs, and Natasha turned her plump cheek for a kiss and he went out of the room, closing the door with soft finality behind him.

He recognized one of the men at the door. Handsome, almost too handsome with that wavy blond hair and those long-lashed eyes, he had been a member of the President's ExCom in Geneva. Rather hawkish, and there had been an argument with Matthew Olds. High up in the CIA, that was it. What was the name?

"I hope you remember me, Mr. Ambassador."

"Of course. You're Whitney Stoughton."

They shook hands.

"And this is my colleague Mr. Cash. Al Cash. Ambassador Hauser."

Another handshake. Cash, in parka and stretch pants, was a thin, stoop-shouldered young man with flat hard eyes and a smile as sincere as a tax adjuster's.

"I thought," Stoughton began, "because Mrs. Hauser came home—"

"Yes, yes, well, come in out of the cold," Hauser said without enthusiasm. "You needn't worry about my wife. She's upstairs. A headache."

The three of them stood in the entrance hall. Hauser sighed and shut the door. "Can I offer you something? A hot drink? Or something stronger?"

"Something stronger would be swell," Al Cash said.

Hauser decided he was old enough, and had a sufficient reputation for cantankerousness, to be blunt.

"One drink," he said, "and then I'd like you to go. The Chairman—"

"Is he all right?" Stoughton asked quickly.

"He's fine. He'll see the President, when the President gets here."

"That may take awhile yet."

"I know it will. Matthew Olds is on his way up."

Hauser led them past the kitchen to his study. Nikolai Ivanovich and Claudia were in the living room. He could hear the faint sound of their conversation through the kitchen doorway, and Claudia's soft laughter.

"Whiskey all right?" Hauser asked, as Stoughton and Cash seated themselves in matching black leather chairs.

"Swell," Cash said. "Straight up."

"Soda, please," Stoughton said, and Kermit Hauser busied himself making the drinks.

"I hear you have a real showplace here," Stoughton said admiringly, getting up and examining the rich tones of the paneled walls, the great expanse of window that looked out on the snowy afternoon, the floor-to-ceiling bookcases. "Are these first editions?"

"Some of them," Hauser replied brusquely.

"And a rather considerable collection of modern art, I gather," Stoughton said with cheerful respect. "Would that be in the living room?"

"I'm a great admirer of modern art," Cash allowed.

"It would be in the living room," Hauser said. "So would Chairman Andreyev, Mr. Stoughton, as I assume you have surmised." He gave them their drinks. "Shall I be quite rude? I'd rather you didn't see the Chairman. I think you can understand why."

"Understand, maybe," Stoughton said reasonably, "but not agree. It's time he got some reassurance from the Administration."

"He'll get it from Matthew Olds."

They all heard footsteps on the polished wood floor of the hall. Claudia appeared in the study doorway. "Dad wonders if—oh, excuse me. Hello."

"You must be the daughter," Stoughton said with an ingenuous smile. He went over to her. "I'm Whitney Stoughton, Miss Andreyeva."

"Why yes, I've heard of you. Hello," she said again, and offered her hand.

Stoughton shook it and said eagerly, "I hope you don't mind if I stand a little bit in awe of you, and your father, and what you're doing. That takes courage, real courage."

Claudia looked at Hauser uncertainly. The tufted white eyebrows almost covered the deep-set eyes as the old man glowered and grumbled something under his breath.

"My father would be pleased that you think so," Claudia told Stoughton.

"I'd like the chance to tell him personally."

And Hauser finally said, because it probably would do no harm after all, and because he wouldn't be rude in front of the girl: "Very well. If that's all you want to tell him."

6 Nikolai Ivanovich was content to let Stoughton do most of the talking. He was flattering, possibly too obviously flattering, but that didn't seem to bother the Russian Premier. After a few minutes Hauser conceded that the CIA Deputy Director was handling himself well. If at times the eyes behind the black-rimmed glasses glazed like those of a man trapped by an earnest bore at a cocktail party, there was no harm in that. Stoughton was no fool.

The same could not be said for his younger colleague. Al Cash had spent the first few minutes studying the paintings on the walls: a pair of small Braque sketches flanking the fireplace, a few almost Orientally tranquil Bigelow landscapes, some oddly captivating Swiss primitives. He commented banally on the paintings, addressing his remarks to Claudia, who nodded politely every now and then. It was obvious that he wanted to impress her. That didn't surprise Hauser. Cash was young, Claudia was attractive—Hauser wasn't above trying to impress her himself.

Hauser had just about convinced himself that the meeting would do no harm when Cash, gazing moodily at the flames leaping on the hearth, said portentously, "When they get around to writing the history of these times, they could do worse than calling it the age of the defector." The words had been dropped into silence, apropos of nothing, and Cash's pale eyes turned to Claudia as he continued, "It's almost, well, fashionable to defect, you know?"

"Is it?" Claudia said coldly, and Stoughton gave Cash a quick hard look, which the younger man missed.

"I've dealt with defectors on all levels," Cash went on, "and I'll say this: The higher the rank of the defector, the more courage he needs."

"Particularly," Nikolai Ivanovich suggested with an amused twinkle in his eye, "if he defects from our side to yours?"

No damage yet, Hauser told himself with relief. Nikolai Ivanovich was sarcastic, not angry. He almost seemed to be enjoying himself.

"Touché," Stoughton laughed easily. "I guess we just like to think there *is* a moral difference. You can't blame us, sir."

A very nice recovery, Hauser told himself. He began to relax.

"No, I suppose I can't blame you," Nikolai Ivanovich agreed. "In this case, though, it is not a question of ideology. It is a question of one man. It is a question of stopping him."

"Of course. Lysenko."

"Some historians have the idea," Nikolai Ivanovich said, warming to the conversation, "that revolution, real revolution, can occur only from within. That is nonsense. Lenin was ten years outside Russia before he returned in a sealed railroad car. Trotsky was living in the Bronx on the eve of the October Revolution. Sometimes what must be done can best be accomplished from the outside."

"The Bronx," Al Cash said. "I didn't know that." He grinned. "I tell you what. We're not exactly in a position to promise you Buckingham Palace, but I guarantee you it will be several cuts above the Bronx. Or, come to think of it, several cuts above that hole in the wall in Mexico City where Trotsky was hiding when Smersh finally put an ax in his—"

"That's enough, Al," Stoughton cut in savagely.

"A suburb, perhaps?" Claudia asked too sweetly. "With neon blight, and a nice used-car lot nearby, and when we go to a restaurant they will ask how do we want our Idahos, with butter or sour cream?"

She bit her lip. Her eyes were too bright. "What right do you have to assume we are going to the—States?" she demanded, and the way her voice caught made the word sound ugly.

Al Cash gave her a bewildered look. "Hey, what'd I say?"

"Do you think you have a monopoly on everything good and beautiful and ..."

She was crying. She ran from the room. Hauser started to go after her, but Nikolai Ivanovich shook his head. "No, give her a few minutes. The crying will help. This is still a terrible thing for her."

"Jesus, I'm sorry," Al Cash said after a while.

Hauser glared at him, and then the craggy old face relented. "Americans," he said. "When will we grow up?"

"Or Russians," Nikolai Ivanovich said gently.

"Of course, or Russians. We're too big. You're too big. Nobody has learned to live with that kind of bigness yet. It produces superpatriots. We're the best, we're the very best there ever was, we say, and to prove it we behave like street gangs, pounding our chests, protecting our turfs.

"I've served my country forty years," Hauser went on, "and I suppose that gives an old man the right to say this. You can have your superpowers. For living, for day-to-day living, I'll take Switzerland. It's small enough. It works. People say that the Swiss are dull. They are not. They are merely civilized."

There was a silence. Nikolai Ivanovich got to his feet. "I'd better go to her now."

As he started to cross the room, there was a knock at the door.

Kermit Hauser went into the hallway, a look of relief on his face now that Matthew Olds had arrived.

He opened the door and stood aside as three men entered, all in overcoats, two of them wearing snap-brim hats and the third bareheaded. He saw the black staff car outside, American flags flying from its front fenders. None of the men was Matthew Olds.

"Where is he?" he said. "Isn't Matthews Olds with you?"

And the bareheaded one, who was Viktor Malinin, told him, "Just get back inside and nobody will be hurt."

Chapter *THIRTEEN*

1 In the neighboring chalet, one of the CIA agents stood at the window, field glasses to his eyes.

"Well, we're about finished here," he said.

"How come?"

"Take a look. Staff car just passed. The brass is taking over."

The other agent raised his field glasses and turned the focusing knob. But the snow was falling so hard now that all he could see was the silhouette of a second car outside

Chalet Elborus. "Are you kidding? I can't see a thing now," he muttered.

"It's a staff car. I saw it. A Mercedes."

"That's funny. What are they doing with a Mercedes?"

"It must be a UN car," the first agent said. "They use them all the time." The first agent was stationed in Geneva, the second had come from Munich.

"Your department, I guess. Who were they, anyway? Presidential party?"

"Search me. Flying the Stars and Stripes from their fenders, though."

The agent at the window put the field glasses down. Visibility had dropped to zero.

The first agent took a deck of cards out of his pocket. "Gin?"

"Sure, why not?"

The cards were dealt on the table in front of the window, and they began to play.

2 Malinin stood in the center of the living room in Chalet Elborus. The KGB agent Sokolov had gone upstairs. Kermit Hauser could hear him moving about. Bayev stood in the doorway, a gun in his hand and a gun that belonged to Al Cash in the pocket of his overcoat. Nikolai Ivanovich and Hauser sat near the fireplace. Whitney Stoughton and Cash stood with their backs to the room, their hands high and flat against the wall.

Kermit Hauser could feel his heart beating too hard. It felt hot and heavy in his chest, and between the heavy strokes was a frightening flutter. He had never felt old, really old, until this moment. He could not stop the trembling of his hands. His knees were weak. Not with fear—with rage and frustration. There was nothing he could do, nothing. Malinin had asked immediately for the documents, as if he had known Nikolai Ivanovich had spent much of the past three days preparing them. It was a logical assumption for Malinin to make. Refusing would have been foolish. He was too old for heroics. The documents were not hidden. Hauser had gone to the study with the agent Sokolov, returning with the bulky envelope. At first Hauser thought Malinin was going to throw it in the fire. He had looked at the contents quickly, nodding, half-smiling, stuffing the papers back into the envelope as he approached the hearth. Then he had changed his mind.

171

Hauser wasn't surprised. The papers might come in handy to Malinin. Power in the Kremlin was based on a lot of unpredictables, and with the Chairman out of the picture there just might be more of a scramble than Lysenko had anticipated. Malinin wanted some ammunition for himself. He folded the bulky envelope and put it in the pocket of his overcoat. Then he waited while the agent Sokolov went upstairs. He looked very pleased with himself.

Hauser heard a door slamming upstairs. Sokolov shouted and there was the sound of wood splintering. Then Sokolov came running downstairs and burst into the room past Bayev, his face flushed.

"The girl went out the window!" he cried.

Bayev immediately turned and ran. Hauser heard his pounding footsteps in the hallway, then on the stairs.

Sokolov, a big Ukrainian with a wild shock of straw-colored hair, looked in bewilderment around the room, then clawed at his pocket to get his gun.

And Kermit Hauser, hardly aware that he was moving, was up out of the chair and rushing at him. Though his heart was pounding, really pounding now, he felt young, young and reckless in his old man's body. He reached Sokolov and got both hands on the man's arm and the hand came out of the pocket empty as the arm moved powerfully, sending Hauser reeling across the room, hopping ridiculously on one foot, flailing the air with both outflung arms as he crashed into the wall near the fireplace.

He could feel his right hip breaking. He could hear it, the dry crisp snap, the sound a slat of wood makes when you break it across your knee.

3 The Munich-based agent drew terrible cards. He was down fifty points in the first box and thirty in the second. He crushed out his cigarette.

"UN car, huh?" he said.

"Sure, they always use them."

"Then why the flags? If it's a secret meeting?"

The other agent gave an elaborate sigh. "Some people are just plain natural-born worriers. Your deal, Chuck."

But Chuck was on his feet. He unsnapped the clip-on holster at his belt, removed the aluminum-frame Colt Cobra, pulled the trigger once to place a loaded chamber under the firing pin, replaced the revolver in the holster, and left the flap open. He got his parka from the closet and put it on but did not zip it.

"I think I'll take a little look around," he said.

4 The footballer Bayev could think of nothing but that Claudia had gone out the window.

He raced through the hallway, found the stairs, went up them three at a time. He found the door that Sokolov had kicked in, went through it into a bedroom where a cold wind and snowflakes were blowing in through an open window. He leaned across the sill and peered out anxiously. There was a tree below, a fruit tree, winter-bare now. It could have broken her fall. If she had jumped just right.

And if she hadn't?

On the white ground to the left of the tree he could see footprints in the snow, long strides for a woman. Running strides. She was all right. She had not been hurt.

Bayev stood there, feeling the cold wind and the snow on his face.

If it were Yegorov downstairs, he thought.

But Yegorov was dead, he had smashed the dead face of his friend himself, stripped the body, buried it. Yegorov had understood how he felt about Claudia Nikolaievna. Sometimes he had even joked with him about it. If it came to this, Yegorov would have let Bayev go after her. Yegorov understood. And Bayev would have tracked her, found her, brought her back without hurting her.

The colonel might send Sokolov. Bayev hardly knew Sokolov at all. He usually did not get along with Ukrainians. They were too arrogant, too sure of themselves. There was no telling what Sokolov might do.

Bayev decided to go after Claudia Nikolaievna himself.

He put the automatic in his pocket and climbed up on the windowsill. He jumped, letting his knees go loose just as he hit. He rolled over, got to his feet, ran after the footprints in the snow.

5 Whitney Stoughton stood, face to the wall, hands over his head and flat against the wall, like a man in a dream. Only one thought kept hammering at him, over and over. You had to play the bigshot. You had to walk in here and see him. You had to get your two cents in before the President, before Matt Olds. And if you hadn't? If you'd obeyed the President's orders? If you'd stayed at the window, glued to a pair of field glasses, you'd have seen Malinin driving in. But no, not you. It had to be done your way.

In a few hours they'll have the Premier on a plane heading for Moscow, and why don't you admit it? That's exactly what Lysenko is waiting for; Matt was right, you were wrong.

You blew it.

Two hundred million dead men thank you, Whitney Stoughton. The ruins of New York and Washington and Boston and Los Angeles and Bear Claw, Idaho, thank you.

He heard the pounding on the stairs, a voice shouting in Russian, the sounds of a scuffle. He started to turn and saw Ambassador Hauser, his arms flailing, crash into the wall; saw Al Cash push off the wall, like a pivoting swimmer at the turn, and hurl himself at the Russian.

Cash moved with blurring swiftness. Stoughton could hardly follow it, going across the room himself after Malinin, who was sprinting out the doorway. Cash used an elbow like a rapier, three, four, five deft slashes with it, jarring the Russian's head back, the Russian all the while clinging to him, bearlike, trying to bring him down.

Then Stoughton had gone through the hall to the front door, looking for Malinin.

6 From thirty yards away, at the head of the driveway, Malinin could see the chalet only as a vague solidness beyond the wall of falling snow. Keep calm, he thought. The Chairman is still in there. You're unarmed, and that was foolish, but you can get help.

He pulled the stem on his watch and calmly issued orders.

7 Bayev could see her.

Fifty feet ahead of him, on the road, running. Everything would be all right. He would bring her back. He wouldn't hurt her.

He was going to call her name, when a figure appeared in the snow ahead of her. She darted to the left, darted to the right. The figure caught her.

"Hey," a voice called. "Hey, miss, take it easy."

Bayev heard her voice, incoherent, laughing, crying. He stood still, completely still, not even breathing. The two figures began to move off together. The American would take her someplace where she would be safe.

Where she—would be safe.

Bayev did not move. His breath swirled in front of his face like steam.

I didn't allow her to escape, Bayev thought. It was the Ukrainian. I tried to cover his blunder. I couldn't.

Let her go. Let her go with the American.

How could he find her, in all that snow? Like the Urals. Or Siberia.

Bayev returned slowly through the trees to the back of the chalet.

8 Stoughton watched Al Cash come outside with Chairman Andreyev. The Russian Premier looked dazed.

Stoughton could not see far in the snow. Malinin was gone. Or watching them, maybe. For an operation like this he wouldn't have just two men. There would be others.

How much time do we have? Stoughton wondered. And how do we use it?

The other chalet?

But Malinin might have a dozen men out there in the snow.

The police?

No, not the police. The Kremlin had already started its campaign to discredit Andreyev. He was mentally ill, according to *Izvestia*. It had happened before. It was one way of getting a defector back. You claimed he was incompetent, and the local authorities were only too glad to get the whole mess out of their hair, give him back to his own people. It could happen that way. Malinin had enough poise to pull it off. As Russia's chief security officer in Switzerland, he had been assigned the sad task of picking up Andreyev, for Andreyev's own good, and the Americans, the American CIA, had tried to stop him.

Definitely not the police. Later, if necessary, an examination by Swiss doctors could establish Andreyev's sanity.

But now?

"Al," he said, absolutely sure he was doing the right thing, the unpleasant thought of just waiting there until

Matt Olds came charging in like the U.S. Cavalry forgotten, "Al, I think you better drive him down to Geneva."

They walked out of the car park and along the snow-covered road to the other chalet.

And Malinin followed them, quite calm, as sure of himself as Stoughton had been.

He heard the argument as Al Cash got into his car, as Stoughton opened the door on the other side for Nikolai Ivanovich. It was a black Peugeot.

"You can't expect me to leave here without my daughter," Nikolai Ivanovich protested.

"It's for your own protection, sir. We'll find her. She'll be all right."

"First find her. Then we'll go."

"Your safety is the most important thing," Stoughton insisted, trying to keep the impatience from his voice. "Nothing else matters."

The near-sighted eyes studied him. "Let me understand this. Are you saying I have no choice?"

"None of us do, sir. Believe me."

"And my daughter? She doesn't matter?"

"That's not what I said." Stoughton sighed. "Okay, Al," he said, and Malinin could even tell what he was thinking. A Peugeot, a common make in Switzerland. Black, nondescript—it would never be spotted.

Al Cash started the motor.

Before Stoughton shut the door on him, Nikolai Ivanovich said, "You're the same as they are. No worse. But no better."

Stoughton stepped back, and the car was moving.

In the cover of the trees, Malinin pulled the stem of his watch. "They've taken the Chairman out," he said. "The Americans. In a black Peugeot." He saw the door of the CIA chalet open and Chuck come jogging across the snow toward Stoughton. "We've got the daughter," Chuck said jubilantly.

Chapter
FOURTEEN

1 Matt was out of the car and running toward the brightly lighted front entrance of Chalet Elborus even before Burt East had pulled to a stop.

A white ambulance stood in the car park, its roof snow-covered, its headlights and dome-light on. The driver sat behind the wheel, smoking a cigarette, looking at Matt with idle curiosity as he rushed by.

Matt burst into the hallway and saw a man sitting on the floor and looking up numbly at another man, older, paunchy, and cherubic of face, who was gently prodding the first man's swollen jaw. The man on the floor bellowed. His swollen jaw hung slack, the mouth twisted to one side. The cherubic-faced man nodded, took a hypodermic from a leather bag, rolled the other man's sleeve up, and shot the needle quickly into his upper arm. Almost immediately the man on the floor settled back, his eyes going blank, and began to snore.

The cherubic face glanced at Matt. "And who are you?" the man asked in English, with the sing-song Schwyzerdütsch accent.

"I'm expected here. Where's the Ambassador?"

"Inside. A fracture of the right hip. They are getting him ready for the ambulance." The cherubic face almost managed to look doleful. The tongue clucked. "At his age . . ."

Matt brushed past him.

A stretcher on wheels stood in front of the fireplace. Two young men in parkas and white duck pants stuffed untidily into boots were easing Kermit Hauser onto the stretcher. His face looked yellow and shrunken. A woman who might have been pretty stood nearby, her round face haggard.

Hauser saw and recognized Matt. He half raised a big gnarled hand in greeting. "Skied fifty years and never

177

broke a bone," he said in a faint voice, the hand dropping weakly. "Now, in my own living room."

"You mustn't talk, Kermit," the woman said. "Don't make him talk," she told Matt.

The cherubic-faced doctor entered the room. "I still would like to give you an injection, Mr. Ambassador," he said.

Hauser glared at him. "I won't be taken out of here like a side of beef. Keep your goddamn needle away from me."

The doctor glanced at the woman, who shook her head. "He always gets his way. You won't change him now."

"As you wish, then."

The doctor spoke rapidly to the two ambulance attendants in Schwyzerdütsch. They had covered Hauser with a blanket. They began to wheel the stretcher across the room.

"Where's he going?" Matt asked.

"The hospital in Saanen. The other one, too. His jaw is fractured."

Matt followed them outside. Burt East was standing over the man in the hallway. "What the hell is going on here?" he said. Nobody answered him.

The attendants lifted the stretcher and carried it across the snow while the ambulance driver opened the rear doors and climbed in to help them. A second stretcher was slid out and carried into the chalet just as the woman, dressed now in a mink jacket and pale stretch pants, came out. She looked at Matt. Her round face was closed and spiteful. "This is what he gets for trying to help you."

There was nothing Matt could say to that. He watched her climb into the back of the ambulance. A few moments later they brought the other man out of the chalet and lifted him in through the rear doors. Driver, attendants, and doctor all got in. The ambulance moved slowly off, dome-light flashing in the falling snow.

Matt and Burt East found Stoughton in the kitchen. He was standing near the windows with a tall girl in white stretch pants, a white turtleneck, and a lime-green vest. The girl's back was turned. The room was cold. Stoughton held a black walkie-talkie set in his hand, its antennae extended through the open window. The walkie-talkie made a squawking noise.

"I can't hear you, Al," Stoughton said. He did not say it calmly.

The girl turned at the sound of their footsteps. It was Claudia.

Stoughton leaned over the walkie-talkie. "Al? Try it again, Al."

Matt looked at Claudia's face as she recognized him. The enormous dark eyes gleamed and the mouth trembled and then quirked in an uncertain little smile, as if she couldn't decide whether to laugh or to cry, as if she were waiting for Matt to tell her.

"You've come," she said. "You've come."

A voice emerged suddenly out of the static of the walkie-talkie.

"—some kind of attack. Jesus, Mr. Stoughton, I don't know what to do. He's just sitting there all bent over clutching his chest."

"Okay, okay, wait a minute. Let me think," Stoughton said wearily. He looked at Matt.

Matt went over to him and took the walkie-talkie. Stoughton seemed almost grateful. "Andreyev?" Matt asked him.

"With an agent named Al Cash. They—"

Matt lifted the walkie-talkie and spoke into it. "Does Stoughton know where you are?"

"Who's this?"

"Matt Olds," Matt said impatiently. "Does Stoughton know where you are?"

"Yeah."

Matt looked at Claudia. "You heard? Is it dangerous?"

"It could be. It doesn't have to be. The medicine—"

"Pills or what?"

"Pills, yes."

"Does he have any pills on him?" Matt said into the walkie-talkie.

And, after a while: "No, medicine, Mr. Olds. He looks real bad."

Matt glanced his question at Claudia.

"Even without the medicine," she said, "it could go away." Her face was white. "Or it could kill him."

"Stay where you are," Matt said into the walkie-talkie. "We'll bring the medicine."

He turned to Stoughton. "How far?"

"Five, six miles."

What sounded like static over the walkie-talkie was

harsh laughter. "It's only a cattle track, Mr. Olds. We're pretty high up. Couldn't turn around if we wanted to. We're not going anywhere."

Matt looked at Stoughton again.

"Cash couldn't get out with him. They almost ran into a KGB car at Saanen. They started coming back here. A second KGB car. Cash got lost trying to find another way out. Then the old man recognized the area. There's a hut—one of those Swiss Alpine Club huts in the mountains. Cattle track halfway, Cash said, and then you walk. They thought if they could shake the KGB car and reach the hut we could pick them up later."

"What happened?"

"The car followed them up the cattle track. Cash took a turn fast and made it. The KGB didn't. They went off a cliff."

Matt spoke into the walkie-talkie. "Try to keep him warm and comfortable. We're on our way."

"Bring him something to wear. He's not dressed for it. And don't forget the . . ." The voice faded under a howl of static.

Claudia didn't have to be told. She got the anorak she had bought for her father in Geneva, fur-lined boots, and a blanket. She found the pills in his bedroom.

Among half a dozen pairs of old boots in the closet, Matt and Burt East found some that fit. They got a flashlight, some chocolate bars, two bottles of Cognac. In the study Matt found a stack of old topographical maps which Kermit Hauser had used for his mountain hikes. They were worn through at the folds. He brought the stack into the kitchen.

"Where is it?" he asked Stoughton.

"A place called Lauenen."

"The Teufelkopf Hütte," Claudia said. She was wearing a parka that matched the lime-green vest.

Matt pulled the right map from the pile and spread it on the countertop. He traced the road with his finger, the cattle track, the dotted red line of the hiker's trail that went up from there to the little flag that represented the hut. He looked at his watch. It was almost three-thirty. Two hours of daylight left, no more.

"What are those huts like?" he asked Claudia.

"The hut?" Stoughton said. "Aren't you going to bring him down?"

"If they're at the end of the cattle track, they're much

180

closer to the hut. We may have to spend the night. Take a look."

"There are beds," Claudia said, "and blankets. There should be firewood. And provisions in the climbing season. Now, I don't know."

Matt opened drawers and cabinets. Water would be no problem. The snow would provide that. He found some links of hard sausage, a long French bread, half a dozen cans of soup, a can opener, cigarettes. Burt East loaded all of it into a rucksack.

"I'm coming with you," Claudia said. "He'll need me."

"You're staying here."

"It's my father. You're not going to leave me behind. I won't let you."

Matt nodded finally. "Come on then." He asked Stoughton, "Think you ought to call the police?"

"The police?"

"When we bring Chairman Andreyev down, I don't want Malinin accusing us of kidnapping him."

"Malinin will claim he's mentally ill, irresponsible. The police would be only too glad to let him take Andreyev off their hands."

"I don't think so," Matt said. "You don't know the Swiss. Besides, there's no guarantee Malinin will wait for us to come down. He could come up after us."

"How would he know where to look?" Stoughton asked.

"He found out Andreyev was here, didn't he?" Matt said.

They were outside. Matt opened the door of the Volkswagen for Claudia. Burt East climbed in back and Matt got behind the wheel.

Stoughton was standing in the snow, watching them. Matt rolled the window down.

"I'd still feel easier if you called the cops."

"We'll find Malinin. If we can keep an eye on him, we won't need the cops."

Matt gave him a last exasperated look, rolled the window up, and started driving. He had no time to argue. He wished there had been a clear chain of command, with himself at the top. But then, Stoughton probably wished the same thing.

2   The *Bezirkspital* in Saanen was, including the few windows under the peak of the high-pitched roof, a four-

story building in chalet style. With murals on its exterior walls and balconies facing across the valley to the mountains and great overhanging eaves already laden with snow, it hardly looked like a hospital. A few cars were parked behind it, their roofs and hoods snow-covered. A small snowplow, its warning light flashing, moved back and forth behind the building, scooping snow up, ingesting it, spitting it in a fine hard stream over the wall behind the parked cars.

Malinin and Bayev sat on the front seat of the Mercedes, Bayev with his head down and his eyes shut, Malinin with a cigarette in his mouth and a worried expression on his face. He still had radio contact with Moskalenko. Moskalenko's car was now at the foot of the hill on which the Hauser chalet stood. Moskalenko had reported seeing Matthew Olds and another man and he thought the daughter in a Volkswagen. Moskalenko had not been able to follow them. A suddenly unresponsive steering wheel, or an idiot behind it, Malinin thought, a slight skid, and they had put two wheels in a ditch. They were trying to dig out.

There was no longer any contact with the third car. They had been following the black Peugeot, keeping it in sight, reporting frequently and optimistically: the highway through Gstaad, a turn at the Rössli Hotel, a second turn beyond it, a road that followed the floor of a valley, and then a village. They had not told Malinin the name of the village. The name on the highway sign was obscured by snow, they said, and then after they passed through the village a sign they could see—the red silhouette of a car, a warning sign prohibiting the passage of four-wheeled vehicles—a cattle track, climbing steeply, and they followed the black Peugeot, Nikolai Ivanovich in it, and then there had been a sudden shout and silence. Malinin had not been able to raise them again.

Describe the route to the woman, he thought. She lived here, she could tell him where they had gone.

He had been waiting forty-five minutes for her to come out of the hospital, but she might spend the night in there while they fought to save the old man's life.

Go in after her?

No, it would be dangerous if they were seen together. But how long could he wait?

One wing of the double glass doors opened, and the woman came out. She glanced at the snowplow and

182

ducked her head to light a cigarette. She stood there smoking, protected from the snow by the overhang. Malinin got out of the car and went to her.

"How is he?" he asked in Russian.

Her head jerked up. "Who are you?" Her eyes were puffy and red.

"We spoke on the phone earlier."

"I should never have called you."

"How is he?"

"He's an old man. They're trying to set the bone, under anesthesia. Go away. Just leave me alone."

She turned her back to him and opened the door. He grabbed her shoulder, spun her, shook her savagely. "Listen to me. You're a fool if you think you can walk away from it now. You're in too deep."

"Keep your filthy hands off me." She struggled in his grasp and he released one shoulder and slapped her face hard. Her eyes flew wide open, showing white all around the iris. She raised one hand to her cheek, the gesture too melodramatic, and cried, "I don't want your money. I don't want anything to do with you."

"It's too late for that," Malinin said calmly. "What if he lives? What if he learns you called us? What would you have left then?"

Her eyes met his, wide and bright and soft, then narrow and bright and hard. Her pink tongue darted out and licked the pale, trembling lips. "What do you want from me?"

"The Americans took Nikolai Ivanovich out in a car. I'm going to describe the route. I want you to listen."

He described the route.

"Can you tell me where they went?"

She shook her other shoulder free. He permitted that. For another moment she gazed at him defiantly and then her eyes dropped and in a flat voice she said: "The place is called Lauenen."

Malinin nodded. A woman, he thought. You could conquer any woman, in any way, if you had the key. For this woman the key was fear.

"There's a climbing hut in the mountains above the village. That's where they went. I'm sure of it."

"How do we get there?"

"The money," she said.

"Yes, of course, the money. I'm sending someone. There's been a small change of plans."

"A change of plans?"

"Nothing important. Come outside and smoke a cigarette. The way you did now. He'll find you and give you the new arrangements. It's of no importance. Now, how do we get there?"

She told him.

3   To become one of the great jet-set watering places, an Alpine town needs accessibility and sunlight.

Gstaad had both. It was a two-hour drive on good roads from Geneva, an hour and a half from Bern and Lausanne, less from Montreux. It was serviced frequently by the Montreux Oberland Bernois Railroad. The small airport at Saanen, three kilometers away, could handle excursion planes.

The valley of the Sarine River, in which Gstaad nestled, was wide. It provided seven hours of sunlight a day even in midwinter, more than anywhere else in the Alps except St. Moritz. Those members of the jet-set who preferred St. Moritz spoke of the high, above-timberline skiing and the big, fashionable turn-of-the-century hotels. The advocates of Gstaad spoke of the rolling meadows, the gentle, pine-clad slopes of the pre-Alps, the relaxed comfort of the chalets on the hillsides instead of the glittering hotels and the beauty of the narrow, gorgelike satellite valleys that twisted and writhed their way through the foothills to the high mountains.

A two-lane highway followed the floor of one of the satellite valleys to the southwest, through grazing land and then a pine forest and a lumber town called Enge, where the milled pine stood in cross-hatched stacks twenty feet high, and finally to Lauenen, which was as far as the road could go. South of Lauenen loomed the great thrusting peaks that stood between the Oberland and the Valais— two miles high, snow-covered always, with vast snowfields in the *cols* between the crests, and blue glacial ice on their shoulders; the high home of chamoix and the rare Alpine eagles, like a wall at the end of the world.

A narrow cleft made ascent by car to the small upland meadows and the lake possible. It was not a road. It was a cattle track, unpaved and rock-strewn under fresh powder snow and so narrow sometimes as it climbed and turned among the pines that Matt had to slow the Volkswagen almost to a stop while he leaned out one window and

Claudia out the other to make sure they had clearance. After they had climbed above the protection of the low hills to east and west, the wind howled in, fiercely driving snow across their path, piling it in low drifts. Soon, Matt knew, those drifts would make the track impassable. Even if they could turn the car around, there would be no driving back down. Whatever happened, they were stuck up here for the night. At least for the night, he thought.

Ahead of them where the track curved sharply to the left, along the edge of a cliff, the guardrail was out. Through the falling snow Matt could see the freshly splintered ends of the pine slats, the uprooted stanchions, the fifteen-foot gap where the Russian car had gone over.

They drove past, Burt East leaning forward, rolling down the window on Claudia's side and peering out.

"Any sign of them?"

"Can't see a thing. Excepting all that white stuff. For a Carolina boy it's mighty pretty. Never did get to see snow, real snow, till I was fifteen, sixteen. Pappy took me up to Washington. Think they're dead?"

"I don't know," Matt said.

"Got me a Magnum .44, boy, that would shoot a hole through a steel door. Pretty good shot. That was old Pappy again. But I'd hate to tackle a car full of KGB people."

Burt East always troweled on the red-clay-and-hominy accent when he was worried, as if a retreat to the status of simple country boy would somehow help. Matt usually found the exaggerated Southern babbling amusing, but now it grated against raw nerves and made him realize how tense he was.

The track widened suddenly, opening on a small wind- and snow-swept meadow and a lake where dead reeds stood in the still-unfrozen water. Matt could just make out the gap in the pines beyond it, where the track continued. This was the last place they could turn around. Once they left the meadow they weren't going anywhere but up.

They reached the dubious shelter of the higher pines. The track was steeper there, and Matt switched into first gear for better traction. That's it, he thought. There is no gear below first.

Claudia touched his hand on the knob of the stick shift. Her fingers tightened. "We'll make it," she said. "I know we will."

The falling snow seemed to burst at them from a point

185

exactly ten yards ahead, like the spreading pattern of a
shotgun blast. The white-laden branches drifted slowly
past, the engine of the Volkswagen whined in first gear,
the wind howled. Their breath fogged the windshield so
that every few minutes Claudia had to rub it clear with
her sleeve. Once her shoulder brushed Matt's, lightly, and
she tensed as he drew away from the contact awkwardly.
She feels it too, he thought.

"Can you see?"

He could see.

"Pappy always used to tell me . . ."

He could see, where a moment before there had been
nothing beyond the metronoming windshield wipers but
the falling snow, the rear of the black Peugeot.

4 The overladen pine branches, every now and then
dropping a clump of snow with a soft thud. The wind,
whipping the snow against their faces, into their eyes. The
fresh snow underfoot, making every step upward more
difficult than the last. The small yellow arrows visible on
the leeward sides of tree trunks, pointing the way to the
hut. The hiking trail two feet wide and sometimes so steep
that you climbed over exposed tree roots and rocks like
going up a flight of stairs.

Matt had debated remaining in the Peugeot for the
night. Warm and secure with five of them in it, perhaps
enough gas to keep the heater going—it had been tempting. But drifts had already reached the height of the door
handles and if the blizzard kept up, they might be buried
under ten feet of snow by morning.

They had waited a few minutes, Claudia thrusting a
small white pill into her father's mouth, getting it under
the tongue while he sat there, hunched over, his eyes
looking at her and his lips working but saying nothing, his
face a dirty-gray color. And then the pill worked its small
temporary miracle; nitroglycerine, Matt thought, to dilate
the constricted blood vessels, and in a few moments he
was talking calmly to Claudia in a weak voice, in Russian,
and even smiling. He looked at Matt.

"You are Mr. Olds? Of course, I recognize the face,
always at the right hand of your President. The National
Security man, yes." His mouth made a bitter turned-down
crescent. "Tell me, was it in the interests of national

186

security to rush me out of town and leave my daughter behind?"

Matt looked sharply at Al Cash, who was a stoop-shouldered man of about thirty.

Cash shrugged. "Mr. Stoughton's orders," he said.

But then Nikolai Ivanovich relented. The eyes behind the heavy-rimmed glasses twinkled. "Tell me, Mr. Olds. Do you know a nice hotel around here? We'll want a suite, naturally, and a good view of the mountains."

"I know just the ticket," Matt said.

"The Ambassador's hut, of course. Can we make it?"

"We'd better get started, sir. There's not much daylight left."

Claudia helped her father into the anorak, zipping it for him. Burt East went back to the Volkswagen for the loaded rucksack, slung it on his back, and got the thumbs of his gloved hands under the straps. "I guess we don't have to lock up," he said. "I hear the natives around here are honest."

"How far is it?" Claudia asked Matt while Al Cash helped her father from the car.

"A few kilometers, that's all."

She winced. "He won't make it, not steep like that. Sometimes it hits him going up a flight of stairs, just an ordinary flight of stairs. A few kilometers—that's the distance from the earth to the moon for him."

"We'll get him there," Matt said. They assembled, Burt East first, then Claudia, then Matt with her father's arm draped across his shoulder, and Al Cash bringing up the rear. The bumper of the Peugeot was at the very end of the cattle track. It simply stopped there. A faded yellow arrow on a pine trunk pointed the way upward through the trees.

They began to climb.

Nikolai Ivanovich managed a hundred yards, most of his weight on Matt's shoulder, and then his legs crumpled and Matt had to keep him from falling. The knuckles of one clenched fist were digging at his chest. Almost falling, he had lost his glasses. Claudia found them in the snow. She worked another pill into his mouth. Her face looked stricken.

"He can't," she said. "I told you he can't."

Burt East had quickly slipped off the rucksack. Nikolai

Ivanovich was sitting on it, breathing in little shallow gasps.

They waited five minutes. It grew noticeably colder. An hour at most, Matt thought, then absolute darkness.

"I'm taking him back to the car," Claudia said.

Matt shook his head. "It'll drift over. Shut the engine and you'll freeze. Keep it on and you'll die of monoxide poisoning."

"I'm taking him back. I've got to."

Matt didn't argue with her. Instead he got down on one knee in front of her father, lifted him, draped him in a fireman's carry across his shoulder, and heaved himself upright.

They began climbing again. Nikolai Ivanovich was a dead weight that pushed Matt's boots deeper into the snow. Once he almost fell sideways. Cash caught him, steadied him. After a few minutes Burt East took over, then Cash, then Matt again.

Half an hour later they had reached timberline. Above them was a snow-covered moonscape, rock-strewn and barren. It was snowing harder.

5   The Russian had seen their car drive by.

He had almost poked his head above the splintered guardrail when he heard the sound of the motor. He waited. The left side of his chest was on fire. Every time he breathed a red-hot needle went through him. Ribs broken, he thought. More than one. He could smell the car's exhaust before the wind swept it away. They were going up. Slowly. He did not know where they were going, or how far it was. But if he stayed here he would never survive the night. He climbed slowly up to the cattle track and started walking. Keep moving, he told himself. Stop now and you'll freeze to death.

The others in the car had not survived the crash. They had gone over the edge, plunging thirty meters into a ravine. He had been driving. The steering wheel had done that to his ribs. The seatbelt had kept him from going through the windshield. He had been unconscious. He did not know how long. His wristwatch was smashed, his chest was smashed, his head ached fiercely. In the pocket of his overcoat he had a Luger.

He reached the end of the track, where the two cars were parked, Volkswagen behind the Peugeot. He approached them cautiously. Nobody there. He saw the footsteps beyond them, heading up through the trees.

He looked at the cars, tried the door of the Peugeot. It was not locked, but he had to stamp the drifting snow to open it. He got in, pulled the door shut. It made a solid, satisfying sound. He shut his eyes, let his mind drift. Alma-Ata, where he was born, and the heat of the southern sun in the big market square, and the Chinese look of so many of the people. His family came from Moscow, his father had become a minor functionary of the Kazakhstan Soviet. We Great Russians, his father always said, have a duty, here among the barbarians. . . .

He was out of the car. A duty, here among the barbarians. What an odd way of putting it. He grimaced. It was meant to be a smile. His father, the petty Kazakhstan functionary, was a frustrated poet.

Following the footsteps in the snow, up among the trees, he looked back once longingly at the two cars and kept going.

Soon he reached a place where they had stopped. He could tell from the way the snow had been trampled. He wondered how long they had remained there, wondered if he would overtake them before dark.

6 Burt East wondered what it would be like to freeze to death.

Al Cash led the way now, a dozen yards ahead. He called out, pointing. Another of the yellow arrows, blazed on the leeward side of a boulder. He climbed above it, turning and probably grinning at them confidently, in that way he had, except that Burt East could not see his face. Matt, carrying the Russian Premier again, followed Cash as he plunged ahead through the snow. The girl was at Matt's side.

That Olds is all right, Burt East thought. A desk jockey, who ever would have figured he had all that stamina? If anything, he had carried the stricken man more than his share. The old East legs felt like lead, but there was Matt stalking ahead, the Russian over his shoulder, his head down, his steps unfaltering. He even turned every now and then to give a word of encouragement to the girl, not that she needed any. She seemed as tireless as Matt, her long legs moving in a slow, steady climbing rhythm. Good-looking dame, too. A real beauty. And unless you're miles off the beam, Burt old buddy, there's something between those two. They practically ate each other up with their eyes, back at the chalet.

East plodded after them. They were approaching a high ridgeline. Hell of a time to find out a guy ain't as young as he used to be, Burt East thought, breathing raggedly in the thin air.

The Russian saw them silhouetted fifty meters ahead. They spread out and walked along the ridge, looking for something. One of them shouted and waved his arm. One of them was carrying the inert figure of a man over his shoulder. They came together in a tight group, conferring for a moment, then set out to the left along the ridge.

The Russian took two steps after them, tripped over a snow-covered rock, and fell. He screamed with the sudden new searing pain in his chest, the sound lost in the wild shrieking of the wind. He dragged himself up slowly and ran stumbling toward the ridge, falling twice more, getting up, brushing snow from his eyes. A final spurt and he might reach them. Or else the slow dragging steps, following them through the fading light to nowhere, following them for just a little while longer because falling like that he had used up what was left of his strength.

He fell a fourth time, and after that he went wild. He tore the Luger from his pocket. He yanked the slide back. He was running, the gun in both hands, swinging from side to side, his chest on fire, his right ankle throbbing with pain.

The bastards, he thought. Oh the bastards. They're going to get away. I'm going to die here.

When he was close enough he fired the Luger, still with both hands on it, to steady it.

One of them spun around and was jerked off his feet by an invisible hand and sat down in the snow, facing him.

Burt East felt the hammerblow against his back. It spun him, ripped his feet out from under him, ripped his consciousness out and, when it was back, he had the Magnum in his hand, the big FBI gun, the feebie gun, his buddies in the Secret Service had always called it, kidding him, telling him it was overkill, who needed the tremendous muzzle velocity of the Magnum shell in a handgun, almost forty-five hundred foot-pounds of energy, you weren't expected to shoot elephants, and his back was a vast numbness and he knew he had been not just hit but hit badly, and he heard a shout and saw the man through the snow, downslope, below the ridge, calmly getting ready to fire his automatic again, not really aiming it but pointing it the way you point a finger.

Burt East fired twice, the tremendous recoil of the Magnum knocking him flat on his back. He had enough time left to see that the man was hit, and then he coughed up a hot thick wetness and saw Matt Olds's face and tried to smile up at him before he drowned in his own blood.

Chapter

FIFTEEN

1 They were walking again, north along the ridge. The wind howled across their path, whipped stinging snow against their faces. Once Claudia went down, suddenly, as if a trapdoor had opened under her feet. Matt found her, ten yards below the ridge, floundering waist-deep in a drift. He saw Al Cash, waiting, with her father. He toiled back to the ridge with her. Burt East's big revolver was an unfamiliar weight in his pocket. Cash had insisted that he take it. He did not argue. He was beyond argument, or thinking. That would come later. He remembered Burt East, on his back in the snow, the snow red all around him, dead. Remembered the Russian shot in the face, half his face gone, dead. He had stood there. Cash had said something. He had looked at Cash woodenly. The weight on his shoulder was gone. Cash had taken it. A hand prodded his back. He had begun to walk. Burt East, with that slow grin on the bland freckled face. Burt East, insisting he would never again eat three turkey legs at one sitting. His body would be found next spring, by climbers, when the snow thawed.

He walked, thinking that he was not thinking, telling himself there was warmth and safety up ahead, some-where up ahead, and soon he was aware of a light, a thin beam in the gloom and the falling snow. Al Cash was using the flashlight. It danced this way and that. It flashed on something and went past and swept back, and by then he had reached Al Cash and saw the post sticking out of a snowdrift, and the arrow-shaped sign that said TEUFEL-KOPF HÜTTE—500 meters.

2 The Devil's Head Hut was two stories high and larger than he had expected. He could just make out the rough stone façade, the weathered wood of the side walls, a pair of chimneys. The recessed windows and the door were boarded up for the winter.

Al Cash went around one side of the hut while Matt left Claudia and her father under the protection of the balcony over the front door and went around the other side. They met in back near a great wedge-shaped cairn of rocks tapering away from the hut, an avalanche-break. Raw pine planks had been nailed over all the windows and the rear door.

They looked at each other. Cash shrugged and scrambled up the cairn of rocks with the flashlight. Matt could hear him stamping around on the roof. Soon he came back down.

"Nothing," he said.

They trudged back around one side of the hut. The windows on the ground floor were low. Matt attacked the pine boards with his hands. He couldn't budge them. They might as well have been part of the wood siding.

Al Cash smiled suddenly and went around behind Matt, his hands working at the buckles of the rucksack. He took out the can opener, still smiling, and worked the handle under one of the planks. His hand twisted and the smile became a grimace. He showed Matt the can opener. The handle had been snapped neatly in two.

Again they looked at each other. The chimneys meant a stove, a fireplace, the boarded windows meant protection from the wind. They would be secure in there, they could wait out the storm in the hut—all the amenities, even including the usual gingerbread balcony over the front door. It was too ironic.

The balcony.

Matt climbed the rocks of the avalanche-break, finding footholds and handholds through the snow. He reached the rear of the pitched roof and walked crouching onto it. The snow, almost knee-deep, supported him and gave him

192

balance as he moved ahead slowly along the slope of the roof. There was just enough light left to see the footprints Al Cash had left, a ragged circle as far as the second, larger chimney.

Matt reached the front of the roof. He looked down past the overhanging eave. A five-foot drop, maybe six, but the roof projected further out than the balcony. He stamped back and forth at the edge, trampling the snow hard. Crouching, he turned, let his legs dangle and eased his weight over. When his hands started to slip he swung his legs inward and let go. He dropped onto the balcony and reeled back against the railing, almost going over. Claudia called out and he shouted down to her reassuringly.

Recessed into the wall were a door and two windows. The door was locked. Both windows were shuttered but not boarded. When he kicked hard at one of them with his heavy hiking boot the wood splintered. He kicked again, and it gave.

No glass in the window. He groped his way over the sill. A floorboard creaked underfoot and he stumbled against something soft. He struck a match, saw a mattress on the floor in the brief flare of light. He walked carefully, arms outstretched in the darkness like a sleepwalker. He stopped, lit another match, cupping the flame in his hand. Another mattress, a wall, upright beams supporting the low ceiling, and on each beam a hook and hanging from each hook a blanket. He reached a door, not locked. A staircase going down. He took it one step at a time and reached the ground floor. He collided with a table.

He carefully lit another match, shielding it. He saw a large room, the walls bare wood. There were three plank tables, chairs of rough-hewn lumber, a huge cast-iron stove with a chimney pipe, a shelf behind the stove with a few battered pots and pans, a great stone fireplace across the room. The front door would be behind him. The match burned his fingers and went out. He lit another one. Ahead and to the left was a doorway. He went in there. To the right, a water closet, the door partially ajar. Beyond it, a small room. Firewood, neatly stacked, an ax protruding from one log, awaiting next year's hikers.

He worked the ax free and went with it to the front door. He unbolted the door, swung it in, called out a warning and set to work on the pine planking.

3 Matt was seated in front of the fireplace, boots off, legs stretched out, socks steaming, trying to operate the walkie-talkie. He had pulled papers out of the flue, heaped them, fetched tinder and logs. Flames were roaring up the chimney.

He had gone upstairs with Al Cash, carried a mattress and two blankets down for Nikolai Ivanovich. They had dragged the mattress near the fireplace. Nikolai Ivanovich had fallen asleep immediately.

All Matt could get from the walkie-talkie was static. He gave up after a while. He took a long swallow of Cognac and felt it burning all the way down. Claudia had found some old jars to use as glasses. She had also found three lamps and a can of kerosene. One lamp stood on each table, its wick trimmed low, the ruddy light making the large downstairs room seem snug and cheerful. Al Cash had removed the cast-iron stove lids and piled wood inside. Now the lids were back on and beginning to glow a dull cherry-red. The damp chill was off the air. In a little while it would be warm, really warm.

Claudia was heating soup at the stove, two cans of it with a pail of snow for water. She found a red and white checkered cloth, covered one of the tables with it. At first Matt didn't know what it reminded him of, but then he remembered the restaurant in Geneva. She even found a couple of candles, lit them, let the wax drip on heavy chipped plates, set the candles on the plates and the plates on the table. Matt watched her as she moved efficiently from stove to table. Her long dark hair was caught up in back and hung in a ponytail. The firelight played on the angles and curves of her face, highlighting the fine high cheekbones, making her eyes glow.

She took a cup of steaming soup to her father, and woke him. His face had a little color now, but the large myopic eyes looked vague and vulnerable without the glasses. Claudia spoke softly in Russian. Her father's lips parted, his mouth worked, he swallowed soup.

Matt blinked. It was hard just keeping his eyes open. Then he was aware that Claudia had joined him and Al Cash at the table.

"He's sleeping. He's going to be all right."

Matt passed her a bowl of soup. Their hands touched. Her dark eyes met and held his and it was almost as if they asked the question neither of them was ready to put into words yet—Do you feel it? Do you feel it, too?

194

4 An hour later Matt sat on the edge of a bare mattress, smoking a cigarette. He couldn't sleep. He was overtired and his mind moved back and forth like a shuttle: The President waiting in Geneva, Whitney Stoughton in Gstaad, Malinin, Red Army troops in Yugoslavia, the walkie-talkie not working, Claudia sleeping so close that he could lean over and touch her.

He went silently to the door and opened it a crack. It was still snowing hard. He shut the door and heard Claudia sigh in her sleep. He stood over her. A lustrous strand of dark hair was down over one cheek. In the firelight he could see it moving slightly each time she breathed. She sighed again, one clenched hand going to her cheek, her eyes shutting more tightly, her lips clamping shut. He wondered what she was dreaming, wished he could comfort her. Then the moment passed. The tension left her face and she was sleeping deeply again.

Matt lit one of the kerosene lamps, turning the wick low. It threw his elongated shadow across the floor as he padded toward the storeroom. Firewood, he decided, looking at the pine stacked against the wall, would be no problem. They had enough for two days, maybe three, and even if the storm lasted longer than that, they could use the plank tables, the chairs, the wide floorboards if necessary. Food was something else again. Enough for two days, if they rationed it carefully. And if the storm didn't stop conveniently in two days?

Beyond the stacked pine was a bedroom, hardly more than a monk's cell, with the only real bed in the place, some empty shelves against one wall, a small shuttered window. Opposite the shelves a tattered topographical map was tacked to the wall. A red circle had been drawn around the flag that represented the Teufelkopf Hütte, and around the circle, also in red, a childishly drawn starburst. The unknown caretaker, Matt thought, alone at night, giving himself and his isolated world some meaning. This is where I am. I will mark it. The center of the universe.

Altitude, the topographical map said, three thousand meters. Just short of ten thousand feet.

Matt heard a sound behind him.

"Can't you sleep either?" Claudia said.

"I thought I'd take stock of things. There's plenty of wood. Food could be a problem, though. It depends how long we're here. How's your father?"

"Sleeping like a baby. The change will be amazing in the morning. You'll see."

They stared at each other in silence.

"You ought to get some sleep yourself," Claudia said. "But I'm glad you're awake. I wanted to apologize."

"What for?"

"The tablecloth, the candles. To celebrate that we were alive. It was foolish." She waved a hand vaguely. "Down there, he was your friend."

Matt said nothing for a moment. Then he nodded. "He was my friend."

"I'm sorry."

"No. You did exactly the right thing."

Claudia sat down on the edge of the bed. "What a sheltered life I've led. I'm my age and yet I've never seen a man die. I was having nightmares. It could have been my father. That's what I thought, when he died. That I was glad it wasn't my father."

"That's only natural," Matt told her.

"Was he married?"

"No."

"But he had loved ones?"

"I guess so."

"Such selfishness!" Claudia said. "The world needs Nikolai Ivanovich now. But I wasn't thinking that. Only that he was my father. I hate myself for it."

"Don't be so hard on yourself," Matt said.

"What's going to happen now?"

"The Swiss. They'll send help when the storm stops."

"Yes? And will my father go to America? Will I go with him?"

She was on her feet again, close in front of him. The room was so small there was barely room for the bed and for the two of them standing there.

"I don't want to be rescued. I need more time." She looked down at the floor and spoke so softly he could hardly hear the words. "When your friend died, there was something else. I was glad it wasn't my father lying there in the snow." She looked at him defiantly for an instant, and then her eyes fell. "And I was glad it wasn't you."

"You knew me," he said harshly, not understanding his own anger. "You didn't know him."

Again the defiant look. "Two hours in a restaurant," she said. "Can you know someone in two hours? Can he become that important?"

Then Matt understood his anger. How had the President put it? *Does the daughter like you, too? It's a place to start. Andreyev won't just open up to you.*

He felt tired and cynical. Not this night, he thought. And maybe not any night.

"What's the matter?"

"Nothing," he said. "Why don't we get some sleep?"

"No, what is it?"

"I told you it's nothing."

"I'm sorry. What did I do?"

"You didn't do anything," he said wearily.

Her lips quirked. "We sound like lovers arguing about nothing, or about everything. But we're not lovers. I wish—"

That, he thought, is going to stop right there. "How old are you, Claudia?" he asked, very fatherly.

The question surprised her. "How old? I'm twenty-six."

"And I'm thirty-eight. I had a wife, I have a son. You're just a kid yourself."

"I'm not a 'kid.' Georgian women mature early," she said. "Besides, thirty-eight isn't old. In Georgia they say a man needs a first love to appreciate a second. The first fades, like a summer storm. The second lasts."

Just how, he thought, did we get into this?

"In Georgia," he said, searching for a way out. He smiled.

"Why do you smile?"

"I always think of the other Georgia. It's not my favorite place."

"You would like my Georgia. The mountains are high. Like the Alps. Higher. In the spring, when the snow melts, wild flowers cover the slopes like a carpet. I can't believe I'll never return." Her face looked pained then. After a while she asked him, "Where were you born?"

"Santa Fe, New Mexico."

"Mexico?"

"New Mexico. It's a state."

"Is it beautiful?"

"It's stark and savage, almost a desert. Real Indian country."

"Yes, I read about that. You keep the Indians on reservations. It's not fair."

"No, it's not fair."

"People should be free. But they're not, anywhere."

"My father spent his life working with the Indians. Trying to help them."

"He must have been a good man."

"He always wanted to do more than he could. He was never really happy."

"To be happy is to strive. For something you believe in."

"Maybe," Matt said.

"Is your father still alive?"

"No," Matt said, and then, to his surprise, he began talking about it. His father had worked for the Bureau of Indian Affairs, as a teacher and as a one-man employment agency for the Hopi Indians who lived on their reservation outside Santa Fe.

Some of them had real talent, he believed, real brains, real ability. These became his special charges, and he pulled strings to get them college scholarships. He became a fixture, when he wasn't on the reservation, in the tidy air-conditioned offices of the new khaki-colored adobe State House. He rarely made a mistake about his students. He was proud of his work in those days, and the drinking was no problem.

Then Washington sent its glib young civil servants to New Mexico to fight the battle of the Pueblos, twentieth-century style. They took a rather more arithmetic approach. There were so many bodies on the reservation, they said. For each body, you found a job. Equal opportunity, demonstrated in press releases by the number of cogs you fit into the machine. The machine was building superhighways and suburban developments, repairing and selling used cars, putting up and staffing shopping centers. So a young Hopi who should have been designing irrigation projects or bridges worked on a construction crew. Another, who could breathe life into a blueprint, who understood the high mesa country and the sort of civic planning that wouldn't make a neon wasteland of it, found himself digging fill for a new cloverleaf turn. They worked, they ate, they got drunk on Saturday night, and the clever, well-meaning reformers from Washington, without malice, stole their lives.

Maybe in another decade, Mr. Olds, they told the anachronism who was Matt's father. We'll worry about the special cases then. Now just get them work off the reservation. Now we have jobs to fill and bodies to fill them. Why, we've got five times as many Pueblo Indians working in gas stations and garages as we had ten years ago, did you know that? They're pretty good around a car. A Hopi who might have been a poet.

Matt's father was not glib enough or patient enough to defend his position against the cleverly worded, optimistic press releases. He took his work rather than himself seriously, and his way of surrendering was—quietly, steadily, and without any flamboyance—to drink himself to death.

"Anyway," Matt said, "that's what he was like."

"Perhaps," Claudia suggested, "it explains why his son works for the President."

"How's that?"

"You are at the seat of power. Nobody who knows less than you do can come from outside and destroy your work."

Matt thought of Congressional committees, the State Department, the CIA—all the bureaucratic apparatus of Washington that sometimes made him feel as frustrated as Matthew Olds, Sr., had ever felt. But still, in a way, because he was closer to the top, Claudia was right.

"My father was a teacher too, of economics. He was the youngest professor at the University in Tbilisi. It was going to be his life. But then he saw the revolutionary dream betrayed. The life of the people was of no importance to the economic planners in the Kremlin. A country's greatness, they said, depended on how much steel it produced, how many power plants and intercontinental missiles—not on the life of the people. A whole generation under the thumb of the Secret Police, because to defy the steel-eaters was treason. My father left the university in disgust. He entered politics. He's been fighting the steel-eaters ever since. No country, he believes, can become great unless its citizens can aspire to greatness individually." She smiled. "That doesn't sound very Marxist, does it? I told you in Geneva my father was the least doctrinaire man I ever met. He would have understood your father, I think. But he's stubborn, like a Georgian peasant. That's why he's here now. They beat him at home, the steel-eaters. But he'll go on fighting them, any way he can, even if it means destroying himself.

"He has an image of himself as the most sophisticated man in Moscow. He's not. He loves the land. Not the fatherland, but Mother Russia. There's a difference. It's almost a religious feeling. He'd die for it if he had to. Or be called a traitor for it. Or both. But he—expects too

199

much of me. I don't have his strength. Oh, I know what he thinks. He'd never say it. He has enough strength for both of us. All I ever wanted was—I don't know. To be left alone, maybe. To find out who I am. That's not easy, in the Kremlin."

"It's not easy anywhere. Most people don't have time to find out who they are. They have to run as hard as they can just to stay in place."

"That makes it sound like a very ugly world."

"It doesn't have to be. The trouble is, the steel-eaters have been in the driver's seat too long. I don't mean just in Russia. People are getting fed up with the military-industrial complex in the States, too. Eisenhower warned about it back in the sixties. More and more people began to ask questions. What's it all about? Where do we go from here? And they've been turning to men like Clay Huntington and your father for the answers."

He gave her a rueful look. "I'm a great one to talk. The papers call me the most pragmatic man in Washington."

"No, please go on. It's fascinating, what you're saying."

What fascinated him was the fact that she could draw it out, as she had drawn out the memory of his father. With her listening, with those big dark eyes intent on his face, he wanted to open up in a way that he hadn't in years, not even to Tracy in their good days.

"Maybe the papers are right," he said. "If you spend your life manipulating people and playing with forces nobody really understands, you're bound to get hard-headed. And a little cynical, too."

"You don't understand yourself at all," Claudia told him. "You're not cynical. You're just like a Georgian. Sometimes you take yourself too seriously. And sometimes you don't take yourself seriously enough." Then she said with the sort of feminine logic Matt would never understand: "I wish I'd known you when you were a little boy," and "Is it still snowing? I want to see the snow."

So he took her upstairs, leading the way with the kerosene lamp through the dormitory, past the bare mattresses on the floor and the beams that supported the low ceiling, and he opened the door to the sudden cold of the balcony.

The falling snow, so thick now that it seemed to fill the air, looked black in the dull-orange glow of the lamp. Snow stood two feet deep on the balcony railing.

Claudia, hands on hips and head uptilted, breathed

deeply. "You can smell it," she said, and Matt could—the clean cold scent of winter.

They stood without speaking on the balcony. Snow dusted Claudia's hair. Her eyes were closed, her lips parted in a smile of delight. A gust of wind whipped her long hair about her face, and when she turned to Matt like that he took a single step forward and said, "I couldn't get you out of my mind all week," and parted the hair with his hands and kissed her.

Her lips were cold and tasted of the snow. He kissed her again, and her hands were hard on his back, pulling him close, away from the storm, away from Geneva and Yugoslavia and a body lying in the snow.

"It's cold out here. Aren't you cold?"

"Yes," he said, and got the lamp, and backed through the doorway with her, their hips bumping awkwardly as he kicked the door shut.

5 For the footballer Leonid Bayev it was like a vision.

There had been the cold, and the darkness, and the whipping fury of the wind, and the snow that pulled at his legs and tried to drag him down. And then suddenly, hanging suspended beyond the dense swirling flakes he saw light, an orange glow ahead of and above him, and he raised one arm and shouted into the teeth of the wind; the sound of his voice lifted and swept away.

In the light, so close, so clear despite the snow that there could be no mistake, he saw Claudia Nikolaievna.

She was smiling up at a tall man, her face glowing in the light that hung in the air, and she went easily into the man's arms, holding him close so long that Bayev stood in his tracks in the snow, not breathing, not even blinking his eyes. It was like the night visions that Bayev had of Claudia Nikolaievna, her beautiful face suffused with light, with the tall man taking his place as in real life Colonel Malinin had for so long taken his place. And seeing it now, through the blizzard, he cried out in pain for what he could never have, and he shouted her name into the wind, her name becoming the wind, his eyes tightly shut so that he could imagine the lips kissing Claudia Nikolaievna's lips were his own, and when he looked again the light and the vision were gone.

He plodded on toward where they had been. He found

a place where the snow was less deep, found a wall, a door.

He threw himself against the door with the last of his strength.

6 Claudia came into Matt's arms hungrily. He can feel it, she thought, their bodies hard together, the way my heart is beating for him, and then she leaned back against the strong circle of his arms and looked up into his face in the ruddy light of the lantern. His lips were parted, the grooves on either side of his mouth pronounced. She traced the line of his cheek with a trembling finger. She touched the shaggy hair at the nape of his neck and pulled herself close again and said against his throat, "I couldn't get you out of my mind either. No matter what was happening. All week."

He kissed her, holding her face the way he had on the balcony. She could feel everything else start to slide away—her father, Viktor, the storm outside, and the whole waiting world down below. It was like the reckless night they had met, when it was not the world but herself she had wanted to leave behind. She could be Tamara again. She felt tears stinging her eyes.

There had been no tears that night in the hotel with Viktor, she remembered. Then Matt broke into her reverie.

"Hey, you're crying."

She pulled him close, her arms tight around his back. His heart was pounding too, as hard as hers.

With Viktor it was all cold male arrogance and certainty.

"I'm so happy, that's why," she said, but now that she had thought of Viktor it had become necessary to speak the words, and she could feel herself pull a little way back inside herself, seeing Viktor in the hotel room and hearing the rain rattling on the window as he calmly and expertly seduced her in the remembered way, and she knew that nothing else could begin until, finally, that had ended.

She could feel the hardness of Matt against her, demandingly. His hands were strong but gentle. She wanted them all over her. But she drew back, stiffening, and the hands trailed through her long hair and away.

"What's the matter?" Matt said. "What is it?"

"I don't know. Nothing."

"You want me to stop, don't you?"

"No. Yes. I don't know." How could she make him understand?

The hint of a smile touched his lips. "There'll be other times," he told her softly. "We've been through too much. It doesn't have to be tonight."

She did not say anything.

How had Viktor put it? *It makes no difference if it is for the rest of our lives or just one more night. We both want the same thing.*

She looked up at him, so gentle, so grave now but ready to smile, and everything else began to slip away again, even the need to explain that he must be patient with her.

And then Al Cash called from downstairs: "Mr. Olds? You better get down here quick. It looks like we've got some company."

Chapter
SIXTEEN

1   Waiting in the darkness outside the hospital in Saanen, fingering the two plastic sticks of the Okinawan flail in his trenchcoat pocket, Dmitri Trofimovich Moskalenko was jealous.

He wondered who had been sent to Belgrade. The Department of Wet Affairs of the KGB was not large. Pyotr, he thought. But Pyotr had developed that nervous twitch after the royal assassination in Jordan last year, and the rumor on Dzerzhinsky Street was that Pyotr would be reassigned to office work or possibly to the Lubianka prison that was housed in the same building as KGB headquarters. Rodya, perhaps. Plump-faced Rodya with the baby-blue eyes. But Rodya's specialty was the knife, and the President of Yugoslavia had been felled by an assassin's bullet. Grishka, then. Grishka was probably the best marksman in the Department of Wet Affairs of Children's World.

Children's World, Moskalenko thought. The euphemism

for the KGB always amused him. Children's World, because across Dzerzhinsky Street from Lubianka was Detsky Mir, the Children's World department store.

Pyotr, Rodya, or Grishka. One of them had journeyed to Belgrade to assassinate President Ilić while he, Moskalenko, was waiting in the snow, outside the hospital in a picture-postcard Alpine village, to murder a woman.

It wasn't fair.

Moskalenko took pride in his work. He was a specialist with an odd little device, like a gun really, that contained a cyanide capsule. When fired at close range at the victim's face, the capsule dissolved and the cyanide spray was fatal in less than a second. Moskalenko had used the device three times in his career, twice in Berlin and once long ago in New York. He fondled the Okinawan flail again. It was saved for special circumstances, usually inside the Soviet Union. Used with skill it could shatter a skull like the tap of a knife shatters an eggshell. He did not remember how many times he had used it to kill. It was his trademark and its value was the fear it imparted. Be good from now on. Or Moskalenko can get you, too.

He was the second best marksman in the Department of Wet Affairs, after Grishka. He had killed half a dozen times with a rifle, at long range. Unless he was using a powerful scope, the range bothered him. He liked to see the victim's face.

Moskalenko enjoyed his work. He had no family. He had no close friends. He accepted his enthusiasm for work the way a ballet dancer does, or a Hero of Sport. Like them, he had a specialty. His specialty happened to be killing people. Moskalenko was not a complicated man. Soul-searching was foreign to him.

He had brought a Finnish Lion Free rifle to Switzerland. It had a removable stock and a twenty-nine-inch barrel. Assembled, it weighed less than fifteen pounds. The gun case also contained a variable-power hunting scope and a bridge mount. The bridge, which wedded the scope to the rifle for accuracy at long range, was sufficiently light to have no adverse effect on the perfect balance of the Lion Free. It also held the scope solidly enough to keep its zero even after recoil. Using the Finnish Lion Free, Moskalenko usually did his work with a single squeeze of the trigger, but it did not pay to take chances. Once, on a bad day in a rented room overlooking the

Kurfürstendamm in Berlin, he had had to fire three times. The affair might have ended in fiasco, except for the bridge mount.

The cyanide gun, the Okinawan flail, and the Lion Free rifle were Moskalenko's usual stock in trade, but he had rejected all of them for tonight's assignment. The cyanide gun worked best indoors. Outdoors in this wind it would be ineffective. He felt an odd reluctance to use the flail on a woman, not because of any squeamishness—as foreign to Moskalenko as soul-searching—but because it would give him no satisfaction. Satisfaction was very important to him tonight because he was jealous of Pyotr or Rodya or Grishka in Belgrade. The rifle was out because visibility was almost zero in the blizzard, and it was dark.

That left Moskalenko's bare hands.

He would strangle the woman. He had never killed a woman before. It would be an adequate diversion before his really important work could be undertaken.

Let Grishka, if it was Grishka, have his moment in Belgrade. Moskalenko's time would come.

There was a chance that Moskalenko would get to use the Finnish Lion Free rifle yet. Ideally they would want to take the Premier alive, fly him back to Moscow, make much of his mental breakdown. But there was always the possibility it wouldn't work out that way. Thinking of it, Moskalenko could almost feel the smooth cold stock of the Lion Free against his cheek, could almost see the victim through the reticule of the scope, the dot in the tack hole centered on Andreyev's chest.

The President of Yugoslavia was small game compared to Nikolai Ivanovich Andreyev, Chairman of the Council of Ministers of the Soviet Union, Premier of Russia.

Moskalenko wished the woman would come out. He was cold. He removed his gloves and thrust his hands inside his ill-fitting trenchcoat and into his armpits. She had come out once and smoked a nervous cigarette before going back inside. The snowplow operator was busily clearing the car park then, and Moskalenko had remained unmoving in the darkness. Now he wanted to experience the barehanded killing of a woman, but he was impatient, too. He wanted to prepare for bigger game, the biggest game of all.

The woman came out, cupping her hands to light a cigarette.

2 They had wheeled Kermit from surgery to the intensive-care room. They were making no promises, but she thought they were more optimistic after they had set the fractured hip than before. She watched them wheel him past, his body looking pathetically flat under the sheet. They had not used a cast. They had set the hip with a metal pin. A bottle of plasma hung over the movable bed, the clear fluid dripping slowly into an opened vein. They would put him in an oxygen tent. At his age, the doctor said, clucking his tongue, shaking his head, you couldn't be too careful.

Natasha wondered if she wanted him to live. Too much had happened, and she was no longer sure what she felt. She went along the linoleum-tiled corridor toward the door, paused for a moment to gather the mink jacket around her shoulders, and went outside.

A gust of wind sprang up and the snow was like swirling white smoke.

Natasha lit a cigarette. She wondered what the problem could be with the money. A simple transaction, an anonymous deposit in a numbered account in the Union Bank in Geneva. A great deal of money. More than enough so that what happened to Kermit would be of no consequence. She wondered when her contact would come.

Perhaps later, she thought. She had made arrangements to spend the night in the hospital anyway. She turned to go back inside.

"*Grazhdanka.*"

The voice wasn't loud. She could see nothing.

"Where are you?"

"Over here, *grazhdanka.*"

Somewhere in the direction of the snowplow. *Grazhdanka*, she thought. How quaint. Citizeness. She hadn't been called that in years. Just where did they get this country bumpkin?

She waited, but he did not come to her.

"It's about the money, *grazhdanka*," he said.

She threw her cigarette away and walked out from under the protection of the overhang and into the snow.

"What about the money?" she asked impatiently.

He materialized so suddenly in front of her that she almost jumped back. A small man in a trenchcoat two sizes too big for him.

"Could you conceive of any circumstances," he said

with a funny smile, only the mouth smiling, "in which you would not require the money?"

He had thrust his face so close she could smell his breath. She turned her head away. "What are you talking about?"

The small hands emerged like knobby white sticks from the too-long sleeves of the trenchcoat.

"I can," he said. He seemed to be enjoying himself.

"Just what is this?" she demanded.

"If you were dead," he told her, and then the hands fluttered in front of her face and closed on her throat.

She tried to scream. She managed a single squawk. Then all her breath was cut off. She struggled. She tried to kick him. Her own plump hands clawed at the hands fastened on her throat. The face was very close. The lips were parted, the lower lip hanging. The eyes had become slits. She tried to scream again. Deep inside herself she screamed. There was no sound. She ducked her head and butted him. He did not let go. She could feel snow stinging her tongue. The face so close to her own face became blurry. Stop, she tried to say, I don't want the money, stop, you can keep the money, I won't tell, stop, just only please please stop.

And then, incredibly, she was down in the snow, half-buried in a snowbank at the side of the car park, and in a jumble of impressions she heard voices shouting, a car door slamming, footsteps pounding across the hard surface of the car park under its fresh dusting of snow.

They helped her to her feet. A man and a girl. They spoke to her in Schwyzerdütsch. The man had ruddy cheeks. He was young, hardly more than a boy. The girl, even with a large old overcoat wrapped around her, looked very pregnant. An older man appeared, and then she began to make sense of the Schwyzerdütsch.

"He got away," the older man said breathlessly.

"Can you walk?" asked the younger man.

She could walk with the older man's help.

They were inside the hospital. A nurse was expecting them. She beamed at the very pregnant girl. "*Ach*, what a night to have a baby," she said.

3 Moskalenko felt exposed and vulnerable in the glass-walled phonebooth on the railroad-station platform in Gstaad.

The lights of the Bernerhof Hotel across the street beckoned cheerfully. The two agents who had driven up in Moskalenko's car were in there now, having dinner probably. They would have to leave. Moskalenko would have to leave. It had been dark, but the woman might be able to identify him. He wished he had spoken English to her instead of Russian. That had been careless. But who would have dreamed a car would materialize suddenly in the blizzard?

Moskalenko dialed area code 022 and the Geneva number that the Embassy had given him. He heard the phone ringing. What if Gros-Claude wasn't there? Seven rings. Eight. Then:

"Allô?"

"This is Calvin," said Moskalenko, identifying himself. Calvin, he thought. That's really amusing.

"William Tell," said the Swiss Communist Gros-Claude. "What do you mean, calling me? Weren't you enough trouble in Coppet?" He was speaking English, the language he had in common with Moskalenko.

"I need three things," Moskalenko said. "People. A place to hide. And a pilot with a helicopter or a ski-plane."

"People? What kind of people?"

"As many as you can give me. Armed. Experienced."

Gros-Claude's mocking laughter vibrated in the receiver at Moskalenko's ear. "Where do you think you are, Berlin? This is Switzerland."

"All able-bodied Swiss are in the militia, aren't they? An automatic rifle in every household," Moskalenko said reasonably. "Get me people."

"You do not understand the Swiss," Gros-Claude told him testily. "Some of us vote Communist. We're not delighted with American foreign policy. We're not delighted with yours either."

"You take orders from Moscow."

Gros-Claude chuckled. "If you really believe that, you know nothing about the Swiss. 'People,' as you put it, are out. What else did you want?"

"A place to hide. The use of a helicopter or a ski-plane—that can take off in secret."

"A plane? I thought it was snowing up there?"

"It is snowing. I'll need the plane when it stops."

"To do what?" Gros-Claude asked.

Moskalenko said nothing.

"Will the pilot have to break any laws?"

"What kind of agent are you?" Moskalenko exploded.

"I know my own countrymen."

A man carrying a snow shovel over his shoulder like a rifle walked slowly past the phonebooth. He looked in at Moskalenko incuriously.

"A law or two," Moskalenko said contemptuously, "might have to be broken. Can you get me a pilot or can't you?"

"A man named Ruedy Stücki," Gros-Claude said after a while. "Try him."

"Is he one of us?"

Again there was the infuriating sound of Gros-Claude's laughter. "One of us? I'm not even sure *I* am one of us. He is young and reckless, he's a pilot, he owes me a favor, and he will do almost anything for money."

"Can he hide me? Can he hide three of us?"

"That too perhaps. The phone number is four-ten-twenty-nine. Why don't you ask him?"

"And if he refuses?"

"Don't call me again," Gros-Claude said.

It took Moskalenko awhile to realize his question had been answered.

"Listen, if you knew how important this was."

"I don't want to know," Gros-Claude said, and hung up.

The Swiss, Moskalenko thought. No one should have to do business with them. He found a twenty-centime piece in his pocket and dialed the number Gros-Claude had given him.

4 Matt could hear the rattle of the doorlatch as he followed Claudia downstairs to the ground floor of the Teufelkopf Hütte. He looked questioningly at Al Cash, who stood to one side of the door. The fire had burned down to a bed of glowing embers, but the room was warm. Nikolai Ivanovich was still asleep near the hearth. The doorlatch rattled again. Cash had a gun in his hand.

"Get over near your father," he told Claudia. She looked at Matt and obeyed.

"Open it when I tell you to," Cash instructed Matt. "Then get behind it. All right?"

Matt nodded. "Now," Cash said, and Matt pulled the bolt and yanked the door in hard, moving with it as it swung toward the right. A blast of cold air hit him. Cash moved with deceptive slowness, one arm and shoulder out and then back, and a man came hurtling in, stumbling, sliding on the floor, knees bumping, head bumping.

Cash stood over him and said, "Don't get up just yet," a lazily spoken command that was hardly necessary. The man was barely conscious. He lay where Cash had flung him, face down, his head covered with snow, his coat covered with snow, his breathing labored. He groaned and his right hand scrabbled at the floor and he began to cough. Cash kneeled near him and patted pockets and stood up with a gun in each hand. Every movement, every gesture, every word Cash had spoken was stylized and understated, as if, Matt thought, he did this sort of thing two or three times every night.

Matt went back across the room for the kerosene lamp. He adjusted the wick high while Cash shut the door. The man on the floor sat up. His bare hands were red. His face was red except for the tip of his nose and an area the size of a quarter over each cheekbone. These were bone-white. His mournful eyes stared up at them. He was shaking and still coughing. The eyes softened when he saw Claudia.

"Comrade Bayev," she said.

The footballer Leonid Bayev just looked at her.

"KGB?" Al Cash asked.

"He was my bodyguard."

Bayev began to talk haltingly in Russian. He couldn't stop shaking. Several times he gestured toward the door. Claudia's eyes became hard and then uncertain and then not hard. She looked from Bayev to Matt and back again. She said, "Colonel Malinin's out there. Not far. He hurt his leg."

Claudia got a bottle of Cognac and a glass. Bayev had to hold the glass in both hands. It clicked against his teeth. He drank and looked up at Claudia gratefully.

Al Cash looked at Matt doubtfully. "Who the hell knows how long we'll be stuck up here? Maybe one extra Russian is all we ought to handle," he said. "And we've already got one."

Claudia said, "If you leave him out there that would be the same as murdering him."

Al Cash did not deny that. He shrugged and waited for Matt to speak.

Five of them, now, to share what little food they had. Malinin would make six.

The decision Cash wanted him to make was callous, Matt realized, but not unreasonable. Cash was no amateur. One way a professional stayed alive was by avoiding trouble.

Matt could think of no reason in favor of rescuing Malinin. Except that he was a human being, and his life was in danger, and they could save him.

"Where's the flashlight?" he said.

He found his boots and put them on. Their fleece linings felt warm and almost dry. He shrugged into his coat. Al Cash brought him the flashlight. "I hope to hell you know what you're doing."

Matt belted his coat.

"You got that gun?"

The gun, Matt said, was still in his coat pocket.

"On your feet, pal," Cash told Bayev, but the Russian needed assistance. Cash helped him up and toward the fire. He came back. "I'll go if you want. Comrade Bayev won't be giving us any trouble."

"No. I'll get him."

Claudia looked at Matt. "Be careful," she said. "Be careful, Matt." She wanted to say more, but he opened the door and was outside.

Chapter
SEVENTEEN

1 *One by one, reports reached Bern from the meteorological stations in the high Alpine country of the Bernese Oberland, the Valais, and the Grisons.*

The reports were not optimistic. By noon on Sunday, 30 November, the first real snowstorm of the season was still blanketing the mountainous spine of Switzerland. The intensity of snowfall was measured, at Les Diablerets near Gstaad, at four centimeters per hour. It was even greater at the Jungfrau station to the east. It tapered off to three at the Simplon Pass and at Andermatt. Farther east in the Grisons, reports from the high stations at Davos and St.

Moritz indicated an intensity just under three centimeters per hour.

When snow falls at the rate of two and a half centimeters per hour it piles up too fast to settle stably. There is then the danger of avalanche. This danger increases when the water content of the snow exceeds ten percent, a common condition if the air temperature rises toward the freezing point. By noon on Sunday the air temperature had climbed to twenty-eight degrees Fahrenheit at Les Diablerets and the percentage of water in the falling snow stood at more than eighteen.

The wind remained gusty, seeming to blow from all points of the compass at once. Its force was rarely less than twenty miles per hour. At fifteen miles per hour or more, the action of wind further increases the probability of avalanche.

At Les Diablerets, at the Jungfrau, the Simplon Pass, Andermatt, Davos, and St. Moritz, the penetrometers and the precipitation- and snowfall-intensity gauges continued to record their findings.

Shortly after noon Bern issued the first avalanche warnings. The danger was slight in the eastern part of the country, moderate in the mountains of the Valais, and acute in the Bernese Oberland.

All day Sunday the snow kept falling.

2 Below two thousand feet it was raining—a heavy cold, pelting rain that reduced visibility at Cointrin Airport in Geneva to zero. On Sunday morning a few flights had taken off. None had landed. Incoming flights were rerouted south of the Alps to Milan, where the weather was bright, sunny, and unseasonably warm. By noon Sunday no flights were taking off. Landing remained out of the question.

Shortly after noon Cointrin radar picked up the blip of an incoming aircraft. Radio contact was soon established.

The plane was a JAT Caravelle, en route from Belgrade. JAT, the Yugoslav national airline, had no regularly scheduled service to Geneva that day.

"JAT special flight zero-zero-one requests clearance to land," the radio voice said in English, the language of commercial aviation.

"What are you doing here, JAT zero-zero-one?" demanded the Cointrin tower.

"JAT flight zero-zero-one requests clearance to land," came the answer.

The radar blip showed that the Caravelle had made a pass over the airport and was banking to come back over the ridges of the Jura Mountains.

"Negative," said the tower. "We're closed here. Milan is your nearest alternate. Repeat: Negative."

"We're making an instrument approach," said JAT zero-zero-one.

"Negative!" shouted the tower.

"See you in court," said JAT zero-zero-one. The American idiom mollified the Cointrin tower personnel somewhat. If the JAT flight crew had been trained in the States, perhaps they would actually be able to bring the big jet in.

A moment later the roar of its twin jet engines could be heard.

Cointrin tower switched on the runway lights and called for emergency procedures.

3 On the terrace of the Bundeshaus in Bern, a lone figure marched back and forth in the rain. Trenchcoat and hat were sodden. He was sodden. The rain came down steadily and drearily, from slate-gray clouds that seemed to hang a few meters above the dome of the Parliament building. The usually fine view from the rocky promontory in the Old Town to the high mountains of the Oberland could not be seen. The Aare River just below the Parliament building could not be seen. Perhaps, the man thought, pacing stolidly back and forth, if he crossed his eyes he might be able to see the tip of his nose. Just barely.

He had a long nose and jowls like a rooster's wattles and a twenty-year habit of pacing on the terrace of the Bundeshaus, whatever the weather, when he had a problem. He was called, usually with affection, the Watchman. His name was Willy Müllener, and he was the Federal Minister of Justice and Police.

Like everyone else in Switzerland, he had followed the newspaper speculation on the whereabouts of the Soviet Premier. And he had wondered all last week—just wondered, because he had not believed it would happen— what he would do if Premier Andreyev really wanted to

213

defect and as a first step had gone underground somewhere in Switzerland.

Then late last night, the *gendarmerie* of the Commune of Saanen had called Bern. Federal Minister of Justice and Police Willy Müllener had been summoned from his home in Nydeggstalden to police headquarters in the former orphanage. He had spent the night there in conference and, after breakfast, had walked through the rain across the Old Town to the Bundeshaus. Another conference, with the seven members of the Federal Council hastily assembled. The President of the Confederation had deferred, was still deferring, to Willy Müllener. The governmental machinery, the federal police, and the army were at Müllener's disposal, if he wanted to use them.

Willy Müllener almost wished he had retired last year, as he could have.

It was an impossible problem.

Either, as the wife of the former American Ambassador to the Soviet Union claimed, Premier Andreyev had spent the night in the Teufelkopf Hütte, or he hadn't.

If he hadn't, and you acted on the assumption that he had, you would be branded a fool.

If he had, and you acted on the assumption that he hadn't, you would be branded an imbecile.

The one thing you couldn't do was pace back and forth on the terrace of the Bundeshaus doing nothing.

Personnel of the Soviet KGB, here in Switzerland in considerable strength for the Summit, would move as soon as the storm stopped.

If, that is, their Premier really was stranded in the Teufelkopf Hütte.

Personnel of the American CIA, if they thought there was a chance the Soviet Premier would defect to them, would also move.

The implications were obvious.

The mountains of the Oberland, eighty kilometers south of the terrace of the Bundeshaus, might become a battleground.

Willy Müllener, pacing in the rain, sneezed explosively. His eyes smarted and his throat felt raw. He was coming down with a cold.

He ducked under the protection of the arcade on the curving south façade of the Bundeshaus, entered the building, sneezed again, walked across the marble floor of

214

the rotunda, and took an elevator to the third floor, where the President of the Swiss Confederation was waiting.

"Catching cold, Willy?" the President of the Confederation asked. He offered a bottle of Williamine and two glasses, and Müllener drank the pear liqueur gratefully, feeling its warmth spread inside him. He removed his coat. His dark suit was just as sodden.

"We will inform several members of the press," Willy Müllener said finally, "that a usually reliable source close to the Bundesrat believes the Soviet Premier is in the Teufelkopf Hütte."

"Is that wise?"

"No," said Willy Müllener. "Whatever we do is not wise. But we have to do something. The Russians and Americans may show some restraint if they know the world is watching."

"That's possible," said the President of the Confederation in a not particularly enthusiastic voice.

"Keep the Air Rescue Service on standby," said Willy Müllener. "Nobody will come down from there on foot after that storm."

The President of the Confederation nodded.

"Inform the Russian Foreign Minister and the American Secretary of State that Andreyev is entitled to, and will have, the protection of Swiss law."

"Don't you read the newspapers? The Russians claim Premier Andreyev is mentally ill."

"That doesn't matter. He is on Swiss soil. He is entitled to the full protection of Swiss law."

The President of the Confederation said, "You really believe that, don't you?"

"Don't you?"

"Yes. Yes, I suppose I do," said the President of the Confederation. "Very well, I'll tell them. Anything else?"

"Yes," said Willy Müllener, and the President waited.

"Alert the army," Willy Müllener said.

4 The President of the United States, in Geneva, was having problems, too.

He swung away from the rain sluicing down the window of the sitting room in the Presidential Suite in the Hotel Beau Rivage and faced his unexpected guest. "Now let's get this straight, Colonel Sumozja," he said. "You're commander of the Yugoslav Army Group in the area between Belgrade and the Hungarian border?"

"In the Voivodina, yes," the little man said in good English. "I have shown you my credentials, Excellency." The little man did not look like a colonel or the commander of anything. Sprawled exhaustedly in a Regency chair, he was wearing a gray sweater and baggy black trousers. His eyes were bloodshot. His gray hair was wild and his broad face sagged wearily from lack of sleep.

"And you claim you represent the new C-in-C of the Yugoslav Army, a Colonel Hamović?"

Colonel Sumozja nodded earnestly.

"What happened to your generals?"

Colonel Sumozja's face contorted contemptuously, almost as if he were going to spit on the floor. "They were too friendly with the Russians. They have been imprisoned. Things are happening in Yugoslavia, Excellency."

"I have only your word on that," President Huntington said reasonably.

Colonel Sumozja shrugged.

"You flew here on a commercial flight."

"Not exactly a scheduled flight," Sumozja said, almost smiling.

"But not an Air Force flight?"

"The Air Force is behind Colonel Hamović and the new All-People's Army," Sumozja said. "But we simply couldn't spare a military aircraft, not under the circumstances. I'm sure you can appreciate that."

The President inserted a cigarette in his stubby black holder, lit it, and blew a plume of smoke, scowling through it at Colonel Sumozja. Yugoslav Defense Minister Cvetković, Whitney Stoughton had said, was a Russian puppet, but from regimental level on down we could rely on the Yugoslav Army. Sumozja's rank would have made him, before the coup—if there had been a coup—a regimental officer.

"What's on your mind?" the President asked.

"In all the Voivodina," the tired little man said, "from Belgrade north to the Hungarian border, what defenses did we have? A few scattered detachments of badly equipped militiamen and a handful of customs guards. The Red Army could have punched through to Belgrade in twelve hours, to the Adriatic coast in twenty-four." A small hand rubbed Colonel Sumozja's face, as if trying to keep the weary flesh from sagging further. "We are moving mechanized units in now, but they will not reach the Voivodina in time."

Here it comes, the President thought. They want help, and I can't give it to them until we know what the Russians are really up to. He looked at the tired, earnest, pleading face. How can I tell him that? he wondered. How can I turn him down?

"Your CIA," the little man said, "assured us last week that five American airborne divisions could be landed in Yugoslavia within twenty-four hours. Colonel Hamović was grateful. I was grateful, Excellency. It gave us the courage to depose Defense Minister Cvetković and his generals. Still, the Red Army could cut through our defenses like a hot knife through butter."

"I wish—" the President began, but a small anxious hand fluttered and Sumozja was speaking again.

"They haven't."

"What?" the President said.

"The Red Army. They crossed the border at Szeged on Friday. A single battalion. There was no resistance. They could have sent in more troops, could have reached Belgrade by now. Instead they dug in just across the border. They are not moving."

"We know that," said the President.

"This is very embarrassing, Excellency," Sumozja said. "We appreciate the assurances given us by your CIA. As I said, it made the coup possible."

"I hope you're aware," the President said slowly, "that the operation outlined by the CIA was just a contingency plan. A final decision on its implementation rests with me."

"Of course, Excellency," Sumozja said eagerly.

"You said yourself that the Red Army isn't moving. It would be a tragic thing for your country if we landed troops to—"

"Our fear was that you would honor the commitment prematurely."

"—fight what may turn out to be a phony invasion. *What did you say?*"

"The last thing we want is a war between Russia and the United States on Yugoslav soil."

They looked at each other, the President of the United States and the tired Yugoslav colonel.

Both began to smile.

Sumozja said, "I'm sorry, do you mind?" He was laughing. "Forgive me, forgive me." He could not stop laughing. Tears were streaming down his face.

"I thought you were going to ask for troops," the President said.

"I was afraid you would insist on sending them," Sumozja said.

He took out a large red-bordered handkerchief and mopped the tears from his cheeks. "For some reason the Red Army is stalling."

"We think we know why," the President said. "There's a very good chance there won't be an invasion at all."

Sumozja continued to mop his face.

"Colonel," the President said, "I think you need a drink."

An hour later President Huntington was having lunch with Sumozja and General Laffont. Miss Priscilla Lee buzzed from her office down the hall.

"I'm sorry to disturb you, sir. Dr. Nancy wants to see you when you have a moment. She says it's important. A call from Washington."

A call from Washington to Dr. Nancy Padgett had to mean Gigi, and the baby. "Where is she?"

"Her room."

"I'll be right there. Excuse me, gentlemen," the President said, getting up. Neither Laffont nor Sumozja seemed to mind his departure. They were busily discussing one of Tito's classic guerrilla campaigns against the Nazis.

Dr. Nancy Padgett, the President's physician, in her thirties and in a smartly tailored tweed suit, removed her granny glasses and said, "They took Gigi to Walter Reed about an hour ago."

"What is it?"

"There's been an unexpected complication. Nothing Dr. Rutherford could have foreseen," Dr. Nancy added quickly, her usually pert face looking troubled.

"Is it serious?"

"It requires intensive care."

"I said is it serious?"

Dr. Nancy nodded slowly. "It could be. It's too early to tell. Here, let me show you."

She got pencil and paper and quickly sketched a uterus

218

with fetus nestled snugly in it toward the bottom and placenta above attached by the umbilical cord.

"This is the normal position of the fetus just prior to delivery," she explained. "The cervix begins to flatten and stretch out." She sketched that too. "Delivery is then imminent, and normal if it looks like this. Once in a long, long while it surprises even the best of gynecologists, which Dr. Rutherford is, and looks like this." Dr. Nancy was sketching again, showing a uterus with the fetus high and the placenta over the stretched cervix.

"Okay, okay, never mind the bedside manner," the President said irritably. "I know Rutherford is good. How dangerous is it?"

Dr. Nancy raised a cool eyebrow at him. "Sorry," the President said, and she continued:

"The unnatural position is called *placenta praevia*. The placenta will then, without warning, pull away from the cervical opening, rupture blood vessels, and cause hemorrhaging. They're giving Gigi whole blood now, and preparing her for a Caesarean."

"Is it dangerous?"

"It happened without warning. She's lost a lot of blood."

"They're operating now?"

"Soon."

"Can I phone her?"

"She's not conscious."

"God," the President said.

Dr. Nancy looked at him. "At a time like this, I know. Can I give you something, sir? A sedative?"

"No, no. Can you keep the line open to Walter Reed?"

"It is open."

They both looked at the telephone on Dr. Nancy's desk. She picked it up. "Howard?" she said. "I've got the President here. Yes, all right, I see." She put the phone down. "They're taking her into surgery right now."

"What are her chances?"

There was a long silence. "She's lost a lot of blood."

"I asked you what her chances were."

And Dr. Nancy stopped hedging at last. "No better than fifty-fifty," she said.

219

Chapter
EIGHTEEN

1 Viktor Malinin looked down the length of his leg at his right foot. The trouser leg had been rolled halfway up his calf. The ankle and foot, bare, were swollen almost twice their normal size. There was just a dull ache unless he tried to move the foot. He could put no weight on it at all.

It had been clever of the Americans last night, he thought, to carry him up here to the second floor of the hut. He looked around the large room at the mattresses on the floor, the blankets hanging on hooks, the patterns of daylight coming in through the intricately designed shutters. He was as helpless as a baby.

They had taken his watch, and the tiny 63-megacycle transmitter-receiver with its nickel-cadmium powerpack, the whole gadget no larger than a package of cigarettes. The American named Cash had been very impressed with the miniaturization. They had taken the envelope containing Nikolai Ivanovich's papers, too.

He could hear them beginning to stir downstairs now, the creak of footsteps on winter-shrunk floorboards, the clank of a cast-iron stove lid. Malinin wondered what time it was. Ten-thirty, he supposed. Possibly a little later. He had been awake for hours, with the daylight. He felt rested and, all things considered, pretty healthy. The recuperative powers of his own body amazed him. If Matthew Olds hadn't come outside looking for him last night, he'd be frozen stiff under three feet of snow right now.

Which, he decided with no malice, made Olds a fool. Had their positions been reversed, he would have let Olds die out there. There was a softness in the childish Western concept of fair play which would bury them all yet. By contrast, the Russian soul had an Asiatic hardness, a realization that life was cheap, and a consequent indifference to death.

In the West, death was a dirty word. Instead of accepting the inevitability, they fought it. Why, Malinin recalled, one of the great newspapers of the United States would not even use the word, as if a clever circumlocution could drive the final enemy away.

He wondered if death was the answer, now, for Nikolai Ivanovich.

Moskalenko, he knew, would think so. Moskalenko, were he here, would conclude that Nikolai Ivanovich must not leave the hut alive. That, of course, was the trouble with Moskalenko and the other experts in death. It was their answer to everything.

There would be one logical weapon—Nikolai Ivanovich's bad heart. Fright could kill a man with a heart like that. A sudden rage could kill him.

But the more Malinin considered the idea, the less he liked it. The time when there was no other way, when Nikolai Ivanovich had to die, had not come yet. You are no Moskalenko, Malinin told himself.

Better, far better to wait for help, to return to Geneva when the blizzard stopped and, somehow, take Nikolai Ivanovich back to Russia. Was that still possible?

He could picture Nikolai Ivanovich, in Moscow, the expert application of brain-washing, a show trial, the Premier recanting, and Viktor Mironovich Malinin responsible for it all.

He settled back, the ankle not hurting now.

General Viktor Mironovich Malinin, Chief of the KGB.

There were the photographs, in the safe in Villa Krupskaya, waiting to be used.

There was Bayev, with his pathetic infatuation for Claudia, but still loyal and eager to please.

And there was Claudia herself.

2   The dog did not like Moskalenko. A black and brindle Alsatian bitch, she sat at the feet of her master in the living room of a chalet on Lauenenstrasse in Gstaad, near the lumberyard. Her eyes looked steadily at Moskalenko's face. She growled.

"Be quiet, Heidi," Ruedy Stüki said. The pilot recommended by Gros-Claude was a red-faced young man with pale-blue eyes. He had a reckless look about him, and Moskalenko did not know if he liked that or not.

"I don't have a helicopter," Ruedy Stücki said. "You won't find any up here until the skiing season starts."

"What kind of plane then?" Moskalenko asked. They were speaking English.

"Single-engined, high-wing, room for five plus the pilot. With fixed landing gear."

"Fixed landing gear?"

"For skis," Ruedy Stücki explained.

"Where do you keep the plane?"

"Saanen Airport."

"That's no good to me," Moskalenko said.

Stücki shrugged. "I didn't think it would be."

"Gros-Claude said you could help."

"Is that what he said?" Stücki smiled.

"The police will be watching the airport, Herr Stücki. No one will take off without their permission."

"Of course," said Stücki calmly. "Not with the Russian up there."

"Gros-Claude knew that. Still, he recommended you."

"So? He was mistaken."

"I don't think so. I will pay anything within reason."

"That of course," Stücki said, brightening, "is something else. How much?"

Moskalenko named a figure, and realized it was too high.

"Are you serious?"

"Yes."

"You have the money with you?"

"No. Gros-Claude will pay you."

"English is not your native language," Stücki said. "I'm curious."

This one, Moskalenko thought, was one you could kill just for the pleasure of it. "No, I was born in Czechoslovakia."

"Yes, it could be Czech, your accent. What do you want the plane for?"

"I want to charter it." Moskalenko said. "For perhaps two hours, when the weather clears."

"The Russian," said Stücki.

"Does it matter?"

"It's my plane," Stücki said infuriatingly.

"I'm hiring it."

"I haven't agreed to that. Is it the Russian or isn't it?"

Moskalenko stared at him. "Yes."

"I don't want any part of that."

Stücki got up. The dog growled at his feet. Stücki

222

looked at Moskalenko, and at the two agents sitting across the room, still bundled in their coats.

Moskalenko rose and fingered the Okinawan flail in his pocket. With this one, he thought, it would be a joy.

"You'll help us, Herr Stücki," he said.

"I don't think so."

Moskalenko took a step toward him. "You have no choice."

Stücki shouted the dog's name: "Heidi!"

The Alsatian bitch made a gargling sound and leaped at Moskalenko's throat.

He swung his arm in a blurring motion, one red stick held firmly in his hand, the other swinging free at the end of its cords. The bitch's growl ended on a single yelp. She dropped at Moskalenko's feet, skull shattered.

Ruedy Stücki's face was white. His gaze lifted slowly from the dead dog to Moskalenko.

"You have another plane?" Moskalenko asked calmly. "Not at the airport?"

Stücki nodded.

3 Not even the accidental clanking of the stove lid as Claudia shoved it back into place with the poker woke any of them.

Her father was sleeping peacefully, Bayev snoring softly, his big sad face relaxed. The American named Al Cash had dragged a mattress to the foot of the stairs and was sleeping there. He had been up most of the night, though, as Claudia had been. She had heard him prowling the room once or twice, had seen the glow of an occasional cigarette. He had drifted off to sleep just before dawn.

Matt was sleeping soundly, and no wonder, Claudia thought. He had been outside almost an hour last night, finding Viktor and carrying him to the hut. Carrying him, after all he had been through. Finally, when Claudia had become frantic with worry, Matt had appeared at the door, breathing hard in the thin air, Viktor slung like a sack over his shoulder. Al Cash had given them both Cognac to drink, and it was Cash who had removed Viktor's watch with the wires and the little box attached to them, Cash who had carried Viktor upstairs while Claudia removed Matt's boots, led him to a mattress, covered him with a blanket. "That was a very brave thing, what you did," she said. But he did not hear her; he was asleep at once.

All night Matt was there beside her, and upstairs, injured and alone—Viktor. She could not think of one without her thoughts drifting to the other.

Of course you think of Viktor, she had told herself as the slow minutes dragged by. It is normal. For a long time he was a large part of your life, he is the only man you ever slept with, what is wrong with feeling pity for him now? It is pity, only that. You're finished with him, you told him that in Geneva.

She tried to blot out the image of Viktor with one of Matt, but Viktor came back like an incubus, and then she saw herself, in the hotel room in Geneva, slapping the cigarette from Viktor's hand, and she shut her eyes and finally slept and dreamed of Viktor and moaned in her sleep.

She awoke remembering the dream and hating herself but feeling pity for Viktor again. Was it warm enough upstairs? The door between the two floors of the hut was open, and the warmth from downstairs would have risen, but still Viktor had been out there for hours last night, struggling up through the snow, hurting his leg, until Matt finally brought him in. Was the ankle broken? Or just badly sprained?

Was Viktor thinking of her now?

No, she told herself, Viktor never thought of you that way. Viktor used you. He used your body and it had not hurt his career to be seen so often in the company of the Premier's daughter.

Maybe he's in pain. And hungry. When had he eaten last?

It would be simple human decency to feed him. Only that.

She selected a can of soup from their meager supplies, opened it into a battered pot, added water, heated it. She lit one of the kerosene lamps and looked at Matt, wishing he would wake up. He did not wake up.

When she reached the foot of the stairs with the pot of soup in one hand and the lamp in the other, Al Cash said, "What gives?" He was sitting up.

"I'm bringing him something to eat."

"Want me to come along?"

It was tempting, it would make everything so much

224

simpler if the American went upstairs with her. "No," she heard herself saying. "Please don't bother."

"If you need me, holler."

She nodded and went past him and up the stairs.

4 "That was good," Viktor said. "I needed that."

The empty pot was on the floor. Viktor sat on the edge of the mattress, his right leg out stiffly in front of him. His face looked haggard.

They had spoken hardly at all while he ate. Now he smiled up at her, a small sad smile, and said, "Poor Claudia. What a terrible thing to go through." His voice was gentle, gentler than she had ever heard it.

"What do you mean?"

"To see your father become a traitor right before your eyes."

"I don't want to talk about that, Viktor," she said stiffly. "He is doing what he must do."

"And you? Don't tell me you went with him willingly. I can't believe that."

She remembered her father's seizure at the Metropole Hotel in Geneva. No, not entirely willingly, she thought, amazed how quickly Viktor could get the nub of things. "I know what I'm doing," she said.

"I can't believe that either. Whatever happens, Nikolai Ivanovich had already forfeited his place in history. You know that as well as I do."

"History isn't written only in the Soviet Union."

"He will be called a madman."

"You know he isn't. And there are competent people here in Switzerland who can examine him, who can prove to the world—"

"I'm not talking about the world. I'm talking about you."

"I can take care of myself."

The gentleness left Viktor's voice. "Do you fancy yourself another Svetlana?"

"I don't fancy myself anything. My father needs me."

"Then you admit you didn't go with him willingly?"

"Please, Viktor. That's enough."

"Your place is at home. You can't sacrifice your life for him. I won't let you."

"My place is with him."

"And when he dies? He's a sick man, Claudia."

225

"That's enough," she said again, picking up the pot and the lamp, turning to go.

He did not try to stop her until she had almost reached the door. Then he called, the old arrogance suddenly back in his voice, the sound of her name like a whiplash: "Claudia."

For a few seconds she stood still, her back to him. She could feel her fingers tightening on the handle of the pot, on the lamp, to keep them from trembling.

"It is not that simple," he said. "It never is."

If she took three more steps, she would reach the door and be outside on the stairs.

"Come back here. You have made an unwise political decision. That has nothing to do with us. For us nothing has changed. I understand you, Claudia Nikolaievna. I made you. Can you deny that?"

She felt the pot slip from her nerveless fingers. It clattered on the floor. She saw herself in Viktor's suite at the Rossiya in Moscow, saw herself in his small country house beyond the southern outskirts of the capital, the wind sighing in the winter-bare birches, echoing her loneliness and uncertainty while she responded to his cynical use of her with a sick excitement. She could feel the familiar helplessness creeping over her again.

"For us nothing has changed," he repeated.

She was at his side, looking down at him.

"Put the lamp on the floor," he said with a bored, superior smile. "That's right, that's a good girl." He patted the side of the bare mattress. "Now sit here."

She remained standing. Her legs felt weak.

"I said sit down, Claudia."

She shut her eyes tightly. She was on the mountain above Gstaad again. If she took three steps forward, just three, she would fall a thousand feet.

To escape Viktor?

But what she had felt then was not despair, it was joy.

"Look at me, Claudia."

She heard Matt's voice, gentle and understanding. *We've been through too much. It doesn't have to be tonight.*

She opened her eyes and saw the look of bored certainty on Viktor's face. It was the face of a stranger.

Malinin was aware at once of the change in her, not of the will to resist but of the fact that something had made resistance unnecessary. It was there in her big dark eyes, a calmness, not an indifference, because Claudia could never be indifferent to a human being who tried to reach out to her.

Malinin dropped his gaze. She's found strength somewhere, he thought. But what did that matter? A clever man could use strength as well as weakness. The strategy of manipulation remained. Only the tactics changed.

"You see," he said slowly, his voice gentle again, almost wistful. "That was the game. It doesn't work any more. Not for you—and not for me. I've changed, Claudia."

He tried to get up. When his right foot touched the floor he winced and sat down again.

"You mustn't," she said.

"Last night," he said, "I almost died. I thought I was going to die. A man makes his peace then, but if he has lived any kind of a life at all, he regrets. Can you see that?"

He sounded so humble now, so unsure of himself. Not like Viktor at all, Claudia thought.

"They say that when a man is going to die his whole life flashes through his mind. That wasn't what happened last night."

He looked at her anxiously, his eyes uncertain. "Instead I found myself thinking if I had it all to do over again . . ." He waved a hand vaguely. "No, you wouldn't understand. It's too late for that now. Go downstairs. To the Americans. I'd be a fool if I thought . . ."

"No, please. What is it?"

"Suddenly, in the middle of my life, I am unsure of myself, don't know who I am—can you picture that? Me? Viktor Mironovich?"

"Yes, Viktor. I can understand that. And you would be a better man for it."

"Because," he said, very quickly then, his voice hardly more than a whisper, "there was one good thing in my life, and I threw it away. That's the kind of thoughts a man has when he is on the brink of death. One good thing in a rotten life." He shook his head and let his eyes drop from her face. You, he said hoarsely. "Only you, Claudia."

Her eyes were stinging then. Two years, she thought, and if he had said it at any other time everything, everything might have been different. "Laugh at me," he said. "Go ahead. I deserve it, after the way I—abused you."

227

"I'm not laughing at you, Viktor."

"One good thing in a rotten life. That's what I understood, when I thought it was too late."

A moment ago it had seemed so simple. But now she was no longer sure. She wanted to believe him. Believing him would make less of a mockery of the past two years. His brush with death, she thought, and mine, the American lying there, his blood gleaming like black oil against the snow, and that had been enough to bring her close to Matthew Olds, away from terror toward an affirmation of life. But what did that mean compared with two years of her life, and the knowledge now, if she believed Viktor, that those two years hadn't been wasted, that Viktor cared for her and had finally admitted it?

But still—

In this very room, just a few hours ago with Matt, and it would have been so right then, and still seemed so right. That was love, born suddenly; this was pity. Or perhaps that was a quick fleeting passion, this was love—

She turned and fled.

Malinin settled back, wondering if he had overplayed his hand. She had been confused. Her reaction to him had been more pity than love. Pity, the most corrosive of emotions. Perhaps I misjudged her, he thought. Perhaps she is stronger than I realized. But still, the woman had not yet been born who could ignore a declaration of love from a man she had once found attractive. There was still time. They weren't going anywhere yet. And if he could turn her against her father, by turning her toward himself, there was no telling what might happen.

Should that fail, Malinin told himself, there was always Bayev.

Chapter
NINETEEN

1 *By Monday afternoon the* foehn *was blowing.
The barometer continued to fall, and the warm south-*

ern wind swept into the low-pressure area already blanketing the Alps, mingling with the cooler air and increasing the rate of snowfall.

You could feel the foehn, *old-timers in the Alps said, in your bones. The* foehn, *they told you, made men irritable and unpredictable, prone to violence. Some outlanders smiled at these quaint peasant superstitions. The* foehn, *they said, was just a wind with a name, like others in the mountains and river-valleys and along the seacoasts of Europe—the* mistral *in the valley of the Rhone River, the* terral *in the south of Spain, the* bora *on the Adriatic coast of Yugoslavia. The canny natives of these regions, all tourist centers, exploited the fame of their fabled winds. Afterward, back home, tourists would perpetuate the legend, would speak knowingly of being stuck for three days in Provence when the* mistral *was blowing, and I swear to God, Uncle Henry, it made you feel funny, you wanted to pick up a knife and stick it into the first person who looked at you crosseyed.*

Old-timers quoted statistics. More people died of natural causes when the foehn *was blowing. More marriages ended in hot anger or with dead-eyed finality. More crimes of violence were committed.*

One statistic was not debatable. The foehn, *being a hot wind, weakens the bonds of cohesion of settled snow, thereby increasing the danger of avalanche.*

Because the Montreux Oberland Bernois railroad was running behind schedule, with each train forced to clear its way through fresh drifts of snow, no newspapers reached Gstaad Monday morning. There was, of course, the radio, and the ten o'clock TV news broadcast, and by noon everyone in Gstaad would know what Bern and Geneva and the rest of the world already knew.

According to usually reliable sources close to the Bundesrat, Russian Premier Andreyev had spent the night at the Teufelkopf Hütte above Lauenen.

Nobody could say why.

Ridiculous, the Russian Embassy in Bern said. As far as they knew Nikolai Ivanovich had spent the night in his bed in Villa Krupskaya in Geneva.

Villa Krupskaya had no comment.

The Bern, Lausanne, and Geneva newspapers had a fieldday.

Surprisingly little was made of the state of Andreyev's

229

mental health. Medicine in Russia was known, as often as not in such cases, to be political.

It was possible, Alphonse Borel speculated in the *Tribune de Genève*, that Andreyev had an entirely fresh concept to present to American President Huntington at the Summit. Perhaps he had wanted to get away by himself to work it out. He had a reputation for doing the unexpected.

It was possible, other papers said, that he wanted to defect. Borel's earlier speculations were resurrected from several-day-old editions of the *Tribune de Genève*. But who would defect to a mountaintop? the papers asked with heavy-handed Swiss humor.

No one could say, least of all the President of the Confederation. But the President of the Confederation was quoted in every Monday-morning newspaper in Switzerland as being confident that representatives of the Soviet Union and the United States now in Switzerland would defer to Swiss authorities in all matters relating to the whereabouts of Premier Andreyev, unless of course Andreyev had spent the night in his bed in Villa Krupskaya in Geneva, as the Russian Embassy claimed, in which event there would be no problem.

Just in case the Russians were mistaken, the President of the Confederation said, he had sent Minister of Justice and Police Willy Müllener to Gstaad to take personal charge of the situation.

If there was a situation.

2 The situation was normal in Tracy Olds's chalet, except that Tracy's luck in the Monday afternoon bridge game, a fixture in Gstaad until the skiing season started, was better than usual.

Tracy's partner was a retired stockbroker named Shields. He was a cautious bidder, but even his caution was soon forgotten in the face of the really splendid hands they had been dealt. They had bid and made a small slam in the first rubber and now, in the second, another—or possibly a grand slam—was in the offing.

Shields had opened the bidding with two clubs. Tracy could scarcely believe her ears. That meant twenty-two or more high-card points and uneven distribution. Tracy looked at her cards again. She was holding thirteen points in no-trump distribution. It had to mean that, between them, they held almost every honor card in the deck.

The player on Tracy's right, the wife of a film director named Swann who had won two Oscars, passed. Tracy licked her lips and said, "Three no trump," letting her partner know she had two aces.

"Four diamonds," Shields said, his eyes under the wavy white hair gleaming.

This is unbelievable, Tracy thought, looking at her hand again. Shields had just named his strong suit. Five cards and two honors in it, at the very least. Tracy was holding four diamonds to the jack-ace. No need to cue-bid her aces, she knew. Shields, from his bidding, had to hold the two missing ones.

She licked her lips again and was about to say seven diamonds.

The telephone rang.

"Damn," she said.

"Let it ring," Shields told her.

But Tracy, like so many lonely women, was incapable of not answering a ringing telephone. She got up.

"You really are a slave to that thing," Shields said with a fatuous little laugh. There was a small suggestion of malice in his laughter, too. A young divorcée, playing bridge with two old biddies and a man in his sixties, of course she'd answer the telephone. The nights were long. And Tracy did, after all, have a certain reputation.

"Hello?" Tracy knew they were watching her, and listening. She forced herself to say, "Can you call later please? We're in the middle of—"

"Tracy?" A man's voice. She did not recognize it.

"Yes. I said could you—"

"This is Whit Stoughton, Tracy."

"Whit? My God, what are you doing in Gstaad?" She answered her own question: "Of course, the Summit Conference, and that business about Andreyev. It's wonderful hearing your voice, Whit. It's been too long."

"Can I see you, Tracy? I need some help."

"Could it wait awhile?"

"It's damn important, Tracy."

The urgency in his voice made her forget the grand slam, or at least lose interest in it. Her place in the pecking order of the foreign population of Gstaad, most of whom were wealthy or celebrities or both, was low, depending as it did on modest wealth and a tenuous tie with an ex-husband.

"I understand, Whit. If it can't wait, it can't. Could you come here?" She gave him directions.

"Ten minutes, Tracy," he said. "And I appreciate it."

"Nothing, Whit."

She hung up. "Whitney Stoughton," she told the three pairs of eyes that were staring at her when she turned around.

"The Deputy Director of the CIA?" asked Shields.

Tracy nodded. "We're old friends. This will have to be the last hand." Almost as an afterthought she added, "So let's make it seven diamonds."

Shields played with his usual slow deliberation. He had no trouble making the grand slam.

3 They opened the last two cans of soup late Monday afternoon. The bread was gone, the Cognac bottles stood empty, the last link of hard sausage had been sliced thinly for a meager meal at noon. Only a few chocolate bars remained as emergency rations.

Claudia stood at the stove, a strand of dark hair down over her eye. She brushed it away with an unconscious gesture, saw Matt watching her, gave him a quick troubled smile, and turned away. Her attitude since their first night in the hut had baffled him. She almost seemed more at ease, these last two days, talking with Al Cash or Bayev. It was as if she were trying to make him understand, without hurting him by saying it, that Bayev's unexpected arrival Saturday night had brought her back to her senses.

Early Monday afternoon, when the wind had dropped and she stood outside under the overhang watching the snow, Matt finally succeeded in cornering her. He still felt the awareness between them. It was an awareness he had felt, immediately, as strong then as now, at the party in Villa Krupskaya. He remembered his cynicism then— drive along the lakefront and if you find you're mistaken about her you can always say thanks but no thanks. He had not said it then. He did not want to say it now. Still, the events of the past forty-eight hours had thrown them together with their emotions bared, and maybe that was what troubled Claudia. Maybe, he thought, she's just a little more objective than I am. Maybe she understands,

232

with a woman's wisdom, that what had not quite happened Saturday night would have been so banal, so predictable that, given time to mull it over afterward, they would have laughed at themselves or, finally, hated each other. Maybe she was trying to tell him, by keeping her distance, that when all this was over, they would see. Because he was sure she still felt the awareness, too.

He waited a few minutes and followed her outside. Beyond the overhang the wind had sculpted the snow in a great concave sweep, waist-high and glistening. There were no trees, no mountains, no earth, no sky. The snow seemed to fill the world.

"It looks like it will never stop," she said.

He nodded. "I wanted to apologize," he told her, the words surprising him because that was not what he had meant to say at all. He remembered how she had wanted to apologize for the homey touches she had tried to give their first meal in the hut.

Her smile was tentative. "It seems one of us always wants to apologize. It isn't necessary."

"I mean Saturday night."

"I know you mean Saturday night. I had some ideas on the subject then myself."

After a while Matt said, "Are you sorry we didn't?"

"I don't know. For me, yes. You know I wanted to. To prove something. That we were still alive, perhaps. But I—I'm glad we didn't. Can we just forget about it? Please?"

"Are you sure that's what you want?"

"I don't know what I want. No, that's not true. I want us to get out of here, and I want my father to do the things he must do, and then I want to go away somewhere, alone, among people I don't know, simple people who are happy with their lives and who don't hold the world in the palm of their hands. . . . But I'll never do that."

"Why not?"

"My father needs me. But if I could . . ." she said wistfully.

He watched the snow. Again he said what he had not meant to say. "I could take you someplace like that."

"Yes," she said. "Isn't it nice to dream?"

He turned her and caught her arms above the elbows. She did not resist. She just stood there.

"It doesn't have to be a dream."

233

But she pulled away from him. "Would you do yourself a favor when we leave here? Would you pretend we never met?"

Her eyes shut softly, and he watched the tears well out from under the long lashes. "Because," she said, "it would be so easy to fall in love with you."

"Then what are you afraid of?" he demanded, his voice suddenly harsh.

She jerked her head up, toward the overhang. "That," she cried. "That, upstairs."

It took him a moment to understand. "Malinin?"

"Yes, Malinin. For two years. Malinin."

So now he knows, she thought. Sooner or later he had to.

She saw the anger leave him. She was twenty-six, she had had an affair, so what? But he didn't really know anything at all. How could he ever understand what it had been like, with Viktor?

She was going to say: I should despise him. But if he snaps his fingers I will come. He knows it, and I know it.

But the words remained unspoken. Viktor had trained her, ruthlessly, for his own use. Wasn't his bid for her pity, here in the hut, the same thing? To use her in some other way—against her father, perhaps?

Suddenly she knew she would not come if he snapped his fingers, not ever again.

Matt, who wanted to give instead of take, had ended it for her.

She looked at him. He was waiting for her to say something.

"It's over," she said. She felt like singing. "It's finally over now."

4 "Hey," Al Cash said, disappearing into the storeroom and returning with the ax, "give us a hand, will you, Lenny?"

The footballer Leonid Bayev smiled. For Leonid, Lenny. But grudgingly he admitted to himself that he did not dislike the American. Sometimes they would sit around talking. Cash glibly, Bayev struggling with his inadequate English, telling what Cash called the tallest tales in the history of spying—whatever that meant. Once the American had stared at him solemnly and said, "If it takes me all year I'm gonna find out which one of us is the bigger liar, Lenny." Then he was off: "Did I ever tell you the time we . . ."

They went outside together, Cash prising the window-boards loose with the blade of the ax, Bayev stacking them and carrying them inside to dry near the stove. Soon all the downstairs windows had been stripped of their boards. Light filtered in through the designs of the shutters.

Later, while Bayev was dozing near a front window, he heard voices outside—Claudia Nikolaievna and the American Matthew Olds.

Bayev listened, concern on his face. Even if he had not seen them that first night on the balcony, he would have sensed something between them. It was as if they wanted to look at each other, to touch each other, but were afraid, and quickly retreated, if they did.

As he did not dislike Al Cash, so Bayev had grudgingly begun to admit that he liked the tall American Matthew Olds. He was friendly, he did not treat Bayev as an enemy any more than Cash did. And somehow, far more than Malinin, he seemed right for Claudia Nikolaievna.

Bayev, knowing it could never be himself, had always hoped that someday a man would come along for her, like the hero in a fairy story come to rescue the unhappy princess. Bayev would resent that man and yet welcome him because Claudia Nikolaievna wanted and needed him. He would scatter the loneliness that surrounded her like a dark cloud.

Was the American Matthew Olds that man?

Listening at the window, Bayev knew before the words were spoken that Claudia Nikolaievna would mention her affair with Malinin. He willed her not to. It would be a mistake, he thought. Accept what the American is offering you. He could be the one. Say nothing. Accept him.

But Claudia Nikolaievna said, "That—that, upstairs," and inside, Bayev sighed and got up to stoke the fire.

A few minutes later Claudia Nikolaievna and the American returned inside. Bayev saw a look on Claudia Nikolaievna's face that he had never seen before. Her eyes were glowing.

And, not understanding at all, but approving, the footballer Leonid Bayev thought: Someday, somehow, I am going to make her eyes look like that.

5 Although their contents were not unexpected, the papers Andreyev had brought out of Russia and the comments he had added at Kermit Hauser's chalet in Gstaad still left Matt feeling numb.

The papers made a hefty package, almost seventy pages of documents and comments. With Andreyev's permission, Matt went through them slowly, alone in the little room behind the storeroom. The documents were in Russian, and rough sledding for Matt until his rusty knowledge of the language, learned during his AP tour of duty in Moscow, came back. The comments were in English.

There were minutes of several crucial meetings of the Council of Ministers and of the Central Committee of the Communist Party.

There were photostats of directives issued by the Council of Ministers to the Foreign Ministry and by the Central Committee to the Army.

Much of the original material was concerned with the occupation of Rumania and the then-proposed takeover of Yugoslavia.

But there was more than that. Running like a leitmotiv through it all was the conflict between Igor Lysenko, First Secretary of the Communist Party, and Nikolai Ivanovich Andreyev, Chairman of the Council of Ministers.

"I do not include this material," Andreyev had written, "to put Comrade Lysenko in a bad light or myself on the side of the angels. But it is essential to show the very grave risks for the world if a nationalistic, power-hungry leader like Lysenko is allowed too free a hand in the so-called collective leadership of one of the world's superpowers."

He showed the risks, all right. Lysenko tried to justify his policy by saying, "We have ten years, comrades, to do what must be done in the West. Ten years, no more. Then we must be ready for China."

Doing what must be done in the West, the documents said, meant, first, ruthlessly crushing all right-deviationism in the satellite countries. "A single monolithic alignment of Socialist states from Berlin to Vladivostok," Lysenko had said, "that is what we must have. Then we can reap a harvest west of the Oder-Neisse line. Already, Finland is economically dependent on us, more than at any time since just after the Great Patriotic War. One out of every three Frenchmen votes Communist, one out of every four Italians. Berlin remains isolated. The Americans are busy with their difficulties at home. If we weigh the risks, if we are sure of our historical role, the entire Eurasian landmass from the North Sea to the Pacific can be a Soviet empire. Then let America and England hide behind their water barriers. Then we can turn to the betrayers of the Revolution, the Chinese."

It was, Matt knew, an elaborate and carefully worked out plan of conquest that almost made Hitler's prison dreams in *Mein Kampf* seem modest.

"The West," Lysenko had told the Central Committee shortly after the military occupation of Rumania, "has accepted the Brezhnev Doctrine to justify our unflinching struggle against the counter-Revolutionary bandits in Hungary, in Czechoslovakia, in Rumania—the West's tacit admission that spheres of influence still exist. But in whose sphere is Yugoslavia? A Socialist state, true, but one that has left the camp of Marxist-Leninism. A test case, comrades. For Ilić's Yugoslavia is neither East nor West. Ilić encourages free enterprise. Thanks to enormous economic aid from the West, Yugoslavia is thriving. Already in Poland, in Hungary, in Bulgaria, in East Germany, there is talk of emulating the policies of the Ilić government. This must be stopped. Ilić must go.

"There are grave risks. The West, to protect its own crumbling empire, may be forced to act. I say these risks must be taken in the name of the glorious Revolution. I say it would be weakness and—yes, comrades—a betrayal of the Revolution not to take them. A time will come, if we are bold, when the six continents and the seven seas are ruled from behind these Kremlin walls, when the Revolution and the single monolithic government of the planet will be one and the same. We are ready. We can open the door. The key in the lock, now, is Yugoslavia."

Nikolai Ivanovich had come in while Matt was reading. He looked rested and fit. His hair was combed now as in the pictures Matt had seen of him, two glossy wings on either side of the bald crown. His eyes were clear. The black-rimmed glasses and beardless jaw still seemed strange, though. It was almost as if an actor who bore a remarkable resemblance to Andreyev had taken off his makeup now that the performance was over.

"Quite an orator, isn't he?" Nikolai Ivanovich said. "Even at meetings of the Central Committee. But of course, he's mad. He has to be, to speak like that and insist records be kept. For history, you see. In his terms, he is the embodiment of history. In my terms, or yours, he could write an end to history."

Nikolai Ivanovich sat down, carefully stacking the papers that Matt had scattered on the bed. "But what is madness?" he said. "There is something about Mother Russia that produces a rare quality in her leaders that is either madness or genius, depending on the direction it takes. It produces a Peter the Great, who built his Window on the West and took Russia out of Asia into Europe. But it also produces a Stalin, or a Lysenko, and if Stalin does not go down in history as one of the world's great tyrants, it is only because Hitler outshone him. As for Lysenko . . ."

For a full two hours Nikolai Ivanovich talked, his English fluent, his ideas incisive. Outside, the snow continued to fall. Gradually the last light of day faded at the window. Soon Matt could no longer see him, except as a deeper shadow in the darkness, and still Nikolai Ivanovich went on. It was almost as if, here, ten thousand feet up in the Alps, with a storm raging, with their food gone, with the recent battle against his illness fresh in his mind, Nikolai Ivanovich wanted to complete his testament, wanted to say all that he had not written down in his careful, professional hand, wanted Matt to listen and remember.

He spoke of what it was like at the seat of power in Russia. "There are two separate and distinct governments in the Soviet Union. The first is the government machinery that confronts the foreigner—the Council of Ministers, the Supreme Soviet. This government, unless the Premier is a strong man willing to fight, is powerless. The real power resides in the secret government—the Central Committee of the Communist Party, working hand in glove with the Secret Police. And since the Central Committee and the KGB are answerable to no one but themselves, it is a vicious system.

"Still, I had reason to hope. I sat on both the Council and the Central Committee. Besides, when you are born and bred to a creed like Communism, it is like a tremendous religious experience. You are part of the inner light. Doubts and self-conflicts vanish. As long as you remain faithful, there is an answer to everything. The alternative is casting yourself adrift in the unknown void. This is very difficult, at the top. Could you imagine a pope," Nikolai Ivanovich asked, "excommunicating himself?"

He spoke of the differences between Russia and the United States, and the less obvious similarities. A hundred years ago both were expanding their frontiers toward the Pacific, into undeveloped territory. Slaves and serfs in each had been freed at the same time. Both took up the European Industrial Revolution and developed an industrial complex that made Europe's pale by comparison.

He spoke of Europe, emerging from the ashes of destruction after the Second World War, to find itself caught between two giants, one in the East, one in the West. "It should not surprise you," he said, "if sometimes your Western allies resent you more than they resent us. You have stripped them of their mantle of power and wear it yourselves now. No father likes to see himself supplanted by his son."

He spoke of the impossibility of war in a way that reminded Matt of Clay Huntington. "Are men better now, intuitively, than Christ was? Better now, intellectually, than Socrates? No, they are not. If technology continues to outstrip morality," he said, "there will be no twenty-first century, it is that simple.

"I want to tell the steel-eaters in my country—as President Huntington has been telling the military-industrial complex in yours—stop, you are fouling the air and fouling the waters of the earth, you are keeping mankind in bondage to uncertainty and fear. I want," he said, "to shake your President's hand, to let him know I understand this as he does. I want to tell him, whatever the difficulties, whatever the obstacles, to continue his fight."

Outside, the storm raged. In the north of Yugoslavia, an invading army was waiting, if, Matt thought, it hadn't already moved. In Geneva, the President was gambling that Matt's guess had been right, gambling that this man he had never met but who dreamed the way he dreamed, who was touched by greatness as he was, could expose his colleague in the Kremlin as a madman, could prevent a war that might be the last war, or the last anything.

Somehow he's got to get out of here, Matt thought. Somehow he's got to meet Clay Huntington, got to shake his hand.

Chapter
TWENTY

1 He walked, wearing a hat for once, the brim pulled low over his face against the driving rain, striding rapidly despite the limp, along the deserted quay in the darkness, across the Mont Blanc bridge, and up steep cobblestoned streets to the Old Town. He had to get away, even for just a few minutes.

Well, he thought, not quite away. Half a dozen Secret Servicemen were prowling the rain-swept streets with him, wishing, probably, that they had a more sedentary President to guard.

He went past the wall around the cathedral gardens and back down the stone steps toward the wide, brightly lit streets and the river. He went along the Rue du Rhône without seeing anything. He was not, for that solitary half-hour, the President of the United States. He was Clay Huntington, husband and father.

The baby had been delivered. Seven pounds exactly, a daughter, Dr. Rutherford had telephoned. Healthy, and bawling lustily. Gigi was in the intensive-care unit. Prognosis uncertain, Dr. Rutherford had said frankly. She was very weak. They just did not know yet. They were doing everything they could.

And Clay Huntington was three thousand miles away, walking in the rain in Geneva, waiting for the word from the mountains, from Yugoslavia, from Moscow.

If it's a girl, Gigi had asked, can we call her Monique? After my mother?

Yes, he thought now, on the rain-lashed street, we can call her Monique, we can call her anything you want, only get well, you've got to get well, I need you.

He went back across the bridge and along the quay to the hotel. He had been away too long, he told himself. Perhaps there was word from Washington. He crossed the lobby swiftly to the special elevator and went up, two Secret Servicemen in the car with him.

General Laffont was waiting in the Presidential Suite, his swarthy face expressionless but his eyes glittering with suppressed excitement.

"It's happened," he said, and waited while the President took off his drenched topcoat, removed his wet shoes, put a cigarette in the black holder and lit it.

"Two hours ago over the Adriatic near Rieka," the Chairman of the Joint Chiefs of Staff said. "A Warlock off the carrier *John F. Kennedy*, flying a routine patrol. Two MiG-27's intercepted it. Our pilot tried evasive action but couldn't shake loose. There was a dogfight, with the MiG's apparently opening fire first. The Warlock released a single air-to-air missile and brought one of them down."

The President ran a hand through his hair and sank heavily into a chair.

"Anything on it from Moscow yet?"

"No, sir."

Picking up the phone, the President said, "Pris, get Secretary Reed in here, please."

Benson Reed joined them a few minutes later. His face was pinched with worry as General Laffont repeated his account of the dogfight.

"It was bound to happen sooner or later," Laffont said finally. "You can't blame our people on the carrier."

"I'm not blaming anyone," the President told him. "As you say, it was bound to happen. What we have to worry about now is the consequences. Benson?"

"It could be the excuse Lysenko's been hoping for. He'll claim we're in Yugoslavia in force. The Red Army could start moving again—to get us out."

"General?"

"That dogfight brought us right to the brink. Anything could push us over now. Anything at all."

The President nodded slowly. He picked up the phone and spoke to Miss Priscilla Lee again. "I want to speak to Foreign Minister Kapitsa at Villa Krupskaya."

"You mean personally, sir? *You'll* talk to him?"

"That's right. Get him, please."

The President waited. Nobody said anything. Then:

"Mr. President? They say he's not in the building."

"Did you tell them who was calling?"

"Yes, sir."

"Do they expect him back soon?"

"They were vague about that, sir."

After the President hung up, Secretary Reed said, "He could be anywhere, of course. Even on his way back home for instructions. But my guess is he's in Gstaad. They want to get Andreyev down off that mountain before the Swiss do and fly him back to Moscow."

"The Swiss won't let them," President Huntington said.

"That's banking on a lot," General Laffont told him.

"Maybe, but they have more than the Swiss to worry about. Yesterday almost six hundred newsmen were in Geneva. There aren't a hundred left. Most of them have taken the train up to Gstaad, and Kapitsa knows they'll be watching every move the Russians make. So will we, by the way. Whit's got a couple of dozen CIA people up there now."

"Just watching?" General Laffont asked. He sounded disappointed.

"If you mean are we going to try to get Andreyev down off that mountain ourselves, the answer is no. How can we? Fail and they accuse us of trying to kidnap him. Succeed and they make the accusation stick."

"And the alternative?" Reed demanded. "What if Kapitsa can pressure the Swiss into letting them have him? We ought to give Whitney more of a free hand," he suggested. "He's level-headed and diplomatic, and he wouldn't—"

"No," the President said. "We're going to rely on the Swiss. We've got to."

"I wish I had your faith in them," General Laffont said.

The President made no reply. Maybe, he thought, Laffont was right. Maybe it's too much to expect of the Swiss. Maybe he'd see things more clearly if he weren't so worried about Gigi. He waited for Laffont or Reed to offer a suggestion. They had none to offer. They were discussing the dogfight. Kremlin, they said. Lysenko, they said.

He could feel the pressures closing in on him from all sides. He had been smoking too much. He rubbed a hand over his face. For the first time in his career he almost wished he were not the President of the United States.

The phone would ring if Kapitsa returned to Villa Krupskaya. The phone would ring if Whitney Stoughton had something to report. The phone would ring if there was news from Walter Reed Hospital.

The phone did not ring.

Clay Huntington, President and husband, waited.

2 Tracy Olds sat up in bed reading, her blonde hair loose on the bolster. The book was a frothy costume romance, the sort that usually worked as a soporific. Tonight it didn't. Nor could she concentrate on it.

She sipped from the tumbler of whiskey on the night table and told herself that, while she felt a slight and pleasant buzz, she was definitely not high. She shut the book and put it aside and thought of Whitney Stoughton, asleep now in the guest room.

Physically he hadn't changed much. Tracy had first known him, let me see, she thought, my Lord, yes, closer to twenty than to fifteen years ago. She was a college freshman, home for the summer in Newport; he was a Boston Stoughton, very eligible and so damned handsome with that blond hair and those long-lashed blue eyes it was almost indecent. He was visiting his family in Newport that summer before flying to Moscow to take up his first diplomatic post.

It had been the sort of quick romance that a girl of Tracy's background found comfortable. Whit's credentials were even more impeccable than her own. They could attend dances and take long evening drives and play tennis and sail with the knowledge that society delighted in them. They could even, for the fun of the game, pretend a certain earnestness that neither one of them quite felt. Tracy had been too young for marriage and even too young to think of marriage, except as a station in life that she would one day assume. Unself-consciously, she and Whit toyed with the notion of it, a sort of what-if game they played.

The romance had not been consummated, as the romances of so many of Tracy's friends were in those days. Whit was attractive and obviously found her attractive, but he had an odd reticence. He would, necking on the sailboat with nothing but blue sky and blue water in all directions to the horizon, bring her to the point where she would not or could not have said no. Then he would stop suddenly as soon as she played that part of the game the way she was supposed to play it—claiming, without meaning it, that she wanted to stop. Whit would sigh and turn his back, staring out over the water while she caught her breasts in the halter top and combed her hair or, once or twice, pushed him over the side with playful fury, suggesting that he cool off.

He had cooled off, reliably, and then afterward the

243

letters from Moscow had cooled off and then stopped altogether, and when she saw Whit the year he got back, he had changed. He had a strange hurt bewildered look in his eyes, she could remember now, and though they met at parties, he never asked her for a date. He was subdued and given to moody silences. He romanced girls Tracy had known, and some of her close friends, but he remained single, switched from State to the CIA, and in a short time was considered one of the most eligible bachelors in Washington.

Tracy had seen him inevitably at a variety of social functions in Washington during her good days with Matt, and had begun to look at him speculatively when the marriage turned sour. Twice, after Whit had seemed to respond to her mild flirtation, she made the invitation more overt. The first time he had pretended not to notice it. The second time he allowed himself a single deep kiss and then he pulled away from her and said thanks, but adultery was not his cup of tea, and then he had apologized for that, saying it wasn't her fault, it was his. After that, they had avoided each other.

Now, in Gstaad, she had been pleased to find he was as charming and handsome as ever. Still boyish, but not quite pretty-boyish any longer, with the wrinkles at the corners of his eyes and the odd challenging hardness in them. She had introduced him, trying to keep the sound of proprietary smugness out of her voice, at the bridge table, and then Shields and the others had left.

He came to the point after a single drink and some small talk. "Andreyev could be up on that mountain. You heard about it, I guess?"

Tracy said she had heard about it. "But is he really?"

"He could be," Stoughton evaded. "I have to assume that he is. I have to assume the Russians will try to get him down from there and back to Moscow before he can defect. It's my job to see that they don't."

"How could *I* help?"

"You know this town. How would the Russians go about it?"

"Whit. Really, I'd like to help you. I don't see how I can."

"There's an outfit called the Air Rescue Service," Stoughton explained. "I gather they're the only people with the right kind of planes. Because it would take a plane to reach him, a special kind of plane and a special kind of pilot."

"Now I'm beginning to get it," Tracy said.

"Do you know any of those people? Can you let me know who they are? And find out if they're in town?"

There were six Air Rescue Service pilots in the valley. Yes, Tracy thought, quickly pouring herself another drink, I know some of those people. Of the six Air Rescue pilots who lived in and near Gstaad, she had slept with four.

They had spent the afternoon at it, Tracy making one call after another, chatting sociably for a few minutes and hanging up, then Stoughton using the phone to assign his CIA agents in pairs to surveillance of the pilots.

One pair kept watch on an empty chalet near the lumberyard on Lauenenstrasse.

Tracy had tried three times to get through to Ruedy Stücki, but his phone did not answer.

"You know this Stücki personally?" Stoughton had asked.

Tracy sipped her whiskey. "Yes, I know him."

"What kind of guy is he?"

Tracy shrugged. "A wild one. He's a charter pilot, and he flies Air Rescue. He always seems to have plenty of money to spend."

"How come?"

"That's the point. Nobody knows. He has something else going for him, that's what they say in the village. It's probably just talk. That's the kind of place this is. I've even heard that the police are trying to get the goods on him."

"The police? For what?"

"Smuggling. The story goes that they aren't after him very strenuously because what he's doing is smuggling American cigarettes into Italy."

"By plane?"

Tracy nodded.

Stoughton picked up the phone, dialed, and said, "It's Whitney Stoughton, Herr Minister. Do you know anything about a pilot named Stücki? Ruedy Stücki? Uh-huh, I see. No, we haven't been able to track him down either. Talk is he does some smuggling by plane into Italy." Stoughton smiled at Tracy. "I have my sources. No, no evidence. But Stücki sounds like a very good bet to me. Sure, I'll let you know."

The crisp authority with which Stoughton had put his

agents into action and the easy terms on which he had addressed the Minister, probably the Minister of Justice and Police, impressed Tracy.

She said so. "You've changed, Whit. You're a damn sight more confident than you were years ago. If you don't mind me telling you, you've turned into one hell of an attractive man. I say turned into because what you used to be was one hell of an attractive boy."

Stoughton smiled and, not unexpectedly, looked her up and down. "You haven't exactly aged poorly yourself, Mrs. Olds."

She made a face. "I hate it when an old friend calls me that. Reminds me of a mistake I made."

"When you married Matt?"

"Maybe. But also when I let you waltz off to Moscow without extracting any promises."

"That was a long time ago."

"Lord, yes. Have you got any wiser since then? I don't think I have."

"Why not?"

"Because I have a very strong urge to make up for lost time."

She got up and went into his arms. She kissed him and felt the good hard leanness of him against her body. "The minute you called," she said against his mouth, "I hoped it would be like this."

He drew away from her and sat down with an odd, twisted smile on his face. "I ought to be getting back," he said.

"Where are you staying?"

"A chalet near the Ambassador's place."

"Brimming over with CIA agents?"

"Something like that."

"Do they know where you are?"

"Sure," Stoughton said.

"Then stay here and have dinner with me."

He looked at her, again with that odd, twisted smile. He's shy, she thought. He's actually shy.

"Okay. But then I really have to get going."

They had steak and salad and a bottle of Gevray Chambertin and Tracy broke out a half-liter of seventy-five-year-old Napoleon brandy. They talked of old times.

After dinner Tracy said, "Look at it out there. It's really snowing."

"I'd better get back."

"The plows call it a day at dinnertime. Do you have chains?"

"No."

"You'd never get up the hill. Why not spend the night? There's plenty of room."

He opened the door and looked outside. The driveway had been plowed that afternoon, but snow now stood a foot deep in it.

"All right," he said after a while. "But let's make it an early night. I'm beat."

They sat around working on the bottle of Napoleon brandy. Once Tracy kissed him, but he did not respond as he had before dinner. He said that the brandy had really hit him. At eleven she showed him the guest room, bringing towels and a fresh toothbrush.

"If you want anything," she said.

"I'll sleep the sleep of the just."

Now, past midnight in her own bedroom, Tracy finished the tumbler of whiskey. She thought about it for ten minutes, told herself what the hell, got out of bed, and padded barefoot down the hall to the guest room. The door was opened a crack, a fact that brought a small, pleased smile to her face. If he really wasn't having any, he would have locked the door. Just an old-school, gentlemanly shyness, that's all.

She went into the darkness of the guest room and quickly climbed into bed beside him. He turned over in his sleep, mumbling something, and she began to caress him. He turned over again, this time on his side, facing her. She ran a hand down his flank, feeling the maleness of him, bringing herself very quickly to a high sexual excitement.

Whitney Stoughton woke up. He was aware at once of Tracy in bed with him. He had thought she would be too drunk, all that brandy on top of all that wine.

He could feel her hands exploring his body. He pretended he was still asleep, but it was no good. Her hands became too insistent. She stroked him and for one glorious instant he felt himself beginning to respond, and he surrendered himself to it, hoping it would last.

It did not last. He could smell the perfume of her hair, the woman scent of her. He lay there, his fists clenched. It was not unpleasant, as sometimes it had been. It was not anything. He threw his arms about her abruptly and pulled

247

the soft curves of her body against his. "Whit," she whispered. "Whit."

His body remained wooden. She was warm and soft and nothing else.

After a while he said with a self-conscious chuckle, "I guess I had a lot of brandy to drink. Forgive me?"

"No, I understand. It's all right."

"Sometimes I have this trouble," he said.

"It's all right. Shh. Just go back to sleep."

"Oh God, Tracy. I really wanted to. I can't. I just can't."

After a long time he was asleep, and she knew it was more than too much brandy, more than, as he had put it, sometimes having this trouble.

"You poor guy," she said.

Chapter
TWENTY-ONE

1 *A stubborn storm can linger in the path of the warm Alpine wind called the* foehn, *but sooner or later the wind brings fine weather. Suddenly the leaden sky brightens, patches of blue appear, and the disintegrating clouds reveal the craggy peaks with their fresh load of snow. The sunlight, when it bursts through, is shockingly bright against the white flanks of the mountains, the white floor of the valley. The storm goes, and soon there is only that incredible deep blue of the high Alpine sky, and the white of the snow gleaming as if sprinkled with a million diamonds, and the dazzling sunlight.*

Minister of Justice Willy Müllener awoke a few minutes after dawn Tuesday morning and saw the brightness at the window of his hotel room. He drew the curtains and squinted out. The last flurry of snow was falling, the sky was bright, rents appeared in the clouds in the time it took him to find and put on his sunglasses. He smiled. The sudden fine weather even made his miserable cold feel better. A snowplow passed on the street below, going by

248

slowly, eating snow like a hungry mechanical monster and squirting it clear of the street.

The telephone rang. Half-dressed, Willy Müllener answered it.

"Ernst Grossmann, Herr Minister. I can pick you up in ten minutes. I'll be airborne in half an hour."

Since the death of the almost legendary Hermann Geiger, Ernst Grossmann was the dean of the Air Rescue pilots. It was Geiger who had developed, and Grossmann who had perfected, the technique of landing a plane on and taking off from the snow-covered mountains, where, naturally, no landing strips were available. What you did was land upslope in a controlled stall, the oversized skis wired to your landing gear skimming over the fresh soft snow, the slope, if it was steep enough, bringing the plane to a stop inside of a hundred meters. What you did was take off downslope—the steeper the slope, up to a point, the better. It is very easy to be airborne, Ernst Grossmann always said, if you fall off a cliff.

Willy Müllener had selected Grossmann to fly the rescue plane. Ernst Grossmann, in his fifties, was known to be a careful, patient man who might not win any races but who invariably got where he was going. The fact that Grossmann said he would be ready to fly in half an hour astonished Willy Müllener. But if Grossmann said it, it was so.

"You're going up with me, Herr Minister?" Grossmann's voice came over the telephone.

"I wouldn't miss this."

"No, I can see that."

"Ten minutes then," Willy Müllener said, and hung up.

He dressed quickly, sure that nothing could go wrong. An Army squad had arrived in Gstaad by train last night. They were camped at the airport now. No plane except Ernst Grossmann's, with Müllener in it, would take off. As a further precaution, word had been sent from Bern to every airport in Switzerland. For the next several hours none but regularly scheduled aircraft would take off, anywhere in the country, without police permission.

But, Müllener reminded himself, the pilot Ruedy Stücki was still missing. Neither the police nor the American CIA had been able to find him. His dog, its skull crushed, had been found in the living room of his chalet.

The American Stoughton's guess had been right, Stücki was a smuggler. The Swiss police had been cooperating for months with the Italian Guardia di Finanza in an attempt to uncover Stücki's *modus operandi*.

About once a month during the winter he flew a plane over the Grand-Saint-Bernard and down into Italy. His Italian confederates had been captured with several thousand cartons of American cigarettes, with watches and camera parts.

Stücki never took off with his contraband from the airport in Saanen.

He had a plane hidden somewhere in the valley.

There were many places, in an Alpine valley, where a small airplane could be hidden. There were not many hiding places it could take off from, except in winter, when the Air Rescue technique could be used on a steep, snow-covered hillside.

Which was why, apparently, Stücki flew his contraband only in the winter months.

It had not been a pressing problem to the Swiss police, and they had tackled it in their slow, patient way.

But smuggling, Müllener thought, was one thing. Flying for the Russians was another.

2 After killing the Alsatian bitch, it had been easy for Moskalenko to put the fear of God into Ruedy Stücki. The tough, self-confident, capable ones, Moskalenko knew, were often easiest to break down. Show them someone tougher, more self-confident, more capable, and they were through.

It had worked that way with Stücki.

"You saw the dog die," Moskalenko had said. "It could have been you. It still can be you. Do you value your life, Herr Stücki?"

The reckless ones valued their lives because they enjoyed them, and Stücki was no exception.

"I am going to ask you once, Herr Stücki. Just a single time. Will you fly us?" Moskalenko held up a hand. "Wait. Before you answer—I said once. I meant once. Give me the wrong answer and you will die. As the dog died. Right here. Right now."

Ruedy Stücki was looking down at the Alsatian bitch. Blood had run from one of its ears and made a stain on the carpet. "I'll fly you," he said.

"Is the plane fueled and ready to fly?"

"Yes."

"Where is it?"

Ruedy Stücki licked his lips. Moskalenko's shoe nudged the dead dog. He tapped the two red sticks against his left palm.

"In a barn."

"You will now go into the kitchen. One of my people will go with you. You will get food. Have you a gas heater? And a portable radio?"

"Yes."

"Bring them, too. We will leave at once."

Twenty minutes later, they had driven off in Stüki's bright-red Land Rover. The words *Ruedy Stücki— Charter Pilot* were painted in large white letters on the side. Moskalenko did not like that, but there was nothing he could do about it.

No one saw them leave.

That had been early Sunday morning. They had driven through the deserted streets of the village and along a road that climbed steeply through a pine wood. Soon the snow on the road deepened, but the heavy-duty snowtires and four-wheel drive of the Land Rover got them through for another mile or so. Then, at Moskalenko's command, Stücki had driven along a lane that went into the pines. A hundred yards and they were stuck.

A hundred yards would be enough.

In a few hours the Land Rover would be hidden, its tracks obliterated. No one would find it.

From there they walked. An hour and a half, uphill, in the snow. It was the hardest physical work Moskalenko had ever done.

They reached the barn. Inside, it smelled of cattle and hay. It was a large barn, and in the rear was an airplane. Not large, but large enough.

They remained in the barn all day Sunday and Monday. Moskalenko had a great deal of patience, but his comrades were restless and irritable. He did not mind. They would be eager to get out and do what must be done when the storm stopped.

Moskalenko had found a coil of rope, and Stücki was bound hand and foot. Even so, one of the Russians was constantly on guard. It was cold, but not dangerously so, and the heater helped.

Tuesday morning dawned brilliantly sunny. Moskalenko had not slept. He had spent the night reaching a decision. He did not believe they would be able to take Nikolai

251

Ivanovich down off the mountain and back to Geneva for the flight to Russia. According to the radio the whole country was in a turmoil. It would be impossible.

He had to kill Nikolai Ivanovich. Then let the subtle dilettantes like Malinin decide what story to tell. It didn't matter to Moskalenko. He admitted to himself, with some reluctance, that they were as good at their job as he was at his. They could pretend shocked innocence. They could somehow blame the Americans. They could blame the Red Chinese or the Swiss or the inhabitants of Easter Island, for all Moskalenko cared.

He woke his two comrades. He woke Stücki.

"How do you get the plane out?"

"The skis."

"Across the floor of the barn?"

"Snow. I shovel snow inside."

Stücki was untied. He rubbed his arms and legs. They opened the wide, dilapidated barn doors. Moskalenko's comrades shoveled snow inside. Stücki tramped it down. Soon he had made a runway of snow from the doors to the airplane. Moskalenko looked outside.

"You take off from that?"

What he saw was a snow-covered field dropping sharply away from the barn doors to a stand of pines less than a hundred yards away.

"It's not as difficult as it looks," Stücki said.

Moskalenko shrugged. They pushed the plane across the barn. It slid easily on its oversized skis. The open doors barely accommodated the span of the wings.

Before they climbed aboard, Moskalenko said, "You can be free of us—or dead—in two hours. It depends on you."

"We'll be seen in the air," Stücki told him. "I won't be able to help that. I usually take off at night."

"Today you take off in the morning."

"It will finish me here."

Again Moskalenko shrugged. He took the case containing the Lion Free aboard the plane. Under his other arm was a pair of snowshoes he had found in the barn. There was room in the plane for four, and even five if necessary. Not that it would be necessary.

Soon the propeller was turning. Thinking of what the morning would bring, Moskalenko felt an excitement almost sexual in its intensity.

They taxied forward and then began to drop down the steep snow-covered field. In less than five seconds they were airborne, barely clearing the pines at the far end of the field.

3 The right rear tire of Ernst Grossmann's station wagon went flat exactly halfway between Gstaad and Saanen.

Kneeling on the hard-packed snow left by the early-morning snowplow, Grossmann jacked up the wagon and unlinked the tire chain. He gave an apologetic look, his third, to Willy Müllener and began to remove the wheel. Müllener got the spare from the back of the wagon. They worked in silence.

Both heard the faint drone of an airplane engine. Grossmann got up, shaded his eyes against the brilliantly blue Alpine sky, and pointed. Behind them, beyond the shoulder of the Oberbort hill and the castlelike Palace Hotel, shut until the winter season began, they could see the plane glinting in the sunlight.

It banked sharply to the right and came flying toward them.

For once Grossmann was talkative. "Our ghost plane," he said. "Twice last winter people reported hearing it. Both times in the middle of the night. The police were never able to learn where it took off from." Grossmann nodded thoughtfully. "I could tell them where to look now."

Willy Müllener was hardly listening. The white, single-engined plane was flying at about five hundred meters. It passed overhead and seemed to be heading straight for the Saanen airport. It had to be Ruedy Stücki. No other private plane would be flying.

Were the Russians with him? Then why was he heading for the airport?

Suddenly, just short of the village of Saanen, the plane began to dive.

It plummeted earthward almost vertically. Grossmann's eyes narrowed. His big hand was squeezing Willy Müllener's shoulder in a powerful grip. "They're going to crash."

But at two hundred meters the plane began to pull out of its dive. At less than a hundred meters, directly over the church steeple in Saanen, it banked to the left, turned a hundred and eighty degrees around the valley, gained altitude, and flew off to the southeast—toward Lauenen and the Teufelkopf Hütte.

Willy Müllener let out a breath. "Hurry," he said.

Grossmann set the spare wheel into place. He picked up the spanner and began tightening the first lug.

4 They were at five hundred meters, Gstaad below them, the highway running straight across the valley floor to Saanen, a single tiny toy car unmoving on it, Saanen and its airport beyond.

Stücki sat at the controls, Moskalenko in the copilot seat, the other two Russians behind them.

"What do you think you're doing?" Moskalenko demanded.

Stücki stared straight ahead. "Are you a pilot?" he asked, his voice cocky. "Can either of your friends fly a plane?"

Moskalenko did not answer him. They were approaching Saanen.

"If you want to live," Stücki said, "just sit still. We'll be on the ground in five minutes."

They hit an air pocket and dropped a few meters.

"Get him away from the controls," Moskalenko said calmly in Russian.

An arm circled Ruedy Stücki's throat from behind. His hands let go of the wheel. He was pinned against the back of the seat. The wheel went forward and the nose of the plane dipped. They began a steep dive. Stücki struggled.

"Are you afraid?" Moskalenko asked. He had to shout over the roar of the engine.

Stücki tried to answer. The arm across his throat made that impossible. He tried to nod his head. He could not do that either.

The toy village that was Saanen grew. The white church and its big wooden steeple became larger.

"I am not afraid," Moskalenko shouted. "Do you understand that?"

He waited another second. Then he said, "Release him."

Stücki's hands flew to the wheel. He pulled back hard, cords standing out on his neck with the effort. Wind shrieked past the thin shell of the plane. He brought the nose level less than a hundred meters above the steeple. He could see people in the street, looking up.

"Now take us to the Devil's Head Hut," Moskalenko said.

Chapter

TWENTY-TWO

1 It was easy for Matt, standing outside the hut, to see how the place got its name.

The hut was perched on a broad shoulder of the mountain, below the summit. Above it in profile loomed the devil's head. A black outcropping of rock high up might have been the devil's ear, a slab of rock two hundred feet long his nose, a snow-filled gully his sunken cheek. With the ground on which the hut stood as one gigantic shoulder, the devil might have been shrugging. A thousand feet above the hut, a high wind whipped the snow in little swirling puffs on the devil's forehead.

Claudia came outside, squinting and shielding her eyes with one hand against the sunlight.

"Will they come soon?"

Matt nodded. He had been listening for the engine of the rescue plane. Nothing yet. "They're probably on their way already."

"I never knew there could be so much snow." Claudia was peering up toward the summit. Except for the slashes of black rock that formed the devil's features, an enormous wall of white loomed over them. The wedge-shaped cairn of boulders behind the hut was pointed straight at its base. "Will we be able to walk out there?"

Matt left the shelter of the overhang, and sank at once to his knees in the snow. He took another step, and the snow reached midthigh. Two more steps and he had sunk no deeper. He returned floundering to Claudia's side. They stood for a while in silence gazing at the devil's head and the high thrusting peaks beyond it.

Claudia heard it first. "Listen," she said, and then Matt heard it, too. He was aware of her reaching for his hand

255

and holding it. Soon they could see the plane, a tiny white toy against the vastness of the sky.

"I'll get my father."

She went back inside and came back a few moments later with Nikolai Ivanovich at her side, shading his eyes to see the plane. Malinin followed them, one arm draped over Bayev's shoulder, hobbling in the shallow snow under the overhang. Al Cash was behind them, his hand making a rasping sound against the stubble of beard on his jaw. "Can I see you, Mr. Olds?"

They walked under the overhang to the side of the hut.

"There's no telling what kind of reception we'll get, down at the airport."

"What do you mean?"

"I just want to know how to play it, that's all."

The white plane was circling the hut.

"I don't follow you."

"The Russians could still make noises about taking Andreyev into custody for his own good. A mental breakdown, and he doesn't know which end is up. What happens then?"

Claudia waved both arms over her head. Bayev grinned.

"Nothing," Matt said after a while.

"Nothing?"

"I don't think the Swiss will let them."

"You could be wrong. Who the hell knows what's been going on down there the last few days?"

"Whitney Stoughton does, for one. Don't worry about it."

"That's my business, worrying."

"From the minute we board that plane, the Swiss call the shots," Matt said. "That's the way it has to be."

As they turned to join the others, Matt saw the plane bank and fly off, so low its skis were almost skimming the snow. Soon it dropped below the far side of the ridge and was lost to sight. The sound of the engine faded and was gone.

The maneuver surprised Matt. With those skis, he thought, they could have taxied along the ridge and come to a stop on a moderate slope no more than a hundred yards from the hut. What were they waiting for? He shook his head ruefully and told himself he was getting as bad as Al Cash.

2 Moskalenko was panting. Sweat stung his eyes and dripped from his chin.

Toiling along the south side of the ridge in snowshoes was hard work. It had taken him a while to find the proper motion—thrusting forward from the hips almost like a skater. He had to hurry. The real rescue plane wouldn't be far behind.

He kept in the shadow of the ridge, certain they wouldn't see the tracks of the snowshoes there. He was climbing at a tangent now, traversing up toward the top. He thought he had covered more than half the distance to the hut. He reached the crest and peered over. Squinting in the dazzling light, he wished he had sunglasses.

Sunlit snow, rising gently and then sharply toward the hut. Three hundred meters, he judged. A long shot, but not hopelessly long. They stood in a cluster under the eave of the hut, six tiny figures. Waiting for the plane to return.

Moskalenko got down behind some rocks and opened the case that contained the Lion Free. He attached the stock and set the variable-power scope into the bridge mount.

He settled into a prone position and raised the rifle with a smooth, practiced motion until the stock rested coldly against his cheek. He set the scope and squinted through the tack hole. Very nice. Really quite lovely. Everything in sharp focus. It was thawing. He could see dripping icicles on the eaves. He centered Nikolai Ivanovich in the tack hole.

He waited. Not yet, he thought. A long shot and, if he missed, they could get back inside the hut. He might not have time for a second shot then. All he had to do was wait a few minutes. Until the rescue plane arrived. They would leave the shelter of the hut, would flounder eagerly across the snow. Plenty of time for a shot then, and a second if he missed.

But he did not think he would miss.

3 At first the plane was a tiny speck against the deep blue of the Alpine sky. Soon it was close enough to see the skis attached to the landing gear.

"That's funny," Matt said. "It's not the same plane."

What they saw now was a high-winged, single-engined white plane with red trim. The name *Diablerets Pilot* was stenciled in bright red letters below the two small portholes on the fuselage.

The earlier plane had been smaller, all white, its fuselage devoid of markings or portholes.

Diablerets Pilot banked steeply and came down in a landing approach.

4 Willy Müllener tried to raise the small plane by radio. It did not answer, and he gave up after a while.

Grossmann had spotted the plane down on the snow, perhaps a kilometer below the hut in the deep shade on the other side of the ridge. He took *Diablerets Pilot* down in a fly-over at a hundred meters. Three figures stood in the snow. One of them had even waved. Willy Müllener could see no tracks leaving the area of the plane but knew it would have been difficult to see any in the shadow of the ridge. A kilometer, he thought. That would be a long way to travel, on foot, in the deep snow. A long way, even, on snowshoes. It would take no more than fifteen minutes to bring *Diablerets Pilot* in, pick up the people at the hut, turn downslope, and take off.

"How near the hut can we land?" he asked Grossmann.

"A hundred meters. The final approach is too steep to come any closer."

"What do you think?" Müllener pointed down at the white plane.

"Try it," Ernst Grossmann said.

"Good. Let's go in."

They flew on to the hut and banked. Grossmann couldn't resist waggling his wings in salute.

Willy Müllener felt himself pushed back hard as they dropped and then he was straining forward against his seatbelt as they raced over the snow, flaps down, snow and black outcroppings of rock hurtling by, and then the skis touched and bounced and touched again, and the hut grew large as they skidded steeply up toward it, snow arching away from the skis like a pair of white wings.

5 The plane came to a stop a hundred yards from the hut, propeller turning slowly and then not turning. The door opened at once, and a man jumped out.

"Hurry," he called.

258

Matt led the way, the others following in the deep footprints he left in the snow.

6 First in line was the big American, and Moskalenko regretted letting him pass untouched through the tack-hole sight of the scope. After all, he thought, their business together had been interrupted.

The footballer Bayev was next, half-supporting Viktor Malinin. Then, a few steps behind, Nikolai Ivanovich and his daughter. An unknown man, another American, Moskalenko guessed, brought up the rear.

The big American, whose name was Matthew Olds, stumbled into a deep drift. Moskalenko could hear his easy laughter as he struggled to free himself. He turned, grinning, and said something and struck out in a new direction, the others much closer on his heels now.

Moskalenko waited until they had covered half the distance to the plane. Fifty meters back to the hut, if he missed. Fifty meters forward to the plane. Plenty of time for a second shot. Moskalenko centered the scope on Nikolai Ivanovich's back, the dot in the tack hole high up between the shoulder blades. He raised it a little. The back of the neck. A single shot there would kill as quickly as turning off a light.

A gentle wind blew from Moskalenko's left across his line of sight. He estimated its velocity and adjusted the scope for windage.

His finger tightened on the trigger.

The Lion Free barked and moved against his cheek and slammed back against his shoulder.

Nikolai Ivanovich did not fall. Moskalenko thought the shot had been a shade to the right. Just a few inches. Too much adjustment for wind. They were scrambling madly in the snow, and shouting.

Moskalenko calmly readjusted for the windage and raised the rifle again.

He heard a distant rumbling, and then a sound like thunder. He looked up.

7 At the flat cracking sound of the rifle Matt was whirling back toward the others. In the time it took him to turn, he understood. The other plane, the Russians, a KGB assassin, all of it clear in his mind even before the first echoes of the shot bounced back from the mountains.

There was no cover anywhere.

He reached Claudia, who was staring at him, eyes wide, mouth wide. He saw Al Cash, a gun in his hand, scanning the ridge to their left. He brought Claudia down, hard, in the snow. He saw Bayev lumbering toward Andreyev.

And then he heard a distant rumbling sound and then a roaring that seemed to fill the world.

8 *An avalanche needs snow, at least a foot of snow and usually much more, at the point of origin. It needs a slope of at least thirty degrees to slide on. And it needs a trigger.*

Overloading, shearing, and a sudden change in temperature are three such triggers.

Vibration is a fourth.

A distant explosion can cause an avalanche. Thunder can start one.

The rise in temperature brought by the foehn had already weakened the bonds of cohesion in the great slab of snow that was the devil's forehead. Left alone, it would have fallen, in some little time, as a comparatively harmless loose-snow avalanche.

Disturbed by the vibration of a single rifle shot, it fractured angularly on a wide front that was measured, afterward, and found to be almost half a mile across. It fell not as loose snow but as a packed-snow avalanche, a solid mass hurtling down the Devil's Head.

Within seconds its great weight gave it tremendous speed. Still in a single enormous slab, it struck the cairn of boulders behind the hut.

The slab fractured and became two slabs crashing downslope, one on either side of the hut. Loose snow rose over the building like a wave smashing over a jetty. One chimney came apart as if a hand grenade had been dropped down it, stones hurtling in all directions. Part of the roof and the rear wall caved in. Above the hut, dirty brown streaks looked like tears on the devil's face.

Below, one section of the avalanche plunged to timberline, crushing and uprooting trees before its force was diminished.

The second section was directed sharply to the left by the avalanche-break with enough momentum to reach the crest of the long ridge in defiance of gravity.

9 Moskalenko wanted to run, but there was nowhere to run. He wanted to hide, but there was nowhere to hide. He screamed and could not hear the sound of his own voice in the roaring of the snow.

The wall of white approached, fracturing. Great angular blocks of snow, some as big as houses, tumbled, struck each other, bounced together and apart.

Then they seemed to hang above Moskalenko. He screamed again. He raised one hand in front of his face.

Seconds later, fracturing and fracturing again, the slab avalanche finally came to rest a thousand feet below. The twisted barrel of a rifle protruded a few inches from the brown-streaked snow.

10 For four of them, the loose snow that spilled over the roof of the hut was no more than a heavy snowstorm. They could hear a distant rumbling. They could see nothing. They waited, helpless, for the crushing weight that did not come. After a while the air brightened, and the sky appeared, and all at once they could see the plane, red and white in the sunlight, untouched, and a small man with a dewlapped face and a larger, grizzled man in a flight jacket, plodding up the slope toward them.

The man with the dewlapped face sneezed. "How many?" he called. "How many?" He sneezed again.

Six, someone said. They counted heads.

And they saw the narrow river of snow, unmoving now, the secondary avalanche that had spent itself before reaching the plane.

11 Tumbling head over heels, Matt was aware of clinging to Claudia. It was like drifting dreamlike in a dense white cloud. His motions seemed impossibly slow. His sense of direction deserted him and he had no idea whether they had rolled just a few yards or all the way downslope past the waiting plane. He remembered wondering, without panic, whether they would be buried, remembered telling himself this was loose snow, the slab had been diverted and even the force of the loose snow had been broken by the hut, remembered thinking it was thawing, the loose snow would be wet and therefore heavy, they would not sink deeply into it as they would have in dry powder, all they had to do was wait it out, ride with it, don't fight it, don't—

He was aware that the motion had stopped.

He was also aware that he could not breathe.

A moment of panic seized him then. He fought blindly against the snow, making swimming motions with his arms, churning with his legs.

He saw suddenly a sky bluer than a sky could be, and the air was cool and sweet. Hands helped him. A man with a dewlapped face smiled at him and said something, and then he was standing on shaky legs only twenty yards from the plane, helping Claudia to her feet, snow on her hair, snow on her face, breathless but unharmed.

He looked back at the ruins of the hut, dwarfed by the jumbled blocks of snow piled high on either side of it.

"Can you walk?" the dewlapped face asked.

They could walk. They reached the plane, and were helped inside. Someone gave Matt a cigarette. His hands were trembling violently. He heard the sound of the engine. The plane turned, its nose pointing downslope. They began to move forward.

In seconds they were airborne. It was, as Ernst Grossmann always said, as easy as falling off a cliff.

Chapter
TWENTY-THREE

1 The bells in the tower of the picturesque wooden church near the airport in Saanen were tolling.

The bells in the two stone churches in Gstaad were tolling.

Men appeared in the streets, some in the coarse gray-green army uniforms they wore for two months every year, some in civilian clothing, some carrying the 7.5 mm *Sturmgewehr*, the automatic rifle of the Swiss Army, some carrying carbines.

They came, in answer to the tolling bells, to the two churches in Gstaad and the wooden church in Saanen. Soon they were marching, in no orderly ranks, members of the least soldierly-looking small army in the world, and possibly the best, from the church in Saanen through the cobbled streets of the village to the flat surrounding farmland and the airport. They piled into cars in Gstaad, and old farm trucks, and some of them pedaled along the hard-packed snow of the highway on bicycles, *Sturmgewehrs* slung over their shoulders.

The bells continued to toll.

2 Vasily Kapitsa, Foreign Minister of the Soviet Union, was a deceptively soft-looking man, short-legged, with shoulders narrower than his hips. Sometimes *Krokodil* caricatured him as a penguin in a white shirt and a tailcoat. The animal they should have used was a chameleon. He had climbed through the ranks of the Foreign Ministry under Khrushchev, under Brezhnev and Kosygin, under Lysenko and Andreyev, never making the mistake of aligning himself with the wrong side, never, it was often said, taking sides at all. His softness hid a brilliant mind and a coldly pragmatic approach to life at the top of the Kremlin power structure. In Moscow they often said, behind Vasily Kapitsa's back, that if war ever came, and no matter who won, Kapitsa would be sitting at the peace table afterward telling the world how to pick up the pieces.

Kapitsa had been in the mountains only overnight. He had taken the train to Gstaad, as six hundred reporters had done, reporters who were waiting outside on the runway now. Their presence bothered him. He had managed to keep aloof from them on the train. He had shepherded his flock of thirty KGB agents, all with cover jobs at the Embassy in Bern and the Russian mission at Villa Krupskaya in Geneva, from the railroad station to the Hotel National in Gstaad. He had used the influence of his office to get rooms for them, which meant that thirty members of the press, arriving on the same train, had had to spend the night in the lobby of the hotel.

He had his instructions from Moscow, instructions he did not like. But, after all, he was a pragmatist.

"I must insist," he told Willy Müllener. "I have orders to return to Geneva with Chairman Andreyev and his daughter."

Müllener blew his nose. "And from Geneva, where?"

"That," Kapitsa said, shaking his head, "is no Swiss affair."

"The Premier does not wish to go."

"The Premier is not responsible for his own actions."

"I believe he is," said Willy Müllener.

"I know he isn't."

"He is tired, he has been through an ordeal, he wants to stay in Switzerland. He will stay in Switzerland."

"Asylum? You're making a mistake. I demand to speak to the Swiss Foreign Office."

"Well, then, if I am making a mistake," Willy Müllener said gently, "at least I am making it in the name of the President of my country."

"Your answer is no?"

"I have been trying to tell you that for twenty minutes."

"Out there," Vasily Kapitsa waved at the window of the control shack in which they sat, "I have thirty men. If necessary, they will defend the right of my government to—"

"Defend?" said Willy Müllener, his voice louder. "Were you defending the Premier, up there on the mountain, when you tried to kill him?"

"I know nothing about that," Kapitsa told him.

"All you have left, Herr Minister, is diplomatic immunity. Be grateful for it. An investigation will determine whether you will be declared *persona non grata* in my country."

"I give you my word," Kapitsa declared solemnly, "that I knew nothing of any attempt to assassinate him."

Willy Müllener's face contorted and he sneezed. "Very well. I believe you. It changes nothing."

"I had hoped you wouldn't make this necessary, Herr Minister," Kapitsa said uncomfortably. "It is my duty to return to Geneva with the Chairman. It is the duty of my thirty men, outside there, to obey my orders. The last thing I want is to resort to force. I do so with grave reluctance, believe me."

Willy Müllener listened to the tolling of the church bells, wishing he were in bed with a hot mulled wine. Finally he decided enough time had passed. He stood up and announced, "We will provide transportation for your thirty men back to Bern, or Geneva, or wherever you wish."

"You just won't understand," Kapitsa said, exasperated, "will you?"

Müllener did not quite smile. He went to the door and opened it. Both men stood in the doorway.

A small squad of Swiss soldiers stood uneasily outside the green tents they had pitched alongside the runway. They watched the thirty KGB agents lounging against the side of the hangar. At a signal from Kapitsa they spread out and faced the soldiers.

"This could be very unfortunate," Kapitsa said.

Close to fifty reporters were poking around the rescue plane. Others had found wood and lighted small fires on the tarmac to keep warm. A great many of them milled about the locked door of the lounge at one end of the hangar.

The soldiers brought their carbines to port arms.

"I hope you are aware," Kapitsa told Willy Müllener slowly, "that you are bringing this on yourself." He did not sound happy. "I ask you for the last time—"

Willy Müllener shook his head.

Vasily Kapitsa raised his arm to signal the KGB agents again. He blinked. His eyes narrowed.

A rag-tag army, perhaps half of them in uniform but even the uniforms looking rumpled, was descending on the airport. A few wore helmets. Scores came on foot. Some came on bicycles, and then more on bicycles, and then cars and trucks were disgorging still more of them.

They came slowly, in no great hurry, but they came inexorably. Some were young, some middle-aged. Hundreds of them were already swarming over the snow-covered runway and still more were coming.

Kapitsa sighed and then, finally, looked relieved, Müllener was certain, like a man who had tried to do an onerous duty and failed but not without honor.

Willy Müllener went through the hangar to the door of the lounge. Not one to delegate authority if he could help it, he had the key in his pocket.

As he inserted it and turned the lock, the church bells stopped their tolling.

Part Three

Chapter
TWENTY-FOUR

1 What would be known, later, as the Schoolhouse Meeting between President Clay Huntington and Premier Nikolai Ivanovich Andreyev took place late that afternoon in a small classroom of the Leman International School, with the two world leaders and Matthew Olds, the President's Assistant for National Security Affairs, present.

The International School had been Willy Müllener's idea. His brother Alfred owned and ran it. The old stone buildings of the school, enclosed by walls on three sides with the fourth side open to the lake, stood less than a mile from UN Headquarters and, ironically, not much farther than Villa Krupskaya. Security, Willy Müllener had said on the flight to Geneva, is a state of mind. To prepare for trouble when what you want is secrecy is to invite trouble. A motorcade, an army of security guards, a harried chase by the press corps, an obvious destination like city hall or police headquarters—all would be unwise. If you want to remain in seclusion for a few hours, the Watchman said, you are wise to select something less obvious and to arrange things with considerably less flair.

He made two phone calls before they left the mountains, and when they landed at a small airstrip five miles from Geneva, a pair of unmarked cars were waiting. Müllener drove the first one himself, Al Cash at his side, and Andreyev, Claudia, and Matt in back. In the second car were Semyon Semyonov and four agents of the Swiss security police.

They drove to the International School, and through the ivy-covered gateposts. They were not followed.

The meeting, Matt knew, could have been so different. It could have been the Council Chamber of the United Nations, with the huge cathedral-like windows and the sepia and gold-leaf ceilings and murals. It could have been all carefully arranged with pomp and protocol, armies of advisers, simultaneous translators, and the press waiting outside in the marble hallway. It could have been an Andreyev as free to speak for his country as Huntington was for his. Instead, it was a small classroom with a slightly battered desk, a few rows of chairs, a green-slate blackboard on which the verb *blanchir* had been conjugated in chalk in a childish scrawl, and a view through the windows to the placid lake. Instead, it was Clay Huntington, one of the most popular American Presidents of the century, and Nikolai Ivanovich Andreyev, the nominal leader of the Soviet Union who hadn't yet been officially deposed.

They greeted each other warmly, the President with the big Huntington grin, Nikolai Ivanovich with a frank, open smile that grew and finally matched that grin while Matt made the introductions. Then Nikolai Ivanovich sat in a front-row seat while the President, performing the ritual of the black cigarette holder, perched on one corner of the slightly battered desk and said lightly, "I guess we both figure the world's worth saving, Mr. Chairman. If you have any idea how we go about it, I'm all ears."

By then Matt was at the door.

"Where does he think he's going?" Nikolai Ivanovich asked.

The President took that, as it was meant to be taken, as a suggestion. "Stick around, Matt."

Surprised, Matt pulled a chair up to the window and sat. He could see the lake and the open end of the quadrangle. Somewhere a bell rang, and students moved in little groups across the cobblestones. Matt's thoughts, oddly at that moment, were of his son. Chris was here, in this school, right now, unaware of the presence of his father, unaware of the presence of Clay Huntington and Nikolai Ivanovich Andreyev, learning the *passé simple* of the verb *blanchir* or discovering with sudden self-conscious insight the beauty of a Shakespearean sonnet or wishing classes were over so that he could enjoy the fine weather— unaware that what he learned, and how he would use it, what free time he had, and what he would do with it, for the rest of his life, might depend on what went on in this room today.

"What is the situation in Yugoslavia?" Nikolai Ivanovich had just asked.

Quickly, President Huntington told of the dogfight in which a MiG-27 had been shot down, sketched an account of the coup of the Yugoslav colonels.

"And the Red Army?"

"They're still camped near the border. The press is beginning to call it the Phony Invasion."

"Before that changes," Nikolai Ivanovich said soberly, "I want to address the General Assembly. How soon can that be arranged?"

"We'll get it set up for tomorrow," the President promised, "if the US Air Force has to fly in the delegates personally. You can expect the biggest radio-TV coverage in history. What will you tell them?"

"The truth. That I was weak," Nikolai Ivanovich said. "Or worse—a fool."

"Now wait a minute, Mr. Chairman. It took courage and foresight to do what you did."

"A man is forced to be courageous," Nikolai Ivanovich said wryly, "when he has been backed into a corner. Mr. Olds has read what I have written. He will understand that."

Matt wasn't sure whether he understood it or not. "Everything you did was an attempt to prevent war," he said. "Opposing Lysenko in the Kremlin, agreeing to meet the President at the Summit, disappearing when you realized—"

"Please." Nikolai Ivanovich raised a self-deprecating hand. "I flew to Geneva like Neville Chamberlain returning from Munich to London claiming he had brought peace in our time. But one does not save a tiger's victim after the victim has been severely clawed. The victim bleeds to death. I knew that Lysenko was determined to have Yugoslavia. But I told myself I was on an errand of peace. That was weakness. Give Lysenko Yugoslavia, and he'll want Finland. Give him Finland, and he'll want Berlin, Austria. ... I have documents, Mr. President, that include nothing less than a meticulous time-table for the conquest of Europe.

"And still I deluded myself. Lysenko, you must understand, had no real lines of communication with the West. He remained in the Kremlin, in a cloak of secrecy. I was his—do you call it, front man? The West knew me, the West had reason to trust me. That was Lysenko's thinking. For me it was seductive. For the world it was diabolical."

The President looked at Matt. "I'm not sure I follow that."

"Lysenko needed me—for one more task. I was to meet you at the Summit. To discuss the Yugoslav crisis, to work for a détente I knew Lysenko would never accept. I was to meet you in treachery. In the midst of our conference, the Red Army would move." Nikolai Ivanovich's face was bitter. "Then I would do some horse-trading."

"I think it would have been a little late for horse-trading, Mr. Chairman," the President said dryly.

"Would it? If I admitted I came to Geneva with knowledge of the invasion? If I told you the vote in the Council of Ministers had been close and I just barely lacked the strength to defeat it? If I presented you with a set of alternatives, one leading almost certainly to war and the other to an uneasy peace?"

Again the President looked at Matt, then back at the Russian Premier. "What kind of alternatives?"

"You could resist the invasion, but if you did, the collective leadership would force me to step down— leaving the Kremlin in the hands of its hawks. The result? A shooting war in Yugoslavia and an irrevocable drift toward total war.

"If, however, you agreed to accept the occupation of Yugoslavia as a *fait accompli*, I would remain in power— the Kremlin dove, wings somewhat clipped perhaps, but still there. A man who thought as the West thought. A man who hated war as much as you did. A man who could work, from the inside, against Lysenko. Tell me, Mr. President," Nikolai Ivanovich asked slowly, "faced with those alternatives, what would you have done?"

There was a silence. Outside, the quadrangle was deserted. At the edge of the lake a boy and girl were holding hands and feeding bread to the swans.

"I see what you mean," the President said. "It would have been tough. Give up Yugoslavia and keep Andreyev. Fight in Yugoslavia and leave Lysenko unopposed in the Kremlin." He shook his head. "I hope I never have to make that kind of choice. I don't know what I'd do. Matt?"

"It would have been tempting to go along with the

Premier," Matt said slowly. "And it would have been a mistake."

"Yes," Nikolai Ivanovich said flatly, "it would have been a mistake. I'd have returned to the Kremlin no more than a figurehead. In time they would have made me step down anyway, using ill health as an excuse. You would have accomplished nothing. Nothing—except to give the West one more reason to doubt American leadership. And then what?"

The question needed no answer. Nikolai Ivanovich had already given it—the irrevocable drift toward total war.

"Instead of forcing you to choose between two evils," Nikolai Ivanovich said with a faint smile, "I disappeared."

"Yes, I can see how that would cut the ground out from under Lysenko," the President said. "The vote in the Kremlin was close. Lysenko was gambling. A set-back and he'd be in trouble at home. It was like Hitler in the Rhineland back in the thirties. If the French had fired just one shot, the German General Staff would have kicked him out of power."

"Exactly," said Nikolai Ivanovich. "Until he knew my intentions, Lysenko couldn't go ahead. What if I defected to the West, bringing documentary proof that the invasion, far from being a response to crisis in Yugoslavia, had been planned for months? World opinion, then, might have made the collective leadership despose him. But he couldn't just call it off either. That would mean a whole new timetable, a whole new set of invasion plans."

"Sure," Matt said, "and the strong chance that the collective leadership, given a breathing spell, would vote to forget the whole thing."

"Lysenko could not afford them that breathing spell," Nikolai Ivanovich agreed. "Ilić was assassinated as scheduled—both as an excuse for the invasion and because Lysenko could not tolerate his policies and was determined to remove him in any event."

"So given the trouble at home, and your disappearance, and the assassination," the President said, "Lysenko did the only thing he could do. He hedged."

"The Phony Invasion," Matt said.

"To be resumed," Nikolai Ivanovich told them, "on my capture or death. To be abandoned, with Lysenko finding a scapegoat in the Red Army, if I brought my case before the world."

"Which," Matt said confidently, "is what will happen when you appear before the UN tomorrow."

"Wrong," said Nikolai Ivanovich promptly.

"Wrong?"

"Wrong, because it will do more than that. It will bring about Lysenko's fall from power. And it will do more than *that*." Nikolai Ivanovich paused.

"I never defected. I never asked the United States for asylum. I never asked Switzerland for asylum. I prepared my daughter for it, I discussed it with Ambassador Hauser, and decided reluctantly it would be necessary."

President Huntington almost bit through the black cigarette holder and Matt found himself out of his chair and standing bolt upright in amazement as Nikolai Ivanovich finished calmly.

"I was mistaken. My defection will not be necessary. Thanks to your wisdom, Mr. President, thanks to your restraint, I am still Premier of the Soviet Union. I intend to remain so. Don't you think it's time we had our Summit Conference?"

2 The needle bit deeply into the swollen flesh of Viktor Malinin's ankle.

"A massive dose of novocaine, comrade Colonel," the Villa Krupskaya resident physician explained. "We use it on our athletes when they must compete despite an injury such as yours. Move the foot. How does it feel?"

"Leathery," Malinin said after some experimentation.

"And the pain?"

"Is gone."

"There will be some weakness, but not much. You will be able to use the foot."

Deftly, the resident physician wrapped the ankle in an elastic bandage. Malinin got up and tried it. Except for the odd leathery feeling and a slight weakness, the ankle felt fine. He dismissed the doctor.

It was then after dinner. He had spent the day in his Villa Krupskaya office brooding over the events at the little airport in the mountains. He would remember them, he realized in an agony of self-pity, all the rest of his life. He had failed. They would give him command of a border station on the Amur River. Or KGB headquarters in a provincial Siberian city. Igor Lysenko did not tolerate such failure.

The plane had come down, and reporters had swarmed out on the runway, the police trying to hold them back while the little group went quickly across the snow toward the hangar. Questions had been hurled at them. Nikolai Ivanovich said nothing. Matthew Olds bantered with the reporters. They seemed to like him. Malinin walked leadenly, his head down, Bayev helping him. A man had broken through to them, bruises faded to dirty yellow on his big, battered face. The pastry chef Semyon Semyonov. Even that, Malinin thought, coming back to haunt him. Semyon had embraced the Chairman. "From now on, Nikolai Ivanovich," he said, tears springing to his one good eye, "I don't leave your side."

On top of everything, Semyon. Semyon, who would be able to say he had been picked up at Malinin's orders and interrogated by Moskalenko in Moskalenko's own inimitable style. And Moskalenko himself? It had been Moskalenko who had fired the shot on the mountain. It had to be.

He remembered the cool-eyed rejection, as final as a pauper's funeral, on Claudia's face. She would never believe Malinin had not sanctioned the attempted assassination. Then, after they had been examined by a Swiss doctor, after they had eaten, the hardy Swiss fare sticking in Malinin's throat so that he could barely swallow, to be held like a prisoner, a common prisoner along with the footballer Bayev, after the others left. And to be flown, finally, with Bayev and the Foreign Minister, to Geneva in a single-engined plane, Bayev as ever untalkative, Kapitsa sunk deep inside himself, weighing alternatives in his wily way, Kapitsa the chameleon-man, who would somehow rise to the surface again as he, Malinin, would not—it was too much.

If anything, it was worse at Villa Krupskaya. Kapitsa disappeared into his office. He did not send for Malinin. Whatever plans he had did not include Malinin.

And soon the rumors began to flow through the high ceilinged halls of the villa on the lake. Nikolai Ivanovich was in conference with the American President at the Hotel Beau Rivage. Nikolai Ivanovich had asked for asylum at the American Embassy in Bern. He was at the headquarters of the International Red Cross, his mental competence being established by an international panel of specialists. He had been flown secretly to Washington in a CIA jet.

The one certainty was that he would talk.

The most consistent rumor was that the General assembly of the United Nations would meet tomorrow at President Huntington's request. But Malinin could get no confirmation even of that. Ordinarily, a summons to the meeting would have gone from the UN building to the Russian Chief of Mission here at Villa Krupskaya. But with Foreign Minister Kapitsa in residence, these were not ordinary times, and all the Chief of Mission would tell Malinin was that he had heard the rumor, too.

Twice Malinin had tried to reach Kapitsa. The Foreign Minister was in conference. The Foreign Minister had left the building.

Malinin finally, in frustration and like any other resident of Geneva, turned to the radio. More rumors. It was suggested, in the liquid accents of Genevois French, that if President Huntington had asked for a meeting of the General Assembly, Soviet Premier Andreyev would address that meeting.

And then? How had Lysenko put it? *An ambitious man who has to live with his own failure is a very sorry specimen.*

Because, if Nikolai Ivanovich talked, Operation Minaret, the conquest and occupation of Yugoslavia, would fail, and Malinin would carry the blame on his shoulders to the post on the Amur River, to the provincial city in Siberia, to the end of his unsatisfactory life.

Andreyev must not be allowed to talk.

There is still tonight, Malinin thought. Moskalenko's way was out. To kill Nikolai Ivanovich now would be as bad as to let him talk.

But to kidnap him? To snatch him away from the Americans on the eve of his triumph? To return with him to Moscow in his own big Tupelov jet? No, no, Malinin thought. That wouldn't be possible, not yet. The Swiss would never let the Tupelov take off. But later? After a few days, after a week?

To take him to the Embassy in Bern, and wait? To call Lysenko on the scrambler? To send to Lubianka for the KGB experts in brain-washing? How long would it take Nikolai Ivanovich, a prisoner, Claudia also a prisoner, to crack?

It could be done, Malinin knew. He felt the good eager tension growing in him, his whole body like a clenched fist. It must be done.

He sent for the resident physician. The novocaine was administered, the bandage wrapped, the doctor dismissed.

Malinin went to the safe. He removed the ridiculous abstract painting, worked the dial. His hands were trembling.

He took out the photographs, the act of perversion, so long ago, in Moscow, there before his eyes in glossy black and white, the face younger but unmistakable.

I will send you a gift, friend.

I will send you a little gift.

He consulted the classified section of the Geneva telephone directory, found a twenty-four-hour messenger service, called it.

Then he took one of the prints and scrawled across the bottom:

"Call me—Malinin."

3 After dinner, Whitney Stoughton went up to the communications center on the second floor of the Hotel Beau Rivage, to send a cable to CIA headquarters in Virginia. He had lingered over dinner working on the cable, a long, detailed report of the day's activities. His heart hadn't been in it, but Old Man McManus would expect it. And, if Stoughton hadn't been at the center of things up in the mountains, still he came off pretty well in the report.

The report was fair, it was objective, and he felt as much at peace with himself as he ever did. It would take some time, though, to get over that fiasco with Tracy. He wondered why he kept torturing himself, why he kept trying. For a time, years ago, it had worked. He had, with a lot of drink inside him and with various women, been able to do what was expected of him. They had seemed satisfied. He had not found them repulsive. He still didn't. But these last few years, no luck at all. And then the surprised look or the mocking look or, worst of all, the pitying look like Tracy's.

Why don't you just let it go? he thought. He was almost at an age when no one would think it peculiar if he dedicated himself to his work. Whitney Stoughton? they would say. He's Mr. CIA, darling, you're wasting your time. He's too busy for women.

He had carefully avoided compromising situations with men. There had been temptations—the lithe young TV repairman in Georgetown, the too-pretty cipher clerk from the National Security Agency, the obvious and aggressive queen during his Damascus assignment last year. That way lay disaster, and his avoidance of it had been complete.

Except once. The hotel room in Moscow, the young Russian information officer and his friend, too much to drink, the poker game, and then—

Whitney Stoughton shuddered. Why am I thinking of it now? he wondered. It seemed almost a lifetime ago.

He entered the communications center with the draft of his cable and a pert young girl approached him and said, "This just now came for you, Mr. Stoughton."

He took the envelope and opened it. He heard the chattering teletypes and the soft babble of talk. A man brushed past him and picked up a phone and said wearily, "If Uruguay can't show up, the hell with them. Tell them to go fly a kite. No, that's not from the SecState, it's from me. No, for Chrissake, I'm kidding. Sure, give them the needle. A little friendly urging. I've got to have the list for that crazy Indian by midnight. You think you're in a stew? You should see him."

Stiff paper. A photograph. At first the light fell on the glossy surface, and Stoughton could not see it. Then he turned it in his hands. His fingers began to flutter. He almost dropped the photograph. He could feel his face going white.

"Are you all right, Mr. Stoughton?" the pert girl asked.

4 He stood in a pay booth in the lobby of the hotel. He heard his own voice say:

"This is Whitney Stoughton, Colonel Malinin."

"I appreciate your promptness."

"What do you want?"

"I will send one copy of that photograph to your President, a few copies to random members of the press. Unless, Mr. Stoughton. There is, of course, an alternative."

The little fan in the phone booth was not working. Sweat stung his eyes.

"What do you want?" he asked again.

"Where's Andreyev?"

"I don't know."

"Then that is your own bad luck. Good night, Mr. Stoughton."

"Wait!"

"Where is he?"

"I can't. I can't tell you that. What kind of man do you think I am?"

"Why, no kind of man, Mr. Stoughton. As the world will know by morning."

A silence. Shame that made him want to scream. He had been first in line for Old Man McManus's job. In a year, or two years at the outside . . .

Again he heard his voice, as if it were not part of him. "The Leman International School."

And once that was out, the rest was easy.

"What are the security arrangements?"

"Six Swiss Security Police, around the clock."

"Six? You're joking."

"More would have attracted attention. It's the truth."

"For your sake, I hope so. Who else is with him?"

"His daughter. A Russian named Semyonov. And Matthew Olds is spending the night."

"Have you been there?"

"No."

"I need more information."

"That's all I know."

"I need a lever."

"What—are you going to do?"

"Do? Why, destroy the photographs. That's all you need to know."

"How can I trust you?"

"Can someone in your position ever trust anyone?" Another silence. Then: "I said I needed a lever. Think."

"I told you that's all I know!"

"Please don't be shrill. Though perhaps it does become you. Any additional item of information. Anything you know."

"There's nothing."

"There is always something. A small chink in the armor. What are the sleeping arrangements, for instance?"

"I don't—wait a minute." Stoughton was now desperate to please. Anything, as long as those pictures were destroyed. Al Cash had taken the President to and from the school. A classroom, he had said. On the ground floor of the boys' dormitory. Erasmus Hall, that was it. "Boys' dormitory," he said. "It's called Erasmus Hall. They're probably in there."

"That's better. Anything else?"

"No." It was done.

"Think."

"That's all I know!"

"You're shrill again. Is Olds still armed?"

"Armed? No, I don't think so."

"These things are important," Malinin said in a patient, reasonable voice. "One never knows what knowledge will tip the balance. You're doing fine. You have almost earned the right to the destruction of those pictures. Is he a light sleeper?"

"What?" All Stoughton could think of was the photograph.

"Is Matthew Olds a light sleeper?"

"I don't know."

"Or anything else? Some unexpected peculiarity? You know all about peculiarities, Mr. Stoughton, don't you?"

Whitney Stoughton's breath caught.

"Shall we say, for a start, the correspondents of the New York *Times* and the Washington *Post* in Geneva? They can't print the picture, of course. But they'll know, Mr. Stoughton. They'll know, and if they are too gentlemanly to spread the good word, there are other ways. How long do you think your secret will be safe?"

Malinin needed a lever, and suddenly Whitney Stoughton knew he could give him one.

"His son," Stoughton heard himself say.

"What was that?" Malinin's voice was no longer unctuous. "Whose son?"

"Matthew Olds. His boy Chris attends the school."

"And he is there right now?"

Stoughton said that as far as he knew the boy was there right now.

"You have my word that I will destroy the pictures."

Stoughton's initial relief, after he hung up, was enormous. It was over now, he told himself. He would have to live with the knowledge of his treachery. What else could he have done?

But the more he thought about it, the less he was convinced it was over.

Why should Malinin destroy the photographs? What if he didn't? What if, for the rest of both their careers, Malinin owned Whitney Stoughton?

How could Stoughton live with a thing like that?

5   Malinin hung up, pleased with himself.

The Swiss, in their quiet, thorough, infuriating Swiss way, were right, of course. Unless a frontal assault on the school by a large band of armed men were attempted, six security police were enough. In Willy Müllener's place, Malinin would likely have reached the same conclusion.

Nobody, least of all Malinin, would mount an attack on the school.

No attack, no violence at all, would be necessary.

Malinin considered the situation. He would need help, but precious little of it.

First, Bayev. Bayev had failed, as he himself had failed, and would be eager to atone for that failure.

Then Department D, here in Villa Krupskaya. The D stood for *dezinformatsiya*—disinformation. Every KGB post, and hence every large Soviet mission, had such a department. To discredit the *glavni vrag*, the main enemy— the United States—with propaganda, with clever forgeries of papers, of documents. And Malinin would need some documents tonight.

Finally, Kolchak. Kolchak, a brash young fellow, was the KGB watchdog on the staff of simultaneous translators here at the villa. He also spoke perfect colloquial American.

Malinin tested his ankle. He could walk easily on it. He picked up the telephone.

Chapter
TWENTY-FIVE

1   Shortly before dawn, a black Mercedes limousine with Geneva plates stopped outside the gates of the school. A man with a flashlight approached the car. Malinin could dimly see another man in the darkness behind him.

"Hi," said Kolchak, who sat behind the wheel. "Do you speak English?" He had an eager, ingenuous voice—a friendly voice.

"Only a little," the man with the flashlight said.

"Better rustle up some guy that does," Kolchak told him. "It's what you might say real urgent."

"Rustle—ah, I see. What do you want here?"

"Mr. Olds. There's been a change of plans."

"Olds? This is the Leman International School. There is nobody here by that name." The man's voice was still polite, but it had hardened.

"Cut it out, Mac," Kolchak said. "We're playing on the same team."

"Please?"

"We're playing—ah, the hell with it," Kolchak said, squinting in exasperation at the flashlight. "Just get somebody here on the double who speaks the lingo."

The second figure stepped out of the darkness. "I speak English quite well," he said. "Who are you?"

"Lew Peters," said Kolchak. "CIA. The President—"

"Identify yourselves," said the second voice. Then: "No! Reach in with index finger and middle finger—so."

"They're a regular bunch of paranoids," Kolchak grumbled, as he and Malinin in the front seat of the Mercedes, and Bayev in the rear, produced their identification folders as instructed.

The folders, Malinin knew, were excellent. With just a few hours to prepare them, Department D had done beautiful work. The folders had a used look. Even their photographs were included behind little plastic windows.

The flashlight went from face to face. Kolchak looked exasperated again, and mugged. "Now is it okay if we see the man?" he demanded.

"What man?"

"She-oot, pal," said Kolchak. "You've got Matthew Olds in there. You've got Russian Premier What's-his-name, and the old man's daughter. Now just how in hell d'you think we'd know all that unless we were the good guys? The good guys, you know? Like in the cowboy movies?"

Careful, Malinin thought. Careful, Kolchak. You're doing splendidly—but don't overdo it.

"Let them in, Henri," one of the voices said in French.

"I suppose that much will do no harm," Henri allowed. "You will stop the car just inside the gate," he ordered in English.

The iron gates were swung back. The car drove slowly in, and Kolchak immediately pulled to a stop.

280

"Leave them wide open," he said, laughing. "For our getaway."

Four figures stood around the car now. Moonlit buildings loomed on either side of them. Directly ahead Malinin could see cobblestones and the shine of moonlight on water.

"Now precisely what is it you wish?"

"Olds. Just take me to him, okay? Oh, yeah," Kolchak added, apparently as an afterthought, "and the kid."

"The kid?"

"Mr. Olds's son," Kolchak said with an elaborate sigh. "Wake him up and bring him to Olds's room. Pack an overnight bag for him. If the rest of them are pulling out, the kid comes too."

"Isn't it an odd hour—" Henri began.

"How would you guys go about moving them?" Kolchak asked. "At high noon with a brass band leading the way?"

There was a silence.

"Well, Jesus H. Christ, howdya think we knew about the kid," Kolchak demanded scornfully, "unless we were—"

"The good guys. Naturally. I'll take you to Mr. Olds. We'll wake the boy. I didn't even know he was here."

"You'll find him in Erasmus Hall," said Kolchak wearily. "Same dorm as his old man. Snap it up, huh? I told you this was real urgent."

Kolchak, Malinin, and Bayev got out of the car.

"Are you armed?"

"Nah," Kolchak said. "We just use our bare hands in case of trouble. You bet your sweet ass we're armed."

Now surely, Malinin thought, Kolchak had gone too far.

But he hadn't. Nobody tried to disarm them. They went across the cobblestones toward one of the buildings.

2 For Whitney Stoughton it was a sleepless night. What he had done was monstrous. That much he knew at once, and he accepted the knowledge. It had been a matter of self-preservation. Malinin could destroy him.

What was worse than the monstrous deed, and his own helpless acceptance of it, was the fact that he had no guarantee it would stop there.

Two o'clock, and the Scotch bottle empty. A dirty

281

metallic taste in Stoughton's mouth. Malinin could call him again, next month, next year—five years from now. It would be exactly as if Malinin and the KGB had a desk at Langley, Virginia, as if every CIA directive passed over that desk. All our agents, all our carefully set-up networks would be blown. As an intelligence-gathering agency the CIA would be as effective as a troop of boy scouts.

Three o'clock. A rippled reflection of moonlight on water on the ceiling of the room. And how many brave men would die, thanks to a single indiscretion in Moscow fifteen years ago? Or because Stoughton lacked the courage to face the consequences now?

Four o'clock. The deep notes of the cathedral bell across the lake. Tolling for Andreyev, for Yugoslavia, tolling for peace.

Tolling for Whitney Stoughton.

He could not let Malinin get away with it.

Call the police, he thought. Call Willy Müllener. The Minister of Justice and Police, now, would be asleep in his brother's house at the International School. He had said he would stay there until Andreyev was delivered safely to the UN. He would move, he would move fast, but afterward he would ask: How did Malinin know where to find the Premier? And how, Mr. Stoughton, did you know that he knew?

Five o'clock. Get Al Cash and his ten-slash-two people. Go in there with them. But sooner or later Cash, or somebody, would ask the same questions.

Five-thirty. An anonymous tip to the police? But how could he be certain they would act on it?

Six. It's too late. Malinin's had plenty of time by now. Or has he? He wouldn't shoot his way in there. Sweet-talk his way in, maybe, using the information Stoughton had given him. But the Security Police would be careful. Words would not be enough. They'd demand to see some identification and, knowing that beforehand, Malinin would have prepared some. That took time. Maybe it wasn't too late.

Not the police, and not Al Cash. Just yourself. You couldn't sleep. You were restless. You wandered over there to see if everything was all right. Kind of lucky you did.

He dressed quickly. The feeling of shame, of helplessness, was gone. Hurry. Just hurry.

"This," said Kolchak with a grin, "is where we take a page out of your paranoid book, friends. That room wouldn't be bugged, would it?"

The Security Police asked: "Bugged?" and, "What room?"

Three of them stood at the bottom of a flight of stairs in Erasmus Hall with Malinin, Kolchak, and Bayev. Another had gone to wake the boy.

"Olds's room, for crying out loud. Bugged means—"

"It is not bugged, Mr. Peters."

"Well, no harm in asking."

"You wish to see him alone?"

"Hell, no," Kolchak said. "Being as how it's top secret, we figured you could call in Eurovision. Now where is he?"

"This way, Mr. Peters," Henri said coldly, indicating the stairs. "First room at the top."

Kolchak, Malinin now knew, was playing it just right. The Security Police disliked him. That was fine. They would be so busy objecting to his arrogance that they would have little time left to doubt his credentials. Not that they had any reason to.

Kolchak made no move to go upstairs. "We'll wait for the kid," he said. "What's taking them so long?"

Then they heard footsteps. The fourth security agent appeared, carrying a small suitcase. A blond boy of about twelve, looking sleepy but excited, was at his side.

"Is my Dad really here?" he asked.

"That's right, Chris," Kolchak said. "Just upstairs there. First door at the top."

"Where are we going?" Chris asked.

"Your Dad'll let you know," Kolchak said, and Chris bolted up the stairs.

"Tell him we—" Kolchak began, then smiled and shook his head. "I guess I better tell him myself."

Malinin went up with Kolchak. Bayev was right behind them. Downstairs, the Security Police heard the boy's voice, and a man's voice, and footsteps, and a door shutting.

Henri was scowling. "What an uningratiating individual!"

"Peters?"

"Who else?" said Henri. "The others never opened their mouths. Would anyone object," he asked suddenly, "if I got the Watchman out of bed?"

283

"The Watchman would object."

There was laughter.

"Still, he likes to be in on everything."

They all admitted that was true enough.

"I'll get him," Henri said.

4 Pale false dawn stood outside the window. Matt wa
still groggy with sleep. "What are you talking about?" h
said.

Chris shrugged. "Search me. They made me pack
bag. They said we were going someplace. What are yo
doing here anyway, Dad?"

It was a small room with two bunks, a desk, a chai
and a sink in the corner.

"Who?" Matt asked. "Who told you that?"

Chris had left the door ajar. It opened wider, and thre
men crowded into the room.

"I did," Viktor Malinin said.

5 Whitney Stoughton had his foot to the floor. The ca
sped along the lakefront. Buildings, trees, the boat basi
the long sloping lawn of the UN fled by. The sky ha
lightened. Dawn was not far off.

Maybe it's too late, Stoughton thought, hunched ove
the wheel. Probably it's too late.

It can't be too late.

6 "Everything is at stake now," Malinin said. "Do I hav
to point that out?"

"No," Matt said.

"The police are downstairs. You can call out if yo
wish. If you do so, the boy dies. Instantly."

Bayev stood with one hand on Chris's shoulder. Chri
looked more bewildered than afraid. There was a gun i
Bayev's other hand.

Matt remained silent.

"Now listen carefully. We are going downstairs with th
boy. There is a car in the courtyard. The boy will be in it
You will then be alone. You are to tell the Chairman an
his daughter there has been a change of plans. You ar
taking them somewhere else. You understand? That is al
you tell them. Then you take them to the car. The polic

may ask some questions. Answer them however you see fit. We are all going to leave here, one way or another."

Chris or Andreyev, Andreyev and Claudia, Matt was thinking desperately. There must be something he could do. He could think of nothing. But there were still a few minutes. He had to dress, talk to the others, go downstairs, see the police—

And all the while a gun at Chris's head.

"Tell the boy what he must do."

"Chris," Matt said slowly. "You're going downstairs with them. Don't be afraid. There's a car. Wait in it with them. I'll be down soon."

"The police," Malinin said.

"There are some men downstairs, Chris. If they ask, tell them it's all right. Tell them I said so."

"I'm not afraid," Chris said defiantly. He swallowed hard.

They took him from the room. Matt could hear their footsteps going down the stairs.

7 Willy Müllener said, "Odd, very odd that I should know nothing about it." He was dressing while he talked.

"Then it was right to wake you, sir?" Henri asked.

Nodding, the Watchman picked up the phone and called the Hotel Beau Rivage. "This is Minister of Justice and Police Willy Müllener," he said. "I would like to speak to Mr. Whitney Stoughton. It's urgent." He waited, and then he was listening, and then he hung up.

"Not there," he said and drew in his breath three times, hard, and managed not to sneeze. Now that he had learned Stoughton was out, he felt somewhat less concerned about the situation. A sudden change of plans in the hours before the dawn, the Deputy Director of the CIA off somewhere in the night to arrange things, possibly there was no need to worry.

But Willy Müllener was not called the Watchman for nothing. "Let's have a look at your CIA agents," he said.

8 Matt was going to say: "I had a call from Whitney Stoughton. There's some possibility the KGB knows where we are. We're being moved."

But he saw Nikolai Ivanovich, polishing his black-rimmed glasses with a handkerchief, an expression of

285

patient curiosity on his face; saw Claudia, her dark hair hanging loose as she ducked her head to light a cigarette, then her head coming up and those big eyes looking at him with trust, and what he said was:

"Malinin and Bayev are outside. They've got my son. They're waiting for us. They'll kill him unless we go with them."

He did not remember what they said. Nikolai Ivanovich dropped his glasses. He groped for them on the floor. Claudia found them, gave them to him, looked at Matt.

"I don't know what to do," he said.

It was an admission he had rarely made before. He had been lucky. He had always managed to keep his private life subordinate. Being where the power was, that was what mattered. But now Malinin had brought everything crashing down on him—Andreyev, the UN, and the world waiting to hear him, Claudia, her life in danger if he let her get into that car, Chris, his life forfeit if he didn't.

"I don't know what to do," he said again.

Let them take Andreyev and Claudia, to save Chris? Alert the police, and watch Chris die?

"Viktor wouldn't—" Claudia began. She stared at her father. She bit her lip.

"He would," Nikolai Ivanovich said softly. "We both know that."

"Yes," Claudia said. "We both know that."

Nobody spoke for a moment.

"Hey, Olds," a voice called from downstairs. "Shake a leg, will you? We don't have all day."

They were in a lounge on the second floor of the building. A big man loomed in the doorway, bald, his face discolored with old bruises, one eye swollen half-shut. He was tucking his shirt tails in to his trousers. He asked a question in Russian.

"He wants to know what is happening," Nikolai Ivanovich said.

Matt nodded. He had understood that much. He looked at Nikolai Ivanovich.

"A little boy," the Russian said. "A helpless little boy. Will they use a gun?"

The big bald man Semyon was waiting patiently. He understood no English.

Matt couldn't talk. He nodded again.

"It would be the same as if we pulled the trigger," Claudia said, watching her father.

Nikolai Ivanovich addressed Semyon in Russian. He cleared his throat. "I explained that we must leave here," he told Matt. "Your President has my papers. We have talked. He will know what to do. Perhaps it was too much to expect that I ... Well, Claudia." He touched her arm. "Are we ready, then?"

"I can't let you," Matt said.

"They won't kill us. They'll take us back to Russia. The boy would die. Tell them we're coming."

9   They were outside in the courtyard.

The sky had grown light. A star or two remained. A fresh breeze blew in off the lake, and Matt could smell the water. He could see the car, fifty yards ahead, between them and the gates, its headlights on. The gates stood open.

Willy Müllener was there, with three of his agents, between them and the car.

"Trouble, Mr. Olds?"

"We're moving. Just a precaution."

It was not yet light enough to see into the car. The young Russian stood beside it. Malinin and Bayev must have been inside with Chris.

They covered half the distance to the car.

Claudia walked proudly, her head high. Her father's stride was firm.

They're waiting for me, Matt thought. They don't really mean it. They can't go ahead with it. But it's my son. They want me to decide.

Chris—or everything.

They had almost reached the car. The young Russian got in, disappearing behind the glare of the headlights. He started the engine.

Chris.

Chris, forgive me.

Matt took a deep breath. He was going to call out to Willy Müllener.

No he wasn't.

He didn't know.

A car came careening in between the gateposts. It struck the waiting limousine with a crunch of metal and bounced back. A man got out, running.

Whitney Stoughton.

287

Willy Müllener and his agents were running, too. Voices shouted. Then Matt was racing for the car, knowing he could not possibly reach it in time.

10 Malinin leaped from the car. His eyes were wild as Stoughton reached him. He backed away, and a gun appeared in his hand. He's going to shoot me, Stoughton told himself with an odd, strange calm. I was in time, I got here in time, but he's going to shoot me, that was why I had to rush, it was an appointment I had to keep, nobody will accuse me of being a—

He saw the muzzle flash, and then something hit his head and destroyed it.

11 In the back seat of the car Bayev made an animal sound, a cry of wordless remorse for what he had almost done.

He had almost pulled the trigger and killed the boy. It was close, so close. But he had not done it.

How could he—with Claudia Nikolaievna watching?

He hurled the gun away and yanked the boy down below the level of the windows, for safety.

12 Kolchak ducked through the gateway and looked both ways on the street. No one. He took two running steps to the left and a man stepped out of the shadows, pointing a gun at him. It was the security agent Henri. Kolchak slowly raised his hands.

"Say something clever in American now," Henri suggested.

13 Matt struck Malinin's hand with the edge of his fist, driving it against the door of the car. When Malinin did not lose his grip on the gun, Matt hit him in the face and Malinin fell down.

Still he held the gun. He was screaming something in Russian. He was sitting on the cobblestones and pointing the gun at Nikolai Ivanovich.

Something blurred past Matt and landed on Malinin. It was the big bald man Semyon. The gun clattered away.

Semyon straddled Malinin and began to hit his head back and forth. He kept on hitting him.

It took three of Willy Müllener's agents to drag him off.

Chapter
TWENTY-SIX

1 When word spread through the Palace of Nations that the press would, after all, be allowed to attend the special meeting of the General Assembly, reporters came rushing from all directions.

Their footsteps clattered across the sand-colored marble of the lobby.

They burst out of conference rooms, where delegations to the General Assembly were being interviewed.

The King of Thailand, in Salle IV, looked up from his notes to find that, except for his assistants, he was quite alone.

They hurried across the Persian carpeting of the rear lobby, leaving a clutch of African delegates in full regalia to answer one another's questions.

They sprinted past the black and white Swedish marble starburst at either end of the main lobby and raced for the great bronze doors.

They streaked past the long windows that looked out over the courtyard, the great cedars of Lebanon, the zodiac globe, and the long slope of lawn down to the lake and the brooding massif of Mont Blanc beyond.

In less than five minutes, six hundred reporters had rushed into the Assembly Hall and found their places. They gazed, most of them breathless, past the gray draperies and the blue carpeting to the podium. It was still empty.

They glanced with some satisfaction at the TV technicians, who had already set up their gear. For once the working stiffs with pencils wouldn't be left out.

They looked again at the podium and rose as the President of the United Nations General Assembly,

Señor Román of Bolivia, took his place. They saw the President of the United States, flanked by Secretary of State Reed and National Security Affairs Assistant Matthew Olds, follow him in. The black leather chair on Señor Román's right remained empty.

Though there had been no official word, there wasn't a man among the six hundred reporters who didn't believe that chair would be filled by Russian Premier Andreyev.

One of them didn't know what to do about it.

Yuri Kirov, the Tass News Agency correspondent, was like a lone swimmer against the tide. Fighting his way in the opposite direction through the mob of reporters streaming into the Assembly Hall, he bolted downstairs and found an empty phone booth in the visitors' lobby.

He got through to Villa Krupskaya quickly, and asked for the Foreign Minister's office.

"Kirov," he said breathlessly "They're letting the press in!"

"Yes, naturally, we had expected that," Vasily Kapitsa's secretary said calmly.

"They're saying Chairman Andreyev will address—"

"Why don't you find out for yourself, Comrade Kirov?" the voice asked sweetly.

"At what point do I walk out?" Kirov demanded.

He thought he heard a mocking little laugh. The woman was talking to someone else at her end. Then: "Don't you want to hear what he has to say?"

"What?" asked Yuri Kirov.

"The Chairman. Don't you want to listen?"

"No walk-out?" Kirov asked, puzzled.

"Comrade Kirov, are you a reporter or aren't you?"

Kirov said he was a reporter.

"Then—report."

The line went dead, and Kirov was running again. The bronze doors of the Assembly Hall were closing just as he reached them. He showed his credentials and slipped inside and leaned against the wall in the rear of the crowded hall. President Huntington was on his feet and speaking.

2 "I have been told that the largest radio and television audience in history will hear these words this morning. More than one billion people, one out of every four human beings on the face of the earth. This is as it should

be. This is no time for secret meetings behind closed doors."

The famous Huntington grin flashed. "On the other hand, with that kind of audience, I will be mercifully brief. This day is not mine. It belongs to another leader of a great nation. I met with him yesterday, and again this morning. He has much to tell you."

President Huntington looked up. The bronze doors had swung wide, and then Nikolai Ivanovich Andreyev, Chairman of the Council of Ministers of the Soviet Union, Premier of Russia, was in the hall.

He wore a dark suit and a figured black tie. The silk cord of his pince-nez disappeared under the lapel of his jacket. His hair was brushed in two wide glossy wings away from the bald dome. Only the neatly trimmed beard was missing. He strode briskly to the podium, shaking Señor Román's hand, shaking the President's.

President Huntington sat down and then rose again as the applause continued. It was for both of them. After five minutes of it, Nikolai Ivanovich beamed and, in the Russian manner, he himself began to applaud. Finally he raised both hands for silence. Five minutes more, and he had it.

"President Román," he said, his voice sure and powerful, "President Huntington, delegates, people of the world. I have been a long time coming here. We Georgians, as you know, are inveterate sightseers. And Switzerland is a beautiful country."

Yuri Kirov heard the easy laughter all around him. The old man was still a spellbinder. Just a few words and he had them in the palm of his hand. But with Operation Minaret, the invasion of Yugoslavia, already underway, even if temporarily stalled, what could he say? What could he tell the world?

"It is a privilege to address you in French, the language of this city and one of the languages of this country. I have much to thank the Swiss for. I would like particularly to thank Minister of Justice and Police Willy Müllener, whose very considerable efforts helped make it possible for me to be here today."

There was a loud sneeze from the left side of the hall.

"And I hope his cold is quickly better."

Laughter and applause.

"I also want to single out, for special thanks, one member of President Huntington's staff—his Assistant for National Security Affairs, Mr. Matthew Olds." Nikolai Ivanovich grinned at Matt. "Somewhere in the Soviet Union there must be a man like him. I would like to find that man."

In the visitors' gallery, Chris felt a tingle race down his spine. That's my father, he thought. That's my Dad.

Chris still couldn't get over the events of the morning. President Huntington had spent almost ten minutes alone with him, after giving him a pass to the visitors' gallery.

"I ought to be mad at you, Chris," the President had said. "I have a hunch I won't be seeing as much of your father in the future as I'd like."

Chris, tongue-tied, waited.

"He tells me you'll be going home with him after the school term."

"I am?" Chris blurted.

"That's what the man says. Just don't hog him, Chris, okay? We both need that father of yours."

Chris, who had felt like crying and laughing at the same time, solemnly promised not to hog his father.

Nikolai Ivanovich adjusted the pince-nez on the bridge of his nose, and scowled at his audience. "There have been rumors that I would be prevented from appearing before you today. I wish I could lay those rumors to rest as being false. I cannot. An attempt was made, early this morning, to kidnap my daughter and me. The attempt almost succeeded. I must tell you that it was made by a high officer of the Russian KGB. It was thwarted by the efforts of Justice Minister Müllener, Mr. Matthew Olds, and another brave American, Mr. Whitney Stoughton, the Deputy Director of the Central Intelligence Agency. In order that I might appear here this morning, Mr. Stoughton gave his life."

Two thousand delegates, reporters, and visitors waited in stunned silence.

"The Ministry of Justice of the Swiss Confederation has asked me to waive diplomatic immunity in the case of Viktor Malinin, a colonel in the Committee for State Security of the Soviet Union. I have agreed to do so.

"Other rumors report a crisis in the Kremlin. These rumors are correct, and I will return to them later.

"Still other rumors say that I will seek political asylum, if not in the United States, then in Switzerland. These rumors are false. I have, after painful consideration, delivered some papers to the President of the General Assembly of the United Nations. Señor Román informs me he will make the contents of those papers public later today. As the world will soon learn, many of them are secret state papers which ordinarily would be kept under lock and key in the Kremlin. But these are no ordinary times. It is no betrayal of the trust of leadership to take one's country off a path that would lead, inexorably, to war. To do that, under the threat of the ultimate weapons in which so many of us have for so long taken such foolish pride, is to act with honor and indeed with patriotism.

"That conclusion did not come easily to me. I needed help. When I needed that help most, it came from Mr. Kermit Hauser, the former American Ambassador to Moscow, who in the wisdom of his years—"

In his hospital room in Saanen, his right hip pinned, his body immobilized from the waist down, Kermit Hauser watched the television screen. Nikolai Ivanovich had raised his hands for silence, then gave up, and stood there as the applause continued.

Wisdom? Me? Kermit Hauser thought. Well, perhaps in eighty years you learn a few things, and I thank you for the testimonial, old friend.

Hauser remembered the scene with his wife earlier that morning. If he lived to be a hundred, and at the moment he hardly knew whether he wanted to or not, he would probably go right on making a fool of himself over women.

There had been the obvious assumption, the painful accusation, the not unexpected denial. Only Natasha could have told the Russians where to find Andreyev.

"A divorce? At your age?" Natasha had bleated.

"I may be too old for a lot of things. I am not too old to divorce you."

"But what—"

"Tell me you didn't contact the KGB."

Natasha had begun to cry.

"It had to be you."

He was relentless, and finally she admitted it.

"He came to me in trust. He was my friend."

293

"And I am a Russian," Natasha had cried. "I couldn't let the Americans—"

"There isn't an ounce of patriotism in you. That wasn't the reason. Did they pay you? Was it money?"

"They cheated me. They lied. They paid me nothing."

"He could have been killed."

And Natasha had said: "You don't understand. You never did. What it's like to have an—older husband. I was always so frightened. What would happen to me after you —died?"

Kermit Hauser stared at the ceiling, surprised to feel a touch of pity for this selfish, fatuous woman who was his wife. He did not want to talk any more. They would divorce, that was final. After a while, sobbing, she left.

And Kermit Hauser continued staring at the ceiling, wondering if he had lived too long. An old man's final question, unanswered except by death.

Then the nurse came in to adjust the TV set. She fussed with the bed, with the tray of medicines on the night table, with the plants at the window. It was clear that she wanted to stay for the speech. She was fortyish and pretty in a buxom, outdoors way, with plump, pink cheeks, twinkling blue eyes, and breasts under the starched white uniform like sails before a good following wind.

"Stop fussing, woman," Kermit Hauser glowered at her. "You can stay for the speech."

She sat down on a chair near the bed. She thanked him. She had lovely eyes.

It took Nikolai Ivanovich fifteen minutes to reveal, with an almost mathematical precision, the Kremlin plan for the invasion of Yugoslavia. He related his unsuccessful efforts to make the Council of Ministers abandon the plan. Except for his voice, the great room was absolutely still. He told of the excuse the Council of Ministers would fall back on—the Brezhnev Doctrine. Told of the provocation—the assassination of Ilić. Told, with shame, of what his role here in Geneva would have been. Then he leaned forward, both hands on the smooth surface of the podium:

"I accuse Igor Lysenko, the First Secretary of the Communist Party, of bringing the world to the brink of war. I accuse Igor Lysenko of betraying his trust to the Russian people and to the people of the world. I accuse him of the cold-blooded murder of President Ilić of

294

Yugoslavia, and I will today invite the United Nations Security Council to consider these allegations. I can assure you there will be no Russian veto.

"Earlier, I mentioned a crisis in the Kremlin. This crisis is being attended to. We are putting our own house in order.

"Yesterday I sent Foreign Minister Vasily Kapitsa back to Moscow with instructions to begin that house-cleaning. I have heard from the Foreign Minister this morning. The work, the very considerable work that must be done before the Soviet Union can show its face with pride in the community of nations, is well underway."

Snow was falling on the vast enclosure of the Kremlin.

Looking out the window of his office in the mustard-colored building in the center of the complex, Igor Lysenko could not even see the Ivan the Great bell tower, or the gilded cupolas of St. Basil's.

His eyes returned to the television screen, where he could see Nikolai Ivanovich talking and hear his voice translated from French into Russian. That was typical of the Premier's bourgeois cosmopolitanism, Lysenko thought—to address the world organization in an alien tongue.

And surely, now, he had gone too far. To betray the secrets of the Council of Ministers to the world, to accuse the First Secretary like a common criminal.

Nikolai Ivanovich had been lucky. The world had been stunned by his reappearance. They would listen. They would listen to anything he said. But the world and the Kremlin, Lysenko told himself, were as far apart as the earth and the stars.

Foolishly, vindictively, Nikolai Ivanovich had let his luck dribble through his fingers. He was finished. Of that Lysenko was sure.

But a small doubt nibbled at the back of his mind. Kapitsa, here in Moscow? That was news.

On the television screen, Nikolai Ivanovich was saying: ". . . with pride in the community of nations . . ."

And the voice stopped.

The face went away.

A small glow of light receded on the screen and was gone.

Lysenko tried the dials. He checked the socket. The television set had gone dead.

Lysenko picked up the phone.

"Yes, Comrade Secretary?"

"The television," Lysenko said angrily. "It doesn't work."

He waited. There was no answer.

"Hello," he said. "Hello!" he shouted.

The phone too was dead.

Lysenko stalked outside. He heard the voice, calmly translating Nikolai Ivanovich's words into Russian, everywhere.

He had given strict instructions that the broadcast not be heard, except on the highest levels. That was possible, he had been told. A special hook-up. He didn't understand such things.

He ran down the corridor, opening doors, shouting, "Shut it off, it is forbidden, shut it off!"

Panting, he returned to his office.

The Minister of Defense stood near the window.

The Minister of the Interior was just inside the door, General Chuikov of the KGB at his side.

Foreign Minister Kapitsa, plump and narrow shouldered, stood behind the desk.

A single sheet of crisp white paper was on the desk, with one of Kapitsa's plump hands on either side of it.

"You will sign this, Comrade Secretary," Kapitsa said.

"Sign it? Sign what?"

The Mininster of Defense brought him a pen. "Your resignation, Comrade Secretary," he said.

Lysenko looked at their faces. Kapitsa was a clever man who could be bent by any wind. But in the Council, the Defense Minister and the Minister of the Interior were Lysenko's closest allies.

All their faces were hard, implacable.

"We are waiting, Comrade Secretary," General Chuikov said. Chuikov, who for years had been little more than a toady.

Igor Lysenko's face sank into his thick peasant hands. He rubbed his eyes. He looked up. They were watching him. Waiting.

At the last instant, as he took up the pen, he saw a calculating look pass across the face of the Minister of the Interior. After Lysenko, the Minister was the most voracious steel-eater in the Kremlin. Lysenko knew he had not been mistaken about that look on his face. The Minister was young, and ambitious. He controlled the police and the means of transportation. He would not bow before the wind, like Kapitsa. He would not roll over and play dead, like General Chuikov. If the others were ready to follow Nikolai Ivanovich, he was not. If the others were willing to sell out the steel-eaters, he was not. He would bide his time.

For a moment Lysenko hated him more than he hated the rest of them. But the hatred gave way to reluctant admiration as his eyes met those of the Minister again.

Lysenko had gambled and lost. The Minister would coldly usher him on his way to political oblivion.

So that the Minister could take his place.

Nikolai Ivanovich would not defeat the steel-eaters without a fight.

The Minister of the Interior would see to that. It was his turn now.

Almost with a sense of relief, Lysenko signed his resignation.

"I have instructed the Foreign Minister to deliver to the Minister of Defense, in Moscow, the following order: 'All hostilities in Yugoslavia are to cease at once. All Red Army units are ordered to return to Hungary and, as soon as practicable, to the Soviet Union.'"

Nobody in the Assembly Hall heard the last three words. A single enormous roar of approval drowned them out.

Finally Nikolai Ivanovich could resume: "In the name of the Council of Ministers of the Soviet Union, I have also instructed the Foreign Minister to ask the First Secretary of the Communist Party for his resignation."

This time it was a roar of astonishment. Nikolai Ivanovich waited, raised his hands and spoke:

"The collective leadership, in its own time, will elect a new man to that post. For though today I have opened our secrets to you, the Soviet Union must, and will, remain master in its own house."

President Huntington was on his feet, leading the applause.

"For the rest," Nikolai Ivanovich continued, "we Russians and the world were fortunate. If President Huntington had acted impulsively in response to what clearly was Soviet aggression, those few of us left alive might be in fallout shelters now. May I offer President Huntington thanks, on behalf of all of us, for his judgment and wisdom."

The President sat down, listening to the cries of approval. He was aware of someone approaching behind the chairs that lined the podium. Dr. Nancy leaned over his shoulder.

"Walter Reed," she said breathlessly. "They just called. The crisis is over. Gigi's going to be all right."

Suddenly Clay Huntington's eyes were stinging.

"This time we were fortunate. This time we survive.

"But what about next time? Before this vast public forum, I ask the world for forbearance. The people of the Soviet Union, like the people of the United States, or Switzerland, like the people of all countries, do not want war. The people of the Soviet Union now have a responsibility to the world. They must be very clear about this. The time they have is short. All our time is short.

"No nation that considers itself enlightened can turn a deaf ear to the pleas of the world. The people of the Soviet Union must enter the last quarter of the twentieth century ready to share the dream—no, to participate in the realization—of world peace.

"If a national leader willingly risks war, that leader must be removed from power. It is the very grave obligation of his own people to remove him through the legal means at their disposal. And, should those means fail, it is their obligation to remove him any way they can."

Young army officers on the banks of the Nile heard those words, and wondered about the despot in Cairo.

East Germans heard them, with sudden bright hope.

Peasants in Cuba heard them, and tribesmen in Nigeria. Half the population of Moscow heard them.

An immensely powerful old man in Peking heard those words. A billion people, he thought, and how many, secretly listening, here in his own country? Were those words the handwriting on the wall?

A strange chill passed over his body.

"Later today, my daughter and I will board our plane for the return flight to Moscow. There is much to be done at home. I take a father's pleasure in the fact that Claudia Nikolaievna will be at my side."

In the front row of the visitors' gallery, Claudia felt a flush of pride warm her face.

He needs me, she thought. I will stay with him for as long as that is so.

Her eyes moved past her father along the podium and she saw Matt, who had glanced up in her direction at the mention of her name. He was confused now, she knew, he was finding himself again in a way he never dreamed would be necessary.

His son to start with. Chris would be joining him in Washington later. Matt would make a home for him.

And the rest? "You can't stand up there all alone, where the power is," Matt had told her this morning, fumbling for the words because they did not come easily.

"All of a sudden you know you're like all the little people in the streets, pushed by events, crowded by circumstances, doing their work, hoping for luck, praying to their God, understanding—I don't know."

"Humility?" Claudia had suggested.

"Maybe. What it's like to be a human being, I guess."

Would it last? Claudia wondered. The very special ones —like her father, like President Huntington—needed it most of all. Without it, they were nothing. Without it, they could become an Igor Lysenko. Or a Malinin.

Please let it last, she thought, now, in the gallery. He can be one of the great ones.

And I want him to be.

On the podium, Secretary of State Benson Reed was looking at Matt, too. A thin Vermont smile touched his face. He still felt piqued that Matt had been in on the conferences and he hadn't.

Matthew Olds was no diplomat. He would never be a diplomat. But he's all right. He really is all right. It's sort of nice having him around. The thin Vermont smile became wry. I must be getting old, Benson Reed thought. I like the lad. I actually like him. Which is a secret I intend to keep.

"President Huntington has agreed to send to Moscow later this month his Special Assistant for National Security Affairs. I will at that time make with Mr. Olds the arrangements for a later meeting with the President.

"The purposes of this Summit Conference—which after

a fashion was held in a schoolroom yesterday—have been served.

"The aggression against Yugoslavia has ended.

"The people of Yugoslavia have the right to pursue their national destiny proudly and without interference.

"As all people, everywhere in the world, have that right.

"But if the purposes of this Summit Conference have been served, the urgent need for another one remains.

"The vast power of the United States, the vast power of the Soviet Union must be put to good use.

"There is nothing—nothing—that cannot be accomplished for mankind if we turn our efforts, our resources, to the task.

"President Huntington has a dream which I humbly would like to share. It is this:

"By the year two thousand, there will be no poverty, no hunger on the face of the earth.

"By the year two thousand, the diseases that have plagued mankind will be eradicated.

"By the year two thousand, the air we breathe and the water we drink will be clear and sweet.

"By the year two thousand, there will be peace not in our time but for all time.

"I pledge myself to this dream, as President Huntington does. To make it a reality will be no simple matter. We will need all of your help, everywhere."

3   Matt eased his way through the crowd of reporters at Cointrin Airport. He turned and watched the huge Tupelov racing along the runway and then lifting into the sky and climbing over the ridge of the Jura Mountains.

"When do you leave, Mr. Olds? Date been set yet?"

"Christmas with luck. Before New Year's anyway."

"Will they get together in Moscow or where?"

"Moscow first," Matt said. "Then Andreyev will visit Washington. Figure two meetings by early spring."

"Would you give us a comment on what Andreyev called the President's dream, Matt?"

For a moment some of the old cynicism fought to return. The military-industrial complex wasn't going to roll over and play dead at home, any more than the steel-eaters would in Russia. Clay Huntington would have his hands full convincing Congress, convincing the voters that we could live in peace with Russia. And even with Lysenko deposed, Andreyev would still find opposition in his Council of Ministers.

What did they expect him to say? Matt wondered. That we'll snap our fingers and usher in the millennium?

"It's a good dream," he told the reporters finally, his voice subdued. "But, we've got to make it more than that. We've got to make it happen."

At first the words sounded foolish to Matt, and then they sounded just exactly right.

Claudia would have liked them.

He would see her in Moscow in a few weeks. His steps quickened as he went through the international departures building to where Chris was waiting.

SIGNET Titles You Will Enjoy

☐ **NUREMBERG DIARY by G. M. Gilbert.** Written from the author's own experience as a prison psychologist at Nuremberg before the start of the trials, this unduplicated document records the atrocities committed by Nazi leaders. "Although much has been written about the Nuremberg trials, this book is original in form and content."—**New York Times**   (#W4551—$1.50)

☐ **THE HERO SHIP by Hank Searls.** Episodes drawn from the World War II aircraft carrier Shenandoah, whose crew refused to give up while under heavy Japanese attack, serve as a backdrop for this novel of naval heroism, personal intrigues and cowardice.
                                                             (#Q4286—95¢)

☐ **IT CAN'T HAPPEN HERE by Sinclair Lewis.** Written in 1936 as Hitler rose to power—a famous, frighteningly realistic novel about the coming of fascism—with terrifying parallels to today's politics.   (#Q4412—95¢)

☐ **THE OCCUPYING POWER by Gwyn Griffin.** A superb tragicomedy about the corruption of absolute power on a British-occupied Mediterranean Island during World War II.   (#Q4092—95¢)

Have You Read These Current Bestsellers
from SIGNET?

☐ **THE FRENCH LIEUTENANT'S WOMAN by John Fowles.**
By the author of **The Collector** and **The Magus,** a haunt-
ing love story of the Victorian era. Over ten months on
the **N.Y. Times Bestseller List** and an international bestseller. "Filled with enchanting mysteries, charged with
erotic possibilities . . ."—Christopher Lehmann-Haupt,
N.Y. Times   (#W4479—$1.50)

☐ **LOVE STORY by Erich Segal.** The story of love fought
for, love won, and love lost. It is America's Romeo and
Juliet. And it is one of the most touching, poignant
stories ever written. Now a major motion picture star-
ring Ali MacGraw and Ryan O'Neal.   (#Q4414—95¢)

☐ **JENNIE, The Life of Lady Randolph Churchill by Ralph
G. Martin.** In JENNIE, Ralph G. Martin creates a vivid
picture of an exciting woman, Lady Randolph Churchill
who was the mother of perhaps the greatest statesman
of this century, Winston Churchill, and in her own right,
one of the most colorful and fascinating women of the
Victorian era.   (#W4213—$1.50)

☐ **SONS by Evan Hunter.** By the bestselling author of **The
Blackboard Jungle,** this is a powerful novel about three
generations of Tyler men, portraying grandfather,
father, and son; their changing world and values.
                                        (#Y4288—$1.25)
